Red Ribbons

by

Jillian Allen

ISBN: 978-1-887339-03-2

Red Ribbons

CHAPTER ONE

Birth, Death, and all that

Except for having two mothers, I was pretty much like any other eight grader. I was the scrawny kid you remember from school, with shaggy hair and wearing ill–fitting hand–me–downs and glasses held together with paperclips and black tape. When I was born, Mom went into a deep depression and would not even hold me, much less let me nurse. Back in the late fifties, there weren't all that many facilities and support structures in our little town and my future looked pretty bleak.

Fortunately, Aunt Jean had just delivered my cousin, Daisy. So, being Mom's wonderful sister, Aunt Jean took me, just as if I were her own baby. And, to me, she became Momma Jean. That is what she was then, and that is what she will remain as long as I live.

For the first three years I grew up with the most wonderful mother and father imaginable, along with my sisters Jeanie and Daisy. Daisy, oh..., my wonderful, sweet Daisy. The love of my life. Closer than my twin. We had nursed at the same breast, played together, been dressed and undressed together, bathed in the same tub, played with the same toys, slept in the same crib. She was exactly three weeks older, and a girl, but otherwise, we were the same person.

On my third birthday strangers arrived and took me from Momma Jean and Daisy. I still have bad dreams about that day. It took a very long time for me to understand these strangers were my real family, and that Momma Jean and Papa Henry were only my aunt and uncle. Now I had another family, this one as cold and hard as the first had been warm and loving. My new older brothers were as unenthusiastic about having a new kid around as I was about having them. After a few years everything settled a little, I learned to stay out of the way and they learned to tolerate me.

What kept me going was knowing that every Friday afternoon I could walk the eight blocks back to my real home, where I was always greeted with kisses and hugs and my favorite snacks, but mostly I went back to Daisy and Momma Jean.

In late January the world turned inside out. Dad was a real hell–raiser. Most weekends he would go hunting or fishing with his buddies and they would get roaring drunk and do stupid things. No two stories ever agreed, except that they were deep in the swamp and Dad tripped or fell or was pushed, and his shotgun went off. It didn't take his buddies long to sober up and figure out something bad had happened. By then, Dad was dead.

If that wasn't enough, by the time we returned from the funeral, Mom had a list of Dad's creditors long as your arm. It was clear our backs were against the wall. Without waiting for anyone to change clothes, Mom had us seated around the kitchen table with a bunch of papers spread before us.

"I'll tell you boys, things are not looking good. That worthless father of yours has left us a mountain of debts and no way to pay them."

William, my oldest brother looked even more confused than the rest of us. "But..., but, Mom. What about Dad's insurance? He always said he had plenty of insurance to cover us if anything happened."

Mom took a deep breath. "I'm sorry, William. I know you idolized your father, but he only had ten thousand insurance, I've already uncovered more than that in bills. We still owe three thousand on that new '58 Buick sitting in the garage." Her head slowly shook. "He hadn't paid the mortgages in three months, or the utilities, and that second mortgage has a penalty clause if any payments are missed."

William, snatched a piece of paper from the table. "Look at this, almost $1200 from the jeweler for a bracelet. You can return that."

Mom's expression did not change. "He didn't buy that for me. I assume it went to one of his girlfriends."

Buddy, my middle brother leapt so fast his chair tumbled across the linoleum. "You lie! Dad didn't have any girlfriends. Grandpa Jones said you'd try to cover up doing him in. It's all to get his insurance money. Dad said he had plenty of insurance. You're lying."

William let his head sink into his hands. "Oh, Buddy. Don't be an idiot. You know Grandpa and Grandma hate Mom, almost as much as they hate Robbie."

I was relieved to learn William at least knew my name. He normally just called me Little Bit or Doodlebug because I was always doodling and drawing in my notebooks or any piece of paper that was handy. I had never been able to sit still very long and drawing was better than squirming, which always lead to a bop to my head by Dad, or getting yelled at by a teacher.

"Sit, Buddy." Mom began writing in a green journal. "Today is Friday. We have to come up with a plan and we'll have to start putting it into action on Monday."

A tiny smile crossed her lips. It was the first time I had ever seen her display any pleasure. Her face actually lit a little.

"Normally I'd say we start today, but it's only proper to show a little respect to that rat of a father. Okay, William. I know you hoped to go to college next year. That's got to be on hold… at least for a while. I've talked with Uncle Henry. He can get you a job at the dealership. Just until we can put our finances into order."

William and I glanced at each other. I know how much he wanted to become a scientist or engineer or something that would take him away. He was smart as a whip and a great athlete, all wrapped into one. I was neither.

He simply nodded. "I'll call Uncle Henry first thing tomorrow."

"Buddy, you've got to quit wasting all your time on sports and find work that pays. Maybe you can get a job stacking shelves at the market."

Once more William and I glanced at the other. We both knew Buddy would never give up sports and get a job.

Unlike William, Buddy had no talents or ambitions beyond anything that involved a ball.

"But, Mom. When I go pro, there'll be oodles of money. You won't have any worries."

This time it was William who sucked in a deep breath and slowly let it ease out. "Buddy, you're a sophomore in high school. We can't wait till you graduate from college and turn pro. We need money now!"

Clearing my throat, I tried to take Mom's hand. She pulled away. "I can get a paper route. Maybe Papa Henry would let me wash cars at the dealership. They wash them every day."

"That's silly, Robbie. Anyway, I have a job for you, right here."

I glanced at William, then Buddy, then turned to Mom. "Here?"

Mom sat up straight. Now a real smile lit her features. "During high school and two years in college I studied Home Economics. Sewing was my specialty and my love. I always thought I'd have a passel of little girls to sew for." Here she glanced at me. "That wasn't to be. But, now I'm going to start a sewing business. In the next few weeks I'm going to make a dozen of the prettiest girly outfits you've ever seen. When the Garden Club has its first meeting, just before Easter, we're going to have a fashion show and sell those dresses to the highest bidder. All of those rich biddies are going to fall over themselves to have their daughters dolled up Easter morning. That will get us started."

All three of us stared at Mom. At last, I whispered. "But, Mom. What am I supposed to do?

"You, my dear little Robbie, are going to help me keep house and sew."

"You mean, like clean and cook?"

Mom beamed benevolently.

"And, I'm going to learn to sew? Like…, like a tailor?"

"No, of course you' won't be a tailor, that's for men's clothing. You're going to be…," she hesitated, as if searching for the proper words, "Well, you're going to be…, like a seamstress, and help me make all those pretty dresses."

CHAPTER TWO

Pretty in Yellow

Mom continued to talk, but I was too stunned to listen. Surely, she was joking, but Mom never joked, and we had just returned from Dad's funeral. I understood he wasn't the best father in the world, perhaps he was the worse, but he was our father. Really, he was no father at all, at least to me. Not that Mom was much better, or my brothers. I was always like a third left foot, something you had to buy a shoe for, but otherwise only a bother. Actually, not much was bought for me. Every piece of clothing I had was a hand–me–down or stuff Momma Jean gave me. The only work I did around the house was to set the table and take out the trash. Not much to show for thirteen years of life.

At last, Mom turned to me, as if I was being dismissed. "It's Friday, shouldn't you be heading to your other family?"

"Well…, I thought…."

"The Boys and I can take care of this. Go play with Daisy." She turned back to William, then hesitated. "And, don't walk through that damned cemetery. It's not safe."

I tried to kiss her on the cheek, she brushed me aside.

Actually, getting out of the house had been what I wanted to do, but not like this. It was my family too, and I needed to become a part of it. I had thought Dad's death would bring us together, yet it looked like I was going to be an even smaller part of whatever we melded into. A sewing girl and cleaning lady. Was that all Mom thought I was capable of? I stumbled over a crack in the sidewalk. Damn! Couldn't I even walk? Perhaps Mom was right. Not about the girl part. She was simply putting me down. But, maybe cleaning and sewing was the limit of my capabilities.

The walk to Momma Jean's was pretty straightforward. Our house was right at the edge of downtown. In the distant past this was the swankest region in all the county. Now it was half tumbled mansions and half converted offices. Momma Jean lived in a much newer and nicer neighborhood. We were closer to the old fashioned stores, she was near the new schools and something called a Mall that was being planned for the edge of town. I traveled straight down Center Street, then had a decision. Ahead and shortest was the Confederate Cemetery, turn left and pass through the edge of the colored section, or turn right and pass by the playing fields.

The Cemetery was creepy and overgrown. It was also where the town drunks passed around their bottles. The colored section was safe most of the time, and I recognized many of the older people. I would wave to them, and they waved back. The problem was that any teenage blacks out and about would throw rocks at me. I had absolutely no idea why they would do that, since I had never done anything to them. On the other hand, if any white boys were on the playing fields they would attack me with words if not rocks. Several times I had tried to join pick–up games, but I was such a klutz they laughed me off. To them I was a sissy since I played with my girl cousins and wasn't good at sports. Come to think of it, perhaps I was a sissy.

I decided on the Cemetery.

The path twisted right and left, almost seeming to fold back onto itself until you came to a dilapidated stone structure containing the remains of unknown Confederate soldiers. There were also some Union remains, but they had names and were in regular graves. At one time this had been the town's main cemetery and there were hundreds if not thousands of overgrown graves all over the place. I didn't mind the graves, it was all the untended weeds and bushes, the lengthening shadows and silent mosses that seeped into your shoulder blades. That, and the scruffy scrape of drunks pulling back into those shadows as you approached. Mother and Momma Jean went ballistic every time I walked through there. So, I just didn't tell them. Anyway, no one would be desperate enough to attack a skinny boy.

*   *   *   *   *

It was a relief to be greeted by Daisy soon as I stepped inside, with Momma Jean adding her own smooches and hugs. Jeanie didn't join in, she leaned against the door jam and wrinkled her nose in greeting. You never knew with Jeanie. She was seldom effervescent like Daisy. Most times she grunted hello, other times she completely ignored me.

It wasn't long before we were in the kitchen munching fresh brownies and Coke. Momma Jean had coffee, of course, and only nibbled at a brownie, but Daisy, Jeanie and I made sure the plate was completely cleaned. Nothing was said about Dad or the funeral, but you could tell it was hanging over us like a sword.

When Papa Henry came in from the dealership there was another round of hugs and kisses. In reality, he just shook my hand and slapped me on the back, but he surely loved–up his 'babies' and patted them on the fanny, then kissed them some more.

Papa Henry and Dad had some sort of silent battle going on that I never understood. Dad had only been a Shipping Clark on an Army base in New Jersey during the war, but he bragged about being in the service all the time. Papa Henry was a Marine in the Pacific for over three years. He fought in every major battle as we marched up the islands until he was wounded for the third time while they were taking Iwo Jima and got sent home. Papa Henry never said a word about the war except one day when Dad was spouting off. Papa Henry ran his hand through my hair and pulled me close.

"War is Hell," he said in a very quiet way. "I pray you boys never have to fight, but if you do, I'm sure you'll make me proud."

All through dinner we chatted gaily, but Dad still hung silently about the room. I thought about Dad and Papa Henry, and suddenly I felt I couldn't stand it any longer. I had to do something that would make Papa Henry proud of me.

"Papa Henry, would you give me a job. I could wash cars, or sweep, or anything. I'll work hard and never complain. Mom really needs the money."

"Robbie, if I could, I'd take you on tomorrow. You'd make a good worker, of that I'm sure. But..., legally I can't even hire you part time till you're fifteen. You know Momma Jean and I will do all we can. But..., that ornery mother of yours...." His voice trailed off.

"She has finally agreed to accept my old sewing machine," added Momma Jean. "As usual, she's determined to do this by herself."

"Yeah, she wants to turn me into a sewing...."

Jeanie snickered. "Yeah is right. Into a sewing girl. That'll be a real hoot."

Momma Jean made a funny sound deep in her throat. "Don't be unkind to Robbie. Especially now."

Once more Jeanie scrunched her nose. Oh, oh. She was in one of her moods.

*   *   *   *   *

We watched The Patty Page Show on their new Zenith color set, then I realized how late it had become. "Gosh, it's completely black outside. Papa Henry, may I borrow a flashlight?"

"You're going nowhere," said Momma Jean. "I told Pam you'd be spending the night. That's why Daisy has twin beds."

Mom and Momma Jean fought all the time, mostly over me, yet they still called each other several times a day. Sometimes they would be on the phone for hours talking about food and clothes and books, but when it came to how I was to be raised, neither would budge.

Momma Jean was silent for a while, then added, almost as an afterthought. "There is no way I'd let you spend tonight in that dreary house. You're going to breakdown soon, and we need to be with you." Her hand slipped into mine. "You're still my baby."

"I didn't bring anything to sleep in."

"I'm sure Daisy can find you something."

"I couldn't do that. If its okay, I'll just sleep in my underwear."

"Men! You're all alike." She gave me a quick peck on the cheek. "Let's see what we can work out."

Daisy and Momma Jean dug through Daisy's bureau while I removed my shirt.

"Oh.... My.... God!" Momma Jean poked a finger through one of the larger holes in my dingy undershirt. Pamela Jones lets you out in public wearing that!"

"Its clean. Its just kind of old."

"Kind of old? You call that, 'kind of old!' How many of your brothers wore that?"

My face was growing hotter by the second. "Momma Jean, we have to conserve. Dad—"

"Was too cheap to buy you underwear! Out of that disgusting thing now. And the shorts..., they're probably even worse."

Hopping fast as I could, I undressed and handed her the shorts and undershirt. As quickly, she pitched them into the waste basket. All the while, I was becoming more aware of just how naked I was, and in front of the two most important women in my life. A snicker from the doorway announced that Jeanie had chosen that instant to show up.

"Wow, somebody hasn't been in the sun lately," was all she said.

"Jeanie, you stay out of this. Daisy, give Robbie a pair of panties."

"Momma Jean, I can't...."

"Would you prefer a panty girdle?"

Before I could answer, Jeanie chimed in. "Actually, he does need a girdle. His fanny is big as mine."

By now Daisy had handed me a pair of pale lavender panties and I almost jumped into them with both feet. "Momma Jean, I really shouldn't do this."

"Why not? Didn't you and Daisy dress up all the time?"

"But, that was years ago. We were babies."

"You're still my babies. There, it's settled. Daisy, that yellow set is getting small on you, it should be lovely on Robbie."

In moments I was stepping into the most awful pale yellow puffy pants with all kinds of lace at the legs and yellow satin bows dangling from each side. The top was even worse, with more puffs, these passing for little sleeves with more lace and bows. It only reached the middle of my hips, so at least half the awful bloomers stuck out. The neckline was scooped to show off my flat chest. Of course, there was still another ribbon bow right in the middle where boobies should have been. The gown would have looked absolutely stunning on Daisy or Jeanie, but on me it was horrid and I could imagine how stupid I appeared.

Then it happened. Dad's death and funeral, the overpowering debts, my accumulated sadness, now this. It was as if my life caved in and the flood burst from deep behind my eyes. I cried for hours, cradled between Momma Jean and Daisy. Even Jeanie and Papa Henry soothed me, until at last I could cry no more. I became aware I was in bed, across from Daisy. The room was dark, but I could make out her shape as she slipped from her bed and into mine.

"Turn over so I can rub your back," she whispered. "My dearest, sweetest Robbie. You mean so much. I'd give anything to help you through all this. Just remember you're my truest love."

Her soft fingers moved slowly across the smooth fabric. I could feel the tension easing from my shoulders.

Now her voice became even less than a whisper. "Wouldn't it be wonderful if you were my real sister. We could have so much fun together."

Sleep was now enveloping me. I could barely understand her words.

"Know what, my love. You're pretty in yellow…, but you'd be absolutely beautiful in pink.

CHAPTER THREE

The Shop Around the Corner

The aroma of sizzling sausage and fresh biscuits brought me around. At first, I couldn't figure where I was, or why I was wearing frilly yellow nylon, then the evening flooded back over me. Daisy had draped a matching housecoat like thing across the foot of my bed. It tied together at the neck, but billowed open as I walked to the bathroom. After cleaning up a little, I headed toward the delicious aromas wafting from the kitchen.

"Look what the cat drug in," Jeanie said, with more of a laugh than her sarcasm of the previous evening.

Daisy gave me a quick hug. "Mornin' sweetie, you want milk or coffee with your biscuits? Mom's letting me cook breakfast, so no kibitzing."

"Milk, please."

Sticking my head close to the pan I could see that she had broken at least half the sausage patties into the thick gravy, just the way I loved it. Momma Jean leaned against the sink, cradling a cup of coffee beneath her nose. Like Daisy and Jeanie…, and like me, she was wearing a similar

housecoat that tied at the neck. Peeking from the slit in
front I could see she was wearing a dress–up girdle and
stockings.   That meant the girls were going shopping,
which also meant I should be heading home right after
breakfast.   Like Mom, Momma Jean wore a girdle and
stockings from sunrise to bed time. Jeanie wore them to
school and Sunday, while Daisy only wore them on Sunday
and special occasions.   And, shopping, especially for
clothing, was a very special occasion.

I didn't feel anything seeing Daisy changing clothes or
even wearing nothing, but glimpsing Momma Jean or Jeanie
in their undies was not the same at all.   Perhaps it was
because their bodies were so much more exotic than mine.
Even their aroma was foreign, not to mention how they felt
when I hugged them.   Daisy was just different.   In some
ways, seeing her was like seeing other boys in the shower
after gym.   I mean, I simply didn't care one way or another.
Now, some of the fellows did seem to notice the other
boys.   Some of them, especially Moose Hanahan and Butch
Spence, were always slapping me on the rump or tweaking
my nipple in the shower, but that just had no interest for
me.

My face suddenly felt extremely hot, which happened
if I started thinking about girls and undies.   I felt certain
Momma Jean knew I was looking at her girdle and
stockings, so I quickly scurried around the kitchen helping
set the table and fix everyone fresh drinks and orange juice.

"Papa Henry?"

"Already off to the church.   The Men For Christ are
meeting with your mother to see how they can help..., after
your father...." Mamma Jean sipped at her coffee. "Well,
to see if they can help."

"Is Aunt Pam really going to start making clothes?"
Daisy made a dramatic gesture, as if she'd become an

actress. "I mean, wonder if she would make me something special, like a princess dress."

"Mom says I'm to help her sew," I said, tickling her in the ribs. "If she will let me, I'll make you anything you like."

"With lots of lace and ribbons..., and petticoats that stick out. Course, you'll probably be real expensive."

"As much lace and ribbons as you like. All you'll have to pay is a big kiss."

"Oh, Jeezeeee!" Jeanie acted like she was going to gag. "And, what'll you make me?"

"How about a head girdle?"

Momma Jean let out a whoop. "Good one, Robbie. Sometimes I feel the same. Come on girls, brush teeth and finish dressing. We're going to get Robbie some new underwear."

*   *   *   *   *

Everyone piled into Papa Henry's newest Eldorado convertible. Being manager of the Cadillac dealership meant he received a new car every six months. The difference was he didn't have to pay for them, not directly anyway, while Dad spent a small fortune trying to keep up. At least Papa Henry would be able to help Mom trade in our new Buick for something reasonable.

We headed downtown to Minx Department Store, the biggest little shop in America! It actually wasn't a shop and certainly not the biggest anything, except in our little town, but it was the only place you could get some of almost everything. I mean, if you wanted a suit, you went to Wilder's, if you needed a wedding dress, you went to Ye Bridal Shop. Mom and Momma Jean got their girdles and bras at Miss Lillian's, but panties and slips came from Minx.

As we entered, I turned right, toward the boy's section. Before I got two steps Jeanie had grabbed my hand and we headed upstairs at a trot to where all the woman's clothing was displayed…, and right into Lingerie. Without stopping, we marched to a huge display of panties and slips and things that looked like nylon undershirts with spaghetti straps, like Daisy used to wear. Instantly, I knew this was not going to end well!

Momma Jean pointed out a bin overflowing with panties. "Daisy wears size six, you can choose a pair to replace the ones she gave you."

While Jeanie and Momma Jean started digging through several other racks, shelves and bins, Daisy drew me over to the panties.

"Oh, this is so sweet," she cooed. "Pick out something daring."

Once more my face felt aflame. Certainly, every woman in town was gawking at me. My head tried to retract between my shoulders, like a turtle. Without thinking, I picked up a pair of the brightest red.

"No red or black," ordered Momma Jean from across the room.

Slinking ever deeper into humiliating shame, I slowly fingered through every wisp of nylon and rayon and satin until I finally settled on a pair in light peach. The entire tummy area bathed in delicate lace and the fabric flowed across my fingers like liquid. They were beautiful, and I knew Daisy would love them. She was almost vibrating with excitement, and her squeals were attracting ever more attention. At least none of my teachers were shopping for undies.

"Okay, Girls, let's hit the dressing room." Momma Jean herded us toward the line of little rooms between Lingerie and Corsetry.

A prune–faced harridan barred our way into a room until she counted the stacks of frillies in Momma Jean and Jeanie's hand, and the single panty I was holding. After giving them number tags indicating the items they were taking into the rooms, the lady pointed to the far corner. "The young man can wait over there."

"The young man needs to try on these panties," replied Momma Jean.

The woman opened her mouth, then closed it with a pop, like a disturbed oyster.

"Don't worry, he's wearing clean undies." With that, Momma Jean herded us into the changing room. Under her breath, she mumbled. "That old biddy should have retired ages ago. She frightened everyone when I was a kid."

First, Daisy tried on my panty right over the ones she was wearing, which meant she first had to wiggle out of her panty girdle. They fit beautifully, which made me beam with pride. Which then made me feel foolish, since all I had done was pick something out of a huge jumble.

"Always try on intimates over clean panties," said Jeanie.

Momma Jean nodded in agreement. "Very good, Robbie. You have exquisite if expensive taste. Perhaps you'll select something as lovely for Jeanie and me at Christmas."

Once more I felt as if my face would catch on fire.

Next, Daisy tried on several bras. After a half dozen it was decided that a Teen-B fit her perfectly. After wiggling back into her girdle and fastening the stockings, she re–dressed and was hustled off to choose two more bras in the same style and size.

Meanwhile I had to undress right down to the panties. When the door shut behind Daisy I was left standing almost naked in front of Jeanie and Momma Jean inside a woman's dressing room within the Intimate Apparel department. Neither said anything for several moments. At last, Momma Jean poked very gently at my hips, waist and chest.

"You've put on a little weight. That's good. You were looking very pale and drawn. I'll tell Pam to feed you better."

Momma Jean had been Doc. Pricher's nurse until Daisy was born. Of course, when she took me in addition to Daisy, any thought of working full time was forgotten. However, she was still a nurse at heart and was always doctoring her three ducklings, as she called Jeanie, Daisy and me. Which was good and bad. If one of us got the sniffles, all three were treated. If one of us had tummy problems, all three got a laxative if not an enema. If Jeanie made too much fuss, all three of us were stood in a corner of the dining room.

The suspense was killing me. I knew what was about to happen, but I was absolutely powerless to prevent it. No mere mortal could stand up to Momma Jean, any more than they could to my mother. Those blasted sisters were so different, yet exactly the same. Once they decided on an action, resistance was impossible. The only way Dad had defied Mom was to hide in the swamp behind a bottle of hooch. As a result, he ended up killing himself, intentionally or unintentionally, we would never know.

Now I was facing my alternate mother and she intended to put me into panty prison. And, there was absolutely nothing I could do about it.

CHAPTER FOUR

A Change of Heart

"There. Absolutely perfect. Don't you agree, Jeanie?"

Jeanie's grin, which had started large and had grown bigger each time I tried on another panty or vest, now fairly burst from her face.

"Oh, yes. Perfect. I can't wait to tell the girls at school. That idiot Buddy Jones is simply going to die when it gets out his little brother wears panties." Her grin grew even more mischievous. "Can we have him fitted with a training bra?"

"No, of course not…, at least not yet."

Momma Jean made one last check of the waist and leg bands, then applied her seal of approval of the panties I was wearing. "Okay, Robbie. You can get dressed. We'll get you two pair each of these," she picked up several panties, "and two of these, for Sundays." She glanced at Jeanie. "You'll tell no one. How could you think of hurting Robbie?"

"Alright, Mom. But it won't be easy."

Her grin faded, but I could tell by the way her lips pursed she was not happy. If there was one thing I knew about Jeanie, it was that one day, sooner or later, she would have to tell someone about my panties. There was no way she could sit on a secret about me. It simply gave her too much pleasure to watch me squirm. I don't think she wanted to hurt me, just make me suffer a little. Except, what was a little to her usually was not small to me.

By this time Daisy had selected her bras and Momma Jean paid the old grump. I almost died when I saw how much everything totaled. It was a good thing they had not turned me into a complete girl, even Papa Henry and the Cadillac dealership couldn't afford a full outfit!

We stopped at the Tin Skillet Diner on the way home. You could either sit outside in your car, or go inside and use a booth. In either case, you could not be there more than a couple of seconds before a waitress would zip up in her pink costume and roller skates and take your order. We went inside. The three Ducklings had ice cream sundaes while Momma Duck drank black coffee. Momma Jean and Jeanie sat on one side of the booth while Daisy and I occupied the other. Daisy kept poking out her chest to show off her new Teen–B breasts, while I tried to shrink as tiny as possible. No matter how hard I tried, I could not believe that everyone in the Diner didn't know I was wearing panties. At any minute I expected Jeanie to jump up and spill my secret. She quietly ate her ice cream as if nothing had happened. But, every few minutes she would glance at me through her long eyelashes and give me a sickening smile. She was already planning the time and place. Jeanie was going to spill the beans, and I was going to end up in the stew.

After they dropped me off at the house I bundled the package beneath my arm tightly as possible, hoping I could make it to my room without anyone noticing. That's when I realized there were cars and trucks parked all over the yard, while men in red caps swarmed about like locusts. Oh, God! The entire contingent of Men For Christ had descended on us. As I stood frozen, four men struggled from the front door lugging the oversize chest of drawers from my room and headed toward the garage out back. Had Mom decided to move me to the garage!

As I entered, another group of men were lugging my bed up the stairs. The house had originally had four rooms and a big hallway on each level. Downstairs was the kitchen and pantry across the back, with the parlor and dining room in front. Upstairs were four bedrooms and a bath. Perhaps fifty years ago someone had combined two of the bedrooms into one master suite with its own bathroom. Mom and Dad had the master, with William and Buddy on the other side. When I came along the pantry had been converted into my bedroom. That was okay, except the room had no window and Buddy had convinced me there were thousands of monsters and spiders beneath my bed just waiting to eat me as soon as the light was turned off. I spent the first couple of weeks with a blanket stuffed in my mouth to keep from crying.

Now I stood watching my bedroom torn apart, with the pieces flying in all directions, while a swarm of fellows hammered and sawed like madmen. Who knows how long I would have remained inert if Mother hadn't arrived.

"Ah, Pumpkin. I'm glad you're back. You can help move your stuff."

"Mom! My bed…. My dresser…."

"Yes, we decided to turn your room and the parlor into work spaces. Eventually, the dining room will become a display area.

"But, my bed."

"It's in my room. Your dresser wouldn't fit. The men had a heck of a time getting it up then back down the stairs. I'll clean out your father's drawers. We'll be just fine." She took the package from beneath my arm and looked inside. "Well, well. What have we here?"

"Mom, please. Not now. Not here."

She held a pair of pale pink panties against me.

"Very nice. Jean always had excellent taste. I wondered how long it would take…, now that your father is gone." She gestured to all the activity hurtling about us. "After all, she is just like me. Never put of till tomorrow what you can mess–up today."

"But, Mom. I can't wear these. What if someone finds out."

She didn't say anything for a while. "Robbie, you know how much Jean and the girls love you. Are you willing to hurt their feelings?"

I stared at the floor and swallowed hard. "No, of course not."

"Then, I don't think we have much choice."

"Mom, you won't tell my brothers? Buddy will kill me."

Her hand brushed through my hair. I glanced up, just as she leaned forward and gave me a slight kiss on the forehead, the first time I ever remember her touching me. "It will be our little secret, at least for now. But, secrets won't last long in this house. Now, run upstairs and change, we've got a lot of work facing us. Oh, Robbie. Of course, you won't be changing your undies."

The truth crushed down on me like a glacier. Mother already knew. She knew exactly what had happened, and what was planned for me.

"No, Mother."

Once more she kissed me. "That's my good boy. That's my very good little boy."

CHAPTER FIVE

Sew and Sew

By the time all the Men For Christ left we were exhausted. Well, not Buddy, because he had just come in from a date or something. I had spent most of the afternoon baking cookies and distributing iced tea. Actually, Mom baked the cookies and yelled at me when it was time to remove them from the oven. I did make the iced tea, which was about the extent of my cooking expertise. Between forays with the tea, I located most of my clothing and hauled it upstairs. Mom's bed was a jumble, but I finally sorted out almost everything and got it hung in the closet or stuffed into Dad's old bottom drawers in the chest. Everything, that is, except my old underwear, so I couldn't have changed out of the lavender panties and vest anyway.

After a silent dinner of cold cuts and the remaining tea, Mom and I walked slowly through the house, taking in all the changes. What had been the pantry, then my room, was now our main fitting area. One corner was partitioned as a changing space. In front of the partition was a big mirror backing a foot–high platform with a six inch step on three sides.

"It's much easier to mark hemlines with the customer on a platform," said Mom.

One entire wall was now covered with shelves. Not only that, but the door to my closet was now a cutting table in the old parlor. The dining room table was set up with our two sewing machines, Mom's old one for me, and Momma Jean's almost brand spanking super dooper, 'do everything except make coffee' machine for Mom. She slowly surveyed our restructured home.

"Jean wanted a newer, even better machine, so taking this one helped her." Mom smiled to herself. "You can't imagine how long I've wanted to do something real, to be somebody, not just a wife taking care of her family, but a real businesswoman. I never thought my dream would come like this, but I'll take it. I had not intended to steal your childhood, but we'll need to work ourselves nearly to death to make a go of this." She wiped at her eyes. "Time for bed, after church tomorrow we begin turning you into a professional seamstress."

As we climbed the stairs, I looked up at her. "Mom, I couldn't find my old underwear."

She didn't reply until we reached the bedroom. "We've discussed this, Robbie. The subject is closed. Oh, I've put out a different nightgown. You can't wear those slinky things Jean bought. This ancient house gets too cold at night, you'll freeze what little fanny you have.

Getting ready for bed was a real chore, what with me terrified I might glimpse Mom half–undressed, but we soon discovered the bathroom was a good place to do any actual changing. Having my bunk crammed into such a limited space was not the best idea in the word, since I had to climb over Mom's bed, my bunk, or the dresser to get in or out of bed, and no matter which I chose resulted in a stumped toe or bumped elbow. My new gown was light blue with dark blue flowers. The inside was fuzzy like flannel, the outside shiny satin. I lay awake a long time, listening to Mom's slow breathing, and knew she was deep asleep. What had she planned for me? Or, were she and Momma Jean actually planning anything? Maybe all this was simply happening. Perhaps God was directing a game from Heaven. Could one of the Angels have checked the books and discovered a mistake. Was I that mistake? After all, I had been terribly injured just being born. I really wasn't supposed to live, but Doc Pricher stitched me back together and somehow I survived. Possibly I had been slated to be a dog or cow or something, and got sent to the wrong mother. Was that why Mom had so much problem with me? Deep down, did she know I wasn't really hers, that I was actually an animal, not a human at all?

* * * *

Morning came far too early. I had to put my panties and vest into a wicker basket in the bathroom before climbing into a scalding tub of bubbles.

"It's your job to hand wash our undies every few days. The soap is beneath the sink. If the weather is warm hang them on the back porch. If not, use the line over the tub."

Safely in one of the Sunday pantie sets, I joined Mom in the kitchen. In days past I would have set the table and called my brothers. This morning Mom had me frying bacon and toasting bread beneath the broiler. It was clear no grass was going to grow beneath her wheels.

After church, William went up to do homework, who knows what happened to Buddy? Mom sat me in front of the old sewing machine and my education began. At first, I couldn't get the blasted thread to fill the bobbin, then I became terrified flying needles would stitch my fingers together. After a couple of hours I could complete a half—straight seam. Before I could congratulate myself, out came last night's gown. I had to undress while Mom stood me on the platform in front of the big mirror. She explained in excruciating detail as nips and tucks were taken beneath the arms, the sleeves were shortened and the hem raised to mid calf. Then, almost before I knew what was happening, she slipped out of her dress and stepped into her own gown. Now it was my turn to pin her sleeves and raise the hem to mid calf.

After a much needed break for coffee, it was back to the sewing machine. I had discovered my biggest problem was being unable to see the tiny stitches unless I removed my old glasses and held the fabric an inch or two from my eyes. By the time I finished the first gown, my eyes were so tired I could no longer focus.

"We have a real problem, Robbie. I had no idea your eyesight had gotten so bad. You'll never be able to sew like this."

"I'm sorry, Mom. It's all my fault."

"Don't be ridiculous, you can't help being nearsighted"

"I should have borrowed some glasses from Daisy. Her eyes are almost as bad as mine, and she just got two new pair."

Mother stared at me. "Truly, Robbie. If I didn't know better, I'd swear you two were twins."

She disappeared into the kitchen and was soon yammering on the telephone. I went back to the hem on the second nightgown. It was a darker blue and the navy thread simply disappeared into the fabric. It was all I could do to keep from crying. On my first day I was a complete failure. My one chance to impress Mom was a dismal disaster. How could I sew if I couldn't see the thread?

The front door crashed open and Daisy bounded inside and thrust a handful of glasses beneath my nose.

"I brought all my glasses, see what works best." She had already yanked my old specs off and tossed them into the trash. "I absolutely hate those." One by one she fitted the eyeglasses, stepped back, shook her head and replaced them with another. At last, she nodded. "Perfect. The little dapples of purple bring out the blue of your eyes and the shape really accents your hair."

Mom and Momma Jean now leaned in above Daisy's shoulders.

"They do look nice," cooed Momma Jean.

Mother nodded in agreement. "I can't believe how much nicer they look without all that black tape."

"And the paperclips," added Daisy.

"Maybe I should check if I can actually see anything. That's why I need glasses."

Mom pushed the nightgown beneath my nose.

"I can see the thread! I can actually see it, a little fuzzy, but it's there." I glanced up. "Your faces are almost clear."

"Then its decided," said Momma Jean, making everything sound final. "Tomorrow I'll order Daisy a new pair and make you an appointment with the Optometrist."

Instantly, I felt the tension shoot between Mom and Momma Jean. There was no doubt, I was right back in the middle. Which one was going to be my mother?

CHAPTER SIX

Panty Raider

Life was falling into what could pass for a routine. Mom got up first and used the bathroom, then put on her girdle and bra before calling me. I'd drag out of bed and into a quick bath while she finished dressing and fixing her face, which mostly consisted of some lipstick and a little rouge. We'd go down together and one of us would start breakfast while the other put on a load of wash and swept the sewing area. Working with fabric produced a lot of lint and threads, and it was a constant struggle keeping the work area tidy. I still required a lot of guidance in the kitchen, but had already learned to make passable eggs, bacon or sausage and toast. Biscuits were next on my list, but fried chicken was far into the future.

It was funny, not ha, ha funny, but interesting funny, how much pleasure I received when breakfast went well. Buddy seldom got up early enough to eat anything solid and ended by gulping disgusting protein powder stirred into milk and topped with a raw egg. I absolutely refused to make it for him, even though he threatened to wring my neck every morning. William, on the other hand, actually complemented me several times.

School, however, was not going very well. Not only was I taking a lot of ribbing about my girly glasses, but I'd also started falling asleep in class because Mom and I were working past midnight. At least no one had discovered I was wearing girl panties to match my girl glasses. I was still waiting for Jeanie to drop the hatchet on me. Anything she started in high school would reach us in junior high within minutes. Disaster, however, didn't come from the high school.

In eighth grade we had gym every Friday afternoon. Many times it only consisted of running around playing tag or dodge ball. Occasionally we'd have to change into gym shorts and tee shirts and play at basketball or tumbling. Since that would work up a sweat, we'd have to shower, which ended up with a lot of shouting and shoving and popping people on the fanny with wet towels.

It turned out this was one of those sweaty Fridays. That's when I remembered I was wearing the pale lavender panty set. White, I might have been able to hide, but there was absolutely no way I could get my pants off and shorts on without someone noticing those lavender panties, and the vest would be even harder. My stomach began flipping right and left. Half the guys were already in their shorts and crowding toward the door.

"Come on, Jones!" screamed Coach Myers. "We ain't got all day, you know."

Grabbing my shorts and tee, I charged toward the toilets. "In a minute, Coach. Gotta pee." The cubicles didn't have doors, but by pressing into the back I was able to change without anyone noticing. I bundled the nylon vest inside my shirt and trousers and dropped them on the bench in front of my locker.

Oh, God! Never again. I'd have to steal some underwear from Buddy!

We were tumbling, and every time I flipped I expected someone to notice the panties beneath my floppy–legged shorts. But, even though I'd taken God's name in vain, She smiled on me throughout class. We piled back into the locker room en mass and I used the chaos to whip off my shorts and panties together, then stuff them beneath the shirt and towel with the lavender vest. Hey, this wasn't so hard after all. You just had to be smarter than–"

I had made it halfway to the showers when Moose Hanahan yelled.

"Hey, Jones. You forgot ya' towel!"

I turned to see my towel and two very lavender, very slinky pieces of nylon sailing through the air. Everything became deathly silent. Moose leaned down and picked up the panties. As if in slow motion, he opened them out and suspended them by the waistband."

"What th' hell? Jones is wearing purple panties."

Then I said the stupidest words possible. "That's not purple, it's lavender."

*   *   *   *   *

Jeanie didn't need to spill my beans. By the end of day everyone in junior high and high school knew I was wearing panties. Right in class, Mrs. Hanahan, my English teacher asked if I also wore a training bra. There was no way I could stay in school, yet there were still months to go before summer. I also knew Buddy was going to kill me. He didn't, but not for lack of trying. As for Jeanie, she did not say a single word about my humiliation. She just looked up at me through those long, luscious eyelashes. I felt her smirk follow me every time we were together.

My name for the rest of the year became Purple Pantywaist, which was not much worse than Zipper Belly, from the huge zigzag scar across my tummy. My only revenge was that after the girls tired of teasing me, they actually began talking with me, not just about panties, about real subjects. Before that time, no girl other than Daisy and Jeanie knew I existed.

One girl in particular, Mitzi Johnson, about the most beautiful girl in the world, began to pop out of nowhere whenever I was changing class. Mitzi and I were in History, Science and Algebra class, but she never in eight years had spoken to me. Now she would suddenly appear and ask something about class or homework. There would be a pause, then she'd drop the bomb.

"What color today?"

I'd stammer out, "Pink!" or whatever.

She would nod and whisper, "I'm white, as usual."

Then she would siddle off as if I no longer existed.

Life was hell, but at least now I was a person. Well, at least everyone in school knew who I was.

CHAPTER SEVEN

Manikin, you Dummy

Mom and I were making real progress on the Easter dresses, and on me becoming a sewing girl. We had purchased patterns and fabric, zippers, buttons, snaps and hooks as well as more accessories that I had ever imagined. I knew the fabric shops and the church's Good Shepard Exchange by heart. The Exchange was especially valuable since there were all kinds of half–used sewing items for five and ten cents. They also had a whole row of really interesting underthings on hangers, but I was always too embarrassed to snoop through all that pink elastic and satin panels.

I learned how to cut out and keep track of all the myriad pieces to a pattern, and had even started to get the hang of creating one from big sheets of brown paper. My chief problem had been in understanding how the flat pieces fit together on a solid person. For a long time, the parts were only bits of paper. Then, as if by magic, one day the flat sections transformed into a dress inside my head. I could actually foresee how making a tiny alteration here or there could morph into a sleeve or waistline that could flow around a living body. Breasts were something we weren't concerned with as yet, since these were outfits for young girls. As Mom said, we'd worry about boobies and hips and fannies later.

Every few minutes Mom would take some obscure measurement off my body, such as from my shoulder to an elbow, then scribble odd numbers onto a pattern. The next moment a sliver would be trimmed here, or extra paper taped onto another section. Then, voila, scraps of cloth could be sewn into living shapes.

She showed me how to add extra fabric in the seams so we could let out a size, or take up to go down a size or two.

"We've got to make these so they'll fit a wide range of girls. We wouldn't have to be so generous in the seams if we knew who might purchase what."

I would nod as if I understood. And, after a few days, I actually did. We now had the basis of twelve dresses sorted into piles, with all the required zippers, laces, ribbons and buttons selected and ready to assemble.

"Mom, don't we need some of those…, I don't know what you call them, but those dummies to fit the dresses on? I mean, how can we make sure they look right, or do the hems?"

Putting down her scissors and taking a dozen pins from between her lips, she smiled at me. "You mean a manikin? Why, Sweetie, I have the finest manikin in town."

"You do?"

"Certainly, darling." Her fingers ran through my bushy hair. "How about my little Robbie?"

"But…. But, Mom. I can't try on these…, these…."

"Well, I don't believe your brothers are going to volunteer. Who did you think was going to do it? Anyway, you'll only need to have them on while I check the fit and mark the hem."

"But, Mom. They're going to be so short..., and so..., girly."

"I certainly hope so. That's what mothers and girls want for Easter. Frills, ribbons and lace. That's why we selected these fabrics and colors. After they're fitted, lined and finished inside and out, they'll be works of art. If we had customers they would tell us what they wanted. But we're making these cold. Our only hope is to make them so adorable every mother's heart will melt. I want them so girly that I'll dream of having you in one come Easter."

"Mom! You wouldn't!"

"You bet I will, if that's the only way we can sell them. Now, get on that machine and start sewing the rose one in satin." She gave a merry laugh. "If you mess it up you'll be wearing it to church next Sunday."

Then she gave me a huge hug, almost like she loved me. Of course, I knew she could never love me.

*   *   *   *   *

As we finished each item I'd have to take off my pants and shirt and slip the satin or silk or taffeta over my head, then stand on the platform while Mom pinned a little or marked a seam. All the while I'd be trembling, expecting William or Buddy to burst through the door and see me in those God–awful outfits. As a last step she would pin the hem. I felt all the dresses were sinfully short. I'd be afraid my undies would show, if I had actually been wearing them.

"That's the way little girls dress these days," Mom chuckled. "Don't you ever look at people?"

My head shook.

"Well, if you're going to be a successful dressmaker you've got to know what people are wearing. If you make a hoopskirt today, nobody's going to buy it."

"But, I'll never be a dressmaker. Not actually. This is just to get you started. Soon as I'm old enough, I'll need to get a real job. Maybe at the dealership or down at the grocery store."

Mother smiled. "You don't know. I never imagined I'd become the mother of three such different boys. I always thought I'd have little girls to sew for, just like my mother or Aunt Jean. You just have to take what life throws at you…, and make the very best of what you've got. Sometimes, you take peaches and make a mess, but you hope you can take persimmons and make marmalade."

"I'm sorry you got persimmons."

Mom didn't say anything for a long while, then she whispered. "Perhaps two persimmons and one peach."

For hours I wondered if William or Buddy was the peach. There certainly was no doubt who was a persimmon, and a green one at that.

*   *   *   *   *

Mom was pinning the hem of the third dress when I turned so she could reach the back. Now I faced directly into the big mirror and for the first time actually began to look at myself. For a boy like me, the dress was a horror, and I was even more of a horror. How could anyone actually go out in public looking like this. At least I had long hair, Momma Jean made sure of that, not the crew cuts now so popular. Patting at the sides of my hair, I tried to imagine it with the curls Momma Jean put into Daisy's. I did have some natural waves, which softened my face. Daisy, even with her Teen–B boobies would look absolutely marvelous in this dress. She was at that exact wonderful state between girl and woman. So sweet, so…, well, fresh as a daisy. Now, Jeanie or Mitzi Johnson would look almost as stupid as me. Mitzi, with all her curves…. No! I couldn't think about Mitzi, not with Mom pinning a hem only inches from me.

"Robbie? Are you alright?"

"Ummmm…, huh?"

"You've been staring at yourself in that mirror for ten minutes. I finished the hem ages ago."

"I was only thinking, imagining how Daisy would look in this. I promised…, umm…, when I learn to sew. I mean, I promised to make her a dress…, you know, after I learn…."

Mom returned to her machine and began working on the next dress. "Perhaps you think too much about Daisy. It's not…, safe…, to become so attached to another person. No matter how much you love her, it doesn't mean she loves you in the same way. Finish that dress. I'd like to complete one more today."

I worked on the dress for the next hour, until it was as perfect as I could make it. Daisy did love me, no matter what Mom said. She loved me, just as I loved her.

CHAPTER EIGHT

Flying down the Runway

Everything was ready. Mom and I had worked till midnight to make sure all the dresses were perfect. Even William had helped to triple check every detail. Papa Henry had one of his mechanics make us a collapsible rack on rollers so we could display the dresses during the bidding. It was noon on Saturday, two weeks before Easter, and the date of the Garden Club's first luncheon of the year. William had taken off from work. Mom was in her nicest outfit. I was in my best suit…, well, actually, my only suit. We were going to have the best fashion show ever. Mom would read a description of each outfit as I carried it from table to table, so the ladies and their daughters could see and handle it. Then, while I got the next dress ready, the ladies would make what was called a silent bid on the previous one. In the end, the highest bidder would get each garment. Half the money would go to some Garden Club charity, half would go to Mom.

What could possibly go wrong?

Well, Mary Williams! Wife of the Mayor and social ruler of our little world. She stood before us like a Spartan ready to defend Her Garden Club, with my life.

"No, my dear," she smoothed. "You can't expect My Ladies to select an outfit trotted around by...." She stared down her nose at me. "This..., young man. It just isn't done. They must be upon a proper model. If you can't find someone, I shall be forced to cancel the entire proceedings."

With that, she spun on her expensive high heel and traipsed through the swinging doors separating us from the dining room.

Mom clinched her fists. "Why, that Bitch! Can you believe how she spoke to us? How an I suppose to find someone this late?"

Suddenly, Mom looked at me. "Robbie, sit! William, bring me that pink outfit, the one with the red ribbons." She fished into her purse. "Robbie, stick you lips out like this. Don't move. Blast it, sit still."

She carefully worked across my mouth with her lipstick and blotted the lips with a tissue. Then she rubbed a spot of rouge onto each cheek and topped everything by dusting my face with powder.

"Mom! What are you doing to me?"

"Quiet. William, there's a girl about Robbie's age at the first table. See if you can borrow her shoes. Hand me the dress."

Taking a tiny pair of fingernail scissors from the purse, Mom snipped two red bows with dangling ribbons from the dress and held one against the side of my head. "Yessss. This will work perfectly.

With every second, my terror leapt. "Mom, what are you doing? Please don't think what I think you're thinking."

By now she had fastened the ribbon in place with bobby pins. Moments later, the second one was attached. I could feel the ribbons brushing against my earlobes.

"Take off your shoes. The socks too. Out of your pants and shirt."

Sinking to my knees, I clutched her legs. "Please, don't do this to me. I'm already a laughing stock at school. Don't make me a fool all over town."

She lifted me to my feet and wrapped me in her arms. "Sweetie, this is really, really important. If we aren't successful we're going to lose the house. The family might get broken up. You've got to do this for me..., you've got to do this for your brothers..., you've got to do this for all of us. I won't force you, but if you don't walk through those doors, all of our work is lost."

I felt frozen in place. I could not breath, much less think. At last, my head nodded. I was already dead. What more could the kids at school do to me? Black slippers slid onto my feet. Some paper was folded and stuffed behind each heel. They were slightly big, at least they didn't fall off. A petticoat went over my head, then a second, followed by yards of satin. Lace, ribbons everywhere..., a sash about my waist.

"William, when he comes back, help him into the second outfit and bring the first to me. We'll work through them just the way they're lined up." She knelt before me. "Robbie, Baby. Are you ready?"

Once more I nodded. My mouth was so dry I could not make a sound. William and I stood behind the swinging doors. Mom's voice sounded clear. She introduced herself and how the auction was to work. My legs felt heavier and heavier. I couldn't move. There was absolutely no way I could possibly walk through those doors. Suddenly, the doors swung aside and a firm hand pushed me forward. I stumbled a few steps, then froze once more. There must have been ten thousand faces staring at me. A titter came from a hundred thousand astonished mouths. Another hand now, this Mom's, turned me slowly right, then left, then so my back was to the throngs. Finally, she eased me toward the first table and I walked right to... Mitzi Johnson!

I must have snapped out of it. Mitzi stared at me. I stared at her. Her mouth opened, then closed. Her hands were on the hem of my skirt by then and she whispered, "What color?"

"Pink"

"I'm pink too." For an instant, her hand squeezed mine. "You're really pretty today."

By then I'd been pushed to the second table and I realized that there weren't thousands of women, only sixty or seventy. Through some miracle I made it around the room and was guided back toward the swinging doors.

I still felt frozen inside, but somehow I survived all the outfits without throwing up. As I completed the final round I felt hands on my shoulders. Mrs. Williams voice cut through the silence.

"I'm sure we all enjoyed today's presentation and you can imagine how hard we worked to provide you enlightenment and entertainment. Now, I think we should show our appreciation to little Robbie Jones for being such a brave warrior today. He truly must be the bravest little boy in town. And he certainly has fine taste in clothing."

My mind woke up when Mom was lacing my shoes. My pants and shirt felt hard and stiff after the soft petticoats and dresses.

"Mom, did they all laugh at me?"

"It sounded more like applause than laughter." She pushed the slippers into my hand. "Return these to the young lady and be sure to thank her."

I stumbled through the doors and looked around. The only young lady was Mitzi. Oh God! On top of everything else, I'd been wearing Mitzi Johnson's patent leather slippers. She stuck our her foot. I could see her red nails through the stockings.

"You'll have to put them on," she said, sliding her skirt well above the knee.

I knelt and brushed the bottom of her soft foot. Inside the stocking, her skin felt incredibly slick. Beneath her skirt, just in front of my eyes, was a dark band of nylon and a tiny metal loop of a garter. Once more my mouth became so dry I could no longer swallow. My hand trembled as I worked the right shoe into place, then the left.

Her fill lips curved upward. "You owe me, Robbie Jones. You owe me big time."

CHAPTER NINE

Ruby Red

William dropped us in front of Tin Skillet Diner and headed back to his job at the dealership. Mom brushed some nonexistent lint from my shoulder, then straightened my collar. All of a sudden she pulled me close.

"I'm so proud of you, Robbie. That horrid Mary Williams was right for once in her life. You are the bravest boy in town." After checking inside her purse, she frowned as she held up a dime. "Jean and the girls are meeting us to hear all about our adventure. You deserve a big treat, but we can only afford one Coke. Just say you aren't hungry and we'll dig up something after we get home."

As always, I nodded, even though I was starving and my stomach was still doing flops from all the tension.

Momma Jean and the girls were already waiting inside. We had only gotten halfway down the aisle when they jumped up and surrounded us. Everyone in the Diner stared, of course, since we made as much noise as a band of marauding Apaches. At last we settled enough for a very brave waitress to approach and take our order. She gave everyone a disapproving stare, but she saved her most penetrating glare for me.

"I'll just have a small Coke," I quickly said. "I'm not hungry."

Before Mom could say anything, Momma Jean corrected me.

"The three ducklings will each have your super banana split with your biggest Coke."

Mom quickly added, "I'll just have a glass of water."

Momma Jean made a face. "The big duck and the old hen will have large slices of apple pie topped with vanilla ice cream…, be sure to add lots of whipped topping and cherries."

"Jean, I can't eat all that. My figure…."

"Then get a new girdle, right girls?"

The three of us replied in unison, "Right!"

Leaning in, Momma Jean said in a stage whisper. "Okay, we want every gory detail."

By the time our calories arrived Mom had given every blow–by–blow. Since I'd mostly been in a trance, I learned a lot about all that had happened. Not only had all the dresses been taken, but Mom had gotten two new orders for Easter dresses, and one query about a prom gown.

All this time Jeanie had been softly singing beneath her breath.

Oh, those ribbons, scarlet ribbons, scarlet ribbons for her hair….

I slowly touched the sides of my hair. "Dear Jesus! That's why everyone is laughing at me."

Desperately, I clutched at the ribbons. As fast, Mom and Momma Jean grabbed my hand.

"Don't you dare!" they said in unison.

Momma Jean gave her most mischievous smile. "Well, girls. I think it's time we began using Robbie's real name.

"Not now," said Mom. Her eyes shifted from Momma Jean, to me, then back to Momma Jean.

"What real name?" asked Jeanie.

Momma Jean settled back into the seat. "When Aunt Pam and I were expecting, I was certain that Daisy was a girl. Little Robbie had been so quiet inside your Aunt Pam, she also was certain he was a girl. There just wasn't any question at all. Aunt Pam had selected the name Ruby, and I selected Daisy. Two beautiful names for two beautiful girls. First, Daisy came as we expected, but when Ruby was born, she wasn't a Ruby at all..., then everything went bad."

"Jean, this isn't the time or the place."

Momma Jean raised her hand. "This is exactly the time. It's almost too late, in fact."

Daisy squeezed my hand. "I love Ruby. I think we should all call him Ruby from now on."

Taking a slip of paper from her handbag, Momma Jean slid it in front of Mom. "I've made an appointment with Doc Pricher for 10:30 Tuesday. Either you take Ruby, or I will. We can't put it off any longer."

Mom shook her head. "I've got to think. Give me more time."

"No. You're going to wake up one morning and realize it's too late. Now is the time."

Tears filled Mom's eyes as she stared at me. "Please, God. Don't let us make the wrong decision."

"I've prayed too." whispered Momma Jean. "For thirteen years I struggled. I love both of you and don't want to hurt either. But, now is the time."

Jeanie slid her hand into mine. I sat, dumbstruck between my sisters. A slight breeze from the overhead fans wafted the scarlet ribbons against my earlobes. Both girls snuggled tight against me. What on earth were Mom and Momma Jean going to do?

CHAPTER TEN

Doc Pricher

Doc Pricher was an institution. He probably should have retired ages ago, but he simply loved his patients and job too much. He had delivered Mom and Dad as well as Momma Jean and Papa Henry, not to mention my brothers and sisters and me. He knew all of us by name and what flavor Tootsie Pop we liked. He remembered all our aches and illnesses. He was slowing down a little with age, but not much. He visited patients in the hospital at daybreak, had office hours till noon, then spent the afternoon reminiscing with shut–ins. If you were too ill to come to his office, he actually still made house calls. He had taken on two 'whippersnappers' to inherit his practice, but the two of them could not handle half his load.

Usually, I loved visiting Doc. I would be placed in a tiny examining room and a few minutes later he would enter, fire off a joke or two, ask what was wrong and take care of my problem. Then he would reach into his coat pocket and pull out a grape Tootsie Pop and I would be off.

This time was going to be different. First, Mom was with me, and instead of the tiny examining room we were in the big room with the funny examining table that had metal poles and things called stirrups sticking out. What was even worst was that Nurse Spence was in the room with us. Nurse Spence was Butch's mother. After Moose Hanahan, Butch was my biggest tormentor. Sitting in my panties and vest in front of her was almost like being in front of Butch. My other big worry was that no man had ever seen me in panties. What on earth was Doc going to think?

There was little time to worry. Doc bounded through the doorway in his normal herd–of–buffalo way.

"Hullo, Pam," he almost shouted. "Hullo, Robbie. Oh, your Aunt Jean tells me you want to be called Ruby now. Pretty name. Quite pretty."

He was already listening to my heart through his stethoscope, then my lungs, both front and back while he thumped as I breathed in deep. Next came the light up the nose, then into the back of my mouth while I said 'AAAAAh,' then 'eeeeeh.' Finally, he did the light through the ear trick so it showed on the far wall while he exclaimed about how empty my head was. After making each leg jerk by tapping my knee, he had me lie back and Nurse Spence set my heels into the stirrups and clicked my legs apart. He had me hunch up, and almost instantly my panties were below my wide–spread knees.

I had never felt more naked and exposed in my life!

Doc ran a finger along my zipper scar. "Well…, it's looking better, but definitely not one of my finest jobs." He turned to Mom. "Pam, I understand you're a dressmaker now. Suppose you could do a better looking seam with your eyes closed. Perhaps I should have done a hem stitch."

Mom stared at my tummy. "It looks fine, Doctor Pricher. At least you saved...." Her voice trailed off.

"Yes, my dear, those were dark days. Dark, indeed. You're not having those thoughts any more, are you?"

"No, Doctor." Mom seemed especially pale.

Turning back to me, Doc began searching for my backbone through my tummy. When he had no luck, he measured the width of my hip bones with his huge hands. All the while he was doing a lot of humming and hawing. Next his attention shifted under my vest as his fingertips pressed firmly into the soft tissue around my nipples.

"Never too young to think about breast cancer. That's the coming disease. One can't be too careful." His hand rested on my tummy. "Did you like playing with dolls, Ruby?"

"If Daisy, wanted to. I mean, we always did what she wanted, unless Jeanie took over. Then we played whatever Jeanie wanted."

"Yes, Jeanie is somewhat the Queen Bee, isn't she?" Doc nodded as if in agreement with his question. "Did you play house?"

"Sometimes. Jeanie always was the daddy, and Daisy was Mommie..., I was the baby."

"Were you a good baby?"

"Of course, otherwise Jeanie would punish me."

"Did she actually punish you? Like spank you?"

"Not really. Once she gave me castor oil. It was terrible."

"Ahhhh! Jean's famous castor oil. It'll cure anything that ails a young'un."

Once more Doc nodded, as if he had discovered all he needed to know about my play habits. I could not have been more lost as to what he was getting at, but I knew he had one more place to examine and that was going to be the most embarrassing of all.

There wasn't long to wait. Doc's gigantic hand moved to my little thing and began its gentle exploration. With Mom and Nurse Spence staring directly at my crotch I shrank even smaller. His touch was unbelievably soft but that's an extremely sensitive location, and Doc kept discovering ever more tender places to press and kneed. Just as I was about to crawl beneath the examining table, he stopped and pulled my panties up my thighs. I humped and he slid them to my waist.

"Healthy as an ox. Well, whatever a young ox is called. You've a mild sinus infection which may be spreading into your right ear. I'll have Nurse Spence give you an injection and prescribe a course of antibiotics." He turned to Mom. "Looks a little anemic. Get some daily vitamins with extra iron."

With that he reached into his lab coat and drew out a grape Tootsie Pop, whipped off the wrapper and stuffed it into my open mouth. A moment later he was unwrapping a cherry Pop and handed it to Mom.

"Cherry, I believe. Pam, if you'll follow me into the office we can discuss a few things. Ruby will need to come in the first of each month for an injection. In addition, there'll be a daily tablet." At the door he turned back to me. "You may have a little morning sickness for a few days. Let me know if it lasts longer than a week. Don't miss any tablets or you'll mess up your system."

With that he and Mom were gone. I looked at Nurse Spence and she stared back.

"Well," she said. "I suppose we should punch a few holes in you."

She disappeared for several minutes, then returned with a tray containing two hypodermic syringes. One was tiny, the other looked like something you might use on an elephant. The small one she poked into my arm. It didn't hurt too much.

"Okay, Sweetie, pull down your panties and lean over the table. Doc prescribed a double dose and it's going to sting."

As I pulled down my panties, I glanced over my shoulder. "What is that?"

"Something to make you pretty."

After rubbing alcohol on my right fanny, she pressed a roll of fat between her thumb and forefinger. The needle drew back and plunged right into the roll. At first there was only a slight prick, then the sting began. Wow! I was on fire.

"Perhaps I should give you one in the other cheek. You don't want to be lopsided."

"No thanks," I moaned.

Nurse Spence made several notes in my record as I dressed.

"Am I really going to have morning sickness?"

She glanced up. "Probably. You got quite a jolt there. It should only last a few days." She smiled sweetly. "I'll be sure to tell Butch what a brave little girl you were."

"Thanks," I said.

"My pleasure," she grinned.

*   *   *   *   *

As we drove to the pharmacy my fanny was really burning, but a much bigger quandary was building inside my head. I didn't know how long I could stay quiet.

At the pharmacy we handed in my prescriptions, picked up some supplies for Mom, then went to the vitamin section. The ones with extra iron were in pink bottles and had something like '*Extra Iron, for a girl's special needs,*' plastered in bold lettering. I could already imagine what Buddy would say when he saw them on the kitchen counter.

My desperation was getting deeper and deeper.

As we waited for my prescriptions, I couldn't keep silent any longer.

"Mom, am I going to have a baby?"

She just stared at me for several moments.

"That's the silliest thing you've ever asked. Why on earth would you think that?"

"When Mrs. Jennings down the street was pregnant she had morning sickness. You said you were sick with William and Buddy. Momma Jean said she was sick for nine months with Daisy. Doc Pricher and Nurse Spence both said I'd have morning sickness."

Mom giggled, then covered her mouth. "Oh, Lord. Didn't you have sex education class last year?"

"Coach Myers talked to us in the training room. He said sex was like screwing in a light bulb."

"Screwing in a bulb? What else was said?"

"Everybody but me laughed. Then Moose asked how many women it took to change a light bulb."

"And, how many does it take?"

"One man and six women. The man changes the bulb and the women talk about it."

She closed her eyes and slowly shook her head. "My God! Our tax dollars at work."

Just then my prescriptions were ready. Mom paid, and we headed home.

She should have realized how woefully ignorant I was about birds and bees, not to mention girls and boys. I knew exactly how Daisy looked, and had a very good idea about Jeanie. But, I was absolutely clueless concerning how all the pieces fit together, and how everything worked. What was worst, far worst, was that I had no real idea what had just been done to my mind and body. I had been turned into a ticking bomb and was too ignorant to understand what was happening.

All I knew was that for some reason I did not understand I had been sentenced even deeper into panty prison for an unknown transgression, and that life was going to get much more complicated before it got better.

CHAPTER ELEVEN

School Daze

By this time I was almost living a double life. During the day I was a mild mannered eight grader, and at night an even milder mannered sewing girl. For two days following my visit to Doc Pricher I was fine, except for a sore fanny. It looked as if the dire warnings about morning sickness were unfounded. Actually, I was mainly worried about Butch Spence. What had his mother told him, and when was he going to clobber me with it? The executioner's sword that normally hung over my head now felt as if it had turned into a battle ax.

But, everything at school was quiet. Perhaps I could get through an entire week without a disaster of embarrassment. I began to breath easier. Except, on the third morning I woke not feeling too well, and the queasiness got worse as I approached school.

When I entered homeroom, Moose and Butch greeted me me with a sneered, "Good Morning, Ruby!"

I turned just in time to barf all over both of them. The good part was they were so grossed they didn't beat me black and blue before running to the restroom to clean up. The bad was I lost the rest of breakfast into the nearest trash basket. I also lost lunch and dinner that night. Then, everything I ate the next couple of days came back within moments. What with the nausea and hot–flashes and chills and stomach cramps, the remainder of the week pretty well melted into oblivion. By the time Monday rolled around I was feeling better and Butch had lost interest in tormenting me about my new name. Moose, of course, never gave up on any distasteful behavior.

My school life settled into a dreary bore, with the occasional case of stark terror, such as when Moose and Butch decided to take off my trousers before history class. All the kids except Mitzi just stood around and giggled. Mitzi kicked Butch in the knee, but that didn't stop the assault. A teacher finally pulled Butch off me, but my pants were already around my ankles. I was sent to the office for causing a distraction. What amazed me was that my brothers never came to my defense. Not once, not in my entire time in school did either of them ever help me. I thought that's what brothers were for, to help and protect each other. Clearly, I was wrong. In the lower grades Jeanie did help. As long as she was bigger than Moose or Butch she could bonk them on the head and send them running. Of course, now she was in high school and both boys outweighed her by fifty pounds. She could scream at them, but they simply ignored her.

For the next couple of months there were no extra horrible reactions to my injections and tablets, and I drifted into a state of suspended animation. The week of my injection I always felt lousy and had a lot of problems with sweating and freezing, then my ankles started swelling and my dreams really got weird. None of that freaked me out. By now I was used to weird feelings. Everything was not completely bad. I was even able to get Momma Jean to purchase a few pair of plain white panties to wear on gym days. I had wanted cotton, but that was out of the question. The oddest thing was that by the end of the school year all of them had been stolen. I could not imagine why any boy would steal another boy's plain white panties. But then, I could not imagine another boy in the world was wearing panties of any color.

My hair really started to take off. As long as I could remember, Momma Jean had cut my hair along with Daisy's. With Daisy, she would just trim it a little, then shape it on the ends. Every few months she would put a lot of rollers in, squirt some smelly liquid on the rollers, and by the time the rollers were removed, Daisy would have a cascade of curls that lasted almost until the next treatment. In my case, Momma Jean would put a bowl over my head and trim around it. Then she would level my bangs and I was ready for the next few weeks. Well, not actually, because Momma Jean was always snipping little bits here and there to keep both of us shaped. She never seemed quite pleased with our hair, but did not want to take us to the beauty shop. Not yet, anyway.

Now I began to realize that Momma Jean was not trimming the length of my hair at all. Soon, it was going to be as long as Daisy's. In fact, the only real difference between us was that Daisy had curls and I only have waves. Whenever I mentioned getting a real haircut, Mom or Momma Jean would just laugh.

"Don't you like your hair?" they would ask. "You look lovely and it smells so nice after you shampoo. Anyway, you don't want to look like all the boys with their crew cuts do you? Now, let's not hear another word."

It was almost as if they had practiced the little speech. And, keeping my hair long really was not that hard. Not with four women constantly snipping, combing, brushing and patting it into place. To really seal my fate, Mom started mumbling about getting me a perm if I made too much noise. I had enough problems with waves, I certainly did not want Shirley Temple curls all over my head.

Science class was my favorite. It came right after lunch and break. Miss Griffith, our teacher, always had some mysterious reason to visit the office and I was left in charge. Mostly we watched movies about wildlife and chemistry or stuff like that. I would load the projector, read the teacher's intro, switch out the lights and start the projector. The boys would immediately go to sleep and the girls would start filing their nails or doodle in their notebooks, while I devoured the film. As it ended Miss Griffith would return and class would end. Another class without being humiliated or embarrassed! That was also a plus.

Sometimes we were supposed to do experiments, but we usually had no idea what was supposed to happen. One time we had a frog and a big static electricity wand. I charged the wand according to the directions and Mitzi set the frog on Miss Griffith's desk. I was suppose to zap the frog and make it jump, but before I could act, the stupid frog sailed onto the floor where Moose 'accidentally' squished it with his size thirteen EE brogan. I accidentally jabbed Moose smack in the butt with the wand. He jumped twice as far as the frog. That was one time I enjoyed getting beat up.

We had lunch the same time as high school, but us snot–nosed kids were suppose to sit at the far end of the dinning hall. The tables held eight, and usually girls ate with girls and boys ate with boys. With my strong feelings for Daisy, I always ate at her table and if I was late, she would hold a seat for me, which usually caused a lot of tittering. As the year progressed I noticed a subtle change taking place. Girls and boys started sharing tables, and a lot of whispering and giggling was taking place.

One day I was late because I had been sent to the office for causing a distraction. By the time my plate was served, Daisy's table was full, and not just with girls. With Moose and Butch and two of their buddies to be exact. I stood like an idiot, with all the tables around me filled to capacity. Was I supposed to sit on the floor? Should I sit with the big kids? My desperation was increasing by the second.

"Robbie, over here!" Mitzi Johnson waved at me from across the hall.

Slinking as quietly as possible, I slid in beside her.

"I saw your girlfriend had taken up with your best buddy, so I saved you a seat."

"Girlfriend?"

"Yeah, tousle–top. I've seen you kissing and holding hands after school. Don't you carry her books every day?"

"Oh, that's Daisy. She's my sister. Well, my cousin. She's like my sister. We were raised together."

She smiled. "Thought that was why you hadn't asked me for a date. Every other boy in class has."

"I didn't think...."

"That's the problem with you, Robbie Jones. You don't think. Come on, eat, we'll be late for class."

All I could do was nibble at my food. Had Mitzi asked me for a date? That was so preposterous it was funny. That had to be the answer. Mitzi was making a joke. The prettiest girl in school..., no, the prettiest girl in the world, would never want to be seen in public with a Purple Pantywaist, especially one named Ruby.

*   *   *   *   *

One day I became a hero, even if it cost me a bloody nose.

As the weather warmed and we kids became more unruly, the teachers began planning outings. We were suppose to learn stuff and write reports, but no–one ever paid enough attention to complete our assignments. This day Miss Griffith had taken us to a local dairy to see where our lunch milk originated. We tramped through the mud and fed hay to the cows. Butch tried to vault over a fence like cowboys do in the movies, caught his foot and fell face first into a huge pile of cow droppings.

Then we entered the barn and a gruff old man brought in a cow to milk. The poor critter looked like she was going to explode down there. The cow placed its head between two metal bars which clicked tight, locking her in place. Although the man seemed really gruff, he gently patted the beast on her big boobie.

"You have to be gentle," he said. "Then she'll relax and let down her milk."

While the man talked, drops of milk started to drip from the nipples.

"Now, we place these four nozzles on each of the teats, and switch on the pump.

There was a throbbing in the distance, and gobs of milk started flowing from the cow and along glass tubes. Mitzi had moved in next to me and stood as transfixed, watching all that milk come from one cow. I hardly noticed as Moose sidled beside Mitzi and stage–whispered into her ear.

"How would you like having that hooked to your tits?"

Mitzi sucked in her breath. I hauled back and let Moose have it right in the kisser. At first, Moose just blinked. Then his fist met my nose. The next thing I remember was Mitzi helping me stand and Miss Griffith blotting the blood with her handkerchief.

Moose and I got expelled for a day. After I came back to school, Mitzi caught up with me on the corridor and slipped her hand into mine.

"That was the bravest thing I've ever seen," she whispered. "You're a real hero."

We walked a couple of minutes. She didn't let go of my hand.

At last she said, "What color?"

"Blue"

"That's amazing. I'm blue also. We must be linked by some unseen force."

CHAPTER TWELVE

Clothes Pony

After school I would hurry home and begin helping Mom, either with sewing or housework. In fact, I was making more headway in learning housekeeping than in sewing. It is amazing how much work is involved in keeping a family of four clean and fed. Meals have to be prepared, then you have to clean up all the mess that entails. But, before you can cook, you have to purchase the food, bring it home, put it in the fridge, pantry or cabinets. Then, when you're ready to cook, you have to locate all the ingredients, do the preparations and actually fix the mean. Of course, you then have to clean all over again. It was an all–encompassing, endless task. Before Dad's death, Mom essentially did all the housework. Now she was working twelve or more hours a day at the sewing machine and someone had to take up at least part of that load. That someone was me.

My very first job, which started as soon as I moved into Mom's bedroom, was hand washing our undies. It was really strange, in that scrubbing Mom's panties and girdles was highly embarrassing, it also was extremely satisfying to at last have a personal relationship with her. I had never felt that she loved me, certainly not the way she loved William and Buddy. It was as if I were a stranger who had been taken in off the street. Now I was taking care of her most intimate clothing and I could show her my love by being especially tender with her personal belongings. I always made certain to hang my panties touching hers. She might not hug and kiss me the way Momma Jean did, but at least our panties could touch.

Now that Dad was gone, we all had to pitch in. William was trying to graduate from high school and also work nearly full time at the dealership. He also kept our accounts, maintained the car, polished everyone's shoes and took care of the yard. Buddy was a full time athlete and goof–off. He had assigned duties, such as taking out the trash, but he never got around to doing them. What made me absolutely furious was that whenever William or I would complete one of his duties, he would say, "Oh, I was getting ready to do that."

After a few weeks I was doing the laundry, vacuuming, cleaning the bathrooms as well as cooking breakfast and some dinners – with Mom's directions – washing and drying the dishes, and shopping for groceries. Cleaning the boy's bathroom was my worse job, buying groceries was the best. Best, because it made me feel grownup that Mom and William would trust me with all that cash. Mom would make a list and each Thursday evening one of the boys would drive me to the Winn–Dixie and read magazines while I shopped. They were allowed to select one item, which I would add to the groceries and pay. Then they were supposed to load everything into the car, drive us home and unload all the paper bags into the kitchen. From there it was my job to put each item into its proper place.

That was how it was supposed to work. With William, it usually did. But not with Buddy. Half the time when I was ready, Buddy would have disappeared with one of his friends. Then I would have to push the cart the three blocks to our house, unload the groceries and push the cart all the way back to Winn–Dixie. At that point Buddy would reappear and want me to purchase his magazine. By this time I would be so mad I'd start peppering him with gravel from the parking lot. Actually, I got pretty good at it and could hit him for twenty paces. What made it even worse was that while William would select a good magazine such as Scientific American, Buddy always wanted a grubby mystery or girly magazine. Little did I know those grubby magazines would come back to haunt me.

*   *   *   *   *

Once Mom and I had completed the twelve Easter dresses, she got serious about training me as a seamstress. She had started using one of my old three–ring binders to keep track of our clients. Turning to a blank page, she printed my name at the top and added some notes about my height and weight, hair color and some other information I did not understand.

"Okay, Ruby. You're a new customer and you want us to make you some clothing. First, I'll measure you, then you'll do me. Now, if you would be so kind, please remove your shirt and trousers, then stand on the platform. If we were going to make something form–fitting, I would make sure you were wearing proper foundations."

"What are foundations?"

"The proper brassiere and girdle. You need different types for different dresses."

"Oh! Does it make a difference? I mean, your and Momma Jean's girdles have satin panels and Jeanie's are all stretchy. But, don't they just hold up your stockings?"

Mom smiled. "You are either very observant or extremely nosy. A girdle doesn't make you smaller, but women are very soft and a good girdle can alter your shape quiet a bit. Different bras can also make a dramatic difference in your shape. When you begin actually making an item for a girl you'll need to be very aware of what else she's wearing…, without being too snoopy. Remember, we are trying to be professional in all regards. We want our clients to feel absolutely comfortable, and also feel they are getting special treatment. They can buy off–the–rack clothing anywhere in town. Most of our work will be alterations, but we can provide hand made and fitted items, like the Easter dresses. Understand?"

I nodded.

"Good. Now, I'm going to take your measurements and enter them on this sheet. We'll be able to take that information and make a garment that fits you almost perfectly. With a final adjustment on your body, it will become perfect."

"But, Mom, can we afford to waste all that fabric and stuff just so I can learn?"

She laughed. "Don't worry, I'm sure we can find someone who can use everything we make."

With that she began taking dozens of measurements and jotting them on my sheet.

"Hold the tape snug, not tight. It helps to put your forefinger inside the tape. It's easier to take up a little slack than have to add fabric after you've cut. It is much easier to measure from the client's back. Sometimes it can feel a little too intimate having someone stare right into your boobs." Mom gave an even merrier laugh. "Be extra careful measuring the bust and bottom. Women want to be big on top and small in the hips. We are actually built exactly the opposite."

Soon my sheet was filled with numbers and notes. Mom slipped out of her dress and handed me the tape. I could feel my face getting hot.

"But.... But, Mom. What if I accidentally..., you know, touch you..., up there?"

She ran her hand through my hair. "Ruby, you're not a grubby old man, you're barely more than a child forced into a grown woman's job. If you accidentally touch someone, carry on as if nothing happened. Remember, you're a professional seamstress. Act like one and no one will notice you're an embarrassed little boy."

After I completed Mom's measurements, we looked through our stacks of patterns until we found a dress I liked. The interesting thing about most patterns was that you could make the same dress in dozens of ways by altering the skirt or blouse part, changing the fabric, adding pockets, using different collars, making the sleeves short or long, adding trim or decorations, as well as dozens of other options.

First, Mom helped me make a straight skirt. Next, she had me make a full, then an A–line. By changing fabric and finishes you could hardly have guessed they were basically the same garment. Finally, we combined the skirt and blouse into a dress and went through the same iterations.

When we turned my room into the fitting room, my old closet became our storage area for completed items. As each skirt, blouse or dress was finished it was added to the closet, which now held a growing wardrobe for some lucky girl.

While I was working, Mom had taken out a bolt of fine cotton in a pale shade of blue and began assembling what appeared to be a uniform. At first it was quite plain, but Mom added a white trim at the sleeves and a white Peter

Pan collar. It really looked like an old–fashioned British nurse's uniform. Since I was our only manikin, I had to try it on several times for her to get everything just right. I was certainly glad the uniform was not for me since the hem was almost at mid–thigh, which seemed sinfully revealing.

As my graduation exam I had to select a pattern for Mom, choose the fabric and accessories, then complete it with the finest details I could imagine, such as lining the skirt with silk and adding a hand embroidered label.

"This is absolutely beautiful," she said. "I'm so proud of you, Ruby. You have a great eye for fashion. I would never have combined this fabric with this pattern, but the way you trimmed and finished it looks…, well, it looks like a designer gown. I'll wear it to church this Sunday."

I knew she was only being nice, but she did look stunning. And, I had never noticed how pretty she was, or just how nice a figure she had.

*   *   *   *   *

At last I had finished all the skirts, blouses and dresses and Mom had completed three of the uniforms. Of course, during all this time she had also been completing other jobs, such as completely reworking a wedding dress and making six bridesmaids dresses. We were both exhausted.

"Time for a break," she said, collapsing back into her chair. "Let's have a treat."

A treat usually meant we'd brew a fresh pot of coffee and sneak a couple of sinfully rich cookies she kept hidden on the top shelf of the pantry.

Instead, she led me upstairs to our bedroom and told me to undress while she started filling the tub with steaming water. When I entered the bathroom wearing only my housecoat she was sprinkling strawberry bubble bath over the tub. Something big was about to happen.

Every year for Christmas, Mom would purchase a large glass container of strawberry bubble bath which she carefully wrapped and labeled as if it were a gift from Dad. Of course, Dad never bought gifts for anyone. Mom bought all the gifts and pretended they were from Santa or Dad. Anyway, Mom would carefully hoard the bubble bath and use it for the most special occasions. What I couldn't figure out was why she had me undress if she was going to take a long soak.

Mom pointed to the tub. "Be careful, the water is hot. You've earned a good soaking."

With that, she walked out and I could hear her in the bedroom, then as she descended the stairs. I knew something was going to happen, but what? Mom would not give up her bubble bath without a reason. I settled into the hot water and was soon enveloped within the warmth of endless bubbles and the aroma of ripe strawberries. We had been working very hard and I was exhausted from scrunching over my sewing. The heat soaked into my muscles and there was nothing to do but relax. I must have drifted off, because the water was much cooler when I became aware Mom had enter the bathroom and settled onto the edge of the tub.

Taking out one of those weird pink safety razors used by women, Mom unscrewed the bottom so the top swung open like double doors. After ejecting a two–sided blade from a dispenser, she rewound the bottom knob so the doors swung tightly shut.

My hand ran across my chin. "Do you think I need to shave?"

"Not your face, silly. This is for your legs and beneath your arms."

"But, Mom! I'm already a laughing stock. The boys in gym will kill me."

"Nonsense, no one will notice. Put your foot up on the tub. Now, work up a good lather..., right up to your thigh. You just let the razor glide along your skin and off come all those tiny hairs. Careful around the ankle! It'll be even easier next time."

"Next time! You want me to do this again?"

"Every week. We don't want any hairy legs running around the house, do we?"

"Well, how about William and Buddy?"

"What about them? They're not Ruby are they?"

I did not say anything else. Life at school was already hell, what more could Moose or Butch and their gang do? Shaving beneath my arms was more difficult than the legs until Mom showed me how to keep the skin tight and shave against the grain, so to speak. After I drained the tub and rinsed, there was a lot less hair on the drain than I expected. Maybe I had less stubble that I thought. Perhaps there was not that much difference and no one would notice my legs were naked.

After drying and slipping into panties, I wrapped a towel around my hair and walked into the bedroom. Mom was sitting on her bed with the most serene expression on her face. Spread out beside her was one of the blue uniforms. She had added a patch pocket in the same white material used in the collar and sleeves. In bright red thread she had embroidered 'RUBY.' A dull ache clutched my chest. She expected me to wear the uniform. Not underneath my clothes, like my panties. This would be on the outside..., where everyone could see it. She expected me to wear a dress in front of my brothers. In front of anyone who came into the house. I could not do it. I would not do it!

"No, Mom! I can't let William and Buddy see me like that. What will they think? What will Daisy and Jeanie think? Do you want me to look like a.... Like one of those boys? I just can't do it. I'll wear anything underneath, but not on top so everyone can see."

Taking my hand, Mom had me sit beside her, then circled my shoulders with her arm. I was slightly chilled, and her warmth felt so comforting, her voice little more than a whisper.

"I'm not punishing you, Ruby. This is strictly for business reasons. Think how much more professional you'll look. Our customers will feel more relaxed. The skirt is nice and short, so it will be easy to kneel when you're pining a hem or taking measurements."

"It's so short I'll look like I'm four, not almost fourteen."

Mom hugged me tighter. "I could punish you. Stand you in the corner in your pink panties. You don't want Buddy to see you like that, do you?"

"No Ma'am."

"William is the man of the house, I could have him take down those panties and warm your fanny. You don't want that, do you?"

"No."

"But, you do want to please me, don't you?"

"Yes Ma'am."

"And you will wear the dress, won't you."

"You won't make me go outside."

"Certainly not. Except for business reasons, such as if we were dealing with a client."

"Promise?"

"Promise. When you come in from school you'll change, and on Saturdays when we're working. Anyway, we need to save your regular clothes for school and church. Now, lets get you dressed. Just as well let your brothers see their new sister at her finest."

"Ohhhhh Mom!"

"Ohhhhh, Ruby!" She hugged me even tighter, then kissed me hard on the cheek. It was the first time she had really kissed me.

*   *   *   *   *

First came the slip, which slithered down my body like a satin flow of cream. Mom adjusted the straps, then slid the dress over my head. It took several tries to figure out how to close the zip part way from the bottom, then reach over my shoulder and pull it to the top. The uniform fit perfectly, of course, since I had been the manikin, but Mom still took forever patting and smoothing it into place. At last, she turned me to face the mirror. We reflected side by side, almost like mother and daughter. The expression on Mom's face was priceless. She glowed with pleasure.

"Oh, my sweet Ruby," she whispered. "You're perfect. Exactly as I always dreamed you'd be. We're going to be wonderful together."

I turned sideways and ran a hand across my chest. "It's a little loose here. Maybe I should get some of those pads girls wear."

Mom smiled. "No, dear. You only need a little time. Everything in its own time. See, I've waited so long for this day. So very long. And now my little Ruby has come home to me."

CHAPTER THIRTEEN

Oh, Brother

The worst thing about working every day after school was that I seldom had an opportunity to visit Daisy. I would glimpse her at school, but more and more she was busy with friends. I couldn't even walk her home, because she had started taking piano lessons after school. I did see Jeanie and walk with her. She even let me carry her books a few times. But, Jeanie was too independent to want any boy, especially a Purple Pantywaist, getting too close to her.

Unlike Daisy, who never was serious about anything, Jeanie was always serious and curious. She was forever asking embarrassing questions about how it felt to be a boy in panties, and if I had ever worn any of Mom's clothing, and if I played with myself more now that I was in panties. It was so difficult to answer her, because I really had never thought of wearing anything girlish before the panties, where as now I could hardly keep from thinking about anything except frillies and foundations. And frankly, unless I touched the panties, they really didn't feel that much different from undershorts, just smoother, cooler, and softer. As for touching myself down there, didn't everyone say it was a sin and would make you go blind?

All of these thoughts flooded over me now that Mom had me in a slip and dress. She said it was a uniform, but I knew it was intended to be a dress that I would accept, not at all like the blouses, skirts and dresses I had just finished sewing. Then, when Mom said that Jeanie and Daisy had sent me a little gift, just for this occasion, I knew my feelings for the girls was going to get all mixed up with my feelings about being in a dress. Mom brought out two grocery bags of their shoes and I began trying on each pair as she took them from the bags. It turned out that Jeanie's shoes fit me almost perfectly, whereas Daisy's shoes were almost all too small. Actually, one pair from Daisy did fit, that was some black and white saddle shoes, along with several pair of those silly socks with pompoms at the heel that barely reach the top of the shoe. The shoes must have been too big for Daisy, because they had never been worn.

"This is great," said Mom. "Now you can save your shoes for church."

"Mom, I can't wear girl's shoes to school. You don't know what the boys do to me already."

She made a face. "We'll see," was all she said.

I knew what that meant.

After fifteen minutes we had seven pair of shoes lined up beside my bed. Actually, eight with the saddle shoes. Five pair were what Mom called flats, although they all looked quiet different. One pair had stacked heels about an inch high, and the last were skyscrapers at least three inched tall.

"Well, I certainly can't wear those. I'll fall and break my nose."

"No, they're too high for regular wear, but they might come in handy when you're trying on a fancy dress for hemming. It would give us a better idea of how the skirt would actually look."

"I still think I'll break my nose."

"We'll see."

"They're kind of scuffed. Jeanie must be hard on shoes."

"Jeanie is hard on a lot of things. Don't worry about the scuffs. I'll have William shine then so bright the boys will be able to see your panties."

"Mooommmm! Don't say things like that."

"Oh, Lord! Now you're a prude. Slip into these Mary Janes and come over to my dressing table."

As I feared, Mom started with foundation, added a little rouge and lipstick, then finished me off with a dusting of powder. I started to get up, but she stopped me and brought out a big red bow which she fastened just above my left ear. Stepping back, her hands planted firmly on her wide hips.

"You should have stockings, otherwise you are simply perfect. Go check yourself in the mirror."

I kept telling myself I was seeing a boy in a dress. But, I had to accept that the boy was only there if I looked at the chest. Even there, my chest was no longer flat as a pancake. Not mounds like a teen girl should look, but definitely not flat like a boy. What was most disturbing was the second set of bumps, right in the middle of the mounds. Perhaps band–aids would keep my nipples under control. Then my eyes lowered to the little bulge of my tummy. Boy's did not have poochie tummies. Girls had poochie tummies.

"Stand up straight and suck in your tummy. Shoulders back. Stick our your chest. Tell yourself that ten times a day."

Mom slipped a white apron around my waist.

"This is part of the uniform. Keep your scissors in this little pocket and your tape measure here. There's a pad in your breast pocket to hold pins. You look very professional. I am extremely proud having you work next to me."

Once more she kissed me on the cheek.

"Okay, Sweets, we've earned a cup of coffee and a handful of cookies.

*   *   *   *   *

After our snack Mom located the old Kodak Brownie and snapped a few shots of me standing beside William's flowering crabapple tree, which was in full bloom. The tree was in the front yard and all the while I was terrified a neighbor would pass and recognize me. I heaved a huge sigh soon as we stepped back inside.

Mom pulled my shoulders back and patted my tummy.

"Suck in. I can put you in a girdle if necessary."

"Yes Ma'am."

"You wouldn't like that, would you?"

"Yes Ma'am."

My hand shot to my mouth. Mom and I stared at each other. I had no idea where that had come from. Of course I had no desire at all to be put into a girdle. That would be a fate worse than death.

"Okay, Sweets. Back to the salt mine."

We worked on the bridesmaids' dresses for several hours. Once or twice I had to hold one before me in front of the mirror to make sure it was coming together properly. Each time, I could not help comparing myself in my uniform, and with the dress held tight against my midriff. Girls were so silly to spend so much on bridesmaid dresses they could only wear once. And that time was on another woman's big day. Weddings themselves seemed ever more silly. Why spend all that money making yourself look foolish in front of your friends and family. Then, the certainty of my future settled over me. I was never going to get married. No woman would want to date a Purple Pantywaist, much less marry one. What had I done to be cursed? I had always tried to be honest and friendly. Only once in my entire life had I ever struck anyone. That was when I hit Moose. And, what had it gotten me? A bloody nose and suspension from school.

"Ruby? Ruby!"

"Ummm, yes Mom."

"If you like that dress so much, we can make you one."

"Ummm. No, ummm. I was only thinking."

"You've been staring at yourself for ten minutes, with the most crestfallen look on your face. What's wrong."

"I was only thinking..., about getting married."

"Married? Are you planning to get married?"

"No, of course not. That's the problem. No girl would ever agree to marry me. I'll spend my whole life as an old maid, or whatever unmarried boys are called."

"Why, that's silly. You're a wonderful person. Loving, intelligent, trustworthy, hard working, attractive. I'd marry you in an instant. So would Daisy or Jeanie if the circumstances were different. Finish that dress and start supper. Your brothers will be home soon. I can't wait to see their reaction when you show off your uniform."

After I completed the dress I hung it on the rolling rack Papa Henry had made for us. Five of the six dresses were now ready for their final fitting. I surely hoped someone would place another big order soon, our cash supply was really precarious. The only meats we could afford were Spam, baloney and tripe. I had decided on Spam for tonight, now the question was what to fix with it. After opening the can, I sliced the Spam thin, so it would fry up nice and crisp, the way William liked it. I didn't care about what Buddy liked, because all he would do was bellyache about not having steak. Well, if he wanted steak, he'd have to eat with Grandpa and Grandma Jones. They could afford to buy him whatever he wanted.

A knock came at the back door. I must have locked it when I brought the wash in. I snatched the door open, expecting William, and faced a stranger. No, it wasn't a stranger, it was the guy from the power company. Oh God, I'd forgotten about him, and he had seem me dozens of times.

He grinned. "Ain't dis th' Jones'?"

"Ya…, yes."

"Must be visiting. Ain't seen ya' a'fore. Got to read th' meter. When they wired these ol' places they put th' fuse box and meter in th' kitchen. Don't know why. Don' make no sense ta me."

He brushed past me, accidentally on purpose letting his hand slide across my hip, stared at the meter for a while, then jotted some numbers on his clipboard.

"Ya from out o' town?"

"Yes." I had no idea why I lied. After all, this was my house…, or at least Mom's.

As he brushed by me on his way out, I felt another pat, followed by a sharp pain in my fanny.

"That hurt."

"See ya around, Babe."

With that, he was gone. It was then I realized Mom was standing in the doorway to the dinning room.

"Did he pinch your rear?"

"Yes. And he patted me too."

"You're growing up faster than I thought." Mom patted me on the fanny. "Big girls get lots of attention. Put on some rice and open a can of beans. I'll make a salad. It sure will be nice when the butter beans come in. I hate caned vegetables."

We worked silently until William's car pulled into the driveway. All the fear and uncertainties that had been deviling me all afternoon welled inside. What if William rejected me completely. There was no doubt I was a continual source of embarrassment and shame for him. What man wanted the biggest screw–up in school as a little brother? What man wanted a brother who wore panties and dresses?

What man wanted....

William burst through the door, tossed his jacket across a chair and began to loosen his tie. He froze, staring at me. I could see his gaze move from my face to my scruffy shoes, then back to my face.

"Aren't you going to say hi to your ol' Ma and sister," asked Mom.

He continued to stare at me for what seemed hours. At lase, he cleared his throat. "Hi, Ruby. Your shoes need polishing. I'll take care of them after supper."

Mom squeezed him tightly. I heard her whisper.

"Thank you, Darling. Thank you, thank you, thank you."

*   *   *   *   *

We delayed supper half an hour, waiting for Buddy, then began without him. Everything was pretty quiet for a while before we began to loosen a little.

"How was your day, William?" asked Mom.

"Better than good. I sold an Eldorado to Doc Pricher."

"Good Lord! Was that wise? He's always thinking about a dozen patients at the same time. He'll probably run over someone."

"Well, at least a doctor will be handy," I said.

"Ha! Good one, Roo..., Ruby."

William looked sheepish about my name change, but he wasn't having nearly as much trouble keeping all this straight as I was. Suddenly, Buddy crashed through the back door and flopped down at the table.

"Not much time. Hot date tonight." He emptied all the remaining rice and beans onto his plate and reached for the Spam. "Damn! What's this? You know I don't eat imitation meat. I need beef to keep my energy up."

"Hello, Buddy. Nice you could join us, Buddy. Thanks for asking about our day, Buddy!" Mom made a face. "You know we can't afford steak. You're lucky to get a meal at all, considering our finances."

"Grandma Jones will fix me steak every day if I ask her."

"Then ask her," said William. "If you'd get off your butt and find a job, maybe we could have a steak once in a while."

Buddy opened his mouth, as if to say something even more sarcastic, when his eyes fell on me.

"Holy Shit! Is th' fagot turdhead wearing a dress now? My God, it is a dress!"

"It's my work uniform. Mom made it for me. See, she even put my name on the pocket." I pointed to my chest.

"This is too much. Bad enough I've got to be in th' same house with a queer. I don't have to eat with one too."

He slammed from the table and took the stairs two or three at a time. Mom put her hand atop mine. William stared silently at his plate, absently stirring the few grains of rice beside even fewer beans. I took the plate of Spam and distributed the three remaining slices onto our plates.

"No need to let this go to waste."

"No, I guess not," added Mom."

A bloodcurdling howl came from upstairs. Buddy descended four steps at the time.

"I don't have any clean shirts. Where are all my shirts?"

"I washed and ironed everything in the hamper. If it ain't in th' hamper, it don't get washed."

Buddy shook his fist at me. "I had plenty of dirty shirts. What have you done with them?"

"Oh, you mean those crumpled piles of cloth on the floor? Maybe I kicked them under your bed."

"Kicked…. Under my bed! Why, you little fart."

"Do you think I like washing and ironing your shirts? Do you think I like picking up your junk? Do you think I like scrubbing after you in the bathroom? Why can't you learn to hit the toilet like a real man? At least William doesn't pee on the floor."

"That's enough, smart alack. I'm going to pull your ugly head off and stick it up your ass."

He took a step towards me, but William blocked him with his shoulder.

"Enough! Can't you at least act civilized? You can't expect Ruby to wash and iron two and three shirts a day for you. If you throw stuff on the floor, she doesn't have to pick up after you."

"His fuckin' name is Robert. Where in hell did all this Ruby shit come from? Why do I have to put up with this tripe? I'm going to Grandma's. Least she knows class when she sees it."

We sat silent at the table for a while. Silent, except for my muffled sobs. Finally, Mom blotted my eyes with a tissue, then had me blow my nose.

"I'm going to finish that last bridesmaid's gown. After you wash up, come in and we'll talk."

Mom left, then William. I remained, head buried in my hands, for a long time. Everything was my fault. If I wasn't such a hopeless son, Mom would not have to put me in dresses. No wonder Buddy was unhappy. Who wanted a queer turdhead for a brother? If I only had the courage to end it all. Dad's guns were still out in the garage. I didn't have to know how to shoot. How could I miss my head if the barrel were sticking in my mouth? All I'd have to do was pull the trigger. Well, I was such a klutz, I'd probably miss and shoot my ear off, and I wasn't even a painter.

At last I found the energy to get up and clean the kitchen. I covered the remaining Spam in plastic wrap and put it in the fridge. William would get hungry before he want to sleep. Mom or I could make him a sandwich.

After clicking off the light, I sat next to Mom as she began stitching the hem on the final gown.

"You need to rest your eyes," I said, taking the needle and thread from her hand.

"Said the little girl who can't find the door without her glasses."

"I can find it, I just can't tell if its open or closed."

She scrunched my shoulders, then began twirling a strand of my hair about her fingers.

"I'm sorry, Mom. It's all my fault. I should have washed Buddy's shirts, even if he just throws them on the floor. Doesn't he understand there's no money to buy him new shirts? That we can't afford Spam, much less steak?"

"No, he doesn't understand. He's just like his father. William is already an adult, the man of this house. Buddy will never grow up."

"I'll never be a man either, will I? I'll always be a turdhead."

"Don't use words like that. You may or may not become a man, but you will always be a wonderful person…, and you'll always be my baby.

William entered with a pair of freshly polished slippers. He knelt beside me and slipped them onto my feet.

"There, you can see your face in them."

"It's not her face she's worried about," laughed mom.

William looked perplexed.

"It's just a little girl humor. Something a boy couldn't understand."

In a way, she was right. Soon as William slipped the shoes on my feet and I saw how they glistened, I immediately wondered if a boy really would be able to see up my dress.

Mom stood and yawned deeply. "You know, my pets. I think a cup of hot coco would go well with a cookie about now." She glanced at me. "And no one is going to have bad dreams tonight."

Later, when Mom and I went upstairs, I opened the closet to hang up my new uniform. Lined along the bottom, right next to Mom's, were all of my new shoes, and hanging on my side were the dresses, skirts, and blouses that I had made. There was no doubt soon I would be entering the next stage of my new life.

CHAPTER FOURTEEN

Spurts

Most of the kids in my class had already started having growth spurts. The girls were first, then the boys began to catch up and pass them. A couple of fellows already had some whiskers and deeper voices. I had almost reached Daisy's height, but Jeanie was still a good two or three inches taller than me. Mom kept telling me I'd soon pass both of them, but I was starting to have real doubts. A couple of months after I began getting injections my body did start changing a little, but not in the way I imagined. First, my butt began to plump up. Fortunately, that only lasted a few weeks. Then my hips seemed to spread and my waist actually shrunk an inch, even though I had gained several pounds. All this time my body turned flabby. Soon, I was going to be as soft as Daisy.

Most disturbing was when my boobies started swelling. Well, actually, it wasn't really the boobies, just the nipples and the dark area right around them. And, boy, did they get sensitive! Then it was my fanny again. In fact, Mom had to show me how to let out the seat of my trousers while taking in the waistband. Then my hips widened and I lost another inch in the waist. Then the boobs started expanding like crazy for a week or so. All this while I was absolutely exhausted. It wasn't as if I were working hard or anything. Mostly I was just sitting at school or in front of my sewing machine. My major exercise was chasing the vacuum all over the house and lugging damp clothing from the washing machine to the drying lines. The minute my head hit the pillow I was out for the count.

Which brought up my other major problem. I had always had a lot of dreams, chaotic nightmares, actually. They had started when I was taken away from Momma Jean, and grew much worse because Buddy was always scaring me about the horrid monsters and bloodcurdling spiders that lived beneath my bed. Momma Jean had given me a little nightlight shaped like a pony, but soon as Mom plugged it in, Dad had yanked it from the wall and smashed it into tiny pieces.

"No son of mine's gonna sleep with a fuckin' nightlight," he screamed. "You trying to turn th' boy into a damn sissy?"

That was the end of my nightlight and my pleasant dreams. Anyway, my dreams had always been spooky and filled with fog and mists. I could never remember what had happened, only that I had been terrified. The good thing about sleeping on a separate floor was that no one ever heard me crying and yelling, so I would eventually cry myself back to sleep. By the next morning, the dream would be gone and I'd only be left with a nagging sense of dread.

All that now changed. Soon after I started the injections and pills, my dreams changed from black and white into living widescreen technicolor with surrounded sound. And, instead of monsters and spiders, I began to relive stuff from what passed for my real life. The dreams would last for about a week after each injection, then they would fade away.

If Mom and I were altering a wedding gown, I might dream being forced to wear a transparent version and walk down the aisle in church while the entire congregation looked on and laughed. Mom or perhaps Jeanie would be behind me with a shotgun, marched me towards a mysterious man I was being forced to marry. I would cry and beg, but no one would come to my aid. It would seem to take forever to reach the alter, where at last the man would suddenly transform into Moose Hanahan or Butch Spence and I would wake exactly as I made a terrible mess in my panties.

This was followed by the most intense feeling of release and pleasure. Unfortunately, within moments I would be overcome with unbelievable remorse and embarrassment. How could I possibly do something so dirty when I knew it was deadly wrong? I knew that all the women in my life would hate me forever if they found out I was having such evil thoughts.

Mom would shake me awake and tell me I'd been screaming and thrashing. She would ask what I had dreamed, but of course I couldn't tell her about having to marry Moose, so I'd lie and tell her some silly story about falling down the stairs or any tale that had absolutely nothing to do with sex. I certainly didn't want her to think I'd become a fiend, or that I was messing my panties. She would talk gently to me and rub my back until I went back to sleep. Mom acted like she believed me, but after a few of these episodes she bought me something called sanitary panties and put little pads in them for sleeping. It surely made cleaning up a lot easier.

Most of the dreams were singles, but several occurred almost every month. These always included Jeanie or Mitzi and Moose. Once I was the frog in science class. Mitzi came at me with the static electricity wand and I jumped far across the room. Just as I landed, Moose lifted his huge foot and started to stomp me. Of course, everything happened in the slowest of motions so it took forever for the shoe to squish me. I don't need to say what happened at that exact moment. Again, thank God for sanitary panties and Kotex.

Another common dream involved milk. We were at the dairy, except this time I was the cow and I had these huge breasts that contained gallons of milk that just had to come out. Mitzi and Moose each hooked a sucker to one of my boobies while Jeanie fastened another to my tongue. It felt like my life was being sucked out along with all those gallons of milk. At last, Mitzi said, 'We've still got another sucker. Wonder where it should go?' 'I know,' said Jeanie. She took the nozzle and slowly reach between my legs. I was terrified, but there was nothing I could do. At last it clomped onto me with a huge slurp and I exploded and passed out at the same instant.

By far the most disturbing dream took place in Mitzi's bedroom. I had never seen her bedroom, of course. In fact, I had no idea where she lived. But, in the dream I knew every nuance of that room, because I had been there a very long time since I was a stool or bench in front of her gleaming white princess dresser. She sat on me for hours, doing her nails, brushing her hair or doing her makeup. I could glimpse her feet and hear her, but otherwise could not see her no matter how hard I tried to turn my head. There were little lamps with pink ballerinas in them that spun as they played music. She was preparing for a date. Slowly, oh so slowly, she undressed, languidly dropping each item onto her bench..., which was me, of course. I could hear her enter the bath and the little sing–song she hummed, hear the gentle splash of water against her skin.

At last she stepped from the bath onto a pink bathmat. She danced about, toweling off. Her naked feet padded across the floor towards me. Down she plopped, her full weight cushioned by her unbelievably soft and bouncy fanny. She leaned over and stepped one foot, then the second into soft pink panties. As she stood to pull up the panties, my head was at last able to turn and for the first time I could gaze upwards along her legs to the little tufts of hair, to her rounded tummy, her lush breasts, her glorious face. That was when I exploded…, and that's when I inevitably was overwhelmed with the greatest feeling of disgust imaginable. How could I even conceive of spying on the only girl who had ever befriended me? In my heart, I knew she would never speak to me again, nor should she, for I had to be the most loathsome boy in all the world. On the nights of those dreams I could not get back to sleep. How could I sleep knowing what a monster I had become?

Mom's solution to all this was to move me into her bed.

"I need to be able to wake you faster," she said. "You're going to hurt yourself one of these nights. Perhaps we should stop the injections."

Each time she mentioned halting the medicine, I always said no, even though I felt yucky for several days after each shot. For, I knew how much pleasure mom got from making clothing for me, brushing my hair and making up my face. Not only that, once the awful head and tummy aches were over, once the outlandish dreams and thoughts ended, once my hands and feet stopped swelling and my breasts quit aching, I would sink into the most glorious pink haze until it was time for the next injection. Already I could tell my monthly reactions were decreasing. I only had to survive for a while longer, and my body would probably get used to whatever I was taking.

Not only that, I enjoyed working with Mom and having her make over me. Sometimes she actually seemed to like me. Even if she could not love me, at least I could be her sewing girl. And, I was getting better each day. It would not be long and I would turn into a real seamstress. Perhaps then Mom would accept me. It was worth any pain to win her approval. After all, no matter how much I loved Momma Jean, Mom was my real mother. And a boy should always please his mother.

*   *   *   *   *

Moving to Mom's bed was a godsend. Both of us had black and blue spots on our legs from stumbling over my bed. After it was unceremoniously condemned to the garage we could maneuver without bashing ourselves to death. The major issue was that now Mom could wake me as soon as I started thrashing. It turned out I only dreamed while on my back, so Mom would have me roll onto my tummy and I'd go right back to sleep…, without all the trauma.

At first, I was terrified that I might touch her during the night, so I would sleep right on the edge of the bed.

Mom just laughed. "Ruby, you're going to fall out of bed soon as you turn over. It's not going to kill either of us if we bump into the other. We're sleeping, not making love."

Then she'd tickle me until I squirmed all over the bed and up against her.

"See, that didn't hurt anything did it? Now, turn over and go to sleep."

This was always followed by a swat on my rump.

Actually, it turned out we were both so exhausted that after a few nights we simply climbed into bed, said goodnight, and immediately went to sleep. Anyway, Mom was used to sleeping with Dad and she knew how to move me back to my side if I rolled her way.

My growth spurts were another issue. The more I filled out and softened, the more Mom seemed to accept me. It was almost as if we were having another chance at being mother and child. I was becoming more confused and befuddled as to what gender I was supposed to be, and Mom now had an opportunity to direct my life the way she desired. I felt utterly devastated in a dress, while Mom absolutely relished making me as girlish as possible. She never put makeup on me while I was in pants, yet the moment I stepped into a dress she simply had to paint my face and polish my fingernails. She never touched my hair when I was a boy, but in a dress she could not keep her comb out of my waves. And, while I was ever more terrified of the bulging mounds on my chest, they sent her into ecstasy.

As to those ever–expanding mounds, Moose Hanahan was attracted to my sprouting breasts like a hippopotamus to water. As soon as peaks became noticeable beneath my shirts Moose felt it was his designated fate to make me the charter member of the PTA — The Purple Tittie Association. Perhaps he had no idea how much squeezing hurt an expanding nipple, but the bigger and more sensitive my breasts became, the more pleasure he took in bringing me to my knees with a quick pinch between his gigantic thumb and forefinger. It became so bad that some of the girls in my class actually started trying to protect me. Mitzi even complained to the Principal, but his attitude was that I was the problem since I was always drawing attention to myself. If I wasn't such a showoff Moose wouldn't be encouraged to misbehave.

As for Mitzi, she just became ever more perplexed as to what was happening to me.

"Are you okay," she kept asking. "Maybe you should see a doctor."

Explaining that I was already under the care of Doc Pricher did not seem to count as seeing a doctor.

"Well, maybe you should see another doctor, or at least start wearing a bra. After all, you don't want to get stretched out of shape."

All this concern was funny in a way, because Mitzi was already much bigger up top than Jeanie, and while Jeanie wore very supportive bras, Mitzi wore ill-fitting bras that appeared to provide almost no assistance to her shape at all. She never wore girdles either, and her luscious body seemed to have a life of its own each time she moved.

Daisy did not appear to notice my changing body at all. Partially because she didn't have any interest in that sort of thing, and also because she had become extremely involved with a group of girls in high school. As long as they talked about clothing I could keep up, but as soon as they switched to boys and periods I was utterly lost. Soon, I wasn't welcome in their little clique. It was as if Daisy had already graduated from junior high, and I had been left behind.

Jeanie took ever more interest in me as my body changed, partially because we were walking to and from school together, and partially because she apparently just found my situation fascinating. Before, she would hardly acknowledge my presence. Now we hugged and kissed each morning and afternoon. Before she never touched me. Now she was always squeezing my hip or patting my fanny, 'to see how I was filling out' she would say. We couldn't be together ten minutes without her asking some really embarrassing question about what I was going through. Had I worn the high heels she sent? Had Mom put me in a bra and girdle yet? Had she taught me how to douche and wear tampons? Not only was this mortifying, but many times I had no idea what she was talking about. What was a douche? What exactly were tampons? Did she know about the special panties and pads I was wearing because of the dreams? Or, was she talking about something completely different? While we walked, I normally carried both our books, so my hands were occupied, which left both of her hands free to poke wherever she pleased.

One day she slipped a hand about my waist and pulled me against her hip.

"I've asked Mom to let me be in charge of your figure. She's going to talk with Aunt Pam about it."

"What do you mean, be in charge of my figure?"

"You know, chose your bras and girdles, that kind of thing."

"Jeanie, do you want to hurt me?"

"God, No! I'd never hurt you. I only want you to suffer a little."

We walked for several minutes with her clinging to me. Then, she nibbled on my ear.

"My dear, dear, Ruby. I want you completely under my command. If we weren't cousins I'd probably marry you. That would be so nice. To have you all to myself forever."

Spinning me, she planted a huge wet kiss, not on my cheek, but right on my lips. "Daisy is such a child, not to mention being an unmitigated prude and bore. You're, oh so different. We're going to have a wonderful time together."

I had always loved Jeanie as a sister, but she frightened me. Now I understood she was far more than a sister. We could never be lovers, of course, but I realized she was going to play a gigantic roll in my life. Jeanie did have power over me, it was not simply the tingle of fear, it was an animal attraction that meant she could do absolutely anything to me, and I would hate it..., and love it.

CHAPTER FIFTEEN

Alone in the Dark

Dressmaking had been furious for over a month as brides–to–be swarmed out of the woodwork. Actually, it was mostly mothers nagging their daughters to finally choose dresses and bridesmaid's ensembles in preparation for their coveted June weddings, but the result was that this had turned into our best month by far. Not only that, but I only had to survive one more week and school would be over. I couldn't wait! Three whole months without getting beat up or have my boobies pinched.

In the meantime, my greatest problem had been Mom's old sewing machine. As if I weren't batty enough, that blasted machine had beaten me into submission. Just as I reached the critical point of a seam, the bobbin would take a siesta. After I fixed that, a needle would snap, or the thread would tangle. Next the feeder foot would break an ankle, bunching up the fabric. Until I started getting injections I never cried. No matter how bad any situation became I could remain stoic, keep the stiff upper lip, as the

British say in movies. Now, Mom's machine could reduce me to a blubbering idiot in minutes. Once the flood started, I lost all control and would weep bitterly for ten or fifteen minutes before I could regain composure. Sometimes, if I really lost it, I would be out of commission for half an hour. This was not extremely efficient when we were fighting half a dozen deadlines at once. In addition to everything else, neither Mom or I seemed to grasp that I was undergoing boy and girl puberty at the same time.

We continually patrolled the Good Shepard Exchange and pawn shops hoping someone would post a decent sewing machine, but none materialized and we certainly could not afford a new one. Meanwhile, I was beaten deeper into submission every day.

On the few days I got to visit Momma Jean, I found a new release for my building frustrations. The first thing I would do on entering was to gather all their dainties and hand wash them. Momma Jean kept telling me I was not their maid, and I could not explain how much enjoyment it gave me to be so intimately connected with the women who filled my life. There was nothing erotic involved, only an almost religious feeling of being attached to the innermost portions of their lives.

Next I would sit down at Momma Jean's new sewing machine and take care of all their mending. It was the best machine made in Europe and simply sliding my hands along the finely crafted pieces filled me with joy. It was extremely powerful and could easily zip through half a dozen layers of thick cloth. Not only did it have all the basic stitches lacking on Mom's old machine, but it had dozens of intricate cams, pulleys and levers that allowed an unbelievable assortment of stitches from straight to stretch to zigzag to embroidery. It would stitch forward and backwards. It churned out button holes faster than you could move the fabric. You could write names or make tiny dogs or cats, and it was possible to make dozens of flowers and designs.

Sometimes I did nothing more exciting than repair a seam or hem. Other times I had to figure out how to make a bra that 'just doesn't feel right,' into one that, 'thank God, finally fits!' One of the joys was discovering how to do something on my own. At home, Mom could always tell me how to make a difficult repair. But, at Momma Jean's I had to figure it out for myself, since Momma Jean could not sew a straight seam.

The other thing I loved was to make little surprises for Daisy and Jeanie. If Daisy had a pair of panties with an open seam, I might repair the seam, then add a pink kitten to the hip. With Jeanie, my tactic was quite different. With the same panty I might fix the seam, then add **Pet me** right across the fanny. She always threw a fit, but then she'd proudly show off my handy work to all her friends.

I did love those girls, but in such amazingly different ways.

*   *   *   *   *

A couple of other things also gave me trouble. Mom purchased a patent leather hand bag for me at the Good Shepard Exchange. Actually, it wasn't a hand bag as much as a hanging bag with a long strap that went over my shoulder. At first I really fought carrying it around all the time, especially since I didn't have anything to tote. Then I realized the uniform didn't have practical pockets like my pants, so there was no place to carry a wallet or handkerchief or anything a boy normally sticks in his pockets.

"A bag is a girl's closest companion," explained Mom. "Except for her girdle, perhaps. Without a handbag you won't have tissues or money. You've got to learn to keep track of a handbag. Otherwise, you're always dreaming and you'll just walk off and leave it somewhere."

"But Mom, when we're out, I'll be wearing my pants."

"We'll see. Anyway, learn to hang onto that handbag like it was your best friend, just for me. Otherwise, if we have to go shopping or anything, you're going to walk off without it."

"Mooommmm! I don't have anything to put in a darned handbag"

Mom plopped my wallet, some tissues and one of her old compacts, a small brush and comb, and a half–used lipstick in the bag and hung it around my neck.

"Now you do. If you say another word, I'll take you shopping and make you fix your face in public."

"Will I even have to take it when I'm in pants?"

Mom tapped her foot. "Would you prefer wearing pants with the handbag, or your uniform with the handbag?"

My mouth felt very dry. "My uniform," I whispered.

"Good, I want to see this bag by your side whenever you're in your uniform." She leaned forward and kissed me gently on the cheek. "That's my sweet little Ruby. Mommie's little helper. Now, we've earned a nice break for a cup of coco."

The funny thing was that Mom never actually threatened to punish me, and she certainly never did more that pat my fanny. She didn't even stand me in a corner like Momma Jean. The options usually centered around if I actually wanted to disappoint Momma Jean or the girls or if I really desired to displease Mom herself. She would usually give me some options and I always ended up choosing what she wanted. Partially because I desperately wanted to please her, and partially because I usually was not too sure what I was accepting. It always ended up with me agreeing to be an even bigger sissy.

I still had a terrible time keeping track of that idiot handbag.

My other nemesis was taking big steps. No matter how often Mom corrected me, as soon as I got in a hurry I would begin running up the stairs or charging here or there. I simply couldn't seem to get the hang of taking dainty steps when there was so much to do. After correcting me a gazillion times, Mom purchased some heavy muslin and sewed it into a tube with an industrial zipper at the top.

"Pull up your skirt, Ruby," She said. "Step in here." She pulled the muslin tube up my thighs and over my hips, then zipped up the rear. "Drop your skirt. See if you can climb the stairs."

Soon as I took a step I almost fell over.

"Mom, I can't walk. It's too tight. I'll never get up stairs in this thing."

"Well, you may have to sleep on the couch. Put one foot in front of the other. That's right. Shift your foot to the side on the stairs. Good, step a little higher. Beautiful. Very dainty. You'll soon have all the boys following to watch your fanny swing.

"Mooommmm!"

"Rubyyyyy!" She gave me a huge bear hug. "My little baby is becoming so dainty, I hardly recognize her. Now, give Mommie a big kiss."

I certainly didn't feel dainty. I felt stupid and trapped. But, it surely was wonderful to feel Mom's arms around me. I could stand anything for that feeling.

*   *   *   *   *

It was during this time that I came to appreciate Mom's foresight in putting me into the uniform. When I was wearing pants, many of our customers were less than happy to have a grubby boy taking their measurements and snooping under their skirts. In the uniform, I suddenly became invisible. I was simply Mom's helper and obviously was passable as an unattractive and exceedingly undeveloped girl. My worry was that sooner or later one of my schoolmates would walk through the door and my charade would be exposed in a most unpleasant manner.

At last, Friday afternoon arrived. The wedding onslaught had settled into a reasonable flood and Mom felt we could take a little time off.

"Go up and change, I've put some clothes out for you. Jean wants you to come over. She has a surprise."

I charged towards the stairs and almost tumbled over because of the blasted prison slip. So I dainty swung my behind side to side as I pranced up each step like the lady Mom desired. All the while I was trying to imagine the surprise. Maybe Momma Jean had baked me a cake. We didn't celebrate my birthday, but Momma Jean always included me in Daisy's party, with my own tiny cake and presents. This year Mom and I had been too busy for me to attend. Missing Daisy's party had been really hard, but I realized that from now on, work was going to take precedence over trite things like birthday parties. At the very least it was going to be a relief to get out of that uniform and torture slip. It's tough for a boy to take small steps and keep his legs together all the time, while also remembering not to lean over too much or plop into a chair without straightening your skirt. By now it was second nature to sit on the toilet to pee–pee, and it made drying myself second nature, which surely did reduce the problem of yellow stains. If I could teach William and Buddy to sit, it would make laundry and cleaning their bathroom so much easier.

As I entered the bedroom I almost toppled over trying to stop. Instead of my boy clothes, Mom had laid out one of the dresses I had made. In fact, it was by far the most girlish one. I had added all that lace and ribbon to please Mom, and because I though I was making the dress for a real girl, not a boy in panties. Mom could not possibly think I could walk all the way to Momma Jeans in a dress and that terrible hobble slip, much less such a frilly one.

Mom placed her hand on my shoulder. "Jean and the girls are dying to see you in a dress. What could be better that one that you designed and made?"

"But, Mom. Being in the house is one thing. I can't go outside. People will see me."

"Well, of course they will see you. Haven't our customers seen you? It doesn't seem to have hurt, you're still alive and well."

"But, Mooommm! Those were women. What if a man sees me?"

"He'll think you're a lovely young lady." Mom's face hardened. "Now, Ruby, you don't want to make me angry, do you?"

I swallowed hard. "No, Mom."

"And you want to make Jean and the girls happy, don't you?"

This time it was harder to swallow. "Yes, Ma'am."

"And you don't want to walk all that way in high heels, do you?"

"No, ma'am."

"There, it's settled. Change and come give me a kiss before you leave. You don't want to be late for your surprise."

"Yes, Ma'am…. Mom, you're not mad with me, are you?"

"Of course not, Sweets. I could never be angry with my baby."

After Mom left I stared at the dress for a long time. At last, I just had to let out a long sigh. Mom wasn't going to back down, and I didn't have the strength to defy her.

Maybe the dress wasn't as bad as I thought. Perhaps, if I tried it on it wouldn't look so girlish. No that wasn't the problem. I was going to look and feel ridiculous in any skirt. Why had I added all that lace and those ribbons? Didn't I have any foresight at all? From now on I would have to play defense. Expect bad and be prepared for even worst. Lord, I sounded like William. Buddy surely would never think about playing defense, he was always on the offensive. In fact, he was the most offensive person I knew…, except for Moose Hanahan, of course.

By now, I was out of the uniform and into the dress. Mom had set out another pair of flats, these were also black except they had red leather bows across the instep. Glancing at the mirror I was surprised. The dress actually didn't look too bad, if you forgot it was a dress and I was a boy. The lace and ribbons really were not that obvious. Whomever had designed the dress actually had some taste. Oh, Hell! That was me. I had designed the stupid dress. That was all the evidence I needed. Obviously I was losing my mind.

After brushing my hair and fixing my lipstick, I wiggled down the stairs and into the fitting room where mom was putting the finishing touches on a wedding gown.

"Better take a good look at me. I'll probably be in jail by sundown."

Mom glanced up. Slowly, her face softened.

"You look absolutely fabulous, Sweets. I could not possibly be more pleased with my little girl. Under absolutely no circumstances are you to walk home. Uncle Henry will drive you, or we'll come get you. No walking outside after dark. The world is filled with dreadful people."

"All right, Mom. I'll remember."

I headed out the door, not at my normal trot, but carefully placing one foot before the other. I could feel my fanny swinging side to side as I walked. I could not imagine Mom's concern about the dark. At least people wouldn't be able to see me in the dark. In fact, perhaps I could actually pass for a girl in the shadows. Daylight seemed a lot more dangerous. I certainly could not walk past the playing fields dressed like this, I could imagine what the boys would do to me. And, the cemetery also didn't seem too safe when I could hardly walk, much less run. That left only the black section. Perhaps no one would recognize me. It wasn't as if I had friends there. What if the boys started throwing rocks? I couldn't run, and if anyone pushed me, I'd probably topple over.

It was taking a lot longer to get to Momma Jean's than I had imagined since my steps were so tiny. The longer I was out, the greater the chance I'd be discovered. At last, I reached the cemetery and started to enter to make up time. Then I realized the cemetery really was not safe dressed this way. There was no possibility I could outrun anyone, and the drunks might be a lot more interested in me if they thought I was a girl. I turned left.

I had gone only half a block when a group of boys came running around a house. They stopped dead in their tracks, I hesitated, then kept walking.

"Hi," I said.

None of them said a word. I came even with them, then passed. Again, no one said a word. At any moment I expected a barrage of rocks to descend on me. I could feel their eyes glued to my swinging rump. The harder I tried to walk straight, the more my butt gyrated, and the louder the stiff material of my skirt swished. I became aware of the click of my heels tapping against the concrete sidewalk. Thank God Mom had not put me in the high heels.

At last I turned the corner and had only a few blocks to safety. Never had I felt more helpless and vulnerable. How could a dress make me so conscious of my every step?

I thought panties were the most devastating thing I could wear, but being in a dress under the open sky was worse than being naked. I was still a boy in panties, but the dress had turned me into a girl and awakened emotions I never had dreamed of, much less experienced. Those boys though I was a girl, and I could sense every one of them undressing me with his eyes.

Now I understood Mom's concern. Dresses and makeup could make me appear slightly pretty, but they also stole the night. Unless I could get back into pants I would never be safe alone in the dark. And, the way my body was changing I didn't think I'd be in pants much longer.

What had I done to deserve such punishment? Was it fate, or had I broken some terrible commandment? How far were Mom and Momma Jean going to take me? Was there any way to escape? Did I want to escape?

CHAPTER SIXTEEN

Curls

My entire body was trembling by the time I reached Momma Jean's. Was it exhaustion, fear, or the sudden onslaught of girlish feelings that had so overwhelmed me? My heart felt as if it would pound right out of my mouth. At last, I recovered enough to open the door and enter.

Daisy was perched on one of the kitchen stools with a huge pink towel draped around her shoulders while Momma Jean busily wound strands of Daisy's hair on tiny rollers.

"You're just in time," called Momma Jean. "Only two more rollers and Daisy will be finished. Go ahead and take off your dress."

"What…. What are you going to do?"

Daisy smooched my way, like she was throwing a kiss. Momma Jean did give me a quick peck.

"Give you a Perm, of course. That's part of your birthday present."

I almost gagged. "A perm? You can't do that. The boys will kill me at school."

"Nonsense, you want to look your best, don't you? It's not every day you complete junior high."

Jeanie entered and began to unzip my dress. "Oh, good. You're wearing the shoes with red bows. Knew you'd like them."

By now she had peeled off my dress and waited while I stepped out. Her hand went to my hobble slip.

"What's this?" Her nose wrinkled. "Looks like it would hold a horse."

"That's Ruby's hobble slip," said Momma Jean as she squirted some evil–smelling goop onto the last of Daisy's rollers. "Aunt Pam thought Ruby was walking too fast. Bet you didn't run all the way over here as usual."

"No Ma'am," I said.

"Can I try it?"

Jeanie unzipped the slip and lowered it so I could step out of it also. Then she wiggled it beneath her skirt and turned.

"Here, zip me up. Lord, this is tight. How do you walk in this thing?"

"It's not too bad," I mumbled.

"Better on you than me. Unzip me and let's get you back in harness."

Soon I was back in the hobble slip and Jeanie zipped me. But, instead of releasing the zipper, she studied it closely. "This is interesting. The zipper is made to lock, like a piece of luggage. Mom, can I put a lock on Ruby?"

Daisy hopped off the stool and checked the bottom of the hobble slip. "If you did that, she wouldn't be able to use the toilet."

"That's the idea, Einstein! She'd have to ask our permission."

Momma Jean followed Daisy with a pink plastic cap which she snapped over her rollers. "No, of course you can't lock up Ruby's legs. You can wash her hair after I trim it. Be careful not to get any tangles.

Soon Momma Jean had trimmed me to her satisfaction and Jeanie had me in a chair with my head leaned backwards over the sink. As she worked up a lather, she appeared to take outrageous pleasure in rubbing her tummy against my face. She was so close I could smell her dusting powder. All the while, her grin grew until she was beaming. "You have such nice hair. It was always such a shame to waste it on a boy. Now Mom and Aunt Pam have fixed that."

"Well, she's not really a girl," added Daisy, glancing up from the latest issue of Seventeen Magazine. "I suppose there's always hope, though."

"Ruby is a girl to me. That's what's important. She's ours now, we have to take good care of her."

Daisy glanced up once more and made a face, as if she had bitten into a persimmon. "She's not ours. She belongs to the whole family."

Jeanie stopped squishing my hair and stared down into my eyes. "You're mine," she whispered. "Don't you forget it."

After thoroughly rinsing, Jeanie toweled me dry and helped me onto the kitchen stool since I couldn't manage it because of the hobble slip. Momma Jean had opened the Perm box and lined all the items atop the counter. After combing my hair to her satisfaction, she began right behind my bangs by lifting a section of hair at mid scalp and straightened it with the comb. Meanwhile, Jeanie had placed a slip of paper on one of the rollers and handed it to her mother. Moments later, Momma Jean had rolled up the hair and clicked the retaining clip into place.

"One down, nine hundred and ninety–nine to go," sang Jeanie.

"Thankfully, not quiet that many," laughed Momma Jean.

Between fixing rollers, Jeanie pulled out an emery board and began working on my right fingernails. After that, she did the left hand, then moved to my feet where she removed the shoes and the tiny stocking bottom like things Mom made me wear instead of decent socks. The next thing I knew, she was painting each nail with bright red polish to match the red ribbons on my dress and shoes. I was essentially trapped on the stool with Momma Jean twisting up my hair and Jeanie painting anything she could reach. To top off my humiliation, she kept lightly tickling the bottoms of my feet, all the while warning me not to squirm under penalty of having my lips painted. I didn't know much about polish, but I knew it wouldn't wear off for days, if not weeks. All I could do was sit like a china doll while mother and daughter rolled and polished the boy out of me.

* * * * *

Almost exactly an hour later my nails were painted and dried and Momma Jean had finished rolling the last bit of hair. My head looked and felt like a porcupine. It smelled like a septic tank. Momma Jean plopped the pink plastic cap over my rollers. Now it was time for Daisy to get freed from her cap and combed out. At first, her head looked like it was covered in steel wool, but after the combing it was more like she was wearing a Shirley Temple wig.

Don't fret, Ruby," said Momma Jean. "You're not wound as tight and it will relax after a few weeks."

"Yep, but I have to go to school on Monday."

"Don't worry," added Jeanie. "Th' boys will all go gaga. They especially like girls with red nails. You'll have more dates that you can handle."

"One is probably more than she can handle," said Daisy, who had already climbed back into her chair with the magazine.

"Okay, Girls! Get dressed, time to get Ruby fitted. That means you, Ruby, back into your dress. Time is wasting."

"You mean, go out?" I felt the plastic cap, then stared at the red nails. "I can't go out with rollers in my hair and hands like this. Everyone will think I'm...."

"Just like half the girls in town. They're all getting ready to go out tonight or this weekend." Momma Jean helped me into the dress and zipped me up. "There, You look just like any normal teenager."

Grabbing our purses, we all headed toward the garage. Jeanie and Daisy were yammering away, but I was quaking inside and out. Was there no end to my shame? And, far more important, would I ever grow a backbone? I could say no. I could pitch a fit like Buddy. I could say 'this is silly, I won't do it' like William. But, no, I simply scurried to keep up in my hobble slip, with a thousand curlers in my hair all topped with a pink plastic cap. There was no doubt. I was a real He–Man.

We didn't stop at Minx Department Store or Sears, instead we headed directly to Miss Lillian's, the most exclusive ladies shop in town. This was where Mom and Momma Jean purchased their bras and girdles, so I figured we were going to pick up something for Momma Jean.

Daisy plopped into one of the waiting chairs and pulled out her magazine.

Slipping beside her, I whispered. "What on earth are you reading? It must be really interesting."

"Oh, it's the most heartbreaking story imaginable, the boy rejected the poor girl and she was heartbroken, but now she's found Mr. Right and the original creep is trying to woo her back. She's about to give in to his lies. I hope she…."

"Ruby, in here please."

Momma Jean waved me toward the dressing rooms.

I couldn't imagine why she needed me, but I scurried off fast as my hobble slip would allow.

"This is Miss Lillian, Ruby. She will attend to you. Please take off your dress and vest."

Suddenly I felt very small and even more defenseless. "Everything?"

"Yes dear, everything up top."

Once more I was faced with an impossible situation. I certain didn't want to show off my scrawny chest to a woman I'd never met. She looked ancient and reminded me of my first grade teacher who was always whacking me on the hand for daydreaming.

"It's alright, dear. I don't bite, and I certainly won't be staring at you or making any judgments. This should be reasonably quick and painless, then you'll look and feel much better."

Jeanie decided the situation by quickly unzipping me and lowering the dress. Once more I had trouble stepping out because of the hobble slip. Miss Lillian's eyes widened.

"Well, well. I haven't seen one of these in ages." Her fingers ran along one of the seams. "Such fine, loving, work. This was made by an extremely talented seamstress."

"Mom. Ummm. My Mother made it for me. So I wouldn't walk so fast."

"She must love you very much."

By now Jeanie had slipped the nylon vest over my head and I stood bare chested…, or bare boobless before all three ladies. What little courage I possessed sank to my toes.

Miss Lillian measured me below, across and above my little mounds. Then she pressed her fingertips into the flab beneath my arms, across my back, then spun me so she could mash all around my nipples. In a flash, she disappeared through the curtains separating us from the shop. I glanced at Momma Jean. She stared back. I glanced at Jeanie. She grinned back. I tried to cover my breasts with my hands, but Momma Jean shook her head. She did give my hand a little squeeze.

"Miss Lillian will be back in a moment. She is very experienced. She fitted me with my first bra in this very room..., and my first girdle too. No, that was in the room down the hallway."

"Me too," added Jeanie. "And probably Daisy and Aunt Pam."

With that, Miss Lillian burst back through the curtains with about three dozen bras in her hand. Actually, it was only seven different sizes and styles. I had to try each on and undergo triple inspection. Soon it was decided that a 34 Teen A fit best for every day, and a regular A–Cup with padding for dressing up.

Then I had to learn to put the darned things on and get them off without killing myself. Leaning over and shaking my nonexistent boobs into the cups was not too difficult, but getting those blasted hooks into those equally tiny metal loops was the hardest part, especially because I kept trying to reach far too high up my back. Once I understood the bra band was supposed to be set beneath my shoulder blades and the hooks were to be in the middle hoops, it all became a lot easier.

"Believe it or not, most women wear ill–fitting bras and don't hook the band low," said Miss Lillian. "You would be surprised at the number of grown women who cannot hook their bras in back."

"Then, how do they hook them?" I asked, dumbstruck.

"Well young lady, they hook them in front at their waist, turn them around and pull them up like suspenders. Disgraceful."

Actually, that sounded a lot easier than what I had just done.

Momma Jean and Miss Lillian left to settle up on three everyday and two dress bras. I started to remove my bra, but Jeanie popped my hand.

"Don't you dare! You're in those for the rest of your life."

"But Jeanie. I can't go out in public wearing a bra. What will people think?"

She slipped the vest over my head, then held out the dress.

"Ruby, I don't think you understand. You're not Robbie any longer. You don't have any choice. Come on, we've got to get you home and combed out or you're going to look like a wire–haired terrier."

On the way home Jeanie and I sat in the back. She pulled me close to her and held my hand tightly in her lap. I kept staring down at my boobies. They appeared at least twice the size they had been only an hour earlier.

Jeanie's grin grew even snarkier. "They're fascinating, aren't they? Especially when the car hits a bump. I hope you get to be a C–Cup, or maybe even a double D. But, as the boys say. More than a mouthful is wasted."

CHAPTER SEVENTEEN

Surprises

After Momma Jean combed me out I looked more like a poodle than a terrier, and more like Daisy than me. At least I got rid of those ghastly rollers and pink cap. Jeanie grabbed my hand and we charged off to her room where I was unzipped from the hobble slip and swaddled into the softest nylon slip I'd ever seen, much less worn. It poured over my shoulders and hips like warm cream.

"Don't you start having naughty thoughts," giggled Jeanie as she slid her hand down my tummy. "We don't have time for playing around."

"Oh, please Jeanie. Don't do that. You know how ticklish I am."

"Hummm…. Don't think it's ticklish you're feeling right now." She delivered a soft swat to my fanny. Wash you face. Don't get your hair wet."

Next I was unceremoniously plopped before Jeanie's dressing table. Instead of makeup, she started by yanking out half my eyebrows. After slathering me in foundation, she started redrawing the eyebrows that had been yanked out only moments before, then worked downwards, first on my eyes, then the cheeks, and finally they lips. By the time she finished it felt as if I were wearing a rubber mask.

"Don't you dare cry tonight or this mascara will drip all over your face."

"Gosh, Jeanie, I'm afraid to even smile, it feels like my face might crack."

"Nonsense, you don't have on any more than Daisy or I. All things considered, I did a darn good job, taking into account what I had to work with."

"Can I look in the mirror?"

"Good Lord, no. The glass might break. I told you I didn't have much to work with. Come on, we need to get you back into a dress, unless you want to go out in your skivvies."

"Go out! We just got back. My heart can't take much more."

"Yup. Soon as Dad gets home, we're off and running."

I breathed deeply. "Out? To some public place with me in a fright wig and made up like a floozy."

"Do you even know what a floozy is?"

"It's a…, a…, not nice girl."

Jeanie rolled her eyes. "I swear, I'm going to ask Dad to warm your bottom if you don't get off your rump. No, wait here and don't go anywhere. I know how to take care of a gal like you."

She was gone for several minutes and I took the opportunity to turn and gawk at myself. The biggest difference, other than all that hair curling in all directions, were my brows and eyes. The brows were much thinner and arched like a light brown rainbow, and my eyes, especially magnified by my thick glasses, appeared twice as big with huge curled lashes. Jeanie had also drawn a blue line on my lower lid and smeared some blue finger paint below that. My pupils looked almost cobalt, as if they glowed in sympathy with all that blue.

As Jeanie returned, she tossed something frothy pink into my lap.

"Put this on."

I held it up. They weren't panties, nor a real panty girdle with panels and stuff, they were just pink, stretchy and frilly.

"What on earth?"

"It was Daisy's first panty girdle. Well, a girdlet or undergirdle for preteens. That girl never gets rid of anything."

"I can't take her things without asking. Anyway, I don't need a girdle. Well, I won't wear one anyway."

"How are you going to hold up your stockings?"

"Stockings? You mean like..., like..., stockings?"

"Yes, stockings. You can't go out at night without stockings. You want people to think you're a floozy? Anyway, you need stockings to wear open–toe sandals. You don't think I painted your toenails to hide them did you?"

This could have gone on all night, but Jeanie grabbed the girdlet, and spun it around.

"You've got it backwards."

"Well, I'm a backwards girl."

"Step into this. Pull it up. Straighten it. Sit. Bunch the stocking like this, then ease it over the toes, set the heel, work it up the leg. Start at the ankle and smooth out all the wrinkles. Fold the stocking top and hook it into the garter like so. Reach behind and fasten the back. No, you've got the garter twisted. The back needs to be tighter, you're sagging. This gets much harder when you're in a real girdle. Sometimes I have to help mom if she's breaking in a new girdle. She wears real killers to church." Jeanie gave me her classic grin. "That's the kind of girdle you need, to make you into a real girl. Okay, you do the other stocking."

It took several tries, but I finally got the stocking to her liking.

"Not bad for th' first time. I thought Daisy would never learn to get them taunt enough. Nothing looks worse on a girl than stockings bagging about the ankles. These are everyday hose, you need to wear cotton gloves to put on sheers."

"What are sheers?"

"Really thin ones, like you'd wear to church or a wedding. Or..., on a hot date."

"Jeanie, no girl would ever date me."

"Good grief! Of course not. Now you'll have to date boys. I can't wait till one gets you in the back seat."

My mouth opened, but nothing would come out.

At last she slipped an open–toe sandal on each foot and tightened a strap across my instep. The heel was only an inch or so high, but the tips were tiny and I had to work really hard to stay balanced without the ankle flopping over. She had me walk round and round her bedroom while she changed her dress and worked over her makeup. Every so often she would glance at her watch and scurry faster. She finished just as Momma Jean called.

"Okay, girls. Dad's just pulled into the driveway."

Jeanie and Daisy darted into the living room, I hobbled behind, certain I was going to break one if not two ankles before I arrived, which turned out to be just as Papa Henry entered. As always there was the smooching and hugging and patting of fannies. Instead of shaking my hand and slapping me on the back, Papa Henry froze, staring at me. His mouth opened, then closed. I knew what was coming. I was a freak, and Papa Henry was going to throw me out.

"Well, Jean. Looks like I need a second job. We'll soon have three weddings to pay for."

His arms circled my shoulders as I was swept into a huge bear hug. His hand patted my fanny, followed by a big kiss on the cheek.

"I never believed it was possible," he almost bellowed. "Now I have three daughters."

*   *   *   *   *

After the five of us had huddled into a massive hug and smooch fest, Momma Jean herded everyone out the door and into Papa Henry's Cadillac. It seemed we were already late and getting further behind by the second. Fifteen minutes later we pulled into the lot of a place called **Greek to Me! a place for Squares**.

"What is this?"

Daisy let out a sequel. "Just the best pizza you've ever eaten."

"It'll have to be. I've never had pizza."

"Well, this is different than any you haven't had," said Jeanie. "They're square and covered with yummy cheese and all kinds of meat and black olives. I love black olives."

"You love anything fattening," added Momma Jean. We'll need to get you a firmer girdle."

"That's okay. Ruby will break it in for me, won't you sweetie? In fact, Ruby is wearing Daisy's old training girdle."

Daisy let out a whoop as she lifted my skirt and slip. "Oh, Gosh! She is. Where on earth did you find that old thing?"

"In the bottom of your drawer where you stuff everything that doesn't fit."

Momma Jean turned and shook a finger at both girls. "Don't either of you say a word about this once we get inside or I'll pull a girdle inspection on both of you."

"Yes, Mommie," both girls said in unison.

Jeanie made a face like she was going to burst with laughter, then pulled a finger across her throat. Daisy held a hand over her mouth and nodded. They were planning something much worst that telling the world I was wearing a training girdle..., along with a training bra, and a sissy dress, and a nylon slip, and Shirley Temple curls, and.... Oh, God. What else did I need to be wearing?

Jeanie and Daisy helped me across the rock and tar parking lot. It was dark as Hades, which didn't make walking any easier, but it surely provided some cover from spying eyes.

Stepping through the double doors was like being transported to a Mediterranean island. Waiters in floppy white shirts and baggy black pants scurried among the tables carting huge rectangular trays and pitcher of frothy drinks. Lively music was pumping from overhead speakers. I immediately felt a desire to begin dancing around. Jeanie, Daisy and I quickly joined into a triangle and began kicking out feet and giggling. Every table must have been occupied, because families were waiting to be seated. At least half the town must have been there, so I knew it would only be moments before I was recognized.

Then I saw her, sitting with a group of boys and girls. Mitzi Johnson, and she was staring directly at me. I expected her to turn away in disgust.

Instead, a girl at a distant table jumped up and yelled to Jeanie, who darted off at the same second Daisy began pulling me after Momma and Papa. Jeanie rejoined us as we neared a wide opening into a back room. Mom, William and an unknown girl were already seated at a giant round table. Thankfully, Buddy wasn't there, I could imagine his derision at seeing me dressed like this. Then I felt really bad for thinking that way, but I had emotions too.

William stood as we entered. I could sense his amazement at seeing me. After all, the sewing uniform in our home was entirely different than watching his youngest brother totter across a public restaurant in a sissy dress and heels.

After giving me a quick squeeze, he extended his hand towards the girl and shouted over the din. "Becky, this is my baby sister, Ruby. Ruby, this is Rebecca, she works at the dealership."

I tried to say hi, but a gigantic commotion from outside drowned us. Mom simply stared at me with tears in her eyes, so I knew she was really unhappy. About me? About our financial plight, about Buddy? I had no way of knowing, but being me I could only imagine her pain was about me.

Jeanie pushed me into a chair between Mom and Momma Jean, and my fanny had hardly hit the chair when the uproar entered our room as a string of waiters carrying trays and pitchers of drinks encircled us. One of the waiters plopped his huge tray in front of me while a couple of similar trays and pitchers of Coke and Beer were placed around the table. My tray was gigantic, rectangular and covered with a thin layer of bubbling cheese with different meats and olives smeared over the surface. And, their was a single candle flickering right in the middle. It took a few seconds in the dim light to realize that **Happy First Birthday Ruby** was spelled out in black olives around the candle.

A fellow with a strange guitar appeared and began picking out a jived up version of happy birthday. The waiters and half the restaurant joined the fray. Soon I'd been serenaded in English, then in what I took for Greek. Next, the waiters lined arm in arm and kicked their way out of the room, followed by the guitar strumming fellow. Papa Henry toasted me with a frothing mug of beer, followed by William. Mom and Momma Jean gave me a big hug and wished me happy birthday, just as Daisy yelled, "LET'S EAT!"

Everyone began chopping into gooey squares of pizza and guzzling quarts of Coke or Beer. We also tried to talk, but no one could make out much of what was being said. However, I must admit, it was the best first pizza I had ever eaten. Soon I was very happy that I was only wearing a girdlet, rather than a real girdle like Mom and Momma Jean, because I was able to stuff down twice as much as either of them.

After half an hour a large group left from the main area and the level of noise dropped to the only unbearable. Papa Henry rose and cleared his throat. My Dad had always said Papa Henry should have been a Baptist minister, because he could sell rubbers to the Vatican. Everyone always laughed, but I could not figure out why the Vatican would want a bunch of rubber boots, but jokes were never my strong suite. Anyway, Papa Henry congratulated me on making it through another year, and ended by saying how proud he was to have me as a very special daughter, and how he and Momma Jean would always be there for me. It was all I could do to keep from crying, but Jeanie kept wagging her finger at me and pointing to my eyes. God, how could a little bit of black goop be used to control a girl's emotions?

Then everyone gave me cards and gag gifts like baby bottles and diaper covers. Of course, Jeanie gave me a pink pacifier on a red ribbon, which she ceremoniously draped over my head before poking the pacifier into my mouth.

When Becky gave me a pair of silver diaper pins she leaned close and yelled, "I'm sorry. Bill said his baby sister was having her first birthday party. I thought you were a real baby."

All I could think to say was, "It's a long story."

What I was really thinking was that this was the first time I had ever heard William called Bill. Could my big brother actually have a secret life? In fact, could he have any kind of life at all outside school and work? For the first time I realized I wasn't the only person with private emotions and desires.

Then it grew quiet when Momma Jean stood. At that same moment I realized that William and Papa Henry had left the table.

"Ruby, I know it's been difficult being stuck between two mothers, just like tonight. But, there's a lot to be said for having two mothers to love and cherish you. Papa Henry, the girls, and I could not be more proud of the way you've stepped up to help your mother and we know you'll soon be the best seamstress in town. In order to help you along, we have a small item to help you on your way."

With that, Papa Henry and William sat Momma Jean's new sewing machine on the table in front of me.

"Of course, now I don't have a machine, so you'll be responsible for all our mending. But then, you already are."

I lost it then, and began bawling like a real baby. By the time I regained control my face, hands and napkin were a disaster. I looked around for the restroom as someone led me down a long corridor and into the Ladies Room. It wasn't until we were inside that I realized it was Becky. Soon she had me cleaned up and helped me make my face half presentable.

"I still don't understand why your family is making such a deal out of this being your first birthday."

Suddenly I felt trapped. Surely, I could not tell a complete stranger I was actually a boy wearing all girl's clothes while standing in the woman's restroom.

"Ummmm. There have been a lot of changes in me the last few months. You know..., a lot of developments. And, my Dad died. And.... A lot of other things."

She nodded. "Oh, of course. I remember my first period. No one told me what was going to happen. I though I'd bleed to death. Hopefully someone explained things to you."

"Not too much. It's been pretty traumatic all around. But everything is getting better."

I was certain Becky and I were talking about different topics, but the disaster had been diverted, if not resolved. Best to let quiet elephants rest. We hugged. I had already learned that was a good way to deal with woman to woman problems. I suppose real men would shake hands.

"Becky, do you know William…, Bill very well."

"Yes, quite well. I hope to get to know him even better."

By the time we returned to the table the men had loaded everything into the cars. I hugged and kissed Momma Jean and the girls as tight as I could, then let Papa Henry pat me on the fanny and tell me how lovely I was. I could not imagine how his pats could make me feel so at peace. It was as if I had actually become a girl, and actually his daughter.

William dropped Mom and me off at the house, then left to drive Becky home. I helped Mom inside, then had to ask the question that had been burning within me all evening."

"Mom, why were you crying when we arrived tonight? Was it because I looked so silly?"

She touched my cheek and was silent for a long time. "I was crying because you were so beautiful. I knew you were terrified inside, but you were willing to undergo all this to fill this emptiness inside my heart. And because I could finally admit to myself just how much I loved you, and how much I wanted to cherish and protect you."

CHAPTER EIGHTEEN

Disaster

The night was more than stressful as I tossed and turned, wondering if Mom was going to put me into a dress for Church, or even worst, send me to my final week of school in skirts. It was going to be hard enough with my fright wig of curls, there was simply no way I could survive facing my classmates as a complete girl. They already thought I was a sissy, the only next step was full queerdom.

When I emerged from the bathroom the next morning, after practicing dozens of reasons not to wear a dress, Mom had laid out my new Sunday bra and the little boy–leg panty girdle on the bed, but she was also brushing the lint from my good trousers.

"Wear your best blue shirt this morning," she said. "Jeanie is singing a solo today so we'll attend the Baptist Church. Be careful putting on your stockings, they're much shearer than the others."

I was so relieved not having to fight my way out of a dress I didn't say anything about the undies. After all, who except Mom would know what I was wearing beneath my pants and shirt? Of course, I did not think about how much more my boobies would stick out in that blasted bra, or that it had a thick layer of foam rubber lining the cups. At the moment I was fighting getting my boobs to shake down into those same cups, and even worse, getting all three hooks into the proper loops. In the end Mom had to help me. Pulling up the panty girdle was no problem, it really was only slightly tighter than panties, its main feature was having the four garters to hold up my stockings and the fact that it made me a lot smoother between the legs. In fact, it was a little disconcerting when I glanced into the mirror and discovered not even a trace of boyhood down there.

The stockings also proved more than I could manage. Several times I thought they were taunt, but when I stood there were little wrinkles at my ankles. I suspected that by the time we walked to church those wrinkles would become huge sags.

Mom laughed. "It's harder than it looks. Here, feel how tight my garters are stretched." She lifted her skirt and slip and put my hand on the elastic bands attached to her open–bottom girdle."

"Gee, they're really tight."

"You need to feel them give and pull every time you move. Otherwise, you'll have wrinkles. Of course, if you pull them too tight, they'll yank your girdle down."

"I don't think I'm cut out for being a girl. Maybe I should just get a job. Now that I'm fifteen, I can legally work."

She said nothing as her fingers took the slack out of each stocking. "You have a job. In no time at all you'll be doing this without thinking. You'll feel lost without your bra and girdle. You'll look back on those horrid boy's clothes with disgust. Trust me, you'll soon be much happier, happier that you've ever felt."

"Can I at least take the paint off my nails? It's so red."

"We call it polish, not paint, and it's the mark of a lady. Think how long Jeanie spent making you pretty. Do you really want to disappoint her? Not to even wear it for 24 hours?"

I could feel the nails being driven into my coffin. "No, Mom."

"That's my good baby. Now, put on your pants and shirt. I've laid out a new pair of shoes for you. Jeanie selected them just for Sundays."

The shoes were all smooth and highly polished black leather pumps with a heel even higher than the night before, but instead of being spikes the heel was quite large so I didn't totter so much. I felt taller, and had to stand straight to keep from toppling forward, which meant my boobs really jutted to attention. I fluffed out my shirt all around, so it appeared the fullness was in the shirt, not my chest.

After smoothing my hair a bit with my comb, Mom used a stubby pencil to go over my missing eye brows, then took out a lipstick.

"Please don't, Mom. I just can't take more right now."

A crestfallen look fluttered across her face, then she smiled. "Of course, Sweets. All in good time…, all in good time."

We walked hand in hand towards the Square, just as we had done when I was a child, with William and Buddy grumpily following behind. Then it was so I would not wander into traffic, now it seemed because Mom simply wanted to be next to me. I could feel the elastic of my panty girdle give and retract with each step. Last evening I had been so traumatized I had felt nothing, now it was as if every nerve ending was working overtime. The unison click of our heels resounded from buildings as we passed. The slight scuff–scuff of my hose rubbing inside my pants added background music to my every move. Once or twice the back of my hand brushed against her firm thigh, and I wondered how long it would be before Mom and Momma Jean would compress me that tightly. Most every girl my age wore panty girdles except Mitzi. Jeanie nor Mom was going to be long satisfied with what I was wearing. It was almost as if I could see my future stretching out before me into a pink haze. I didn't think that future was going to be very comfortable, and it surely was not going to include pants.

The Methodist Church was on the south side of Memorial Square, the Baptist on the north. We were Methodists, Momma Jean and her brood, Baptist. I pretty much bounced between. I liked the Baptist Sunday School better because it was segregated by gender, but I always attended the girl's class with Daisy. The Methodists mixed boys and girls, and I hated it because Moose and Butch were always making asses of themselves. Plus, I had to deal with them at junior high, I didn't need them on Sunday also.

We were running late because of Mom having to get me ready, so I wouldn't have to face Sunday School, just preaching…, which I hated because Reverend Farmer simply would not shut up once he got the spirit up and running. Church was supposed to be over at twelve, but it was always half–past if not one o'clock by the time he'd wind down. But, today Jeanie was singing, which would make any amount of torture endurable. Even if she was in one of her moods, Jeanie sang like an angel. Even though she was a soprano, her voice was full of body and smooth as a glass of sweet milk. She never screeched, even on the highest notes and I always sank into a delicious trance as she sang. Afterward, instead of listening to Reverend Farmer's boring sermon, I always turned my bulletin over and drew Jeanie as an Angel. I'm sure she tossed the bulletins, but I always gave them to her. How I loved to hear her sing.

As we entered the sanctuary I began to realize I not only loved to hear Jeanie sing, I had started to love her, really love her, just as I loved Daisy. I had never been able to imagine life without Daisy, now I needed Jeanie just as much. Oh God! How could a mixed up, sometimes boy, love his sisters so impossibly much?

*   *   *   *   *

All the way home and through the afternoon Jeanie's rendering of The Old Rugged Cross filled my brain and mixed in with everything that was happening. Soon as we walked into the house Mom sent me upstairs to remove my pants and shirt. I assumed she would put me into the work uniform and I'd spend the day at my new sewing machine. Instead, Mom put me into a much firmer panty girdle, this also supplied by Jeanie, and my most fancy Sunday outfit with two crinolines underneath, designed and sewn by yours truly. After completely painting my face, Mom clipped ear bobs to my lobes and slipped a string of pearls around my neck.

"We'll have to get those ears pierced. No modern girl still uses clip-ons."

"My ears already feel numb."

"Yeah, but when you remove them it'll seem like your lobe's are on fire."

She stood back, hands on hips. "Perfect. You really could not be prettier or more dainty. You've been working hard, you deserve some time off. If only you had a boyfriend who'd take you down to the river for a little walk about, so people could admire you. All in good time."

"I can hardly breath and I can't relax at all in all this taffeta and lace. And, I certainly don't need a boyfriend!"

"Well, girls don't relax when they're in their Sunday best. You're suppose to be pretty, not comfortable."

"At least we've got the uncomfortable right. How do you stand all this pressure on your tummy?"

"You'll feel better when you stand."

"But then my feet hurt. My calf started to cramp in church."

"I could put you in those three inch heels…."

"I'll fall and break my nose."

"Not with those rubber boobs. Now you know why girls have breasts."

"Oh, Mooommmm!

"Oh, Ruuuubbbby!"

Mom had William finish the roll of film we had started earlier, as well as another one, clicking photos of me all over the yard and front porch. Back then taking photographs was an expensive and methodical endeavor. You would think carefully and snap one or two shots. Perhaps months later the roll would be finished and sent out for processing. When the prints returned it was like Christmas as you rediscovered all the events captured for posterity. Taking more than a roll of film on one boy/girl was unheard of, probably monumental. We ended with me lilting high in the swing hanging from the branches of the gigantic oak tree in the back yard. It was only after we were inside that I realized William could probably see up my skirt as I swung.

"What are you going to do with all those photos?" I asked.

Mom poured us a cup of cocoa and settled beside William and me at the table. "Make an album, of course. So I can show you off to everyone. We want to remember this day forever.

"You might show more than you think," said William.

"You could have said something."

"Why? You looked so pretty with all those undies showing."

*   *   *   *   *

Monday dawned clear and beautiful, but a dark storm raged inside. If I could survive one more week, school would be over and I would be free for three months, and released from junior high forever. But, with curly hair, painted nails and girl shoes, five days were going to be worse than five years.

"Mom, I don't have to wear a skirt to school, do I?"

"Don't you want to? You'll be so pretty."

"Of course not, I'm going to be crucified as it is."

"Then wear your old worn out pants and shirt. You'll look rather silly with a bra under your shirt, but if that's what you prefer...."

"The Bra! I've got to wear the bra?"

"And the panty girdle. You don't want to disappoint Aunt Jean and Jeanie do you? After Jean took you to Miss Lillian herself. That wouldn't be very nice, would it?"

I stared at the floor and shook my head. "No Ma'am. I couldn't disappoint Momma Jean..., or Jeanie."

"Then it's decided. Come down when you're ready, I'll fix you a big plate of pancakes and sausage for breakfast."

Jeanie was all smiles when I joined up with her and Daisy. It was good we only had a few books to carry, because they both piled theirs onto mine as we started off towards my execution. Daisy was nattering about how sad she was to leave junior high, but Jeanie sidled next to me and ran her hand down my back to my fanny.

"Oh, very good," she squealed. "I was afraid you might chicken out." Her hand moved to the bottom of the panty girdle and she lightly snapped the elastic of a garter. "I liked the drawing you did on your bulletin. Were those little devil horns you added beneath my halo?"

"No, they were big horns. That other girdle you sent was really tight."

"It's supposed to be tight! Wait till I get you under my full control."

I stopped and stared at her. "What do you mean?"

"I want you near me always. Even after I'm married. Maybe I'll turn you into my maid or something."

She giggled, then bumped me with her hip. Suddenly, her face darkened.

"Ruby, listen to me. I'm not playing with you now. Stay away from Moose. The word is he's planning to play a really mean joke on you. No one will say what, but Moose is sick in the head and his mother isn't much better. Please, stay out of his way and don't let him sneak up on you. I don't know why your brothers don't protect you. It's almost like they want to see you get hurt."

"They just don't care, that's all."

"It's got to be more that that. Any fool can see how delicate you are. You're not like other boys. They're your brothers, they're suppose to look after you. I remember on the first day you went to school. William was suppose to take you to your class. He just left you standing alone on the steps. How were you going to find your room? You'd probably still be standing there staring at the closed doors through those thick glasses if I hadn't found you." Her head shook. "It's just not normal. They should look after you." She stared straight at me. "Since they won't, I will."

* * * * *

Actually, everything went pretty well on Monday and Tuesday. All of the rich kids and athletes were taken over to the high school for special orientation and class selection. This was supposed to make it easier in the fall for us poor trash to get oriented and receive class assignments. Everyone knew it was to ensure the high class people got the pick of courses and clubs and activities. Money and sports carried a lot of clout in our town. Intelligence and hard work were not worth much.

It didn't take long for most of the girls to figure out that I was wearing a bra and girdle. After all, I could look at a girl and know what she was wearing beneath her dress, I assumed they could do the same with me. Anyway, soon after the girls knew, the boys knew also. No one laughed in my face, but I could feel them tittering behind my back.

Miss Griffith was my savior. She kept calling me out of class to run errands and close the science lab for the summer. That took almost all of Wednesday.

Thursday was a near disaster. Mrs. Hanahan, Moose's mother, was my English teacher and she had been instructing us how to diagram sentences. 'To help you in high school,' she said. In actuality, none of us had much of an idea what she was talking about most of the time, but Buddy, of all people, came to my aid by explaining diagramming so I could understand it.

Anyway, on the final Thursday of school, Mrs. Hanahan decided to test our knowledge. She handed out slips of paper with sentences and sent us off to the board. Most people had really short, simple sentences. Mine was over ninety words and so convoluted I could barely figure out the subject, much less the remainder. I struggled at the blackboard while everyone else finished and returned to their seats. First titters ran through the classroom, then giggles, then outright laughing. I realized that by stretching up to write on the board, my bra was clearly outlined through my shirt, and probably the outline of my girdle was showing as well. On I struggled, trying to make sense of the impossible sentence. Right in the middle on the most complex section, Butch Spence hopped from his chair and snapped the back of my bra so hard I let out a yell. Turning as Butch scurried back to his chair, I threw a full piece of chalk as hard as possible and caught him at the base of the skull. Down he went with a thud. He didn't move for a long time, then staggered up with blood gushing from his nose.

Everybody was silent for several seconds, then a girl screamed at the exact moment Butch put his hand to his nose and saw all the blood. Several more screams erupted as he fainted. It must have taken fifteen minutes to get everyone quiet and Butch off to the Nurse's office.

Instead of packing me to the Principal, Mrs. Hanahan lectured me on how stupid I was for not being able to diagram such a simple sentence. She took up her teaching guide and started to correct my errors. That was when it became clear she had miss–copied the sentence. Every time she tried to correct her mistakes, I corrected her mistakes. That's when she sent me to the Office. To top everything, she gave me a B for that reporting period, which broke my string of all A's reaching back to the first grade. I knew Mom would not say anything, but how could she possibly love anyone who wasn't perfection in all things?

What bothered me most was that Mitzi had not said one word to me all week. It wasn't like we were friends or anything, but I desperately looked forward to our fleeting interactions. Not only did she not speak, she didn't even look my way. I knew she had seen me in the dress at the pizza restaurant, which had probably disgusted her, but was that enough that she could not even stand to see me? Perhaps it was the perm, or my girl's underwear. That must be it. I was disgusting.

On Friday I was so jumpy waiting for Moose to play his trick I could hardly breath. By now everyone was tired of ragging me about my curls and bra and girdle that the day was almost anticlimactic. After what seemed like years, the day and the school year ended. Moose had not played his joke, but there was certainly enough humiliation to last till fall.

I moseyed out to the front door to await Jeanie and Daisy. They would be saying goodby to all their friends, so it was going to be a while. Mitzi was standing alone, with her back to me. At first, I simply waited, unseen behind her. At any moment her father's driver would arrive and whisk her away. She didn't want to see me. The least I could do was honor her wishes. But, I couldn't let her leave without saying something. Should I apologize for being the stupid ass I was? There was no way I could explain, it would simply sound as if I were making excuses for my shortcomings. Then, how could I explain what I did not understand? All of a sudden, some power inside forced me forward.

"Hi, Mitzi. Ready for Summer?" God! That was stupid.

She did not respond.

"I'm surely ready for school to be over."

She made a harrumphing sound.

"Maybe I'll see you around somewhere. This is a pretty small town."

"You'll have to be good, then. Grandmother is taking me to Europe all summer."

"Wow, I've always dreamed of visiting Europe. Especially Rome and Istanbul. Most people don't know where Istanbul is located, or that half of it is in Europe."

She turned, I could see fire in her eyes.

"Moose told me what you did. That's the most disgusting thing I've ever heard. We're not friends any more. I don't ever want to see you again."

Her car arrived and the driver hopped out to open her door. She didn't wait, but yanked open the door and dove in, slamming the heavy metal behind her. My hand half raised, but she didn't glance back. In moments she was gone and only a spray of gravel marked her passing.

Jeanie put her hand on my shoulder. "Girlfriend troubles."

"I don't know. Moose told her something…."

"Moose told her that you had sucked him off, then begged him to screw you up the fanny."

I shook my head, trying to make sense of what was happening.

"Suck? Fanny?"

Jeanie squeezed her eyes tight. "Oh, God! You don't even know what that means, do you? Moose has been bragging to the whole school that you sucked his cock till he came in your mouth, then begged him to fuck you up the ass."

I could hardly speak. "But…. But, Jeanie. You don't think…."

"Of course not. But, obviously Mitzi believes it. She'll probably never speak to you again."

CHAPTER NINETEEN

My buddy, Buddy

Jeanie and Daisy walked me home. I was so distraught I couldn't think straight. Mom gave me a huge dose of paregoric which contained enough codeine to put me out for the rest of the day and night. It took several more days before I could get to work, and even then I kept falling apart. How could anyone possibly think ruining my life was a joke? There was no way I could ever be taken seriously in town, no way I could go back to school. My only friend never wanted to see me again. Everyone at school now knew I was a flaming Queen. Even to think of Moose and his gang laughing over my destruction brought me to a complete breakdown.

However, everything passes, no matter how great the hurt, how unjust the situation, life must go on. So, I went on.

The problem was, there was nowhere to go. After the bridal season slowed to a crawl, our sewing work completely dried up. No one even wanted to have a pair of trousers hemmed. There was not one waistband to be adjusted in the entire county. At first I was convinced we had no customers because people were disgusted by my actions, but as the days passed I had to admit it was more. We simply had not considered that nobody would be buying fancy clothing during the summer. We had the occasional swimsuit that needed adjusting, perhaps a dress or suit needed for a funeral. Otherwise, Mom and I sat hour after hour staring at each other.

"Soon as school gets near everyone will start buying and we'll be overwhelmed, just you wait."

"But, Mom, we can't go hungry till August. And, the mortgage needs to be paid. And the utilities, and..., and...."

"I know, Sweets. We'll manage..., some way. If I only had something else to sell."

"You've already sold your engagement ring and Dad's guns. There is no more silver or crystal. We've even sold my old bed and dresser. Unless you sell me, what else do we have?"

Mom bit her lip. "Perhaps I could get a job downtown. You know, in one of the shops. Only until things pick up."

"I'm the one who need to get a job. The problem is figuring out who will hire a punk."

"Don't say things like that about yourself. You're an intelligent, God fearing and honest young lady."

"Mom, I'm a boy who wears dresses. Everybody in town thinks I'm queer as a seven dollar bill."

Now Mom burst into tears as she fled upstairs.

I had to get a job, the question was..., who would hire a useless queer?

*　　*　　*　　*　　*

For all my life Buddy had terrorized me. It began the moment I tottered into the house as a three year old, and continued every day since. Sometimes he just frightened me, other times he punched, pushed, tripped or kicked me into submission. I never understood why, or had any idea what he might do next. It just gave him immense pleasure to torment the living daylights out of his strange little brother.

Actually, his attitude had changed from the day I began receiving treatments. Whereas before he only wanted to torment me, now he seemed fascinated by what was happening to my body. He absolutely could not keep his hands off me, and my expanding fanny most awakened his curiosity. He was always pinching, patting or kneading me, and I could not even think about leaning over without getting goosed. That was the worst, because he always choose my most vulnerable and inopportune moments to slip silently behind me and 'check my oil,' as he loved to say. I never liked it, but I was becoming more sensitive back there with each injection and his every touch had started to produce extremely embarrassing reactions in my tummy.

My revenge came one day when Mom had me in my firmest panty girdle. I was leaning over the work table cutting out a very intricate patter when Buddy crept behind and goosed me. Instead of jumping six inches off the floor as usual, I simply turned and jabbed his hand with the scissors. Thank God for panty girdles!

Just as Moose could not keep his hands off my boobs, Buddy could not stop tormenting my rear.

I was now doing all the washing and ironing as well as house cleaning. Every week I would gather everything that was dirty; wash, iron or fold it, then return the items to the appropriate place. For several weeks some of my panties and one girdle had gone missing. For the life of me I could not imagine where I had misplaced them. I hadn't put them in Mom's drawer. They weren't in the washer or clothes hamper. They had simply disappeared.

Then, one day while returning Buddy's underwear to his bureau, I spied something pink and nylon tucked beneath his undershorts.

"Good grief! How did these get mixed up in here? You're really losing it, Ruby Jones."

Stuffing them into the pocket of my apron, I thought no more about them. That is, until the next time I hung them on the back porch to dry. That's when they disappeared the second time. Now I became interested.

The next week when changing the sheets on Buddy's bed I noticed something beneath his mattress. Not only did I find the missing panty girdle, but also a stack of pages torn from his magazines. At first I couldn't figure why he was saving them, especially beneath his mattress. They were only advertisement pages, not like photos of naked girls or dirty stories or anything. I flipped through the pages, then slowly studied them. Each had a similar advertisement for the most unusual comic books and sets of photographs. Almost all were about women tying girls into impossible positions. All the girls were in their underwear. Some panties and bras, but others in girdles and corsets and strange rubber costumes, and everybody wore impossibly high heels. The women doing the tying all looked strong and dominate with lots of makeup, the poor tied girls seemed delicate and passive. Most important, the passive girls appeared to have been tied for simply ages, and were all resigned to be there forever.

I sat on the bed and studied each advertisement more closely. My heart raced, I became incredibly hot, sweat beaded on my forehead. Never before had I imagined feeling like those rushing through me. It was even stronger than the emotions in my dreams.

Ever so slowly I regained control. Removing a sheet from the middle of the stack, I carefully folded it and placed it into my apron pocket. This time I simply returned the girdle beneath the mattress. Otherwise, Buddy would only steal it again. Besides, it was already feeling too loose on me.

I had no idea what to do with the advertisement, but I had to discuss it with someone. Jeanie was the only one I could think of. Certainly, I could not talk to William or Mom about such things.

That very night at supper a grand scheme began to form in my head.

Buddy would sometimes eat with us if we had fried chicken. Otherwise he ate with Grandma Jones. Mom had decided we would splurge for a few days.

"Maybe we need more protein, so our brains will begin working," she had said.

So, I fried chicken, cooked rice and gravy with fresh butterbeans. We had biscuits and syrup for desert. Buddy belched contentedly and leaned back in his chair.

"They're looking for help down at th' Tin Skillet."

Mom perked up. "That would be perfect, Buddy. You're a wonderful skater. You could wow everyone with your jumps."

"Not me! I don't serve anyone hamburgers for a living."

"You don't do anything for a living," observed William.

Buddy rolled his eyes. "I'm certainly not going to become anyone's slave. I was thinking of th' shrimp."

"I don't know how to skate."

"William could teach you," said Mom.

"William is the worst teacher in the world. Remember when he was going to teach me to drive? 'It's simple, Doodlebug. Just crank it up and stay in the road. Nothing to it.' Ha, if Papa Henry hadn't taught me I'd still be trying to figure out how to crank the blamed car. Now I can sit for my license soon as I turn sixteen."

"Well, I'm definitely not wasting my time teaching no queer how to skate." Buddy hopped from the table and disappeared upstairs.

"I pray he'll stop saying things like that to you, Ruby. He just won't listen."

Stacking the dirty dishes, I cleared the table. "Don't worry, Mom. Buddy Jones is about to meet his match."

Mom stared at me above the rim of her coffee cup. William's mouth hung open.

$$* \quad * \quad * \quad * \quad *$$

After clearing the kitchen I marched upstairs and into Buddy's room. He was sprawled on his bed, staring intently at a page in the back of his magazine.

"What you want, Shrimp?"

I tried to peer over the top of his magazine, he slapped it tight against his chest.

"Those ads are interesting."

"What ads?"

"The one you were leering at."

His eyes darted to the door, then back to me. "I said, what do you want?"

"I want you to teach me to skate. Fancy, like you."

"Ha! That'll be th' day. I don't teach qu—"

"If you call me that again I'll slap your face. You're my brother, at least treat me with a little respect. I've never called you names."

He didn't say anything for a while as he hugged the magazine closer and closer.

"Why should I teach you anything? I'm too busy."

"If you teach me, I won't tell Mom and William what's under your mattress."

"There's nothing under there but springs. Ha ha."

I walked to the door and yelled, "Mom! Could you come to Buddy's room? We have a problem."

"Shut up, Bitch. You'll wake th' dead." His eyes darted out the door, then to me. "Okay, we'll talk."

"It's alright, Mom. I fixed it."

Buddy's face was ashen and his hands trembled. "I'll teach you..., if you get a job, and if..., you do something for me..., it's kind of private..., just between us."

Backing against the wall, I shook my head. "Buddy, you know Moose Hanahan was lying about me. I can't do anything like that."

"Don't be goofy. I wouldn't make love with you for all the gold in Fort Knox."

"What then?"

"Just lift your skirt. I only want to see."

"You're always dating. Don't you have girlfriends?"

"Girls don't go around lifting their skirts. Just do it!"

My heart raced. Was Buddy going to hurt me? I wasn't a real girl, but I didn't want him gawking at me, even if I was wearing panties and a girdle. But, they were panties and a girdle, which was worst than boy's undershorts. Christ, I didn't want him gawking at me in undershorts either. But, I wanted..., no, needed to learn to skate. Back and forth, back and forth. I was tearing myself apart even as I slowly lifted the hem of my skirt to mid–thigh, then to the top of my thighs.

Buddy was almost panting. "All the way, up to your waist."

At last both skirt and slip were bunched about my waist. He reached out. I backed even tighter against the wall.

"I'm not going to hurt you." His fingertips lightly pressed into my hips, then into my tummy. "How does it feel?"

"What?"

"This thing. What you're wearing."

"My girdle? It's tight, like a second skin that's too small. It feels like I'm being hugged around the middle. It…. It makes me feel like a sissy, what do you think?"

His voice was hushed, little more than a whisper. "Does it hurt?"

"Sometimes it's uncomfortable, like a new shoe, you just have to wiggle a little or pull it back into place. Girls have to put up with that type thing." Good grief! I couldn't believe I was saying things like this, and to my brother.

"Turn around…. Please."

That was the first time I'd ever heard Buddy use the word.

By now it was as if I were in a dream that would never end. I could feel Buddy's eyes drilling deeply into my fanny. I was so gross back there. He must be ready to barf just looking at me. His finger tips lightly pressed into the sides of my backside, then underneath.

"You're beautiful," he whispered. "Absolutely beautiful."

After lowering my skirt, I turned and faced him, huffing in deep breaths to quiet my own thumping heart. "We have a deal?"

He nodded.

"One more thing. Have you ordered any of those comic books…, the ones with the girls?"

His eyes started darting again. "Are you going to tell Mom?"

"Of course not, I don't want her to have a heart attack. You know I like to draw. I want to see if I can draw girls like that…, with clothing."

A big grin lit his face. "You really are a girl. Inside, I mean. You see beautiful girls and you want to put clothes on them. Boys want to take clothes off girls." His head shook. "They're hidden. I'll leave some under the mattress tomorrow night." He started to close the door. "Goodnight, Ruby."

As the door swung shut I realized that was the first time he had ever said anything nice to me, and the first time he had used my name. And that name was Ruby.

He was correct, I did want to put clothes on those women, but only so I could them remove them. But, by far most importantly, I wanted to be one of those girls. Not the mean women. No, I wanted to be one of the helpless girls. I wanted a woman to tie me up and do anything she desired. I knew that was the only way any woman would ever touch me…. If I were a helpless girl, and if I let her crush me beneath her heel.

CHAPTER TWENTY

The Wheel McCoy

Mom thought it was hilarious that I might become a waitress at the Tin Skillet.

"One, you can't skate, and two, you couldn't manage those trays full of burgers and fries. What are you going to do when you fall and your skirt flies over your head?"

"I'll wear a panty girdle. If I fall, people will be looking at it, not for any bumps under my panties."

She made a face. "I'd better talk this over with Jean."

Mom always talked with Momma Jean when something new came up. The situation really got interesting when Mr. Green, owner and manager of the Skillet was desperate enough to give me a try. I was supposed to start on Friday afternoon, which did not give Buddy and me much time. But, first, Mom had to talk with Momma Jean once more. Half an hour later I was sitting between Momma Jean and Jeanie as we drove downtown.

"Where are we going?"

"You'll see."

"What are you going to torture me with this time?"

"You'll see."

"I'll probably feel it, more than see it."

Momma Jean smiled at me sweetly. "I know a little girl who's about to get a super dose of Caster Oil."

Jeanie snickered.

"What are you snickering about. If I get one, you'll probably get one too."

Jeanie made a face. "Yukkkk! Mom, you wouldn't do that, I'm too old."

Momma Jean smiled even sweeter. "Probably. I'm sure you've done something to deserve it."

Soon we pulled into a parking space before Minx Department Store. They each took a hand and guided me downstairs to the Bargain Basement and up to a round display filled with tall cylindrical tubes. Each of the tubes was labeled with the name Playtex, and displayed a woman in a girdle and bra with her hands sticking straight up. There was a big sign over the display blaring **Playtex half-off sale**, but the prices still looked really expensive. Momma Jean selected several tubes and Jeanie drug me after her mother into the nearest changing room. Soon I'd been stuffed into a rubber brief with a bunch of holes poked into the tummy and fanny. Momma Jean ran her hand between my legs to make sure I was absolutely flat.

"Wear this when you go skating or swimming. If you fall, no one will suspect you're not a girl."

"It's too tight, and it makes my fanny stick out. Anyway, I don't have a swimsuit and don't know how to swim. See, it makes me look like a beach ball. I feel like one too." I sniffed. "It smells funny."

"Well, Miss Beach Ball of 1958, you'll feel right at home in the pool in any case." Jeanie gave my fanny a pat. "Th' boys go wild when you wear one of these. They'll be sniffing all around you."

"Do you have one of these?"

"Certainly. I wouldn't be caught dead in a swimsuit without a brief. See, it makes your tummy absolutely flat."

"Yea, but it makes my butt absolutely round. Now what are you doing?"

Momma Jean added another tube to her arms. "Getting you a panty girdle too. Pam can put you out in the sun and sweat some of the smartness out of your fanny."

*   *   *   *   *

By the time Buddy and I finally reached the skating rink it felt like my panties were already drenched with sweat, and I sweated even more as we skated. I thought that perhaps I'd sweat off a few pounds of fanny fat, but that never actually happened.

Anyway, Grandma Jones had given him a wad of money to take his girlfriend skating, so we weren't short of cash, but I surely wasn't happy having anyone think I was his date. Buddy had his own skates but we had to stop at the store and get me fitted. He chose several pair and I was soon in some girl size eight–narrow. They were white with startling pink laces and wheels, with some type of rubber bumper at the toe, also in bright pink. Lively organ music blared from every speaker, so loud we had to shout.

Kneeling before me, Buddy slipped off my shoes and little foot nylons and worked a pair of thick cotton socks up my calves. I knew he could see up my skirt, but decided it was better to keep him interested than make an issue of it. My foot slipped into the skate easily, but he soon had me laced so tight my ankles could barely move.

I sat, unable even to stand, while he put on his skates and deposited our shoes and my handbag in a locker. Too soon he was back and yanking me upright. I felt like a baby learning to walk on marbles. He skated backwards holding my hands as we slowly worked our way into the rink and over to a handrail. With one hand on the rail and him holding me about the waist he guided me down the rink. It took a while, but soon I understood the skates would only roll forward or back, not to the side. To skate, I had to press sideways with one foot, while stepping forward with the other. It wasn't long until I grasped that I had to stand right over the skates. If I leaned forward, the skates would zip out behind. If I leaned back, the skates would scoot from under me.

By the end of an hour I could make it all the way around the rink without falling more than a couple of times. If William was the world's worst teacher, Buddy must have been the best. It was hard to believe he was the same monster who had called me so many names and pushed me down a thousand times. But, here he was, patiently guiding me around the rink with an arm tightly grasping my waist. Not once did he try to goose me or rub my fanny, although he easily could have done either. Every time I fell he patiently picked me up, brushed me off, and explained what I had done wrong. This really could not be my brother.

"Always fall on your fanny. It's made to bounce. If you fall forwards you might break a wrist."

"You just want to see my skirt fly up."

He laughed, in a merry way I had never heard.

"I'll have to admit, you do make quite a sight on your fanny with your legs flailing in the air. You look like a fluffy turtle."

All at once the music changed. Boys and girls started linking up and skating rapidly around the rink. Some were actually dancing on their skates. Buddy pushed me towards the railing.

"Just keep going around. Stay next to the railing."

He schussed away like an Olympic skier and into the arms of a really attractive girl. They spoke for a moment or two, then were off arm in arm, dancing to the organ music. I almost fell trying to watch them and struggle along, so concentrated on staying alive. After about thirty minutes the music switched to a slower tempo and Buddy swooped back next to me.

"You're doing great, Sis."

I could see his face grow red. I could not believe he had actually called me Sis. Then, I could not believe this was my real brother.

We shared a burger and coke, then I made the mistake of going to the bathroom and discovered you never, never, never pull down a rubber girdle when you're sweating like a pig. It took me fifteen minutes to struggle back into the blasted thing. My hips and fanny felt as if they had gone through a clothes wringer. When I finally got back to Buddy he just looked puzzled.

"Don't say a word. It's a girl thing."

He simply nodded.

We practiced for another hour, then sat down and took off our skates.

"Where do I return these?"

"They're yours. Consider them a birthday present from Grandma Jones. She doesn't know, but what she doesn't know won't hurt her." He stared down at me. "I'm sorry she hates you so much. You're not a bad kid at all."

I didn't know what to say, so I said nothing all the way back to the house. As we got out of the car, I did a really stupid thing. I threw my arms around Buddy and kissed him on the cheek.

"Thank you so much. You are a wonderful teacher and brother. I really appreciate everything you did for me."

He backed away.

"Oh! I'm..., I'm sorry. I shouldn't have done that."

"No, Sis. Really, you're not bad at all. I.... I just need a little time. Time to figure out what's happening."

*　　*　　*　　*　　*

By Friday I could skate forwards and backwards and even make a single jump, although I was still a little wobbly on the landing. I could easily make ten loops of the rink at full speed without falling. Buddy even taught me several dance steps. Of course, whenever the dance periods came he would dart off to find some lonesome princess to dance with. Once or twice a young boy who was just learning to dance picked me up and I was able to make it through the entire period without falling or even tripping him up. I have to admit, the boys were usually pretty bad, so it didn't take much to keep up.

Mom couldn't let a chance to sew for me pass without going overboard. She made me an absolutely stunning satin outfit. The bodice and skirt were contrasting panels of bright blue and green. The skirt, which barely reached my thighs, was lined with bright yellow, and the bloomers were bright red. Red ribbons dangled from my sleeves and a huge red bow closed my neckline. I was certainly the most visible skater in the state. Every time I moved the skirt would spring up revealing flashes of yellow and red. Whenever I fell those bloomers were far more visible that the rubber brief had ever been.

What was strange was that even though my bottom was covered by a layer of nylon panty, rubber girdle and satin bloomer, I felt far more exposed than ever. I could feel every boy in the rink staring at me. Actually, I think the girls were staring even harder than the boys, and their thoughts were probably not nearly as kind.

The first week at The Tin Skillet, Mr. Green had me work inside the restaurant which was a lot less hectic than outside. He got upset that I was not filling out the order slip as each person said what they wanted. At last I convinced him I could easily remember a dozen orders. If it was a table of teens I would go around clockwise taking orders, then repeat them back. Finally, I'd quickly fill the order slip while skating to the kitchen.

It was a little more different when I was shifted outside. There was no problem if it was one or two boy–girl couples. The boys were on their best behavior, trying to impress their dates. However, it there were four or more rowdy boys in a car, especially a convertible, they would make absolute fools of themselves trying to trip me up by changing their orders half a dozen times. One of the other girls taught me how to deal with them. I'd simply looked bored and ask, 'You want to eat this burger, or shall I dump it in your lap?' That always shut them up.

The Skillet hadn't changed its menu in thirty years, so everyone knew exactly what was available. The best burgers, dogs and fries in town, washed down by the biggest shakes or drinks, and everything followed by ice cream or pie. There were a few other items, like onion rings, or chilli after football games in the winter. Otherwise, you could choose what you wanted on your burger and if you wanted chilli or slaw on your dog. Some of the guys could eat two or three burgers — all the way — along with extra–super–large fries and a giant shake. I could never finish a full burger, especially if I was wearing that darned rubber brief. Which was essentially every day since our uniform consisted of a tiny hot–pink dress even shorter than my skating outfit, with pink bloomers. We were supposed to keep the top couple of buttons undone, so our cleavage would show. Since I only had Teen–A boobs and no cleavage, I buttoned my top all the way to my neck.

Usually, I worked from six o'clock to midnight, except on Fridays and Saturdays till one in the morning. We closed on Sunday, which was good since I really needed the sleep. The pay was good and sometimes I even got tips. Again, family groups or boy–girl couples were great, because the boys wanted to impress their dates. A car full of rowdy boys, the worst. Well, actually the rich kids were the worst. They never tipped and always were the most demanding.

Momma Jean and the girls stopped by almost every week and insisted that I serve them. When she paid, Momma Jean would slip a twenty into my pocket. At first I tried to give it back, then I realized she was desperately trying to get money to us, so I would just squeeze her hand and kiss her cheek. Mom let me add my salary to the household funds, but she insisted I keep all my tips separate. That tip money was going to become very important to me, but I didn't understand it at the time.

Every so often Moose Hanahan and his gang would show up. Like me, Moose didn't have his license as yet, but one of his buddies had flunked a couple of times and as a reward had earned a big new convertible. Each time I served them, Moose would stare at me. It was clear he couldn't quiet figure out who I was. Heck, I hardly recognized myself in that outfit with all those curls and makeup and pink butt sticking out back. By now I was a pretty fair skater, so I really started showing off as I served them, and you could see Moose getting more and more interested as I would zip around their car, balancing their order on one hand as I spun forwards and back. I knew it was a sin, but it gave me the most obscenely perverse pleasure watching them pant after me.

Near the end of summer my plan was complete. One Friday night they came tooling in, hot for leather. There were several beer bottles scattered about the floorboard. Moose was sitting in back, his shirt open with his hairy chest and belly exposed, nursing half a beer. I took their order and sailed off to the kitchen, but not before I circled their car making loops. There was no doubt, I had Moose's attention.

At the kitchen I added a superdog with extra chilli to their order along with a large cup of ice and another of Coke. I was going to lose my job, but it was worth it.

After handling several other cars, I picked up their order and fixed the tray to the driver's window. I distributed the order and collected. Moose jerked awake and stared at the tray.

"Who gets th' dog?"

Grabbing the superdog, I yanked his belt and stuffed the dog and hot chilli down his pants.

"Suck that, you lying bastard!"

"Aaaaa! Hot…, hot."

I dumped the ice on his head. "Maybe this'll cool you off!"

"What th' fuck? You crazy bitch—"

After splashing the Coke in his face, I squeezed his nipples hard as I could.

"How do you like being in the PTA?"

"God Damn! That hurts." His eyes bulged out. "Jones, you…. I'm going to kill you ass."

He started climbing out of the car as I backpedaled.

"You and what army, Moose. Can't catch a little sissy? You can't even walk straight, you shithead."

Moose was stumbling, trying to shake the superdog out of his pants and wipe his face and run after me, which was at least two more things than he could manage in his condition. I skated round and around him, between the cars, up on the walkway, down into the parking lot, back between the cars. The harder he tried to catch me, the faster I skated.

"I'm gonna kill you, Jones. Bash your head in."

"Why don't you try sucking me off, shithead. You can't even catch me."

By now everyone was blowing their horns and yelling at Moose. I would almost let him grab me, then scoot off. I knew that if his buddies sobered up enough they could surround me, but I prayed they would be too dumbstruck to act.

There had been so much commotion that two police cars with lights flashing pulled into the lot. Mr. Green walked up the first car.

"I believe these youngsters have been drinking, Officer. I would greatly appreciate if you would escort them off my property."

"Certainly, Mr. Green. I think we recognize these fellows."

As Mr. Green headed back inside, I skated beside him.

"I'm sorry for the commotion. I'll pay for any damages. I've enjoyed working for you."

He was silent for a while. "It probably is better if you go home, these boys aren't going to be too happy. I'll expect you back at work on Monday."

After taking off the skates and gathering my belongings, I headed outside. Buddy was leaning against the fender of his car.

"Need a lift?"

We didn't say anything on the way home, but after he cut off the engine, he looked over at me.

"That was beautiful, Sis. I'm dammed proud of you."

CHAPTER TWENTY–ONE

Freaky Friday

Summer was almost over. Mr. Green was cutting back at the Skillet, so he let us temps go, but added two weeks pay to our envelopes. Mom had been right, now that school was nearing, mothers had started readying their daughters. We worked a deal with the Catholic School to outfit their entire incoming class, which was a huge amount of work, but also a lot of cash.

Money was still our main problem. Mom, William and I were making enough to pay our daily bills, but there was simply no way we could manage two mortgages. The house had been in our family for three generations and should not have had any mortgage. What was especially galling was that Dad had wasted the first mortgage on worthless oil well stocks, and the second mortgage money on booze and women. Everything seemed so unfair, but the bills came due every month and we had to find the money somewhere.

Once or twice we had become so desperate I considered becoming a prostitute, since someone had said that was a good way to get cash. But, I always had to admit that no one would pay to do things to me, especially when I didn't even know how to kiss a girl, much less a man. It never occurred to me that a woman might pay to play with a boy/girl.

One Friday afternoon I reached a breaking point. I simply could not sew another seam. Mom sent me upstairs to soak in her favorite strawberry bubble bath. When I finally emerged from the bath, Mom helped me dress in one of my favorite outfits and sent me off to visit Momma Jean and the girls.

"Don't come back till your head is clear," said Mom. "I can't afford my best girl having a breakdown."

The fact that I was Mom's only girl didn't make any difference, I suppose. I knew I should have called ahead to let them know I was coming, but I had been too exhausted mentally to think of such mundane stuff. It was no longer like in the old days, when I could just appear. Jeanie and Daisy had other friends and Momma Jean had become much more active in community and church activities. I decided to pass by the playing fields since no one was likely to be messing around in late August heat if they didn't have to. The fields were vacant except for a flock of crows.

"Sorry, crows. I know you come in murders, not flocks."

To bring home the point, I tossed a rock into their midst, simply to watch them fly about in disarray. That was not very ladylike, but beneath my skirt and panties I was still a boy..., at least part boy, anyway.

I still had my key, so I let myself in as usual and walked into the kitchen. Momma Jean was busily decorating a cake for the First Baptist Cake Sale.

"Oh, hello Ruby. Didn't Daisy call you?"

"No, Ma'am." I hugged her and pulled a stool up to the counter.

She squirted some icing onto a saucer and pushed it towards me. "Are your hands clean?"

"Don't need clean hands to lick icing." To make my point, I licked my finger before sticking it into the mound of icing. "Ummmm. Wonderful. I love cream cheese icing."

Jeanie entered and I plopped a finger full of icing into her mouth. She glanced at her mom, at me, then back to her mom. Something was definitely wrong. I should have called. No, I should not have come. By now Daisy had entered and they all kept glancing one to the other.

Momma Jean cleared her throat. "Daisy, don't you have something to say to Ruby?"

I hopped off the stool. "It's getting late, I'd best be heading home."

Momma Jean pushed me back towards the stool. "You'll go nowhere. I don't want you near that cemetery after dark. Papa Henry will drive you when he arrives. Daisy, don't you have something to say?"

Daisy drew a circle on the floor with her foot. "I was supposed to call. You see…, I've got some friends coming over for the night. We're heading down to the beach tomorrow."

I let out a sigh of relief. Everything was alright. I had spent many a sleepover with Daisy's friends. We played games and sang songs. I would end up sleeping with Daisy, and her friends would spread out in the other bed or in sleeping bags all over the room. It was like camping out.

Daisy cleared her throat. "You see, its not like it used to be. We're older now. Some of the girls…. They don't want you in my room. You know, like you might see them. It was okay when we were little."

"Oh?" Then I understood. "They think I'll hurt them."

"It's not that…."

"I'm sorry, Momma Jean. It's best if I leave. Promise I won't walk through the cemetery. Bye Jeanie."

Before I could take a step, Jeanie grabbed my arm.

"You're going nowhere. We'll have a girl's night out, then you can sleep with me. She made a face at Daisy. "I know you won't hurt me."

"But, Jeanie?"

"It's decided. Mom, Ruby and I will be out. Don't wait supper on us."

Jeanie led towards her bedroom. Normally, she hardly let me in there, certainly I had never slept with her, even when we were babies. Jeanie was a very private person and I had learned years ago not to play with her toys or even read one of her books without her express permission.

In a very short while she had me down to my panties and bra and had started tossing items onto the bed like a madwoman.

"I cannot believe that Daisy. Aunt Pam said you were getting burnt out and needed a break. We knew you'd be coming over. Daisy should have called..., not let you walk into something like this. Well, we'll have a great time tonight, just you wait."

"You don't need to baby me. I've got feelings of steel."

"You're a damn pussy willow. Somebody's got to look out for you." More items flew onto the bed. "Can't find it. Well, we will just make do."

Jeanie grabbed a heavy–duty panty girdle and tossed it to me.

"I'll never blast my way into this, it's too strong."

"It's just my dress girdle. At least it's broken in, I'll need to wear the new one. We want to look our best tonight if we expect to be picked up."

"Picked up, does that mean what I think?" I had folded the top over on the girdle and had worked it up to my hips. "I'm stuck."

"Pull the back over your butt. Don't break a nail! Here, let me help. See, you can't even get into a girdle by yourself."

"This isn't a girdle, it's a torture device." By now it was high enough and Jeanie helped me unroll the top so it smoothed out two inches above my waist. "How do you stand this?"

"My waist is smaller, that's how. If you weren't so thick in the middle you'd look better. You need less waist and more hips."

"What I need is more boobs. If I'm going to be a girl, at least I could look like one." I stared down at my little Teen–A breasts. "My fanny keeps growing, but I'm not getting any bigger up top."

"I'll talk to dad about getting you a boob–job for Christmas."

"You'll do no such thing!"

"For crying our loud. Make up you mind."

Jeanie got out a brand new girdle, just like the one I'd struggled into and we removed the tag. After she had wiggled into it without even breaking a sweat, she ran her slender hands down her hips. "Some boys hate it when you're in a girdle. Others can't keep their hands off you. The most important thing to remember is never to take it off, no matter how hot the boy gets you."

"Why not?"

"As long as you're in a girdle like this, a boy can't do anything he shouldn't. I mean, if a boy wanted to rape you, he could cut you out of the girdle, but if you're just smooching in the back seat or something, he'd never get past it and get you in trouble."

"Oh, like do things to you?"

"Yea, like do things. There is one other secret you've got to remember to be safe. Never let a boy inside your bra."

"Why?"

"If he starts kissing you and sucking your boobie, you're going to take off your girdle, then you're going to get into big trouble."

"I don't understand. What do boobs have to do with getting into trouble."

A strange smile crossed her lips. "The first time a boy starts kissing your boob you'll find out. Come on, time to finish dressing."

An hour later I was decked out in one of Jeanie's prettiest dresses, my hair was combed into somewhat of a presentable do, and my face was caked beneath layers of makeup. If felt as if she'd plucked the remainder of my brows, but close inspection at the mirror revealed a few stragglers still remained. My main problem was that she had strapped me into towering open–toe sandals with open backs. I was afraid they would fall off on the first step, but they actually stayed on as long as I pressed down with my toes.

"Sit." She pointed to her makeup bench. "Cross your legs. Not like a field hand, daintily, like you're a lady. Lift your skirt like this, cross your leg, daintily, now lift your toes so the sandal comes away from your foot. Wonderful. I need to check under your panties, you're becoming more of a woman every day."

"I don't understand. Why do I want to do my foot like this."

"Because, Sweetheart, if you sit like that for a few minutes some guy who likes legs or feet is going to buy you all the drinks you want."

I swallowed hard. "Jeanie, where are you taking me?"

"A joint crawling with men with lots of money and not nearly enough women."

Soon we were clomping down the stairs and into the kitchen. Momma Jean was at the stove and Papa Henry was catching up on the papers. They both looked up, but it was Papa Henry who whistled.

"Where are my kittens off to?"

"Just looking for a little action."

Momma Jean shook her stirring spoon at Jeanie. "Don't find too much action, and don't you dare start flirting and forget about Ruby."

"Ah, Mom. I won't."

"Ruby is a lot younger than you and has absolutely no experience gallivanting about."

She took a twenty out of Papa Henry's wallet and stuffed it into the sideband of my bra.

"Listen to me Ruby. If you get separated from Jeanie, call a taxi and have him drive you straight home. You've got your key. No matter what time it is, you come inside and wake us." She shook the spoon at me. "Do you understand?"

I nodded.

"Okay. We love you and want you safe. Jeanie, please do nothing foolish. It's easy for boys to start drinking and showing off. They don't realize how strong they are, and how delicate you girls are. I won't say any more, but remember that you're not too old to have your fannies warmed."

Jeanie rolled her eyes. "Yes, Mom. We'll be safe. 'Night, Mom, 'night Pop."

Soon we were zooming down a darkened lane of trees. Jeanie laughed.

"Mom's been giving that same speech for years. Dad would probably faint if she actually asked him to spank us."

"Are you sure?"

"Certainly." She was quiet for a while. "I'm pretty sure. We'll have to try it sometimes. I wonder what it feels like to have your fanny warmed."

I snorted. "You don't want to find out."

"I don't mean beat the shit out of you with a belt, like your father. That was barbaric. I've heard you screaming when he yanked you into the back room. I wanted to kill him when he hurt you. Barbaric. The bastard! If I'd only been a man."

*   *   *   *   *

We had burgers and fries with Cokes at the Skillet. A couple of guys got out of their car and started talking us up. Soon Jeanie moved me and one of the fellows to the back seat and the other slipped in next to her. We drove around with the guys sliding closer and closer to us. After a while, Jeanie found a really dark place overlooking the river. She switched off the engine, but left the radio on playing soft music. It was almost full moon and I wanted to see the light glistening on the moving waters, by my fellow had other ideas. It wasn't long and he was almost sitting on top of me, with one arm draped over my shoulder and the other across my tummy. I almost said something stupid, but decided telling him I was a boy didn't sound like a very bright idea. He was smooching me all over my face while his overactive hand worked up to my waist, then down to my knee. About the time I realized his hand was under my skirt, he started to kiss my mouth. Every time I tried to say stop, he would stick his tongue deeper inside and at the same time explore into ever more intimate places. I was being torn apart. I wanted to barf, and I also wanted his tongue deeper in my throat. I kept telling myself I was safe as long as I was in the girdle, but I wanted to wiggle out of the dammed thing so he could get to me, I didn't care what happened when he discovered what he had his hands on.

I have no idea what might have happened if Jeanie had not decided to crank the engine and squeal around in the soft sand. After we dropped the fellows off at their car we headed onto an even darker and more desolate road. Out past the edge of town we pulled into a really seedy place. I couldn't tell the name, because half the neon sign was out, and the other half was blinking on and off. The dirt lot was chock–a–block with beat up pickup trucks, with a couple of gigantic rigs pulled over beside the road. A deafening drone of Country music rattled the car windows.

"What is this place?"

Jeanie laughed. "This is where you learn to cross your legs and sip a beer. You'll find it disgusting, but you need to be able to take a few sips without throwing up."

"Why?"

"So you can have fun…, let down your hair…, have a good time."

"Hummmfff. I'd have a better time going home and getting out of this girdle."

"Well, don't get out of it in here or you might be knitting baby booties."

We were already inside before I figured out what she was talking about. I didn't think I could have a baby, but I wasn't absolutely sure, so I decided it was best if I stayed in the girdle.

What passed for music was ten times louder inside, and the smoke was so thick a knife would not have been of much value. We found two open seats and plopped down. Jeanie pulled up her skirt a little and daintily crossed her legs. I did the same. She did the sandal trick, so did I. Within five minutes we had half a dozen men offering us drinks. I ordered a Coke. Jeanie made a face at me and asked for a brew. Everyone was yammering away so loudly, no one could hear anyone else. I did a lot of nodding and smiling. Occasionally I would say something completely nonsensical but no one seemed to notice. It wasn't long before Jeanie was forcing me to sip some of her beer..., it was worse than I had imagined. But, first thing I knew I was sipping more and more, and my silly head was reeling fuzzier and fuzzier. That was also about the time one of the men started feeling me up and I was really happy I'd stayed in the girdle. It wasn't long before he moved upwards to my boobs. I suppose because of my experience with Moose Hanahan, I expected him to pinch my nipple and I almost slapped him. Fortunately, he was more interested in softly rubbing rather than pinching, and I soon discovered how very different a couple of fingertips could feel through a layer of satin. In fact, I was feeling tinglings in places I hardly knew existed. Once more, I don't know what would have happened if Jeanie had not drug me back to the car.

On the road again, my head started to clear a little now that I wasn't breathing ninety percent smoke.

"Oh, God! I feel awful."

"Oh, God is right." She patted my knee. "Think I've got a little slut on my hands. Was that guy inside your bra?"

"No, of course not. I don't think so. I'm not sure."

"Close your eyes and lean back, we'll be home soon."

We rode silently for a while. The hum of the tires and the soft music almost put me to sleep. I roused a little and put my hand of Jeanie's thigh.

"I'm not really a slut, am I?"

"Course not, Sweetheart. You're just learning a little about being a girl."

*   *   *   *   *

We crept into the house. Everything was deathly quiet. There weren't even any giggles coming from Daisy's room.

"Mom and Dad can go to sleep now," whispered Jeanie.

"How do you know they aren't asleep?"

"They never go to sleep until I get into bed. Doesn't you Mom stay awake when the boys are out?"

I though about it while we removed our shoes and dresses, then put them away. "Yea. Then after they come in, she quietly kisses my cheek and turns over. I never thought about it."

"Being a parent is a full time job, you know. We have to be ready for that when we get married. A lot of kids don't think about such things. That's why they have so many problems."

I removed my slip and bra and had started to wiggle from my girdle when Jeanie stopped me.

"No, leave your girdle and stockings on. I'll do the same."

She handed me a babydoll top and slipped into one also.

"Come to bed. We'll talk a while before we sleep."

I slipped between the covers, staying as far to the side as possible without falling out of bed. Pulling me next to her, she snuggled close up against me.

"I can still smell your strawberry bubble bath, it makes me want to eat you." Her hand moved from my waist to the satin tummy panel. "Don't you love the way this girdle hugs your hips and flattens your tummy."

"It's kind of tight."

"It's supposed to be tight, you ninny. That's what girdles are for."

"I thought they were to hold up your stockings."

"That too, and make you smooth and pretty and feminine. Don't you feel feminine?"

"I feel crushed."

She pinched my thigh. "Don't be a smarty."

By now we were giggling and snorting and trying to be quiet all at the same time.

"Seriously, did you enjoy tonight?"

"It's always nice to be with you."

"I mean with the guys. You don't have to marry them, just let off a little steam, enjoy yourself. Clean out the cobwebs. Seriously, how did you feel when they kissed you."

Her hand had moved under the babydoll and a finger was slowly tracing the outline of my nipple, which not only had jumped to attention, but was desperately sending signals to my mouth and tummy. I was really having trouble thinking.

"I asked you a question."

"It was nice, but my mind kept telling me it was wrong..., that I shouldn't be doing that. I'm a boy and they though I was a girl. I was lying to them. They were being nice, and I was lying."

"They were trying to fuck you. They were feeling you up because boys like to feel girls. It's just a little game until you find the one you love. Then you get serious. In the meantime, you have a little fun..., and you don't get into trouble."

She was quiet for a long time while her hands explored my body. Soon I couldn't control myself any longer and I started exploring her as deeply as her hand had been working on me. Her skin felt liquid soft, like satin, and every mound and valley was more exquisite than the last. Even feeling her through the girdle was almost more than I could stand, and I understood that without that elastic barrier we probably would no longer be under control.

Somehow our babydolls had been removed and we rolled together, breast to breast, and satin panel to satin panel. I kissed her, not like my sister, but deep, like the men had kissed me. My hands were exploring ever recess of her girdled body and suddenly I realized how marvelously she felt. I loved her body, but I absolutely worshiped her fanny tightly squeezed into all that elastic.

She pushed me away.

"We've got to cool off," she whispered hoarsely. "My God, you're a great kisser. Breath deeply. That's right."

"I'm so sorry, Jeanie. Please, don't hate me. I'll go sleep on the couch."

"You'll do no such thing. We only lost control a little. This is all learning how to be a girl. This will come in handy when you get married."

We were silent for a long time. I could tell Jeanie was drifting into sleep.

"Jeanie?"

"Yes."

"You know I'll never marry. No girl would have me, and no man would want me."

She didn't say anything for an even longer time. At last she whispered. "Don't worry your little head, Sweetheart. I'm working on it. I only need to find the proper person for you." Jeanie was silent for a while. "I've got someone in mind. She might be a little difficult. Hell, she's going to be very difficult."

Soon Jeanie had drifted into sleep, yet I remained awake for hours. My life was impossible, but I still had Jeanie and Daisy. With a shock I realized that I also had my brothers. Before, they were only shadowy figures on the periphery of my life. Now they were real brothers. I could almost believe they actually loved me a little, that they might even care what happened to me.

But, that could not possibly be. No one could really love me, because I was not a real person. I was only Mom's sewing girl.

Then I fell into a deep sleep.

CHAPTER TWENTY–TWO

In a Bind

When I awoke, Jeanie's side of the bed was empty. After throwing some cold water onto my face, I slipped into a housecoat and tumbled downstairs. The house seemed abandoned until I discovered Jeanie on the screen porch, lolling in a chair with her feet stretched across an ottoman. She was silent and seemed mesmerized by dozens of birds at the feeders.

Starting coffee, I scoured the pantry and fridge, then decided to make Bisquick biscuits and bacon. When the coffee finished perking, I poured a cup, added cream and sugar, then carried it out to Jeanie. She silently took it, then returned to the birds. The biscuits and bacon finished about the same time. I fixed two plates, added containers of butter and grape jelly, and returned to the porch.

Jeanie sat upright and kicked the ottoman aside. Instead of reaching for a plate, she dropped a pillow on the floor before her feet and pointed,

"Kneel."

It wasn't very dainty, but I made it down without spilling anything. She languidly split a biscuit, added butter and jelly, nibbled a morsel with her strong white teeth then settled back into the chair. Following several more nibbles, she sensuously attacked a strip of bacon. Another biscuit, more bacon.

My tummy was starting to complain, and I could not help licking my lips.

"Does my little Rubypoo want a biscuit?"

She didn't wait for an answer, but pressed a biscuit to my lips, followed by a strip of bacon. We continued, except now she would take a nibble and immediately press the biscuit or bacon to my lips. Each time she sipped coffee, the cup would come to me. When both plates were empty, she blotted our lips with a napkin, and once more settled back.

"There's no question. After I'm married you're going to be my maid. Nothing could be more delightful than have you at my feet while my husband watches, all the while knowing I love you more than him."

Her lips brushed gently against my cheek.

"My lovely..., lovely Ruby.

While she bathed, I cleaned the kitchen, washed our girdles and stocking from last night and hung them on the porch to dry. I had almost finished dressing when she emerged, wearing a bulky terrycloth robe and fluffing her hair with a matching towel.

"Got to go so soon?"

I nodded. "Jeanie, will you look at something for me?"

"Sure, Sweetheart, what have you got?"

After I settled on the makeup bench, she scooted in next to me and waited while I took the advertisement from my handbag. She stared at it for a long while, then glanced at me.

"Where did you get this?"

"Beneath Buddy's mattress."

"Does he know you have it?"

"He knows I found them. He doesn't know I took one, or that I'm showing it to you. Do you think.... You know, that he's hurting girls?"

"Buddy has lots of girlfriends. Half the girls in school want to be seen riding around in his car. I don't think any of them would let him tie them up." She stared at me. "If it was you, that would be different."

"What..., what do you mean?"

"I mean, you're so gentle, most girls wouldn't think you were going to hurt them. Buddy is very big and extremely strong. He could hurt a girl without thinking..., not that he thinks that much."

She looked at me even more intently, then tapped the page.

"Which one of these girls is you?"

My mouth felt very dry. One of the girls was blond with curls like mine. She was wearing a heavy white girdle and bra with impossibly high heels while bound to a huge wooden contraption by about a hundred ropes. Even her fingers were tied. The other girl was all in black, but wore only black lacy panties, bra, stockings and heels. If anything, her heels were even higher than the bound girl. I pointed at the blond girl, all the while feeling like I should drop thru the floor.

A smile flitted across her lips. She tapped the other girl.

"That's me. Course, I'd probably wear a girdle too." Her arm slid around my waist. "You don't have to be embarrassed. Not with me. I know you're going through a lot, what with the injections and dressing and everything. You're trying to figure out who you are. Just like me, only ten times worse."

"You won't tell. I don't want to go to jail."

"Jail? For looking at an advertisement? Don't be silly."

"No, for touching you last night. That was very bad of me."

"Oh, good grief! I'm the oldest. If anyone went to jail it would be me."

"But, I'm a boy…, well sort of. I should know better."

She squeezed me tight. "Sweetheart, we were only playing around a little. How else are we going to learn anything. We can't ask Mom, that's for sure. There aren't any books in the library. I know, I've looked. If we don't kiss and cuddle a little, how are we supposed to get ready for marriage? Anyway, I'll never tell anyone. Not about last night, not about breakfast, not about the ad. You have my word, I'll never hurt you, long as we live." Her attention shifted to one of the comic books in the advertisement. "You draw better than this. Maybe you're in the wrong business."

"I don't know how to tie anyone up."

"You could practice on Daisy and me."

"I couldn't do that, I might hurt you."

Jeanie chuckled. "Girls can take a lot more than you think. We're not really flowers or made out of glass."

"Well, I still couldn't take a change."

"Okay, I'll tie you up. I can think up better stuff than this." Her smile faded. "Now, what else is bothering you."

"Nothing."

"Don't give me that. This is Jeanie. I can read you like a book."

I took a deep breath. "Mom's going to keep me out of school this year."

"I know. Aunt Pam and Mother have been arguing about it for the past few weeks."

"Mom thinks we can make it. But, there's no way we can earn enough to pay that second mortgage. Any day now the bank is going to..., what's the word..., foreclose on us. No matter how hard we try, we're going to lose the house and be out on the street."

"You could come live with us."

"We might have to, for a couple of days, but Mom and Momma Jean could never stay under the same roof. Anyway, it wouldn't be fair to you and Daisy, not to mention Papa Henry. No, we'll have to leave town."

"It's not just that, is it?"

"If I don't finish school, I'll never get a decent job. How can I support Mom?"

Jeanie shook her head. "It's not only that. If you don't go to school, you'll never see Mitzi again. That's what is really hurting you, isn't it?"

"I know she hates me. But, I can't live without seeing her. She's the only girl who ever spoke to me. You can't imagine how lonely it is. I know I have you and Daisy, but it's not the same.... It's not the same."

CHAPTER TWENTY–THREE

High Finances

The first day of school came and went. I buried myself deeper and deeper into my sewing. At least we were inundated with last minute alterations for school uniforms and clothing. Then we began to get early requests for prom dresses, then maternity outfits. We both did alterations, but Mom took prom dresses and assigned maternity clothing to me. It wasn't clear at all why Mom figured I could sew maternity outfits, considering I had never really been around pregnant women. Obviously, even I knew they got big in the tummy, especially the last few months, but I had no idea just how big, nor that babies were so low in the abdomen. I'd always thought it was like when men developed a beer belly. How wrong I was about all of this, which meant I had to do a lot of thinking and re–working outfits. Perhaps that was Mom's idea. Keep me busy to keep me out of trouble. Make me spend time designing and re–designing outfits to get them to look and fit properly.

But, nights were horrible, especially after the lights were off and Mom was sleeping peacefully. I'd start wondering what had happened at school that day, then my mind would be filled with images of Mitzi flirting with Moose Hanahan or Butch Spence and I'd fall apart. It was almost as if I were only three once more, having to stuff my fist in my mouth to keep from crying out in the darkness.

Money was flowing in, what with Mom and my sewing, William at the dealership, and even Buddy was working part time as an assistant coach with the Intercity Church Sports League, which actually wasn't intercity at all, since it only covered out little town.

School had now been in session almost a month and I was frantically trying to get a maternity smock to drape properly when Mom went out to get the Friday mail. She was gone a very long time, and I began to wonder what could possibly take forever to walk to the street and open the mailbox. I wandered into the kitchen. Mom was seated at the table, her shoulders shaking with sobs. Pushing an open letter towards me, she whispered, "It's all over."

The letter was straightforward, across the top in big letters it blared, NOTICE OF EVICTION. I scanned the letter, then slowly read through everything in the oversized envelope. It looked like we had two weeks.

That night we sat around the table for several hours discussing all possible ramifications. For the first time in history, Buddy didn't get irritated and stalk out. William laid out all our finances down to the nearest penny. Finally, Mom gave her determination.

"William, you and Buddy will go to Grandma and Grandpa Jones. Ruby, Jean and Henry are going to put a room in the attic for you. I've found a job over in Etheridge. It doesn't pay much, but I'll do all the alterations as well as work retail."

"But, Mom. We won't be together."

"No, Ruby. We may never be together again. We'll just have to wait and see. We did our best, and I appreciate all your efforts. We were just facing more than we could handle."

Buddy piped up, "Isn't there anything we can do? Can't we get a loan from Grandpa? He has gobs of money."

"If he was going to help us, don't you think he would already have come forward? I've begged him for help, if nothing more than to send William to college. He just laughs in my face and says we're getting what we deserve."

"When do we..., you know, start breaking up?" asked William.

"Monday. We'll have one last weekend together. Go to church and out to lunch, as if nothing had changed. There's no need to drag our problems before the whole world. I love each of you in your own special way. You'll always be first in my heart."

As we got ready for bed, I wrapped her in my arms and we clung together. After we dried our eyes, I sat her at the dressing table and removed her makeup, then began to brush her hair.

"Should I get out my old clothes?"

Mom was silent. "No dear, stay just the way you are, at least for a while more. Soon you'll be Jean's. You're to do exactly what she tells you, and don't bother those girls. They're getting older and have lives of their own. Life won't be like it was. Maybe Henry can find a place for you at the dealership. If so, work hard and don't cause any problems. I'm sure they won't treat you like a poor relation, but.... As I said, life goes on, everything changes."

After finishing her hair, I polished Mom's nails and massaged her feet, then helped her into a nightgown. Before she switched off the light, she pulled me close.

"As a mother, I'm not supposed to have favorites, but, I love you, Ruby. I truly love you.

*   *   *   *   *

Saturday was the worst day of my life. We desperately were trying to finish all the work we'd promised, yet it all seemed so useless, so senseless. Why even try any longer? Yet Mom would not give an inch. She was going to fight to her last breath, therefore, so was I.

Early Sunday morning I soaked till I felt like a prune, shaved every bit of fuzz from my legs and underarms, then stood patiently while Mom dressed me like I was three. At last I was polished to her perfection, then sent to wait at the kitchen table while she put herself together. I detoured through the fitting room and perused myself in the wall mirror.

"Why, Sissy Ruby. Hope you're happy on the cover of Seventeen."

"Thank you, Robbie. So nice of you." I curtsied to my reflection, the way Mom had taught me when I met a new client. "I feel, so…, so…, masculine in all this lace and ribbon."

"Well you should, you sissy nuthead. Only a few more weeks and all this will end. Then it's back to school and all that torment. I'm sure Moose and Butch have a well planned set of hoops planned for you." My hands settled over my little breasts. I was sure Moose would soon have my nipples under his control. "These things aren't going to go away, are they?"

No answer came from the mirror.

Mom and I walked hand in hand, William and Buddy followed silently behind. We crossed Memorial Square to the Baptist Church. Daisy was having her first public performance at the piano as accompanist for the Youth

Chorale, but first we had to attend Sunday School. Daisy was fast developing a case of butterflies, so I spent most of the class trying to calm her, so really didn't pay much attention to the lesson or who was in class. Soon as it ended, Daisy darted off to get into her robe and I walked slowly towards the sanctuary, which was connected to the school rooms via a long corridor. Half way along was a tiny side corridor that ended in the family restroom, used mostly by mothers who needed to change diapers, and that sort of thing. As I reached the side corridor a hand grasped my arm and whisked me into the restroom. I was spun around to face..., Mitzi Johnson.

"Why aren't you in school and why are you wearing a dress?"

She was right up close, and had backed me against the sink.

"Because people would laugh at me in just my undies." We were both almost shouting in stage whispers.

"You know what I mean. You could be on the cover of Vogue."

"It's supposed to be more Seventeenish."

"I've looked all over school for you. Your stupid cousin or girlfriend or whatever she is says you're working as a dressmaker or something. Again, why aren't you in school?"

"Because..., because...." I couldn't hold back the tears and blurted out our entire sorted situation, and ended with, "We're broke, the bank is taking our home, we're being thrown out on the street and we'll probably never be together again."

She stared at me, wide eyed. "What bank?"

"Southern. What else, we've used them for generations, but they're still taking our home."

Her head slowly shook. "I don't believe you. They'd never do that."

"Why would I lie? Why won't you believe anything good about me? When I feel the way I do, why do you hate me?"

A hand went to her mouth. "Of course I believe you. It's just...."

There was a loud rapping at the door.

I panicked. On top of everything else I was caught in the bathroom with a girl, while wearing a dress, at church, on Sunday. How many sins could I commit at one time?

Cool as a frozen squid, Mitzi stuck her head out the door. "Sorry. Do you have a safety pin? Thanks."

Ducking back inside, she slowly counted to ten while she innocently fastened the pin underneath her collar. As coolly, we stepped out, to face a flustered woman with two tots in tow.

"Again, sorry. Had a mishap. Rob..., er..., Ruby had to pin me up."

Grabbing my hand, Mitzi hurried us off at a trot.

"Come along, Ruby. We'll be late for service."

As we entered the sanctuary she gave me a wink, then peeled off into the milling crowd.

Service was horrid. Reverend Farmer was worst than usual and got a second, then a third wind. I feared he'd never shut up. Daisy was wonderful. She only missed a few notes, but the kids singing were even more off key. I applauded anyway, even though you weren't supposed to clap in church. The kid's parents joined in, so I didn't seem too outrageous.

We filed out, shook hands with Reverend Farmer and said how wonderful his sermon had been, then headed down the front steps. Mitzi once more caught my arm, then stuffed a piece of paper in my hand.

"You and your mother have an appointment at the bank tomorrow morning at nine sharp."

"The bank doesn't open till ten."

"Pop's there sharply at eight every day. You be at the front door at nine, the guard will take you directly to him."

As quickly as she appeared, she vanished into the crowd.

"Who was that, dear?" Mom looked down at me.

"A friend from school. Well, she used to be a friend. We have an appointment with her father at the bank." I looked at the piece of paper. "At nine o'clock sharp."

"The bank doesn't open till ten."

"We'll be there at nine. What have we got to lose?"

"Wait, what did you say your friend's name was?"

"Mitzi, Mitzi Johnson. Her father must work at the bank."

Mom's eyes grew wide. "Johnson! He doesn't work at the bank, he owns it."

Buddy saddled up behind me. "Girlfriend talking to you again?"

"It was more like yelling."

"I told her about you and Moose. She thought the Superdog bit was hilarious."

I caught his hand and rubbed the back against my girdled rump.

"Thanks, Buddy."

"My pleasure," he said. "Both!"

*   *   *   *   *

At exactly nine o'clock we were ushered into a wood-paneled room twice the size of our kitchen. A small man with hair exactly the shade of Mitzi sat hunched behind a mahogany desk bigger than one of Papa Henry's Cadillacs. Numerous files were spread across the desk, otherwise, not a single item in the huge space seemed out of place. Certainly, not a speck of dust was evident. The man stood, came forward with extended hand, greeted us by name and ushered us to stiff–backed leather chairs before the desk. An older woman entered and served us coffee while the man continued to peruse the papers, all the while making strange noises, as if agreeing, then disagreeing with whatever was in the papers.

Finally, he straightened and looked directly at me.

"Well, Miss Ruby. Mitzi tells me you are a bright and talented young lady. I wish you well." He turned to Mom. "Mrs. Jones. I must apologize. It appears the Bank has made quiet the mess of your account. I do not know who is responsible, but you can be certain they will be found out, reprimanded and properly trained in the future. Southern Bank prides itself on handling even the smallest account with precision and honesty."

Mom cleared her throat. "Thank you, Mr. Johnson. But…, exactly what does that mean. As far as I can tell, we are about to be thrown out of our home, and my family will be broken up."

"Far from it, my dear lady, far from it. As you can see, your husband undertook this first mortgage for twenty thousand dollars. I believe he used that money to purchase shares in Amalgamated Oil, what is known in the business as a Wildcatter. A long shot investment, to say the least. Your home is collateral for that loan. The payments on that mortgage are up to date. However, he also took out this second mortgage for fifty grand. I would have never approved that much, based upon the limited value of your home. To be honest, dear lady, your house is much more valuable as a business location than as a home. The area is what we now call, mixed use, but it is rapidly turning commercial."

"I don't mean to appear ignorant, but once more, what exactly does that mean?" Mom's hand slipped into mine.

"To secure the mortgage, your husband had his father, co–sign the loan and put up his own home as collateral.

Which all means, once your husband passed away, the loan should have gone to your father–in–law. I warned him repeatedly that your husband was not a reliable risk, but the ol' coot would have none of it. To be precise, you do not owe anything on the second mortgage. The Bank will now pursue Mr. Jones, Senior regarding payment."

"You mean, we're not going to be thrown out of the house?"

"Certainly not, dear lady. In fact, I am shocked this situation has escalated to such an extent. You should have been assigned a personal agent to work out an appropriate arrangement. Perhaps we could have traded you into a smaller place and re–worked your home into office space. But, let me repeat, you are completely up to date on your mortgage. And, now that Amalgamated Oil is on the mends, there is always the possibility we shall have…, what do they call them…? Ah, yes. A gusher."

"Amalgamated Oil? We thought they were worthless. My Father–in–law said…."

"Dear me no. They have been paying a penny or two a month for the past year. They have only found gas to date. But…, one can always hope. Now if you will excuse me, dear ladies, I must attend to my duties. I shall have a loan officer contact you to make certain all aspects of your account are in order."

We shook hands. I remembered to do my little curtsy like Mom had taught. Mr. Johnson seemed impressed.

"I hope we'll see you up at the Club someday, Miss Ruby. We've spent a fortune putting in a new Olympic pool. We need lots of youngsters to break it in."

As we neared the office door, Mom turned. "Mr. Johnson. We appreciate all you have done. I don't suppose we would qualify for a loan, to combine all our outstanding debts."

"Another mortgage? No, I'm afraid not. However, we certainly would consider a small business loan. As I stated, your home is quite valuable as commercial property. Such loans are subsidized by the Government and can be quite useful for the business owner and the bank. Talk it over with your loan officer."

Once outside the bank, Mom and I danced in circles until we were dizzy. Then we bounced around like preteens. Everyone on Main Street must have though we were nuts. In a way, we were. At least we were deliriously happy nuts. After we couldn't dance or jump or twirl another step, we clung to each other for ages.

At last Mom pulled her last few dollars from her purse and stuffed them into my hand.

"Go over to the Skillet and get their biggest dish of ice cream with every topping.

"Where are you going?"

"To kill your grandfather. Oh, Ruby. If you learn I'm in jail, have Papa Henry come bail me out. I think there's something called justifiable homicide, and your mother feels damned justified right now."

CHAPTER TWENTY-FOUR

Pulling Wool

Mother didn't kill Grandpa Jones. She did put the fear of something into him, because she came home with our shares from Amalgamated Oil and a check covering the dividends we had earned. She didn't tell him about the visit he would soon receive from Southern Bank. As she said, she didn't want to miss the surprise.

The next week was such a blaze of celebration, elation and disbelief that it melded into a pink blur of happiness. Come Sunday, I settled back into my role as Mom's fashion plate. One Sunday I would be dressed as a young sophisticate, the next as a preteen in ribbons and lace, followed by my mature lady persona. The strategy must have been working because we would always get an order or two for a similar outfit. Along with the prom dresses and maternity outfits, these hi-fashion sales were keeping our head above water. Today I was a preteen drowning in enough lace and ribbons to sink a tugboat, if not a battleship. Once more we were at the Baptist Church, this time because Jeanie had another solo. At Sunday School I was sitting with her on the back row, so she could sneak out of class early, when Mitzi slipped into the next seat.

"Thank you so much," I whispered. "Are you still mad at me?"

"Of course not. Whatever gave you such an idea?"

Our teacher cleared her throat.

I just rolled my eyes, making sure Mitzi could see me.

We sat quietly for a while, then Mitzi slipped something into my hand. It was a page from Vogue, showing a young woman in a gorgeous wool outfit. I almost swallowed my tongue it was so lovely.

She whispered, "Can you sew me one of these? Out of this cloth my Mom found. I need it before Christmas."

The fabric was a purple and blue heather with the finest hand I had ever felt. It must have cost twenty or thirty dollars a yard.

"I can, but I won't."

"Why not?"

"Look at the model. She has no bust, no waist, no hips, no butt. She looks marvelous, you would look like a stuffed sausage."

Our teacher cleared her throat.

"I'm not a sausage."

"I didn't say you were a sausage, I said you'd look like one. Okay, I'll do it, but on two conditions."

"Which are?'

Taking out my pen, I quickly restructured the design so it would flow around Mitzi's shape, rather than fight it. "First, I make it like this."

Mitzi studied the drawing. "Yea, this actually looks much better. You're right, I would have looked like a sausage. What's the second thing?"

"Have your Mom take you to Miss Lillian and be fitted with a proper girdle and bra."

"What! I don't wear girdles. What's wrong with my bra?"

"Whats wrong? Look at yourself in the mirror. This material will show your every curve and line. Do you want to look like a slut? No girdle, no dress."

The girls around us had started to giggle.

"What do you know about girdles? Have you ever worn one?" Mitzi squeezed my hip. "My God! You're wearing a girdle!"

"Of course I'm wearing a girdle. How else would I keep my stockings up."

"With a garter belt."

"Yuk! Look at the lines they make on your fanny."

The teacher rapped on the lectern.

Mitzi made a face. "I'm trying to impress a boy. I want him to know I have boobs and a butt."

"Any idiot can see you have boobs and a butt. Do you want them to bounce?"

"Mitzi and Ruby! What are you girls whispering about? I'm trying to teach up here."

Jeanie shouted, "They're trying to decide if Mitzi is going to wear a girdle."

The teacher threw up her hands. "Dear Lord, help me in my hour of suffering." She threw down her Bible. "They don't pay me enough to do this."

Someone asked, "Do they really pay you?"

"No, they don't have enough money. Class dismissed."

Everyone else hopped up and began filing out. Mitzi and I stared at each other.

"How much will it cost?"

"You'll have to supply the cloth, I don't have that much money. Buy five yards, I'll need to match the grain. Otherwise, there's no charge. You'll need to come in to be measured. But, no girdle, no dress."

"We'll see. You're only doing this because you want to see me in a girdle. Don't you think I look nice?"

"You look marvelous, but not in a fitted wool dress."

She nodded. "I still think you just want to torture me."

As we walked towards the Sanctuary, our fingers intertwined, then she pulled free. I wanted to say I was concerned about how she looked because I worshiped the ground she walked on, that the mere thought of her smile kept me sane, that I would give my life to kiss her feet. I wanted to beg her not to date anyone else.

Instead, all I said was, "I just want you to look pretty for your date."

*   *   *   *   *

Three days later Mom answered the doorbell and returned with a merry, "Customer to see you, Ruby."

I looked up to find a radiant Mitzi standing next to her. Mitzi spun on her toes like a ballerina.

"What do you think. It's a good thing I gave up breathing for Lent, and you can forget about sitting."

Mom shrugged and made a strange face.

"Oh, Mitzi! You look fabulous. Mom, this is Mitzi Johnson. She's the one who got us the appointment with her father."

"Hello, Mitzi. I certainly could never forget you."

By now Mitzi had dumped a large package in my lap. I pulled out the fabric and ran my hand across it.

"Feel this, Mom. It's even nicer than I remembered. I'm going to make Mitzi an outfit"

Mitzi handed Mom the page from Vogue. After studying it intently, Mom nodded.

"I agree with your modifications, Ruby, just remember this fabric is really going to hug the figure. Don't fit it too snugly, and be careful what you wear underneath, Mitzi."

Now Mitzi rolled her eyes.

"Good grief. You people have girdles on the brain."

I hopped up and led Mitzi towards the fitting room, we certainly didn't want to start another round of Who's on First over girdles.

"If you'll step onto the platform, I'll get your measurements, know you have a busy schedule."

By the time I had my tape ready, she had stepped from her skirt and was unbuttoning the blouse.

"Don't I need to remove these..., so you can get proper measurements?"

She stood like a goddess in the sheerest slip imaginable. Both her bra and open bottom girdle peeked through the endless lace with just enough definition to be intriguing, without being fully exposed. From the crown of her blond waves to the bottom of her three inch heels she screamed sensuality and beauty like no one I could imagined, much less had seen. It was as if she were the culmination of every movie star and beauty queen in Hollywood.

"Is this okay?" Her hand swept from her breasts downwards as if she were presenting a new automobile on television. "Miss Lillian called this an Always 21. I asked if it were legal for a fifteen year old to wear an Always 21, but she didn't seem to get the joke."

I could not speak. I could not think. At last, I realized I had dropped the tape measure. Falling to a knee, I fumbled blindly for the tape, yet couldn't take my eyes off her. She stood erect, hands on hips. It appeared she had grown into a twenty foot statue. Slowly, I must have drawn my hands beneath my chin, because I at last realized it must look as if I were praying to her.

Mom tapped me on the shoulder. "You measure, I'll record."

My trance broken, I stumbled upright. "Ummmm. It's okay. I can manage."

"You sure?" Mom glanced at me "This is extremely expensive fabric. You don't want any mistakes."

"No, Mom. I'm okay. Go back to what you were doing, I'll handle everything."

"Don't handle too much," was all she said.

Actually, instead of returning to her sewing, she began fiddling with a pattern, so it looked like she was busy, but actually she was overlooking everything I did. This did not help my confidence in the least.

"What are you doing?"

Every time I tried to get behind her, Mitzi would spin on her heel to face me.

"I'm..., er..., trying to get behind you. It's safer..., er..., better, if I take measurements from the back."

"I can't talk to you if you're behind me. Stay still and take your silly measurements." She giggled. "Every boy in school wants to know my measurements, and you're going to know first hand. Don't you think that's funny?"

"Hilarious," I said.

Every time I attempted to measure across the fullest part of her bust she shifted slightly so my hand brushed her breast.

"I can't imagine why I can't stand still today. It must be there new shoes. Do you like them?"

"Yes." My voice came out almost a squeak.

"Miss Lillian said I was putting on my bra all wrong. She had to show me the proper way."

"Yea, same with me. Suppose I'm not a very good girl."

"Oh, do you wear a bra too?" She shifted again, so her breast almost brushed my nose.

"You know I do. I don't really need it. I'm pretty flat."

Once more the breast neared my face.

"Some people say anything more than a mouthful is wasted. Do you think I'm mostly wasted?"

"No, of course not. You're.... I don't know.... Perfect."

By now my excitement and frustration had reached immeasurable limits. At any second I was going to burst. She took a half step back and let me continue measuring without any more interference. I had finished the bust and worked down to the waist, then the hips. I could also almost breath again, and my hands were hardly trembling. Once more I dropped to a knee, this time to measure the widest part of her thighs. Some girls are widest at mid–hip, others where the legs join the body. Suddenly her hands were atop mine. She pulled my fingers up her hips.

"Do you think this girdle is firm enough? I don't want to disappoint you."

I let my hands linger, only a moment, then slid them back down the satin panel.

"Ya..., yes, you could not be more wonderful."

Instantly, her demeanor changed. She glanced at the gem–encrusted watch on her slender wrist.

"We need to hurry. Dad's driver will be here shortly."

She became all business and we finished the measurements in record time. I helped her dress and escorted her to the door. By now I was completely mystified, not to mention mortified. Obviously, I had highly offended her, but had no idea exactly what I had done. One moment she was pressing her breast against my face, the next second she was a frozen goddess.

"I'm.... I'm sorry if I offended you."

She stared at me through up–curled lashes. Her lips came close, for a moment I imagined she might kiss me on the lips. Instead, she brushed my cheek.

"Nonsense, sweet Robbie. I learned exactly what I wanted to know."

*   *   *   *   *

I leaned against the door, breathing deep to clear my tiny brain. How could any girl turn me so inside out? How could she switch on and off at the blinking of an eye? Was I a boy, or a girl? If I was becoming a girl, how could I feel such fantastic anguish each time I though of Mitzi, much less saw her? And, the touch of her body had been as excruciating as grabbing glowing coals, yet I would plunge my hands into her fires without hesitation.

My heart quieted enough to move back to my sewing machine, but I couldn't clear my mind sufficiently to attack the maternity smock I had been working on. Mom came in and settled before her machine also.

"Ruby, how well do you know Miss Johnson?"

"We've been in class together for ages. She just started talking to me…, you know…, after Moose discovered I was wearing panties."

"And, she talked to you about that?"

"Kind of…. Then the fashion show."

"Ah, yes. You wore her shoes."

"I thought we were friends. Then not. Now, I'm not so sure one way or the other. She did get us together with her father."

"Yes, and that was extremely valuable. You were right to offer to make the dress. But…."

"But?"

"She had you around her little finger. Perhaps I should say her big breasts. Or was it the girdle you found so fascinating?"

"I don't know. I couldn't take my eyes off her. She could have made me do anything."

Mom patted her lap. "Come here."

Sliding into Mom's lap, my arms drew themselves about her neck and my head settled onto her shoulder. I never had sat in her lap, not even as a baby, but now it seemed the only place I wanted to be.

"Miss Johnson is a beautiful, talented and very rich young lady. One day she'll become successful and marry an equally talented and rich young man. Even if she liked girls, rather than boys, you have nothing to offer her. It's not that you aren't wonderful and talented. I could never have redesigned that outfit in a week, much less a few minutes. But, Sweetheart, she offers you nothing but pain and rejection."

"I can't help the way I feel."

"Of course not, and I am not trying to hurt you or run your life. Still, you know I'm right."

I nodded.

"Run upstairs and take a long hot soak, then a nap. Tonight we'll start on this marvelous outfit for your Mitzi."

*   *   *   *   *

Three days later Mitzi was back on the platform swathed in heather wool. After turning forward and back numberless times, she guided my hands to her thighs.

"Does it need to be slightly tighter here?"

"No, it will cup beneath your fanny."

"I see. But I met him on the beach at Saint–Tropez. He seemed completely enthralled with my bikini bottom."

She turned to get a better look at her bumpers. "I wasn't wearing the top, of course."

"No, of course not."

She made a face into the mirror. "You're right after all. You're always right about fashion. You're very talented, Robbie. I've seen some of the drawings in your notebooks. Maybe you should go to art school." She patted her flattened tummy, then ran both hands down over her fanny. "I'm really not sure I can stand all this pressure. Not just to impress a boyfriend. Would you torture yourself like this…, just to impress a boy?"

"I don't have any friends. Mom and I work sixteen hours a day, when anyone is willing to hire us."

"You don't date?"

"Who would date me?"

"I'm sure there are boys out there somewhere." Her face brightened. "Know what, I'll set you up sometimes. Maybe we could double date. Mother gets upset if I spend too much time on single dates. Would you like that?"

I smiled up at her. "Sure, that would be wonderful."

She made one last pirouette. "Okay. The dress is terrific. You were right about the girdle, I would have looked like a sausage. But, if this thing kills me, I'm going to will it to you and you'll have to wear it."

"Agreed," I said.

After helping her change, I carefully wrapped the outfit in tissue and smoothed it into a box.

"How much?"

"I told you, it's a gift. You provided the cloth, that was the expensive part. I think that's your car, I'll carry this out for you."

As we reached the door, she quickly turned. Once more I thought she might kiss me on the lips, once more she brushed across my cheek.

"I can't decide if I like you better as Robbie or Ruby. I like you as Robbie, but as Ruby you excite me terribly. After my friend visits at Christmas I'm going to send you this torture girdle and make you wear it. You're a very naughty boy…, or girl. I haven't decided which."

Her driver closed the Mercedes door with a solid thunk. Moments later they were down the drive and into the street. Mitzi did not look back. I stood in our doorway for a long time, as if I could see her far in the distance. At last, I closed the door and leaned back against it. My hand slipped into the pocket of my apron, almost without my thinking, and pulled out a small pink envelope. On the back, gold embossed letters read, *From the desk of Mitzi Johnson*. Inside were five crisp twenty dollar bills, almost a fortune for a poor seamstress. There was also a note that only said, *Love you, M.*

"Mitzi. Mitzi. You're driving me crazy. Tell me what you want."

Of course, there was no answer.

CHAPTER TWENTY–FIVE

Growing Pains

The wolf was no longer beating down our door, but he was still lurking outside. Now that we were only covering one mortgage we were breaking even financially, but getting ahead was a completely different matter. But, while money – or the lack thereof – was still important, it was no longer paramount in my mind. Now I was obsessed with trying to figure out if I was a boy or a girl. I knew that beneath everything I was a boy. That was how I was born, and how I remained. I still mostly thought like a boy, and had boy desires. Yet, I hardly looked like a boy at all, and I had not worn anything resembling boy's clothing in months. The closest I could think of was a boy–legged panty girdle, which hardly seemed boyish at all.

Nor had I run or jumped or climbed trees in ages. Or yelled or trampled in a rain puddle since school had ended. Instead, I did house work or sat at my sewing machine making woman's clothing. By now my hair was far too long and curled to be in any way masculine. My boobs had stopped growing, yet my hips and fanny simply would not stop ballooning, and my entire body was soft as a pillow. I had essentially no social life and, most important, no school life. For some strange reason, I had always adored school, even though I was certainly not a popular student and had been bullied since the first grade. Until Mitzi, no fellow student had befriended me no matter how hard I tried to be outgoing and friendly. At least most of my teachers, with the notable exception of Mrs. Hanahan, had at least appreciated I made no problems and needed little in the way of instruction. Of course, the primary pain from not going to school was being unable to see Daisy, Jeanie and Mitzi every day. Oh, God! How I missed them.

By now I was pretty well resigned not to be in school. Buddy was still Buddy, and William had blossomed into his role as man of the house. He was working full time at the dealership and was attending night courses at our new junior college. The college had started as a tech school when a new assemble plant had moved just outside town. This was fortunate, since most of the old textile plants that supported our economy had long since gone to that industrial burial ground in the sky. There was talk that the junior would soon be removed from our college, and that it would expand to a full four year institution. William was ecstatic about the new Dean of Men, a Doctor Frank, who was bringing new life to the student body. I could not quite figure out if Frank was his first or last name, but he must have been some guy for all the praise William dumped his way. Of course, I blew everything by asking who was the Dean of Women. All I got from William was a blank stare.

In addition to being man of the house, William was also becoming man about town since he was also showing ever increasing interested in Becky, who also worked at the dealership. For some reason, this did not sit too well with Mom, who kept intimating that Becky was not a proper choice for an upstanding young man like William. I was not sure exactly what sin Becky was guilty of, but it was clear she was soiled in some way. She seemed like a perfectly nice young lady to me. But, what did I know?

What I found most silly about William's new status, was that Mom had started to use him as part of my very light discipline. Mom never scolded, much less struck me. However, if I really got out of hand she would say, 'Now Ruby, you don't want me to speak to William, do you?' The implication was that William would take me over his knee. We had all been beaten on a regular basis by my father, I didn't think there was any chance that William would spank me, even though his giant hands and great strength could have easily twisted me into knots. The other reason was that William seemed absolutely terrified of my changing body. The only way he ever touched me was to brush across my cheek when he kissed Mom and me goodnight.

That did not seem very threatening at all.

*   *   *   *   *

As summer faded into fall I buried myself in sewing. It never entered my mind that anywhere on earth there might be another boy like me, dressing and living as a girl. I could imagine another boy might wear panties. Perhaps his family was really poor and he had to wear his sister's underwear. Other than that, it just did not seem possible anyone would be as sissy as me.

My only breaks came if Mr. Green needed help at the Tin Skillet. Not only did I earn wages and tips, but it got me out of the house and onto my beloved skates. I knew it was probably sinful, but I simply relished showing off on skates. Not only was it thrilling to spin down the aisle balancing a full tray of food in one hand, but acting over the top also increased my tips. Plus, it was so much more fun to jabber with customers about food than belabor yet another hem or over–tight waist line. The only negative was that ever so often while walking home late at night, someone would follow in the darkness. They never said a word or showed themselves, but I knew they were there. At first I figured it was Moose Hanahan, ready to get his revenge. Yet, Jeanie and Mitzi told me that Moose seemed to have accepted his punishment and moved on to tormenting other sissies. So, I was literally left in the dark. Someone was following me. One day, perhaps tomorrow, they would attack, and day by day I was becoming softer and weaker. My only consolation was that Buddy had bought me something called pepper spray.

"Keep it in your hand, Sis. If someone attacks, hit him right in the face. Don't think about it, or hesitate. Just spray and run like hell. It won't stop a rapist, but it should slow him down. If he catches you, knee him in the balls, hard as you can, then scratch his eyes out."

It didn't help my self esteem as a boy having to worry about rapist, but I kept that little spray can in my purse twenty–four hours a day.

Being a boy had become a preoccupation. Day by day it was becoming more difficult to convince myself I was actually still male, and that one day soon all this playacting would come to an end and I'd be my old bumbling self, going to school and getting into trouble. I expected someone from the city to appear and demand I return to school. Yet, no one ever came. There was not even a letter from the school asking if I had died or moved away. It was almost as if I had simply vanished into nothingness.

Several times I thought about running away. Perhaps I could become a freak in the circus. But, the circus came to town in May, which was a long time to wait. The county fair occurred each fall, but everyone associated with the fair seemed pretty grubby. Maybe I was too picky.

One day when Mom was out delivering outfits, I got several boxes of my old clothing from out back and dumped them onto the bed. First I studied myself in the mirror. Even though I was a boy, I looked like a girl. After taking everything off, I again stared at my reflection. Once more I looked like a girl, except now it appeared as if I had a birth defect between my legs. Trying on the best of my old clothing proved two things. Nothing came close to fitting, and I looked even more stupid in boy's clothing than in my dresses. In frills I looked like a boyish girl, in boy things I looked like a girl in trousers. Pulling my hair back and removing makeup made no difference. I was an even worse boy than girl.

Cramming everything back into the boxes I shlepped them to the old garage and returned to my sewing machine. How could I run away? As a boy I looked like a girl, and as a girl I would be far too vulnerable. Then, I just had to admit the truth. I was simply too scared to run away. On top of everything else I was a coward. Nothing but a lily-livered, died in the wool coward.

When Mom returned we had lunch, then went back to our sewing. It was a Monday, always our slowest day, so we worked silently. Mid afternoon Mom made tea, then called me into the kitchen. We sipped silently for a while, then Mom patted her lap.

"Come, Baby. Sit."

Wrapping my arms about her neck, we clung for what seemed a long time. At last, she whispered into my ear.

"We can buy you some new boy's clothes that fit."

"Why would we do that?"

"You don't want to run away looking like a ragamuffin."

"Who said anything about running away?"

"Ruby, this is Mommie. Don't you think I know you're aching inside? Don't you know it's killing me to watch you come apart? You understand how important this is, but I cannot bear watching you suffer. You're entitled to a quarter of what we have. I can't let my feelings destroy you. In many ways the past few months have been the happiest of my life. Even with all our problems, I have my baby Ruby, we have the business, we're still together. You've blossomed in so many ways. As a seamstress, as an artist, as a designer. But…, and this is a major but…, if you are unhappy, we must bring this to an end."

"Mom, I can't disappoint you. I can't leave you. Anyway, where would I go?"

"Jean and Henry will take you in an instant. I will give you up, they will adopt you."

I remained silent for several minutes, mulling everything Mom had said.

At last, Mom cleared her throat. "Well?"

"I feel like a piece of bacon."

"Bacon? What on earth?"

"Deciding if I want to jump from the frying pan into the fire."

"And…?"

"Jeanie will never let me out of girdles, will she?"

"Probably not."

"And, we'd probably end up killing each other."

"Probably."

Then, I'd best stay in the pan. At least my bottom is warm."

Mom didn't say anything, but I thought she would squeeze me in two.

* * * * *

Even though I adored skating, Mom would not think about allowing me to skate alone. In her mind, she considered me much closer to five than fifteen and I believe that by then she had completely shifted me into a girl. She knew I had one boy part, but that had no real bearing. In her mind I actually had been born a girl, now I was simply back to what I had always been.

"No decent girl is going to a public skating rink alone. Do you want people to think you're a slut? Next you'll be asking to go to the cinema by yourself. I simply don't know what modern girls use for common sense."

"But, Mom. I won't be alone, there'll be a hundred people, all skating by themselves."

"Well, one of them won't be my daughter."

"Mooooom, you don't understand, this is 1958. I thought you wanted me to show off my new skating outfit."

"Ruuuubbbbby, you don't understand. You're only fifteen and this is a very small little town with lots of very small people. Certainly, I want you to display your clothing. We get orders every time you go out. But, not to such a place without a chaperone. I don't want people thinking you're a tramp. Now, come along. I'll fix us a nice cup of tea and we'll have a cookie."

Which was how almost all of our 'arguments' ended

Occasionally, if Buddy didn't have a date on Saturday afternoon, he would take me skating. En route, he would lay down the law.

"Sis, this isn't a date, and don't you even think about using that word. You're my little sister and I'm having to take you skating. Okay? Understand? This is not a date."

"Sure, Buddy. I'll enter by the back door and put on my own skates. I'll even buy my own snacks. You won't see me until you come looking. Just don't leave me like last time when you hook up with some lame–headed floozie.

Remember what Mom did to your ear when I had to call a taxi. This time she might twist something else off."

"You don't have to do that. I'll lace your skates and get the snacks. Just don't tell anyone you're my date."

Buddy and I would skate separately until the dance segments started, then he'd be at my side and we'd twirl down the rink. As much as he hated to admit it, I had become one of the best dancers in town. I also weighed less than most of the girls his age, so it was much easier for him to lift me, and Buddy liked to show me off as much as I loved to be on display. One of his favorite moves was to crouch behind so I could sit on his right hand, then spring as he lifted me straight up and balanced me with his left hand on an ankle. I would lean back and spread eagle while he did a slow spin. I would become slightly light headed, but would enter a state as close to ecstasy as I could imagine. The drop always terrified me, but Buddy never let me fall and he didn't even feel me up very much on the way down. I did not like it if he got too familiar, especially up top, but he mostly was interested in my bottom.

It seemed so strange. After all, Buddy knew I was a boy and his brother, yet the rounder and softer I grew, the more he liked my bottom. His touch was nothing like Papa Henry who tapped Jeanie, Daisy and me on the bottom as if he were patting us on the back. Buddy's touch was soft and sensual, more a bashful caress than an erotic grappling, yet it always left both of us breathless and confused. I never knew if I was supposed to relish the attention, or slap his face, so I usually ended up blushing and stammering.

Sometimes we would skate together all afternoon. Other times Buddy would spot some sweet young thing ready to trot and he'd be off like the Lone Ranger to save her from dying of boredom. I would skate alone for a while until I found a friendly looking girl and join her. Some times she would turn me away, but mostly she would agree to dance. I had no problem switching to the boy's part, so I would lead and we would swing together. It was perfectly okay for two girls to dance, of course, two boys skating arm in arm would have caused a riot. My problem was that boys simply could not stand to see two girls having fun together. Within a few minutes some guy would break in and steal my girl. The only thing I could do was slip away and hide my frustration by outskating the macho goons.

Most of the time Buddy was good and remembered to take me home before heading off to schmooze with his new gal. Sometimes he'd forget and I would have to take a taxi, which drove Mom into a tizzy. By far the worst was when Buddy forget my feelings and said something to kill my outing. One day we had just finished an especially beautiful dance. His arm went around my waist and he gave me a tight squeeze.

"Geez, Sis. You're a great dancer. Should have known a queer would be good at girl stuff"

It was all I could do to keep from screaming. Instead, I burst into tears and fled to the ladies room. It took half an hour, at last I quieted enough to call a taxi and head outside to wait. As always happens when you need something, it was shift change time and I waited and waited. At last, Buddy came up behind me and put his arm around my still trembling shoulders.

"I'm sorry, Sis. I don't know why I say things like that. They just come out."

"Is that what you think I am? Do you think I like dressing and acting like a simpering idiot? Do you think it's fun wearing a girdle and heels?"

"I…. I…. Mom says…."

"I do it for Mom. She like me this way. I can't hurt her. You know what she's done for us. It's the least I can do for her."

He squeezed me tighter. "You can whack me if it'll make you feel better. Sometimes I'm a real klutz when it comes to..., you know, being sane."

"I don't want to hit you. But, I don't like being called names. They hurt just like being kicked."

"Okay, Sis. I'll try not to kick you any more. Next time give me a good slap a'side the head.... Just to get my attention."

I never did slap him, yet he surely tried my patience at times.

*   *   *   *   *

My relations with Jeanie and Daisy were even more confused than normal. It was not as if Daisy had turned her back on me, but her attention had definitely shifted to her group of girl friends. At one time they had sort of been my friends also, since we had all played together. Now they were mostly interested in boys. Since I was not really a boy, nor actually a girl, I no longer fit into their gatherings in any way. A couple of the girls thought it was a sin that I was masquerading as a girl, some thought I was dangerous, and one thought I was a freak. Jeanie would have chosen me over the girls, but Daisy chose her friends over me. What made everything even more painful, was that when it was only Daisy and me, she acted as if nothing had changed, but the moment she was with her friends, I vanished.

It took a while, but I slowly worked out that while Jeanie and Daisy were both interested in boys, that fascination took dramatically different forms. Daisy spelled boy h–u–s–b–a–n–d. Jeanie spelled it S–E–X. Daisy never thought about sex, Jeanie could not get it off her mind. Yet, for both of them, sex was completely verboten until after marriage. I knew even less about sex than either girl, but I had both boy and girl hormones boiling through my

body and no way to get any relief except in my dreams.
Since Mom had taken control of my dreams, I was always
in a state of the highest agitation. As Tennessee Williams
would have said, I was a Kitten on a Hot Tin Roof, and
Jeanie was my only ladder.

Although Jeanie was more beautiful than Daisy, she
was not nearly as popular at school. Partially this was
because she was quiet, like me, and because of her mood
swings. Daisy was always up. She talked incessantly
without ever really saying much. She laughed a lot and
flirted outrageously. When Jeanie was up, she was really up.
However, when she got down, she really went low. Doc
Pricher had tried lots of medicines and she was taking
something now that helped a lot. The problem was that
when she got low, Jeanie would 'forget' to take her pills.
She also had a lot of trouble with her periods. I really was
not sure exactly what that meant, but I knew that at times
she would be in agony for several days, during which she
would do nothing but lie curled in a darkened room. When
the bad period and extra low mood hit together she became
a danger to herself and someone had to sit with her
constantly. As Jeanie and I came closer, I became that
someone.

Fortunately, most of the time Jeanie was up and the
down times were less and less frequent. Every couple of
weeks she would stop by and take me out for an evening.
We would take in a movie or go shopping, then she would
drive to the Tin Skillet and get us burgers and fries,
followed by a secluded stop overlooking the river. Mostly
we only talked and did a little smooching and cuddling, but
sometimes it would go far enough that we came up against
each others panty girdle, which signaled it was time to stop.

Jeanie loved to tie my hands behind my back with a
long strip of red ribbon. She didn't tie me tight, and she
always made a big bow with the ends dangling down by my

hands, so I could easily have untied myself if necessary. In fact, it was more mental bondage than the real sort depicted in Buddy's advertisements and comic books. Then, she would use a feather to drive me absolutely bonkers while extracting my most intimate thoughts and secrets, such as all the sordid details of my dreams. When I reached the very peak of frustration, she would coolly play out parts of my dreams while I suffered. Her favorite pastime was to put me on my hands and knees before her makeup table with a folded scarf tied over my eyes. I could hear her remove her girdle and feel her warmth and weight as she gently settled onto my back. She really never sat on me very long, but it seemed an eternity as she squirmed and shifted. When I felt I could hold her no longer, she would suddenly rise and help me stand.

"How was that," she would say. "Was I as nice as Mitzi? Or better."

"Much better," I would answer. But, I always wondered, much as I loved Jeanie, could anything be better than having Mitzi sit on me?

Several times Jeanie included me on double dates. I was always stuck with the bumbling shy friend, or the overaggressive octopus. Jeanie appeared to take a lot more interest in how I was faring in the back seat that what was happening with her date. Being kissed by some guy with bad breath was bad, but getting groped was a lot worse. And yet, it gave me a really perverse thrill knowing that I could be girl enough to tumble with a guy in the back seat and not be detected. Of course, Jeanie made sure I was wearing my firmest panty girdle with a super sanitary pad, which would have hidden the sex of Godzilla, much less a purple pantywaist.

Afterward, we would snuggle in her bed and whisper about our dates and how I felt and what I had though. Then Jeanie would drift asleep in my arms while I lay awake in turmoil. Still, I would not have missed a moment of my time with her

The most bizarre part of our developing relationship concerned Buddy's growing collection of bondage material. Every time Buddy found a new advertisement or bought a new set of photos or a bondage comic book he would accidentally leave it where I'd find it. As soon as I discovered one, I'd make an excuse to meet with Jeanie so we could look at it together. She always wanted to know how I felt about every photo or drawing. Which girls did I like and why? What elements of the drawing technique did I find interesting? Was it the artwork, the girl or the position that most interested me? Which girl did I want to be? Could I actually get into that position and remain like that? What did I think was supposed to happen when a girl was bound? On and on until we had dissected all aspects of the drawings. Jeanie wanted to know my most intimate thought and emotion, yet she never revealed how she actually felt about anything. Was she simply coddling me, or did the drawings affect her as much as they did me? All I knew was that no matter how terribly written the stories were, the artwork spoke to something so deep inside me that I could hardly contain myself. Although I kept wearing out pencils, I simply could not capture the same feeling. It was impossible to understand how so few lines could be used to convey so much feeling and emotion. I had to learn how to draw girls like that. No matter what it cost, there was an artistic firestorm building inside, and it had to be extinguished. Otherwise, I could not live.

CHAPTER TWENTY-SIX

Madonnas and Angels

Mitzi had become by far my best client, yet every time she visited I ended in the most horrible funk. She seemed forever attending proms or important functions with her grandmother, who if anything was more wealthy than Mitzi's family. Well, I suppose they were all the same family, except some of them talked to each other, and others not. Mitzi was the only granddaughter and obviously the plum of the entire convoluted mess of sons and granddads and aunts and uncles vying with each other to become the next family patriarch..., or matriarch. Mitzi didn't appear to take it any too seriously, partially because every time anyone kicked off, Mitzi's trust fund grew larger and she had one less relative to deal with. Every function required a new outfit, and against her mother's wishes, that brought Mitzi to me, which was good because she demanded the very best but was extremely generous. Yet, it was also bad in that by the time she finished teasing me I was ready for the asylum.

She always arrived without warning and I had to drop everything to take care of her. At first she brought photos or advertisements and had me make something similar. Then one day she arrived, mounted the fitting platform and slowly turned a full circle.

"Grandmother is taking me to New York over Thanksgiving. We'll attend the parade and some godawful opera or other. Could you be a real sweetheart and make me something new for each? I don't want to look like one of the Macy balloons, otherwise whatever you think will be stunning."

"Do you want to be stunning, or the star of the Met?"

"You know me. I like to be noticed, but not ridiculous."

By now she had removed her blouse and was stepping from her skirt. Dramatically, she held them out and let them drop into my hands, then waited while I put them on hangers.

"I know your measurements."

"Perhaps you should check. Maybe I've grown."

"Lord, let's hope not."

Taking my hands, she slid them down her hips.

"Will this girdle be sufficient? Don't you dare make me wear that Always 21. I'm saving it for you."

All I could do was nod and quickly grapple for my tape. As always she stared intently into my face as I repeated all the measurements, and as always her smile broadened while I grew hotter and redder. After I had become so nervous I could no longer hold the tape steady, she would relent.

"Okay, you can dress me now"

Buttoning her blouse was more difficult than feeling her hips. She delighted in making me touch her girdle, but I knew that absolutely no girl wanted me to touch their breasts. Well, perhaps Jeanie, but that was a different situation. After the blouse was perfect, I held her skirt while she seductively stepped inside and waited while I tucked her in and zipped her up.

At the door she gently kissed me on the cheek and stared deeply into my eyes.

"You are an absolutely gem of a Ruby. Mother wants me to use her dressmaker, but I wouldn't trade you for all the money in Dad's bank. Ta Ta, sweets."

Then she was gone as mysteriously as she had arrived.

I discussed Mitzi's visits with Jeanie, who always simply shook her head in wonderment.

"I wish I could hate Mitzi," she would say. "She's rich, beautiful, self–assured, and perfect in all ways. But, she's also kind and helpful and always friendly. I'll bet she pays top dollar and leaves you a huge tip. I think she likes you and wants to help, but she can't just come out and give you charity."

"She probably thinks I'm queer as a pink moon. You know what Moose told her about me…, and she believed it."

"She was shocked and hurt. Anyway, she talks to you now, and kisses you on the cheek. I think she likes you."

"Jeanie, think about it. Mitzi dates guys in college. She has no interest in a drop out. To her I'm only someone to make dresses. She doesn't even think of me unless she need something new. Something to impress some stupid guy."

"We'll see." Jeanie made a face. "You're too young to worry about such things right now. All in good time. We'll see."

*   *   *   *   *

In general, Mom and I had divided our work to fit out particular strengths. That worked with everything except prom dresses, which except for Mitzi, were done exclusively by Mom. The problem was that I had a much better eye for what modern girls wanted to match the season and occasion. Anyone over thirty was ancient to me. Children were precious Angels to be coveted, not preyed upon. Pregnant women were Madonnas to be worshiped. None of these held any sexual interest for me. They were only bodies to be made beautiful.

Girls near my age were an entirely different kettle of emotions. Regardless how hard I tried, I could not keep from becoming excited whenever one entered for a fitting. Of course, my panty girdle kept me physically under control, but nothing could quiet my emotions. Finally, more out of frustration than resolution, Mom let me do the designs, while she took care of all measurements and fittings. As long as I stayed well clear of the fitting room all was well, but as soon as I saw a girl my age in her undies I was in agony.

Since I had never seen a fully pregnant woman I was having problems planning for an entire pregnancy. Mom had to continually remind me to leave more material in the smock. Skirts were normally not a problem since the material we used for the tummy panel would stretch to perhaps ten times its original dimensions. I just made flaps on either side of the waistbands with half a dozen buttons at two inch intervals which should have been sufficient for an elephant. Most of our Madonnas were newlyweds having their first child. They usually were ecstatic to be pregnant and wanted to shift into smocks soon as they started showing. However, a few were not so pleased and wanted to hid their condition as long as possible. I soon figured out how to do either, but it surely was more enjoyable to put my Madonnas on full display.

One day a maternity client returned to have her smocks let out. Not only was she in the last weeks of her pregnancy, but she had also added many extra pounds so she looked like Little Buttercup from HMS Pinafore. I had begun to measure her tummy when she suddenly groaned and grabbed my hand. Before I knew what was happening she pressed my palm against her extended tummy. At first I felt nothing except her extreme firmness, which was shocking since I expected her to be soft. Then a powerful thump whopped against my palm, quickly followed by two more.

"Junior is really active today," she laughed. "Last night he almost kicked his daddy out of bed."

Mom came up beside me and placed her hand next to mine.

"Buddy was just like this. He kept me awake all night, then slept soundly all day. One night he kicked his daddy in the family jewels, as if to say, 'stay away from my Mommie.'"

We all laughed as I finished taking measurements.

After the customer left, I sat quietly at my machine making the required adjustments. Now I understood just how large a woman could get while pregnant. I also realized for the very first time that there was more than just a thing inside her. It was a living little person that moved and kicked. Did it think? Did it hear? Was it aware of itself, like you and me? I did not know, but it was alive. It was already alive.

Mom pulled her chair beside me.

"Why so sad, Doodlebug?"

"I was only thinking. About babies."

"Do you often think about babies?"

"This is the first time. I mean, really think about them. I can't have a baby, can I?"

Mom didn't say anything.

"I don't think I can be a father, either. That means I'll just disappear without a trace. There'll be nothing after me. Emptiness, only emptiness."

She put her arms around me. I could feel her tears on my cheek.

"Sweets, oh my sweets. I never intended that. I didn't think. Oh, God! I didn't think about how you would feel."

CHAPTER TWENTY–SEVEN

All Hallows Eve

Halloween was just around the corner and I had imagined we would be swamped with mothers wanting cleaver costumes for their munchkins, but cheap knockoffs seemed to be filling the bill. The good news was that Mom and I were receiving some much needed rest. We used the free time to visit places like the Good Shepard Exchange and stock up on anything we could use in our business. A down side was that Mom was always finding goodies that could be used as torture instruments. Actually, she would go through the foundation garments looking for unusual pieces that might be incorporated into items like prom dresses. If you started with a heavy duty strapless bra, you could build a beautiful strapless evening dress that had all the support built in. But, she also found tidbits that could be used on me.

"Ruby, look what I've found."

Mom held a heavy–duty all in one against me.

"This cost a fortune and it's never been worn. Look, it still has the price tag."

"Mom, that thing is ten sizes too small. I couldn't wiggle into it by Christmas. Look at the cups, they'd swallow me."

"Nonsense. It would fit you perfectly. Well, we might need to pad you a little up top. I could probably use some of that foam rubber we found last week. We could make you a really svelte outfit for church. Ohmygosh! Look at this girdle. This boned panel would make your tummy flat as a pancake."

"This thing weighs a ton. If I walked near a magnet I'd be trapped forever. Anyway, I wouldn't even be able to sit in this thing. There must be thirty bones in the tummy panel alone."

"More nonsense. There are only, lets see..., six in the tummy and three in the back. I can't wait to see you in both of these."

I let out a snort. "Yea, I can't wait either."

Actually, both of them fit perfectly, just as mom said, and I could sit..., with difficulty, but the all in one required a couple pounds of foam rubber to fill the cups, and I looked like Mitzi, which really was not such a bad thing.

We were just closing one evening when Mom answered the phone. A few moments later she came into the fitting room where I was finishing an outfit.

"Ruby, we have a late customer. A man. Under no circumstances are you to leave this room unless I tell you."

I nodded. "We don't get too many men."

"Especially this late. We'll see."

Moments later the bell rang and Mom answered the door. I shifted so I could continue working, yet keep an eye on the door. A well dressed man entered and took off his hat. He was short, dumpy and balding, but not seedy. There was a large paper bag clutched in his left hand, a sheet of paper in the right. He spoke, Mom nodded. This continued for several minutes before the man handed Mom the piece of paper. Once more she nodded, then led him into the fitting room.

"This is Ruby, my daughter and business partner. She is an absolute whiz with special fashions. Ruby, the gentleman needs this in his size. Can you make it?"

I stared at the paper. It was a drawing of Alice, from Walt Disney's movie. Glancing at Mom, I nodded.

"Like, for a costume party? If I used really light-weight material, it wouldn't be too expensive."

"Yes, like for a party, except make it just as you would for a regular dress, with fastenings he can manage."

"The underthings too?"

"Yes, exactly like the drawing. It seems Mr. Young has lost a wager and has to be Alice this Halloween. Can you arrange it?"

The man cleared his throat. "Ummm, cost is no problem, young lady. I made the wager, and aim to abide by the consequences. This is what I get for being a smart aleck."

Mom pointed towards the screen. "You can change here. Do not be concerned about Ruby, she is young but a complete professional. She has constructed many special garments.

After Mister Young disappeared behind the changing screen I turned to Mom and shrugged. My expression must have been one of wonderment, because Mom shrugged back, then held out a fist filled with twenty dollar bills.

"Mom?" I whispered. "What am I supposed to do?"

"Treat him just like Alice herself had entered."

"What about the undies?"

"Use your imagination. What would you wear if you were Alice?"

"But...."

"No buts. It's not for us to judge. He's very nervous, but seems perfectly harmless. He's payed good money, so give him good service."

When he emerged Mister Young was wearing a slip over a terribly fitting girdle and long line bra. I recognized the girdle from the Sears catalog, so assumed he had ordered based on fitting his male measurements into the woman's size charts. Thankfully, he had purchased the girdle to fit his waist, which would make adjusting it much easier. The bra must have been at least a D–cup which he had stuffed with something or other. I relished difficult challenges, but this was not going to be easy. While I completed the measurements, Mom got down several bolts of cloth in appropriate shades and material. As I suspected, he selected a pale blue satin for the body and white satin for the undies.

"Thank you, Mister Young. You've been very patient. Making something from a drawing takes a lot of measurements." I hesitated. "Er…. Mister Young, if you like I can adjust your foundations. So they fit you better."

"You can do that?"

"Certainly. That's what we do, we make things fit. Do you just want the extra material removed, or do you want it to be snug, like on a woman?"

"Oh, snug, of course. If I'm to be Alice, it must be…, perfect."

"And the bra. Shall I pad the cups, or sew the extra material down, so the cup follows your natural shape?"

"You can…, you can do that? Pad the…. Make it look natural?"

"Okay, I'll fill the cups and cover them with soft satin, so it won't scratch you."

His eyes had grown larger as spoke and I could tell he was in a high state of excitement, like some of the guys when they were caressing me in the back seat of Jeanie's car. I figured we need to bring this to a close before we had a mess on our hands. After I had pinned up his foundations he changed and Mom showed him out while I finished all the paperwork. Since I needed to make everything, including the pattern, based only on measurements, it was vital to double check every smallest detail. Mom returned and pulled a chair next to me. Her fingers played through my curls.

"You were absolutely wonderful, Doodlebug. You could not have been more professional, even while pinning that poor man's girdle."

"That must have been some bet he lost."

Mom didn't say anything, but her fingers continued to twirl my hair. At last she whispered.

"Dearest Ruby, there was no wager. Mister Young isn't going to a party. He probably has no one to go with. If he ever was married, his wife probably divorced him and took everything. He is lonely and heartbroken. He has dreams he can never fulfill. When he looks into the mirror, he desperately wants to see Alice or some other figment of his imagination. But, you saw him. He is a hairy man with no shape and no means of becoming the person he dreams of. We have no right to judge, but we can make him an outfit that might bring him a tiny measure of happiness."

Now it was my turn to be silent. It was as if Mom had removed a blindfold from my eyes. I could see into the future, and what I saw was Mister Young.

"Mom, is that how I'm going to end up? An outcast existing in the shadows with no friends and no future?"

She drew me against her breast.

"No, Sweetkins. You are a very attractive, very lovable, very talented young lady. We only need to find the right person. You're still young…, hardly more than a tot. You think the world has passed you by, but you haven't even entered the race."

CHAPTER TWENTY–EIGHT

Giving Thanks

We all celebrated Thanksgiving with Momma Jean and Christmas Eve at our house. For Thanksgiving, my job was to bake two pecan pies and make a sweet potato casserole. All us females were to gather in the kitchen Thanksgiving morning to roast the turkey and bring everything else together at exactly one o'clock. Meanwhile, the menfolk would be mesmerized before the television yelling at the football games. At five till one, Momma Jean would snap off the television and announce dinner was ready. We'd hold hands in a circle while Papa Henry said grace, then we'd sit quietly while he carved the turkey and passed the plates. It had been that way as long as I could remember, except this year Dad would not be there, so there would be no arguments over which games to watch, or which teams were better. At least, that was what I hoped. Dad was hardly ever mentioned anymore, and when his name did arise it usually put a real damper on everyone.

We were ready for a holiday, that was certain. The fall had been hectic, but highly lucrative. As for our special projects, Mitzi adored her outfits. I made sure she showed enough boob to be noticed at the opera, but not enough to cause a sensation at the parade. Well, more sensation than she normally aroused. Mom and I had completed over a dozen prom dresses for the first big dance of the season and I had turned out scores of velvet dresses for Christmas Angels.

Mister Young had been more than pleased with his Alice dress, and even happier with his foundations and undies. After I thought about it, I realized these were probably the first girl's clothes he had ever worn that actually fit. The girdle could not give him female hips, but the bra definitely gave him a bust. I really didn't want to think about how he was going to use my masterwork. I was a simple craftsman..., or craftsperson. Once my dresses were purchased and paid for, they were no longer mine, even if a little of me stayed in each one.

Like clockwork on Thanksgiving morn everyone arrived and ate breakfast together, then the men disappeared into the den to watch the parade and we women tackled the turkey and dressing. Jeanie was in especially high spirits and she kept tickling and goosing Daisy and me every time we leaned over to baste the turkey. There was no doubt, things were soon going to get out of hand. Around ten, the guys yelled for beers. Jeanie popped the tops and slipped a quick sip. On the second round, we all quaffed a big gulp before taking them out to the den. By this time Jeanie was telling naughty jokes and Daisy was yammering nonstop. Even I could tell we were really getting loud, but then, so were the guys. It was almost as if the entire family had decided to relax after such a traumatic and terrifying year.

By the third round of beers, it started. Perhaps it was Jeanie, perhaps it was William, but one or the other pushed the first snowball down the hill.

"Will you hens stop clucking! We're trying to watch football in here."

"Well, we're trying to fix dinner so you guys can stuff your faces. You could get off your duff and help"

William shook his finger beneath Jeanie's nose. "Listen, girl. I can take you over my knee and warm that fat fanny."

"Yea! You and who's army?"

Daisy piped in. "Yea, who's army."

For some reason, I just could not stay quiet. "I don't think William can march anyway. They probably wouldn't take him in the Army."

Before I knew what had happened, William had yanked me over his knee. Since I was wearing a full skirt with two crinolines, everything flew over my head. I could feel William pawing through the crinolines trying to reach my fanny, which was wrapped in a bright pink girdle. Seconds later his huge palm landed on my rump, quickly followed by half a dozen more. There really was no pain, just a lot of popping, but I was embarrassed nearly to death as I yanked upright and fought my skirt and crinolines back into place.

"Alright! Who's next?" yelled William.

Jeanie pushed Daisy forward. William gave her a couple of light taps atop her skirt, then helped her up.

Without missing a beat, Jeanie yanked her skirt and slip to her waist and plopped across William's lap. "Okay, He Man, give me your best shot."

She was wearing one of her nicest panty girdles, a Pirouette, one I loved to see her in, and this was a view I had never gotten. I felt a sudden tightness in my throat and my hand went to my mouth. Dear Jesus, I could not believe how lovely she was.

William's palm rested on her fanny for a second, then he gave her a little tap.

"Heloooowww. I can't feel it."

His hand descended again, this time with a real pop.

"I'm wearing a girdle, you know. Is that the best you can do?"

This time the palm really sailed into the plumpest part of her bottom. Jeanie stiffened and let out a yelp. A half dozen more pops followed. Each time she gave a more energetic yelp. Quickly as it had begun, the spanking ended. Jeanie almost hopped up and straightened her skirt. Without a word she returned to the kitchen. I looked around, everyone had a stunned expression, as if they were not sure what had just happened.

"Come on, Daisy," I said. "Time to bast the turkey."

Jeanie was busily chopping cabbage for slaw. I put my hand on her fanny.

"You okay?"

She nodded. "Now I know how hard to spank you, so you'd best watch out."

"You mean…?"

"I always wondered what it felt like. It's not my cup of tea, his hand is too big and strong, but my palm should fit you just right."

*   *   *   *   *

After dinner we sat around the table with everyone except me telling war stories. Every so often, Jeanie would crack one of her crazy jokes. I sketched everyone on their napkin as a memento, and included William spanking Jeanie on her napkin. Slowly, the guys drifted back to the television, while Mom and Momma Jean took a stroll to enjoy the beautiful weather. I started putting away the leftovers while Daisy and Jeanie loaded the dishwasher with pots and pans. William stuck his head around the corner.

"Doodlebug, could you fix two plates. I'd like to take them to Becky and her mother."

"They don't fix Thanksgiving?" I asked.

"They're even poorer than us. I think sometimes they miss meals."

"Why didn't you invite them to dinner? We always have enough for an army."

Jeanie, Daisy and I all giggled at the word, army.

"Anyway," I continued, "talk to Mom about inviting them for Christmas."

William's mouth twisted. "Don't think that would go over too well."

I got down two large paper plates and heaped a little of everything on them, then covered each with foil.

"Thanks, I'll pick them up a little later."

He shifted awkwardly for a while, as if he had something else to say, then turned away. After he had returned to the Den, Jeanie and Daisy shrugged.

"Why doesn't he just admit he's dating her?" asked Daisy.

Jeanie shook her head. "He never admits to anything. It's like he doesn't have emotions.

They started the washer, then straightened the kitchen and dinning room while I hand washed the silver and crystal. After everything was dry, Jeanie and Daisy slipped on their sweaters and went outside. I was putting away the crystal when I sensed someone behind me. William licked his lips, then looked sheepishly at his feet.

"I'm..., I'm sorry Doodlebug. I didn't mean to embarrass you. I never though your skirt would fly up like that."

I hesitated, not sure what to say. Then, without thinking, I threw my arms about his waist and squeezed as tight as I could.

"You're my brother, William. I love you. Can't we at least be friends?"

At first he stiffened. Slowly, I felt him relax and his arms engulfed my shoulders.

"I never thought about you as my brother. I suppose, because you were always so different, and maybe because I knew Mom loved you more than Buddy and me. But..., now I know why you're different." He squeezed even tighter. "I love you too, Ruby. I truly love you. And, I'm proud to have you as my baby sister."

*   *   *   *   *

For the first time I was thinking about Christmas presents. Because, for the first time, I actually had money. Real money that I had earned as tips.

As long as I could remember, Mom had purchased all our presents. Then she would put labels on them as if we were really exchanging gifts. My only contribution was to help wrap, and to make the labels. For the guys I would draw hunting scenes, and for the gals I would draw lots of hearts and flowers and add gooey sayings. At home I usually got a couple pair of socks and an orange. If it was a big year I might also get a box of raisins or some nuts. I received all kinds of toys at Momma Jean's, but I could never take them home or Dad would go ballistic.

This year would definitely be different. It was almost like I was becoming an adult. A couple of gifts were easy. I made Daisy the most feminine Princess dress I could imagine. Not only did it have two lace–trimmed petticoats sticking from under the short skirt, but beneath all that were satin pantaloons with enough ribbons and lace to sink a sissy. The top was built like a bodice with faux bright red laces crisscrossing down the back. The bodice was tight beneath the bust, with a lot of ruffles above so it really emphasized the boobs. The dress was so outstanding I simply had to try it on and get William to take my photo. For the guys I made sports coats lined with contrasting silk. I needed help with those, since I had never made any male clothing. For Mom and Momma Jean I chose luxury items like bubble bath, chocolates, and all kinds of fancy creams and lotions, since I knew neither of them would purchase such things for themselves.

For all the gals I purchased really slinky panties from Miss Lillian's. Pink for the ladies, and red for Jeanie and Daisy. After all, there were a few advantages to being changed into a girl. As a boy I would not have been caught dead withing a hundred yards of a corset shop. Now I could prance into any clothing store in town and no one batted an eye.

But, Jeanie and Mitzi…. They were a major problem. I simply had no idea what to get either, and I also had no idea how to get a gift to Mitzi. After agonizing for weeks I decided to make a satin blouse for Mitzi. That would be personal, without being too personal. After all, I couldn't get her a girdle or anything intimate, she'd never speak to me again. To make the blouse special I made the collar really wide with long wings that could be tied into a huge bow to be feminine, let dangle in front for a casual look, or crossed and flipped over the shoulders to be sophisticated. Now all I had to do was decide how to get it to her.

The same day I finished the blouse, I happened to pick up one of Buddy's special comic books and suddenly my second problem was solved. I almost ran to the office supply outlet, which was also the only place in town to purchase art supplies. Frantically, I selected a half dozen ink pens and brushes, a bottle of drawing ink, and a pad of ink boards. Rushing home I cleared a space on my dressing table and set up all my supplies.

As long as I could remember I had drawn comic strips. The few times I was taken to a movie I'd end up laying the story out in little panels in my notebooks or the backs of envelopes or whatever pieces of paper I could scrounge. After I saw Snow White, I must have redrawn the entire story a dozen times. Each retelling increased Snow White's beauty, the individual quirks of the dwarfs, as well as the hideousness of the wicked Queen. Now, all that practice would be put to use.

First I lightly laid out the first panel in pencil in my sketchpad before transferring it to an ink board, then took up a pen and dipped it into the ink.

The Adventures of Fifi

Once upon a time there lived a very naughty boy named Robert who delighted in tormenting his two beautiful cousins. No matter how kind his cousins treated him, Robert returned their love with disdain. Then one day, his older cousin found a mystical necklace that had belonged to an Egyptian Princess. And from that day, everything changed....

The story began with Robert, who looked a lot like me but muscled like Buddy, tormenting his cousins, who appeared much like Jeanie and Daisy. Then Jeanie tricked Robert into putting on the necklace. Of course, the necklace was magical so he could not remove it. And, to his horror, he discovered his body changing into that of the Egyptian Princess. Most horrific for poor Robert was that now he was the complete slave of his cousins, for only they could release him from the necklace. The real magic was that all this was in pen and ink. Instead of taking months of discomfort for his body to change as had happened with me, I could draw Robert becoming a girl overnight. In no time Robert was dubbed Fifi, and was now subjected to all the indignities two haughty young ladies could heap upon their servant. Every time the girls relented, Robert..., er, Fifi, would rebel, which resulted in even more torment, bondage and sissyfication. There was no sex, but a lot of suggestion, and everything was in the extreme, but without any hint that Fifi was in real pain or danger.

I worked on the story ever free moment. Soon, Mom was reading over my shoulder, and even making suggestions.

"If you're going to give him boobs, make them bigger. I thought poor Fifi was being punished..., those ropes don't look very tight."

"Don't forget, Fifi really needs to pee pee. He's desperate for the girls to return and release him."

"Hummm. Well, you could have them give him a laxative, then he'd really be desperate."

"Yea, good idea, Mom. Caster oil, I presume?"

By mid December I had reached the end of Book One. Poor Fifi had been reduced to a simpering French Maid and was having to serve tea at his mother's garden party. Fifi was actively planning his escape, and the girls were ready with even more diabolical punishments.

I took up a pen and carefully lettered across the last page:

The End, or is this just the beginning?

Now, I was ready for Christmas. For the first time in my life I did not dread the Holidays.

*   *   *   *   *

The girls and I had been practicing a lot. After dinner on Christmas Eve we always gathered around the old piano and sang. We began with carols, then ended with a lot of popular Christmas songs. Next, we toasted Jesus with Grandma's secret recipe eggnog before we exchanged presents. Grandma's secret was a double shot of Bourbon for the adults, and a couple of drops for us kids. This year we planned to end with Jeanie and me singing and Daisy doing her Jerry Lee Lewis imitation at the piano. I was going to end with a special flourish and had already figured out my props.

During the final days before Christmas I was excited as a four year old anticipating Santa. I just could not wait to watch people open their presents. I knew everyone would be as pleased with their gifts as I had been delighted with their preparation. Everything had been stuffed into boxes and sealed withing bright papers and ribbons. Carefully, I hand lettered each tag and added an appropriate animal, a dove for Daisy, a beaver for Mom, an owl for Momma Jean. At last I finished Jeanie's book by binding the pages with pink ribbon, then carefully wrapped them. As a final touch, I added a tiny mouse to her label with a finger to its lips and the words, *For Your Eyes Only*, beneath her name.

Now, all I had to do was wait for Christmas Eve. But, me being me, it wasn't long before I began to second guess myself. Daisy was going to hate her dress. She was no longer a child, and Princess dresses were for children. The men's sports coats could not possible fit. Obviously, I had completely missed their size and the material was all wrong, not to mention the dreadful colors I had selected. As for Mom and Momma Jean, clearly they would want to select their own candy and cosmetics. And, by far the worst would be Jeanie. Who could possibly want a comic book for Christmas? She would hate it. She would be offended. No, she would hate me.

By Christmas Eve I was a complete basket case. How could I ever survive the humiliation? But, I had no choice. The only thing to do was buck up and take what was rightfully coming to me.

Mom and I cooked all afternoon and by six o'clock when the boys came in from work everything was ready. Since most of our first floor was now work space, we had moved the tree and piano into the kitchen. This was really no problem, since the kitchen was by far the largest room in the house, but it also meant the tree was always in sight and I was constantly reminded what terrible gift choices I had made.

Soon everyone else arrived and I pretty much became enveloped in all the kissing and hugging and wishing Merry Christmas. The men brought all the new packages in from Papa Henry's trunk and added them to the piles already beneath the tree, while we girls loaded the table until there was hardly room for our plates. Papa Henry said grace after we gathered and soon everyone was munching and talking. The adults drank sparkling wine and we kids settled for bubbly grape juice…, except William and Jeanie slipped a little wine into their glasses.

After the meal, we lowered the lights a little, but continued to sit around the table. Soon, everyone began listing all we had to be thankful for during the year, then Papa Henry talked about the tragedy of Dad's passing, and how he was now in a better place. Before it could get too serious, we shifted around the piano and Daisy played while Jeanie directed. As every year, we began with *O Little Town of Bethlehem*, then the songs became lighter and lighter. When we shifted to popular music I joined Jeanie and Daisy at the piano. On cue, I pinned some plastic antlers into my hair, and stuck a red rubber ball on my nose. Daisy hopped from the piano bench and began pounding the keys like Jerry Lee Lewis while Jeanie started belting like Chuck Berry.

Out of all the reindeers, you know you're the mastermind
Run, run Rudolph, Randalph ain't too far behind
Run, run Rudolph, Santa's got to make it to town

As we sang I pranced around like Rudolph, ruffling William's hair, pulling Papa Henry's shirt out, tickling Momma Jean. As we reached the final verse, I realized Mom had left the kitchen. I knew my singing and prancing were not great, but I didn't think they were that bad. As the last words approached I ran to the piano, spun around and flipped my skirt up like a Can–Can dancer, displaying the fluffy deer tail I had sewn to the back of my girdle. I figured if everyone had a glimpse of my fanny at Thanksgiving, they should really get an eyeful for Christmas, so I wiggled to send the tail in circles just as we reached:

Run, run Rudolph 'cause I'm reelin' like a merry-go-round

I spun back to applause and hoots, and right into Mom, standing in the doorway with two strangers. Except, it wasn't two strangers, it was one stranger and Mitzi all decked out in her svelte wool outfit. I yanked my skirt down, feeling as red as my rubber Rudolph nose.

"Ruby, you have visitors," said Mom, as if nothing unusual had happened.

I tried to speak, but only a garbled grunt came out.

The silence seemed endless. At last, Jeanie can forward.

"Merry Christmas, Mitzi. We were going to have some of Grandma's secret recipe eggnog. Would you like a glass?"

Mitzi put her hand on the stranger's arm. "Merry Christmas everyone. This is my friend Peter Goldman. We met in France last summer. He's visiting from New York for the Holidays. Please excuse us for barging in, but I needed to speak with Ruby, just for a moment."

Jeanie grabbed Peter's other arm and began leading him towards the kitchen table. "Well, I know Peter would like to try some eggnog. You've got to be careful, it'll knock your socks off."

Daisy pushed me towards Mitzi. My brain finally kicked back in, so I grabbed Mitzi's present from beneath the tree and led her from the kitchen into the fitting room. It was much dimmer and cooler, with only a faint glow from several electric candles in the front windows. We huddled closely, partially because I wanted to be near her and also from the chill.

"It's so wonderful to see you," I whispered. "I made you a little something, but I was afraid to bring it to your house. Your mother...."

"Yea, that was wise. Mother would have been furious." Her eyes glistened in the flickering candle light. "I only have a few moments. Peter and I will be late for dinner at the Country Club."

She pressed a small box into my hand as I presented mine to her.

"Please open it," we said in unison.

Both of us tore into the boxes. She won, because she had put half a roll of tape almost covering her small gift.

"Oh, it's beautiful," she whispered, holding the blouse against her breasts. Gosh, this is the slinkiest satin I've ever felt, and the cream will go with everything."

"The collar is special. I've enclosed a card which shows all the ways you can fix it."

She had moved much closer to me. "I suspected as much. Here, let me show you how this works. It's a cameo, hand carved by this funny little man in Sorrento. Luckily, I had your school photo, so it's the two of us in profile. It goes around you neck, like this. The ribbon is usually black, but you look better in red ribbons."

The cameo was against my neck and my hands were on her waist. Her nose came forward until it pressed against the Rudolph nose.

"Do you know you have a red ball taped to your nose?"

"I've got a tail, too"

"I know, we saw it in living color."

My hands seemed completely beyond my control, they kept caressing her waist, then working lower.

"This girdle and these heels are already killing me," she moaned. "If I survive tonight I'm going to make you wear them for a month."

"I couldn't wiggle into them in a month...."

"I know...."

Her lips met mine, softly at first, then her arms were about me, crushing us together as her tongue played gently against mine.

"Okay, lovebirds. Time to break for air." Jeanie gently pulled us apart. "Peter is going to be on the floor if he keeps hitting the eggnog."

She wiped around my mouth with a tissue, then turned to Mitzi's lips.

"Thank God, your lipsticks almost match. Mitzi, soon as you can you need to do a patch job."

Mom stuck her head out the kitchen door.

"Is it safe out here?"

Mitzi gave me a quick squeeze.

"Mother is really coming down on me. She says I must forget you, that you're just poor trash with no future. That you're not even smart enough to make it in school. I don't want to forget you, Ruby. I want us to be best friends, but I'm not sure when or if I'll see you again."

By now someone was bundling Peter out of the kitchen and all of us towards the front door. Silently, I saw Mitzi and him down the steps and into their waiting car. Within moments they were whizzing towards the Country Club, and I was standing in the cold, clutching the cameo to my throat.

I'm not sure how long I stood alone, at last Jeanie guided me inside and wiped the tears from my eyes.

"You've got to go back in there. You've got to smile and be happy. This is Christmas Eve. No matter how you feel, you can't ruin the evening for everyone. Understand?"

I nodded. "Jeanie, I'm going to die."

"No you're not. You feel like that and, God, do I know the feeling. But, you've simply got to be a big girl."

"My nose must be as red as this ball."

She patted my on the fanny. "Well, at least you got a little tail tonight."

I didn't laugh, but I did smile.

Despite my worst fears, everyone seemed to love their gifts. I decided it was mostly because of Grandma's eggnog, or at least the bourbon. I held Jeanie's book to the end. She read the card, looked perplexed, but nodded. Later, I did see her peek and her face really lit up, so I guessed she was not too offended. One of her last gifts to me was a pair of pearl studs.

"Monday morning Daisy and I are taking you to get pierced. You've had naked earlobes long enough.

Speaking of naked, here's you final present. I'll let you decide if you'll accept it."

I slowly unwrapped the box. Inside, nestled in pale pink tissue was Jeanie's favorite style Pirouette panty girdle. A fancy card, lettered in her elegant script, read – *I need to be well broken in by Easter.* Without taking time to think, I nodded. An expression of extreme pleasure, and perhaps relief, spread across her face.

There was no doubt, I had just let Jeanie wrap me tighter about her little finger.

*   *   *   *   *

Sometime in the night I was wakened as Mom slipped back into bed.

"Ummmmm, are you okay?"

"I'm fine, Ruby. Go back to sleep."

"Is it Christmas yet?"

"Not yet, go back to sleep. I was only getting Santa another glass of eggnog."

"Did you remember the secret?"

"Certainly, Dear. I gave Rudolph some too."

"Thanks, nite Mom."

The sky was a bright pink when I awoke once more. Mom had already gone downstairs, so I slipped into my housecoat and slippers. I figured on Christmas morning it would be okay to leave the bedroom without a bra and girdle.

I congratulated myself on holding together after Mitzi had left the night before, but it was not going to be so easy beneath the light of day. She had abandoned me once, then returned. I really did not think that would happen again. This time she was gone, and gone for good. Although we had not been bosom buddies, I had felt an incredibly warm connection when she flirted. And, to touch her made me feel on fire. Of course, I only saw her in the fitting room when there were no other kids around. I felt sure that at school we would no longer have had anything in common. I was nothing, only her dressmaker.

And yet, I felt absolutely devastated, as if my very best friend had died. How could I even breath, much less live? Lifting the cameo I held it against my neck. It appeared carved from some sort of shell. There were two girls in profile, facing each other..., almost kissing, just as Mitzi had kissed me last night. One girl was definitely Mitzi, the other was me, but the artist had been working from my school photo, and both girls had tons of ringlets and curls, as if we were ancient roman ladies. I held the cameo over the waste basket, there certainly was no need to keep something that would only remind me of a lost friend. But, no matter how hard I tried, I could not let it fall. Desperately, I stared at myself in the mirror.

"You are not going to cry. You are not going to ruin Mom's Christmas. You're going to be a big girl and go downstairs as if nothing had happened."

I slipped the cameo into the pocket of my housecoat and almost ran down the stairs.

Mom was at the stove, frying bacon and flipping pancakes.

After giving her a hug, I began setting the table.

"I had the silliest dream last night. I thought you gave Santa and Rudolph some of Grannie's special recipe."

"Why would that be silly? They were both exhausted by the time they got all those packages down the chimney."

"What packages?"

"I wouldn't know, they weren't for me. They're beneath the tree."

I ran over, and beneath the tree were several huge packages. One was cylindrical and as long as me, another was at least three feet long by two deep and high, the last was between the others in size. The card read, *To the naughtiest girl in town, you're lucky I ran out of coal, Santa*, but it was written in Jeanie's delicate hand.

Tearing into the cylindrical package revealed an artist's easel, the middle package was half a dozen canvases, the last a wooden box filled with a gigantic array of artist supplies. There was also a large book entitled, The Complete Course in Art. It started with drawing, then stepped through charcoal, pastel, pen and ink, watercolor, acrylic and ended with oil painting.

Plopping down, I cradled the book in one hand, the cameo in the other, and burst into tears.

Mom knelt and hugged me tight.

"Is my baby unhappy?"

At last I managed, "Oh, Mom. I'm being torn apart. I've never been sadder or happier in my life."

CHAPTER TWENTY–NINE

Marking Time

The days tumbled into weeks, which faded into a mist of months. By now I was working half time at the diner and full time as Mom's seamstress. When you added the hours I spent on art and design, I was burning my candle at both ends while desperately trying to light it in the middle. Mom had gotten her loan and was functioning as a business with me listed as her partner, yet I knew I was only a worker, not a Queen Bee. I was a terrible business person. Anytime someone came in with a sob story, I would stop everything to help them out, and you just cannot run a commercial enterprise on sob stories. I never knew when to say no, and I was too softhearted to go after cheats. As it turned out, some of the wealthiest families in town never paid their bills. Mom was strong enough to say no, or make them pay cash. Even then, it usually was only after we had been burned many times.

My other problem was that I simply had very little interest in fashion itself. I was fascinated by beauty and harmony, I loved bright colors and unusual fabrics, and I absolutely adored the art of designing. That, and females, especially girls my age. The curves and softness or their bodies, the way light flashed from their hair and eyes, the ways I could manipulate their size and shape with fabric and color. Boys were so hard and angular. They were loud, large and hairy and they smelled bad, while the slim, smooth flesh of girls sent my creativity into overdrive. As a boy I had been completely satisfied with my second–hand clothing. As a girl, I would have been perfectly happy with a couple of outfits. It was Mom's need to feminize me and turn me into a fashion statement that had morphed me into a clothes horse. In fact, I had so many outfits I was utterly stymied each morning until Mom told me what to wear…, down to the proper foundation garments and shoes. I was allowed flats while sewing, otherwise it was heels, heels, heels!

There was one exception concerning my dress. I had agreed to break in Jeanie's girdles, so I wore them religiously unless Mom told me otherwise. Every six months Jeanie presented me with a new girdle, which I would wear every day for a month or two before giving it back. If she liked my work, she would keep it, otherwise it would return for more stretching. All this was really a game. I knew it, she knew it, and Mom knew it, yet we all acted as if Jeanie was destroying my freedom, when in fact she was a source of extreme satisfaction for all of us. Sometimes I wondered if we had all gone a little nuts, then I would think about how much pleasure I was bringing to Jeanie, a little craziness didn't seem so bad.

Mom was still Mom and Momma Jean was also still Mom, only with a difference. They were always arguing over me, but only in terms of what was best for my upbringing. Of course, I had absolutely no say in what was best for me, because I probably would have said standing at an easel was what I wanted to do. But, standing at an easel paid no bills and put no food on the table. We were barely scraping by as it was. One problem with living in a century–old home was that it always, and I mean always, needing repairs, which drank every spare dollar we earned.

As far as day to day living, Mom treated me as if I were eight, rather than eighteen. In addition to my dress, she decided on my hair, my makeup and how I spend my miniscule free time. With respect to work, I was treated as if I were twenty–eight. I was allowed to design clothing exactly as I desired. If I asked, Mom was always ready to give advise or assistance. Otherwise, she let me run my side of the business strictly as I chose. Since I was such a klutz with respect to finances, I always let Mom set all prices and do the collecting. I wanted some freedom, but I also knew my limits.

What was by far most strange, was that every time we finished a wedding dress or maternity outfit, I would hold it against my body so Mom could get the overall effect we had created. Invariably, her eyes would tear and she'd murmur, "I can't wait until we can make something like this for you. That will be the culmination of all my work."

Yet, Mom knew I could never marry, nor could I ever have a child.

*   *   *   *   *

William was fast becoming an old man as he continued working and studying full time. He was finished his studies at Tri–County, our newly commissioned four year college, and was really proud of being one of the first graduates. I think he primarily liked the intimate feeling of such a small institution, but mostly he talked about all the changes Doctor Frank, the Dean of Men, had made in the college and how I should enter the GED program, as if I needed something to fill my spare time. William had been promoted to Manager of the Chevy dealership, while Papa Henry directed the Cadillac franchise. William was finally openly dating Becky, although he seemed nowhere near popping the question. At least he and I had developed a reasonably stable brother–sister relationship. Most of the time that seemed sane, other times it only added to my confusion. Was I really his sister or his brother, or both. Only Doc Pricher might have a clue.

Everyone was convinced I was going to walk into trouble, especially in the old Confederate Cemetery or while coming home at night from the Diner. So, Papa Henry and William found me an automobile of sorts, but it more than fitted my needs. It was a Beetle of midnight blue that had suffered not so much neglect as misdirection by it's former owner. Misdirection, in that she had serious problems judging distances, and had a tendency to cram the poor bug into spaces slightly too small, For this reason, all the fenders and doors were beat all to heck. The body man at the Chevy dealership taught me how to pound most of the rumples from the body and cover everything else in Bondo. When it came time to paint, I decided on red, yellow, green and orange for the fenders, with baby blue and shocking pink for the doors. On top I painted several large yellow spots and finished by adding **Ladybug** on the driver's door. I thought it was beautiful, everyone else almost threw up.

I still walked almost everywhere, even though every six months someone would get accosted in the Cemetery. Usually it would be a young couple who had gone in to find privacy. Instead, the boy would be beat to smithereens and the girl molested. There would be a commotion and everyone would agree something had to be done. But, nothing ever happened.

Buddy continued to take me skating until he went off to university. The biggest change was that we started to enter dancing contests at local rinks, and we almost always were in the top finalists. This meant our photo ended in the newspaper every few months, and the articles got clipped and pasted into Mom's scrapbook, along with photos of every outfit I wore. Mom also had me design ever more outrageous skating outfits, first only for me, then for Buddy also. Lord, did he complain, but Mom would twist his ear and send him to his room until he relented. It took a long time indeed for me to realize he really loved showing off in the costumes, but his male ego was getting the upper hand. Every time we won Buddy went out of his way to announce that I had designed and sewn our costumes, which brought us a lot of business. I just kept quiet and tried to hide in the background. All this made me realize I had no ego at all since I never complained about anything or took credit no matter how hard I worked. Also, I was pretty much a floor mat for anyone to stomp on. The only time I had defended myself was when I dumped the Superdog and drink on Moose Hanahan. I either had to grow a backbone or find someone to protect me. Since the latter was highly unlikely, it was essential I find a backbone, and I did not think a girdle stay was going to help.

Speaking of Moose, he was now a star of the football team and apparently had long ago forgotten me. I even told myself that Butch Spence had turned human. Even his mom no longer tortured me during my monthly injections. Jeanie, however, was forever threatening to arrange a blind date with Moose or Butch, and that they both expected certain services from any girl they dated. Jeanie was never clear what these services entailed, only that it would require a lot of sucking. None of this appealed to me in the least. The last thing on earth I wanted was to have Moose pinching my nipples or Butch feeling me up.

But, deep in my heart I knew Butch Spence was always there, hidden in the darkness whenever I walked alone. One night he would attack, I just had no idea when or where. He would strike, and I had to be ready.

I liked dating a lot, even if it always was as a double with Jeanie, otherwise I had almost no social life. Dating at least gave me the opportunity to talk with someone my age and it got me out of the house. Sometimes we'd go to movies, but lots of times it was only riding around and stopping for a burger and fries before finding a dark place to park. Kissing and cuddling with an especially nice boy could be extremely pleasant. I didn't even mind getting groped a little since my skin had become extremely sensitive, as long as things did not get too far out of hand. A panty girdle give a girl lots of protection down bottom, and most boys were stopped stone cold when they encountered a sanitary pad, so Jeanie insisted on both. But, my boobies lead to a lot of anxiety. First, because I felt really undeveloped, and two, because my nipples were so unbelievably erogenous. I knew a boy could get me completely under his control if I let him play around too much up top.

Jeanie was still my only friend, but while Daisy was not unfriendly, we simply no longer had anything in common. She was always busy in school or with her friends, so I hardly ever saw her.

As I advanced with my art book I became desperate for subjects. When I asked Daisy if she would pose in her underwear for a painting, she just stared at me like I was insane. The next time Jeanie came home from university, she hopped out of everything except her bra and panties and stretched out on a sheepskin rug before I could finish asking. I sketched while she filled me in on her latest adventures in college, which were not going too well. When Jeanie was up, she was an A–plus student. But, when she was down, she could barely function. Instead of empathizing and helping her, the school was actively trying to get her to leave, since they seemed to consider her a liability. To make matters worse, she was having all kinds of problems with her love life.

"I'll never find a boy who can understand," she would say. "They want to date and feel me up, but none of them would ever be willing to take care of me when I'm sick." Then she would look at me with those big cow eyes. "You're the only one who sympathizes with me, Ruby. You're the only one I trust, the only one who'll always take care of me."

She was right. I would take care of her. No matter what, I would willingly have given my life for her.

The next time Jeanie came home I presented her with the painting. It was the first complete oil I had finished. She was stretched on the rug in front of a roaring fireplace, with a lock of hair covering one of her lustrous cow eyes. Nothing really showed, but you could sense every curve of her luscious form. God, she was stunning. Jeanie wanted to hang the painting above the living room mantle, but Papa Henry almost had a heart attack, so we displayed it on the wall in the family room. After all these years later, I can still see Jeanie staring at that painting as if she were seeing herself for the first time.

Thus, life continued, day by day. I worked, morning till evening and frequently until midnight. I had never been on a real date, never attended a sock–hop, much less a prom, even though I adored dancing. Each year I made an ever more complex Fifi book for Jeanie. I had my hair done in the same beauty salon as Mom and Momma Jean. I shopped for groceries, washed and ironed, vacuumed floors, designed and made beautiful clothing for other women. I now planned and drew all of Papa Henry and William's newspaper advertisements. I painted pictures, made drawings. I kept busy. But, I did not have a single real friend except Jeanie. And she was off limits.

Mitzi had entirely disappeared. I knew she had spent her junior year in Paris, living with a local family, and was now completing her senior year as a student in Switzerland. I was unlikely ever to see her again, much less hold her tight and kiss her. Perhaps it was best not to see her. To know she was near but forever beyond my reach would be the worst torture I could imagine. No, by far the worst torture was imagining her in another man's arms, that was beyond agony. So, I simply refused to think about her at all. Except at night in the dark, then she filled every cranny of my mind. Mitzi, my Mitzi, where was she? How could I live without her? Yet, I did continue to live, even if existence had contracted until I could only stumble along an endless darkened tunnel. A hole with no beginning and with absolutely no light at the end.

* * * * *

Friday lunchtime was always busy at the Tin Skillet, but today was unbelievable. I could hardly complete an order before one of my booths turned and I needed to start over again. I quickly wiped an open table. Instantly, four men in suits slid in and grabbed menus. Most of our customers this time of year were from the college, we didn't get that many businessmen. After I picked up and delivered an order, I skated back to the suits.

"You gentlemen ready to order, or do you need more time?"

One man glanced up, then grunted his order. The others followed. Now the first man sat back and actually looked at me.

"Can you remember all that?"

I pointed around the table. "Double burger, rubber cheese, no pickles, large fries and Coke, Dog with chile and slaw, medium fries, chocolate shake. Burger all the way, Swiss cheese, large fries, Coke. And for you, Burger, no mayo or onions, small fries and Seven–Up. Separate checks."

Now the man smiled and stared at my flat chest, which made me feel very self conscious.

"You have quite a memory. What's a girl like you doing in a place like this?"

The other men laughed.

"Serving you lunch."

I skated away to more laughter. Each time I returned the man stared at my chest, which made me extremely uneasy. Was it because of my lack of boobs, or because he was absolutely gorgeous? The more I looked, the more he reminded me of Cary Grant, except with a more squared jaw and naturally waved hair. And, the more I looked at him, the more intensely he stared back.

The handsome guy was obviously from the college because he was clearly working the others for more funding. As I skated in to collect, he suddenly slammed his palm onto the table. Once more he looked up at me, but this time into my face.

"Now I know why you're so familiar. You're Bill Jones' little sister. You're Ruby, or Doodlebug, as Bill calls you."

"Bill? Oh, you mean William. Yea, he's my brother. Did he tell you I was a failure at eighteen?"

"No, he told my you had to drop out of school to help your mother, that you were a whiz at art and a hard worker."

He took out a business card and scribbled something on the back, then delicately slipped it into my apron pocket.

Most guys would have taken the opportunity to feel my hip. When you're a waitress at a diner you get used to being propositioned and felt up. Some times it wasn't too bad, but other times it made you feel like dirt the way men treated you.

"That's my number and office. Stop by Tri–County and see me. It'll be well worth your time."

"Sure, any day after dark. I've heard every line a dozen times."

"No, this is all up and up. I'm going to put you back in school."

After they had left and the lunch crowd thinned a little, I had time to think about what the man had said. Could this be the marvelous Doctor Frank. Sure enough, right there on his card, *Doctor Richard P. Frank, Dean of Men and Head of Industrial Arts, Tri–County College.* On the back of the card was written, *come see me, I can help you.* I wondered two things. If his middle name was Paul, which would give him three first names, and what the heck was Industrial Arts? Then I wondered something else. Did he want to help me, or screw me? The more I though about him, the more either option seemed quiet pleasant.

*   *   *   *   *

Monday afternoon at three o'clock I drove Ladybug into the parking lot of Tri–County and looked up at the ancient High School building that was now serving as college headquarters. The building had been abandoned before I was born, but someone was spending a lot of money to revitalize it. Right in the middle was a wide set of steps leading up to an imposing entrance, with wings extending forward on either side, so you entered across a wide concrete quadrangle. I expected something like Abandon Hope All Ye Who Enter Here, to be chiseled above the doorway. Instead, there was only a hand lettered note about no parking except in designated spaces.

Doctor Frank's office was the first door to the right, so that it looked out onto the steps. I had hardly knocked when he opened the door, ushered me in and sat me on a big leather couch, while he pulled up a straight–backed chair so we sat facing each other. Almost instantly he was up and yanking heavy purple curtains across the windows, closing us off from prying eyes on the stairs.

"The afternoon sun will soon start blasting in here and we'll be roasted," he said, nonchalantly plopping back into his chair. "This old building isn't air conditioned. There are many things we don't have as yet, but we're making strides towards turning this into a real institution of higher learning."

"It sounds as if you've said the same thing to a lot of bigwigs."

He laughed. "Bill said you were sharp."

"Did he also tell you I dropped out of school after the eighth grade? That I'm good in drawing, okay in English, History and Science, but hopeless in Math?"

Again he laughed, this time he slapped his knee. "No, he said you and your mother ran a successful business, that you were a skilled artist and a fabulous skater. I witnessed your skating today. You made the other waitresses look like beginners. I also saw you drive into the parking lot. I take it you decorated your VW."

I nodded.

"Well, you certainly won't get lost in the crowd." His face became serious. "Ruby, I want you to consider an offer. A large company is ready to build a plant just outside town. They've offered us a grant to start an Industrial Design program. I need bodies. You would take regular introductory courses, plus art and design classes."

"But, I haven't even started High School."

"We also offer a GED, that's the General Educational Development. You pass a test and get the equivalent of a diploma. The problem is that I need students now, you'd have to complete the GED before I could give you credit. It would be difficult, but from what Bill says, you're up to it. What do you say?"

He leaned forward and put his hand on my knee, even as he stared deeply into my eyes. His hand felt incredibly hot, his eyes bore ever deeper into me. I tried to look away, but I felt trapped.

"I.... I'll need to talk with Mother. She depends on me."

"I understand, and you depend on your mother. But, Ruby. This is a chance to make something of yourself." His fingers gently squeezed my knee. "You'll think about it."

Once more I nodded. Oh, God. If only he had just wanted to screw me. That would have been so much easier to understand.

"I'll think it over," was all I could say.

CHAPTER THIRTY

Burning Bright

After many hours of discussion with Mom and William I signed up for the GED and Industrial Design programs. It was clear I could no longer work full time with Mom, part time at the Tin Skillet and attend classes. Even though funds were going to be really tight, Mom hired two ladies and I dropped back to only design and making specialty garments, such as costumes for Mister Young, who appeared as if by magic several times a year. The thing I could not understand was why he would not let me make him regular woman's clothes. I could not imagine putting all that money and effort into costumes no one could see. I suppose I was a small town girl at heart, and still had no idea just how different people could be. All that was ready to crumble around me.

Soon as Jeanie returned home for the summer break she began tutoring to give me a boost when the fall term began. Not only that, she had decided to transfer to Tri–County to be closer to home when she became depressed.

She would be a junior while I was a freshman, but at least I'd have one friend on campus.

By the time September arrived I had been through all the GED materials at least twice and was more than ready to begin the fall semester. The first few days were orientation when we received class assignments and met with guidance counselors and professors, most of whom had been called out of retirement or brought in from India or Pakistan. I suppose they had to scrape any barrel they could find to get Tri–County off and stumbling, if not running.   It didn't take long to figure out that understanding the professors was going to be our biggest problem.

Monday morning I entered Industrial Design 101 and sat on the front row. Even with my outlandishly expensive multifocal glasses I need to be near the blackboard if I were going to see anything. Except now the boards were white with a row of brightly colored markers lined along the bottom. A distantly familiar voice broke my revery.

"Well, well. Look what the cat drug in."

A body flopped heavily into the desk behind me. I turned to stare at Butch Spence.

"Good Lord! What are you doing here? I thought you'd be playing football at some university."

"I'm gonna be a designer, what are you doing here? You on th' cleaning staff or something?"

By now twenty or so other students, all males, had wandered in and plopped into chairs. They were followed by a shriveled man with unruly white hair and an even more untidy mustache. Meticulously, he sat a huge stack of folders, books and papers on the front desk, and rapped his knuckles three times on the decrepit oak.

"Good morning, Gentlemen. I am Professor Silver," he announced in a heavy Eastern European accent. "This ees Industrial Design 101. If you are to be in basket veaving, this not your course, please depart now. My job ees to drive principles of design into thick skulls. If you attention and vork hard, you perhaps one day become designer. If play, you fail. As you see, against my wishes, one female ve have. She probably designing frocks while we undertake serious design. Not let her become a distraction. Keep eye on prize and nose to proverbial vheel, then you succeed. Please to open books, page ten, chapter one. Now, first rule of design...."

I could hear Butch snickering behind me, then I felt his fingers twirl through my curls. After a moment's hesitation, his fingers lowered as he attempted to snap the band of my bra. Spinning from my chair, I plastered my palm across his face as hard as I could.

"Touch me again and I'll blast you with pepper spray."

Professor Silver stopped mid word. He glanced at a sheet of paper on his desk, then looked up. "Herr Spence, please to back of room. Young lady, cause disturbance I remove from class." He cleared his throat. "As I saying. Are many elements to good design...."

As we filed out at the end of class several of the fellows were teasing Butch, but I knew they had already taken his side. I also knew I had turned Butch from an enemy into a mortal enemy, but I could not let him paw over me the first day of class. I would have to be doubly careful, because Butch was simply not the kind of boy who would back off once he got riled. He was not very intelligent or he would have been on an athletic scholarship at some prestigious school. He might be dumb, bullheaded and a lout, but he was also twice as big and strong as me.

*   *   *   *   *

English, History and Math classes really were not that different than what I recalled from junior high, and they were fabulous in helping me prepare for the GED exam. I was terrified about math, since it had always been my Achilles heel, but it turned out mostly a review. Unfortunately, Professor Silver also taught Art. If anything, he was more anti–female than in Industrial Design because there were three of us weepers, as he called us. The good part was that there were not enough freshmen or sophomores to fill two classes, so Professor Silver was teaching one combined class, so I was getting two courses for the price of one. We had one hour of lecture and three hours of practice each week. The class was a combination of history and technique, both of which I found fascinating. I didn't have my run–in with the good Doctor until our second drawing lab.

"No, no! Fräulein . Last week you draw correct. You forget already?"

"I'm sorry, Professor Silver. I draw like I cook."

"Cook? This art, not cook!"

"To me they're the same. The first time I cook something I use a recipe. If it's good, the next time I change it a little to make it better. But, I never look at the recipe again. Where's the fun in repeating something over and over? Also, I never measure ingredients. I just use what looks right."

"Fun? Recipe? Look right? This not de class for cook."

"Well, no, but Momma Jean—"

"Momma Jean? Dis you Mutter?"

"Kind of, she's my second mother. But look, isn't this drawing better than what I did last week? See, I only changed a few things…."

Professor Silver stared at my worksheet, then slowly shook his head.

"For this I am too old."

After that, he pretty well gave up on me. I was thrilled to be learning so much I simply could not limit myself to taking small steps, which was Professor Silver's method. Every week I would incorporate everything we had learned in class and try to leap beyond. Some of the boys and one of the other girls could draw pretty well, the others were absolutely clueless, but I had been drawing long before I could write. Now, to incorporate new techniques, to capture line, texture, shape, lighting and color was causing my mind to nearly explode with excitement. If there was a heaven, there absolutely had to be easels everywhere.

Butch, however was no longer laying low. He started his attack slowly by spreading lies, pushing or tripping me in the halls, letting the air from my tires, that sort of thing. Then he became more vicious. First it was the dead rat in my locker, then a cockroach tossed into my plate at lunch. Next he used an ice pick to puncture all four of my tires, which meant Big Mike and Jake, two mechanics from the Chevy dealership had to come rescue me. Finally, one night I made the mistake of parking tight against a light pole in the lot. It was really late as I headed home, only to discover that Butch had parked his car against my rear bumper so I could not move forward or back. Soon I discovered Butch was nowhere to be found. All I could do was phone William to once more rescue me, which made me feel about two inches tall.

Thirty minutes later the shuttle van from the Chevy dealership pulled next to Butch's car and my two gallant mechanics hopped out. It took them less then a minute to unlock his car and jump start it. Ten minutes later the fellows had driven Butch's car behind the school building and parked it next to the trash dumpsters. One by one the wheels were removed and tossed into the back of the van. In no time the car was perched peacefully atop four cement blocks. To add insult, Big Mike clicked on the headlamps and re–locked the doors.

He tipped his hat. "Tell this joker he can find his tires in Mister William's Office."

I gave them both a hug. These giant men with their calloused hands and grease stained overalls were kinder than either of my brothers. I must have seemed a real klutz to them, with my pink skirt and high heels, but to me they were growing in statue by the minute.

"Thanks, fellows, I owe you big. You saved my life the second time this week."

Again Mike tipped his hat. "Our pleasure, Mam. Mister William said to take care of you. Next time this joker bother you, just call Big Mike and Jake, we'll break his legs."

The next day Butch did get his tires back, although it took him hours to figure out how to work his jack and tighten the lug nuts properly. That was when he discovered his battery was stone dead. Butch had also found a black eye and split lip along with the tires. I never did find out if it was William, Big Mike or Jake.

But, I also knew this was only going to slow Butch down. It definitely would not stop him. He didn't have enough brains to know when to get off the train that was hurtling us to a crash.

*   *   *   *   *

In addition to everything else, I was working on the latest edition of Fifi's adventures. They had turned into Jeanie's favorite Christmas present and there was no way I could disappoint her. Mom had fashioned a carrier for my artworks out of some old upholstery material. It was shaped like an oversized briefcase with dividers for drawings and a side pouch for art materials. Since I never knew when I'd find a few free moments, I started carrying a page or two of the adventures around with me. I knew this was dangerous, not because there was anything dirty about Fifi, but even a simpleton would know most people would be highly offended by such subjects, not to mention the extremely graphic renderings of Fifi's torments.

By mid November I was ready to take the GED. At nine o'clock sharp I knocked on Doctor Frank's door and was shown inside.

"Just toss your purse and carrier on the couch," he said with a smile. You'll only need a few pencils for the test."

He led into an adjoining room and sat me behind a metal desk while he opened a large manilla envelope. Inside were three white envelopes. Snapping the seal on the first white envelope, he checked his watch.

"The test is in three sections. You have fifty–five minutes for each, with a five minute break. You're an intelligent and diligent young lady, I'm sure you will do fine. Even if you finish early, just sit here until I return."

The first section was English, which was labeled as Language Arts. Everything was pretty straight forward. In fact, I remembered most of it as coming directly from the GED workbooks. I finished after about forty–five minutes. The second part was math, which took the full time. In fact, I could have used some extra minutes to check my calculations. But, I probably would have only started to second guess myself. The last section was history and social studies and ended with a space to write a hundred–word statement of why I wanted a diploma. That seemed rather straight forward, but I winged something that sounded high falutin. Well, at least pretentious.

After Doctor Frank resealed the envelopes we returned to his office where he once again sat me on the couch while he pulled a chair close in front of me. Soon he was grilling me – in a most genteel manner – about my classes and how I was adjusting to school, how were Mom and William, and what plans did I have for the future. As we talked he became more and more animated, and more friendly. He really was the most beautiful man I had ever seen, and his elegant words and soothing voice soon had me almost in a trance. That was when I realized his hand was once more on my knee. Actually, it was more on my thigh than the knee, and his fingers were making little circles that sent a magical current right through my skirt and stockings. I could feel my heart racing.

Suddenly, I hopped up. "Oh, gosh! Look at the time. I'm filling in at the diner this afternoon. I'm already late. Thanks so much for overseeing my test. Hope I didn't disappoint you."

He said something, but I had already grabbed my carrier and purse and headed out the door. By the time I reached Ladybug my heart had slowed, but I still felt overheated, and my face must have been as colorful as the beetle. I was a boy, I could not feel so strangely about a man. All of this was because I'd been so keyed up over the exam. That had to be the explanation.

Plopping into the seat, I breathed deeply. *Come on Ruby, get your head straight. Doctor Frank was only being friendly. He wasn't trying to hustle you.*

Then it hit me like a hammer to the head. I had put my purse on top of the carrier, but when I retrieved them, the carrier was on top. I quickly checked the purse, then the carrier. There was no doubt, Doctor Frank had gone through both. I felt certain he wasn't trying to steal my few dollars, but a girl's purse is a very private place. More important, there were six pages from the latest Adventures of Fifi in the carrier. They were now in the reverse order. I could tell the photo section of my wallet had been opened, which contained several revealing shots of Daisy, Jeanie and me playing with a water hose in the back yard. We all appeared as if we were auditioning for a wet tee shirt contest since none of us were wearing bras.

God! Oh, God! He had discovered my most damning secrets. I was going to be thrown out of school. Would he publicly expose my depravity, or would he let me leave quietly?

Or, would he demand some special service to remain silent. If having Butch at my throat wasn't bad enough, now I had delivered myself into the hands of a complete stranger.

CHAPTER THIRTY–ONE

Exhibitionist

A few days later Doctor Frank. Dean of Men, and Head of the Department of Industrial Design called me to his office. As so often happened, there was a sign on his door reading, IN CONFERENCE– PLEASE WAIT! I waited, knowing the ax was about to fall onto my naked neck. Fifteen minutes, twenty, then thirty minutes ticked by. All the while I paced back and forth, up and down the hall, with my stomach ratcheting tighter and tighter.

Finally, the door swung open and Butch Spence ambled out, hitched up his pants, gave me a snarky grin, and ambled down the hallway. A few moments later Doctor Frank emerged, snatched the sign from his door and waved me inside. He collapsed heavily into an overstuffed business chair and pointed to the chair before his desk.

I sat, daintily as I could, making sure my skirt covered my knees. I certainly didn't want him to think I was trying to proposition him in my precarious position.

"Thanks for coming in, Ruby. Have a nice weekend?" he asked, as if he had not found the drawings in my carrier or the naughty photos.

"Er…. Ummmm…. Yes sir, and you."

"Yes, wonderful. I had a relaxing walk down by the river. Did you know that's where the young people go to park? Quite lovely."

I swallowed at the lump growing in my throat. "You wanted to see me?"

"Oh, yes…, yes. I wanted to get your opinion on something."

"Er…. Yes, sir?"

"You know that I've been conducting all types of activities to raise funds. To purchase extra supplies for the school, new books for the library, art supplies, that sort of thing."

I had no idea where all this was heading, or what it had to do with expelling me. "Yes, sir. We've been using the new brushes in art lab."

"Well, what would you think of an exhibition of art pieces from everyone in Art and Industrial Design? Do you think the students are ready? Would they participate? The Country Club has offered to sponsor us, and provide a venue with hors d'oeuvres, drinks, that type thing, which should attract some of the town's bigwigs.

"I think it's a wonderful idea. You could have an auction of our pieces. That might raise a little more money. That's how Mom and I got started. But, shouldn't you ask Professor Silver."

He made a face. "Silver thinks you're all incompetent idiots." Then his face brightened. "Actually, that's how I got the idea. I was visiting with one of our major benefactors who mentioned your mother's auction. You must have been quite a hit."

It felt as if my blood pressure dropped to zero. On top of everything, did he know I was a boy?

"I appreciate your input, Ruby. You've convinced me to try the exhibition. I expect something spectacular from you, Professor Silver says you're his best student." He glanced at his watch. "Best run along, you'll be late for class."

As I reached the door he called out. "Oh, Ruby. You aced the GED, as I expected. We'll have a little ceremony one day when your Certificate arrives."

By the time I closed his door he was already busily going over papers on his desk. He now must know all my secrets, yet he did not expel me, nor did he try to seduce me. Well, if he now knew I was a boy, he certainly would no longer have an interest me. That explained no seduction. But, why didn't he expel me? No red blooded he–man would want a flaming sissy around. And why would Professor Silver say I was a good student when he pointed out my every error? Nothing made any sense. But then, nothing ever made any sense to me. I had to be the most clueless person in town.

*   *   *   *   *

An idea had been boiling inside the vacuum of my head for weeks. Actually for months. It had started as a vague idea, then had become so vivid it was almost as if a photo had been glued behind my eyes. The only way I could find peace was to paint the image inside my head. Perhaps I could talk Papa Henry into purchasing it at the auction. I was sure he would like it better than the nude of his favorite daughter. I would feel better. The school would be helped, and Papa Henry would have a painting of his favorite ladies.

Soon as I arrived home that evening I set up my easel in one corner of the kitchen and clamped my last canvas in place. For a long time I stared at the blank material, arranging and rearranging elements using all facets of proportion, spacing and perspective we had learned in class. Then I began to break those rules until the image took form before me.

By now Mom was stuffing Spam sandwiches and iced tea into my hands, I hardly noticed.

Our beaches were all sand, a hundred yards wide and miles in either direction. My painting required cold black rock, jagged and threatening, with a storm–tossed sky and sea crashing towards a protected cove. Using the rule of thirds, I placed a grouping of Mom, Momma Jean and me to one side. They were Victorian ladies, young and sprightly, who had removed their jackets, stockings and shoes while standing exactly where sea and land joined. I was a boy, perhaps ten, with my back to the viewer, offering them some hidden treasure. At the opposing third I sketched a second grouping. This was Jeanie and Daisy facing the viewer, with a second me, again with back to viewer. All three of us were Victorian girls stripped to our undies and corsets playing in knee deep waves. Once more I was offering them a hidden gift. After mixing colors on my pallet, I took up a wide brush and began laying in the sky.

At two o'clock the next morning, Mom forced me into bed. For the next few weeks I spent every free moment transferring the image from my head into the oils. At last I took my thinnest brush and twirled it into cobalt red, then lettered, *The Gift, Ruby,* in the bottom right corner.

It was as if some gigantic weight had been lifted from my shoulders. All I could do was stare at the painting. Mom put her arm around me.

"It's beautiful, but I don't understand. What is the gift, and are you giving it to Jean and me, or to the girls? I've spent hours just staring at the darn thing."

"You're not suppose to know. That's because I don't know what or who I am, or what, if anything, I have to give."

"You're Ruby, my wonderful daughter. You have more to give than anyone could ever imagine."

She kissed me gently on the cheek, and tightened her hug. We stood silent for a long time.

But, I didn't know. Was I a boy, or a girl? A sewing girl, or an artist? A child or an adult? Was I suppose to select a mate, or wait for someone to choose me? Or, was I to be alone all my life?

*   *   *   *   *

A week before Christmas we were set up at the Country Club. As expected, nothing had gone as planned. Professor Silver disliked everyone's work, especially mine.

"Look," he railed. "This is Art? Someone should pay good money for this? Who can understand? What gift? Show me gift! Here, here! Doppelgangers. Now we need twins? Fifty bucks..., we should be so lucky.

Actually, he did like Butch's painting of what appeared to be dead flowers from a cemetery. At least, they looked like dead flowers, but I was not sure.

The paintings were set up at the Country Club in what appeared to be a ballroom, while the refreshments were in an expansive entryway.

The boys were in what passed for their best suits, we girls were completely dolled up. As if I were not uncomfortable enough having people stare at my painting, Mom had gone out of her way to make me miserable in one of my frilliest dresses. Underneath I was so firm I could hardly breath, while my feet were perched in my highest heels. Mom had painted about a pound of makeup on me, but that wasn't sufficient for Jeanie who took me into the ladies room and completely reworked my face. Hoards of people kept arriving. They would browse through the food and drinks, then mosey into the ballroom. I was so nervous all I could do was find the darkest corner and nurse a cup of ginger ale in a losing battle to settle my tummy.

Every few minutes Jeanie would sashay back in and whisper tidbits about how the bidding was developing. She took extreme pleasure in telling each time the bid increased on Butch's dead flowers. They were soon up to seventy–five dollars, which was much more than Professor Silver had predicted for my painting.

"Has anyone bid on mine?"

"Yea, I think there's been a little activity."

"Well, how much?"

Her shoulders would shrug. "I didn't look. I'll check next time."

But, she never remembered to check. It was driving me bonkers, but I did not have the courage to enter the Ballroom and look for myself. I slunk deeper into the corner, wishing I could dig a hole through the carpet. What made my torment much worse was that also in my corner was a large grandfather clock that methodically ticked towards nine o'clock when the bidding was set to end. I stared as the large hand moved past eight thirty, then a quarter to nine. Second by seconds the minutes faded away. Ten till nine.

"Hullo, Ruby."

I spun, almost into the arms of Mitzi. At first I could say nothing. At last I managed. "Mitzi! Oh, Mitzi. I've missed you so much."

"I've missed you too, Ruby. More than you can imagine. It took all my strength, but Mother was right, I was able to live without you. I've grown much stronger and I've learned to control my emotions. You see, I have so much responsibility now that I control my Grandparents' wealth. I have a duty to society to live up to my station in life, to create jobs and support liberal causes."

Her eyes filled with such sadness it was all I could do to keep from taking her in my arms, but that would have been stupid. She was one of the wealthiest women in town, probably in the state, I was a failed painter. I realized then, that I probably could not even paint a house, much less a piece of art.

We stared at each other. Slowly, my eyes lowered to her left hand, which she as slowly raised.

"No, there's no ring. Lots of men, but none are willing to let me be on top." A sad smile played across her lips. "You know I'd have to be in charge. Most boys aren't interested in playing second. Perhaps I need a wife, not a husband."

"Maybe they just need to be taken in hand."

She wiggled her palm at me. "Perhaps that's what some little girl needs. You might be amazed what this palm can do."

Her hand slowly moved forwards until the tips of her fingers caressed my cheek, then my lips. She came near until we were only inches apart, her other hand was behind my neck, my hands slid to her waist, then around, to crush her against me. As our lips met the grandfather clock chimed and hoards of people streamed from the ballroom. Mitzi pulled free. For an instant our hands clutched, then she had vanished into the milling throngs.

Jeanie was at my side, almost yelling into my ear.

"You can't guess who I just ran into."

I nodded. "She ran over me too. After all these years. How could she turn up, just in time to see me humiliated."

"What on earth are you talking about?" Jeanie stared at me.

"I poured my heart into that painting. I though at least Papa Henry would want it. That he would pay a few dollars for it. I'm so useless. Now Mitzi is going to see how worthless I am."

Jeanie hugged me tight. "My sweet Ruby. You can't imagine what Mitzi has been doing. Just you wait. I'm no longer playing with you, but I won't spoil your pleasure. Just you wait."

Doctor Frank and several men in tuxedos climbed onto a small platform not far from Jeanie and me. Now I realized that Daisy was also at my side, while Mom, Momma Jean and Papa Henry all hovered closely behind. After what seemed interminable speeches, Doctor Frank glanced at a sheaf of papers and read aloud.

"Alllllright! Our first work was by…, Sally Williams. Sally wave to everyone. Sally made a ceramics bowl and the winning bid of eighty dollars went to…, it looks like, Sally's grandmother. Congratulations Sally, and thank you Grandmom."

Several members of our basketball team waded through the crowd and presented the bowl to Sally's Grandmother.

I pretty much went numb as they worked through the other pieces, but did perk up when they got to Butch Spence, partially because Butch was nowhere to be found until he showed up from the Ballroom. I felt a chill, watching him strutting around sporting a broad grin as it was announced his painting of dead flowers had fetched one hundred and twenty dollars from…, Mrs. Spence, my old nemesis, the deadly nurse. At least she had been willing to plop down good money for her son, which was better than I could expect.

Subconsciously I had been counting off the objects, which had been announced in alphabetical order. My painting should have been ages ago, obviously no one had even bid on it. Thank God, the evening was now over and I could slink silently away.

Doctor Frank held up his hand for silence, even as he waved one last piece of paper. That must be the grand total collected for the evening.

"Ooookkkkkay folks! This is the moment you've all been panting over. We've been witness to a bidding war far beyond anything any of us expected. Who is the final winner of the final painting. The bidding started high with over a dozen bidders, but it came down to two mystery contestants, Mister J, and the even more mysterious PH. We all knew they were not the two lovely sisters entering the bids. The real bidders are right here in these two envelopes."

There was a lull as two basketball players brought in an easel and set it up next to Doctor Frank. All this while Daisy and Jeanie had been hopping around like bunnies in heat. For an instant, I thought they were going to pull me in two as they each tried to get me closer.

Once again Doctor Frank motioned for silence.

"Okay folks, this is it. The winning bid is…, he looked down at the paper and methodically read out the numbers. Two thousand…. Four hundred…. Eighty four dollars. From…." Now he slowly opened one of the envelopes. "Mister Johnson, President of Southern Bank. Two thousand, four hundred, eighty–four dollars for the painting, The Gift, by Ruby Jones." He patted the easel. "Bring it out boys!"

The basketball players worked through the crowd and placed my painting on the easel. Everyone went quiet. Someone had used a black marker to write, QUEER across the painting. All the faces had been obliterated and a big penis had been scribbled near the bottom of the painting.

"Nooooo!" I screamed, even as I bounded onto the stage. Whipping off my glasses I stuck my face inches from the painting while I dampened the hem of my slip and touched the marks.

Professor Silver was at my side. "Thanks to all holy," he whispered. "It's no permanent. Let dry completely. Then we clean like new."

Now Mister Johnson and Doctor Frank were leaning over my shoulder.

"I can repair it," I said.

Mister Johnson let out a deep breath. "Who would do such a thing?"

A heavy whack came from behind us, we turned in unison to watch Jeanie pounding Butch over the head with her purse.

"You worthless scum," she screamed. "How could you? How could you be so stinking low?"

Her purse landed with each blow. By now, Daisy was pounding Butch from the other side. As he flailed, something flew from his hand and skidded across the floor. Someone scooped it up and held out a cylindrical object.

"It's a black marker," he yelled. "This young man had a black marker in his hand."

Somehow in all the melee Mrs. Spence had grabbed Butch and was dragging him towards the door. Jeanie and Daisy ended their bombardment as Butch disappeared outside. A roar of approval filled the room. I'm not sure how I got them both in my arms, yet I thought our hug would never end. At last I broke free and went to Mister Johnson, who was standing between his wife and daughter.

"Thank you so much, Mister Johnson. I'll repair the painting so you'll never be able to tell a thing."

"No, thank you, young lady. I was determined to get that painting for my office. I think I was bidding against your uncle, but I was obstinate enough not to be defeated. Anyway, I imagine you could paint him something anytime he liked."

Reluctantly, Mrs. Johnson extended her hand. "It appears I've misjudged you, Miss Jones. You are far more than a sewing girl. I don't understand your painting, yet I could not take my eyes off it. Perhaps that was your intent. I'm left with more questions the longer I gaze upon it." She hesitated. "Perhaps you could design a gown for me someday."

"It would be a pleasure, Mrs. Johnson. Mit..., your daughter knows where we are located."

Mitzi did not say a word, yet as they departed her hand slipped into mine, only for an instant. Then she winked in that wicked way she could tease.

*　*　*　*　*

All evening I had been unable to eat because of nervousness, now I was absolutely ravenous. We convened at the Skillet. Mom, Momma Jean and Papa Henry crowded into one side of the booth while we three girls perched on the other. Everyone else had coffee while I plowed into several pieces of apple pie with tons of ice cream. Soon my girdle was screaming for relief so I slowed to a steady munch.

"Thank you so much for bidding on my painting, Papa Henry. I didn't think anyone would want it."

He lifted an eyebrow. "Well, I was in at the beginning, but soon it got much too rich for my blood."

Daisy shook her head. "I only entered what Mister Johnson told me."

"And I just topped each bid by one dollar," added Jeanie.

"But, what would you have done if you'd won the bidding?" asked Momma Jean.

Jeanie only gave us one of her classic grins. "Oh, I think my bidder knew Mister Johnson well enough to understand when to stop. She wanted him to have it, only she wanted him to sweat a little…, and pay through the nose."

I almost dropped my fork. "You mean Mitzi?"

Her smile grew broader. "No, I mean Mrs. Johnson."

CHAPTER THIRTY–TWO

Prom Fright

Christmas came and went, followed by a startlingly brilliant New Year's Day, the happiest Holiday Season any of us could remember. Once more I could dream of Mitzi without sobbing. She never could be mine, but at least she was near. Soon the new semester had begun and I was once more buried in work, yet supremely happy to be learning once more.

Our local newspaper had carried extensive coverage of the auction, including an interview with Mister Johnson and me with a color photo of my painting. No mention was made of the vandalism, of course, especially since the Spence family were ancient and respected residents of our little town. The notoriety proved lucrative since Mom and I received several new clients including Mitzi and her mother, while I also began designing advertisements for Minx Department Store and Miss Lillian's. In fact, I was earning almost as much from advertisements as clothing designs.

Butch had received no punishment for his vandalism and I was still suspicious of his every action, yet now I had even less idea what he might try next. Since I had not been expelled, perhaps Doctor Frank had decided that Butch's vandalism and my transgressions balanced. To be on the safe side, every week I made a cake or cookies for Big Mike and Jake and dropped them off at the Chevy dealership on my way to class. Sometimes I'd pick up burgers from the Diner and we'd share lunch together. They would tell me about idiots doing crazy things to cars, and I'd tell them silly jokes. For some reason I simply fell in love with those big guys and doted on being with them. They seemed to like me too. In a way it was all absurd, me in my frilly dresses and them all smeared in grease. What did we have in common? Yet, in some strange way they became my best friends. Maybe I was trying to make one last grasp at being a male. Not only that, one could not be too careful when dealing with Butch Spence. Big Mike and Jake were my ace in the hole.

Professor Silver was as acerbic as ever. Almost every week he assigned me extra work, which certainly did not make my life easier, yet I was soon designing far beyond the rest of my classmates. Tri–County had begun to offer a life drawing lab for senior art students. Since there were only three seniors, Professor Silver let me sit in. This gave me a lot of needed experience drawing near–nude bodies, and quickly taught me I had been taking far too many shortcuts with hands and feet, which are just as difficult as the face.

As January drew to a close I had begun to relax. My classes were going well, Butch was not bothering me, and almost every day I was enjoying lunch with Jeanie, which was especially nice since I had no money and she insisted on paying. Not only did I love to spend time with her, but she ate like a bird, which meant I usually got to eat at least half her meal in addition to mine. Then the first shoe fell on my head.

"I've arranged dates for us," she said, nonchalantly sucking the remainder of her Coke, then tapping the bottom of her glass to free a clinging lump of ice.

I stopped munching my burger. "Dates to what?"

"Th' Valentine Prom."

"What Valentine Prom?" I sat the burger back on its paper plate.

"The Valentine Prom, of course. Tri–County is having its first official dance. Actually, it's open to any college student. So, I arranged a date with one of my friends from the University. He'll find someone for you."

"A friend I don't know is going to find some goon to take me to a Prom I knew nothing about? Jeanie, you know how that always work, you'll get a handsome gentleman and I'll end up with some joker with three left feet and wandering hands."

"Oh, don't be such a Princess. Don't we always have a good time?"

"You have a good time watching me fight for life in the back seat. Remember, the last guy you set me up with had my girdle half off before the movie started."

"Yea, but didn't you enjoy the movie?"

"I don't even know what was playing, he was on top of me all night."

Jeanie slid her chair next to me and started playing with my earlobe. "Come on, don't be a spoilsport. It's not like I'm asking you to date Moose Hanahan."

"God forbid!"

"Anyway, I haven't been to a dance all year."

"I've never been to a dance, much less a prom. I don't have a dress. I don't know how to dance."

"Says the girl with a room full of trophies."

"Those were for skating. Anyway, I only followed Buddy."

She rolled her eyes. "Aunt Pam is already working on your dress. See what you made me do, I've spoiled her surprise. She's waited all her life to make you a prom dress, you're not going to disappoint her, are you?"

I let out a sigh, knowing I was defeated. "Okay. By the way, are you going to eat the rest of your sandwich?"

"You eat half my lunch and I gain weight."

After finishing my burger and her ham sandwich I sat back. "I'm trying to make my boobies grow."

"Well, I hope it all goes to your butt."

*   *   *   *   *

That evening we had a surprise visit from Mister Young. This time he had a photo of one of the oddest dresses I'd ever seen. After I had checked his measurements and he departed, I turned to Mom.

"I don't even know what this is, how am I suppose to make it, especially the undergarments."

Mom stared at the photo. Slowly, a smile came to her face. "I think this is an English gymslip. Girls used to wear them in school, perhaps they still do, although they don't appear very practicable do they? Just do your best. Mister Young is usually pretty accommodating. If he gives us problems I'll whack his bottom."

We both had a good laugh. I waited for Mom to say something about the prom dress, but so far she wasn't giving away her secret. Perhaps I was suppose to bring up the subject. At last, I couldn't keep it bottled any longer.

"Jeanie wants me to go to the Prom. She's getting me a blind date."

Mom hardly glanced from her sewing. "That will be nice dear. You haven't ever been to a real dance. It will be good for you."

"What do you think I should wear?"

"Oh, I wouldn't worry about it, Sweets. I'm sure we can find something in your closet."

I returned to Mister Young's gymslip. The photo was black and white and not very sharp. Dark blue seemed appropriate for the dress, with a white slip and pink bloomers, since the skirt was quite short. Anyway, a girl would feel more protected with bloomers. Then an interesting modification occurred to me.

"Mom, do we still have any of that pink rubber sheeting?"

"Yes, dear. There's almost a full roll on the top shelf, right beside where the foam rubber is stored." She glanced up. "What are you planning?"

"Thought I'd line the bloomers with rubber. That should be different."

"Well, it certainly should give him something to sweat over." She was quiet for a while. "Ruby, perhaps you're becoming too imaginative. Maybe you should slow down on the Fifi adventures for a while."

I didn't say any more for a long time. Then, as we were closing for the evening I sat next to Mom and took her hand.

"Do you think I've become a bad girl?"

"No, nothing like that, Dear. It's just.... Girls aren't suppose to know about bodily things like sex. Some men might be frightened if you are too aggressive. You're only eighteen, but you need to think about getting married someday."

"Okay, Mom. I'll try to settle down. And, I'll think about what you said."

I lay awake for hours that night. Did Mom actually imagine any man would marry me? Had she forgotten I was really a boy, and could never become a real girl, no matter how I appeared? Then another idea came to me. Had Mom ever really accepted that I was a boy? Had she always believed I was a girl? Questions! Always questions, and never any answers.

*   *   *   *   *

A few days later Mom still had not said anything more about what I should wear to the Prom. Had Jeanie only been kidding about Mom making me a special dress? I loved Jeanie and I was pretty sure she loved me, but sometimes her idea of a joke turned out to be less than funny, especially for me.

At any rate, there was more than enough to keep me busy and, as Mom had said, I could always find something to wear in my overstuffed closet. At the moment I was working overtime finishing Mister Young's gymslip. Lining the bloomers with rubber had been more of a challenge than I imagined. It was one thing to draw it in a Fifi story, quite another to actually bring it to life at the sewing machine. In addition, I had to keep up with my school work and house chores. Sometimes twenty–four hours seemed more than sufficient for a day. Other times, it wasn't nearly enough.

The gymslip came together only minutes before Mister Young arrived for the final fitting. Mom sent him behind the screen to change. By now we had all become much more comfortable with the situation, and Mom had even found him a long blond wig at the Good Shepard Exchange. I often wondered how the old ladies who ran the Exchange would react if they discovered a lot of their stuff ended up on cross–dressers and others they would probably find highly objectionable..., like boys pretending to be girls.

Soon he emerged in stockings, foundations and the blond wig. Thankfully he had chosen flats rather than the five inch heels he loved. I didn't mind the heels, since I wasn't having to wear them, but it made him so tall I could barely get clothing over his head. First, I handed him the bloomers and watched as his eyes almost popped out over the rubber lining, but at the same time, I could tell he was displeased about something.   Overall, the gymslip fit beautifully. It was only necessary to move the button at the waist, and mark a couple of darts to adjust. He turned back and forth several times before the mirror, then let out a deep sigh.

"The undies should have been dark blue, not pink. Everyone knows girls wear dark blue or green bloomers with slips."

"I.... I'm sorry. I didn't know. I though you'd prefer pink."

"Well, you shouldn't think. You're paid to do things right."

Mom had been watching with her hands planted on her hips. She strode forward on firm steps.

"Just one minute, young lady. What gives you the right to correct your betters? On you knees before Miss Ruby. Kiss the hand that makes you pretty clothing and beg her forgiveness."

"Please forgive me, Miss Ruby, I'm a very naughty girl."

I glanced at mom. She shrugged.

"I forgive you..., this time. But..., don't you even think about doing it again."

Mom grabbed him by the ear. "Alright, young lady. Into this corner. Hands on head. Tummy in. Bust out.

You are not to move an inch until I give you permission. Ruby, go into the ladies room and remove your panties."

Actually, Mom pointed to the back porch, where I had recently hung our undies. Shortly, I returned with my oldest pair of panties. The body was dry, but the crotch was still damp. By this time Mom had pinned Mister Young's skirt and slip so his huge pink bloomers were on full display.

Wadding the panties, she stuck them right before his nose. "Open!" In went the panties. "Close!" The lips popped shut. "You are not to make a sound or move until I return. Come along, Ruby, we have work to finish."

As she passed, Mom gave me a wink and a huge grin.

We worked silently for an hour, then Mom took up a really stiff measuring stick we used while hemming and walked to Mister Young. Back came the stick, then it descended three times right into the center of his rump. Even with the panties in his mouth he let out quiet a yelp.

"You may change your outer clothing. Wear your undergarments until morning. That's when you may remove the panties also. I hope this will teach you to give Miss Ruby the respect she deserves."

He nodded violently, then disappeared behind the screen.

When he had departed, after adding a large tip to our bill, I turned to Mom.

"How did you know what to do?"

She glanced up from her sewing. "I'm your mother. Mothers know everything."

Once more we worked silently until she called me over and patted her lap. I settled into her warmth and rested my head on her shoulder.

"Dearest Ruby. Mothers don't know everything. The other day I said you needed to change, but I was wrong. I love you exactly the way you are. You cannot imagine how pleased I am with your work. Your paintings are marvelous. You are so intelligent, so loving, so gentle. I adore reading your Fifi stories and am still amazed how you can turn a few scraps of cloth into stunning outfits. I don't want you to change a thing. Tomorrow when you return from school I have a surprise. You'll be the most beautiful girl at the prom. All the boys are going to fall over each other to dance with you."

*   *   *   *   *

By the time Friday evening rolled around I was bathed and perfumed. The fellows were to collect Jeanie, then stop by for me. I was still in the absolute dark about my date. Sometimes Jeanie could find really sweet fellows and I would have a wonderful time. Of course, on other occasions my date could barely walk on two legs. I particularly disliked the hairy, athletic types who knew they were God's gift to women. I didn't mind a little smooching and petting, it could be extremely pleasant with the proper boy, but large strong men frightened me. Not only because of the difference in size, but also because they could really hurt me if my secret was uncovered. I did not feel I was cheating them. After all, I was giving them the same attention they would have received from a real girl. Unless, that is, they were only interested in sex. In that regards I could not meet their needs. It never dawned on me that there was more than one way to have sex. I had figured out that boys got on top and went inside girls. What other way could there be? Boys seemed to like it a lot, and girls got pregnant, which changed their lives completely.

Mom had spread out my firmest panty girdle and a corset–like strapless bra. It took a full five minutes to struggle into the girdle, then I gathered up the bra, which must have weighed ten pounds. The cups had foam rubber in the bottom and sides, which pushed me up until I was certain any deep breath was going to pop my boobies completely out. I had to suck in as much as possible while she hooked the long row of eyelets. Taking a really deep breath, I looked down. My nipples didn't pop free, but there certainly was a lot of straining down there. Mom had to hook my stockings since I could no longer lean over. The shoes were black pumps with skyscraper heels and red ribbons at the toe. Next came three stark white and starched crinolines. About a pound of makeup and an equal quantity of hairspray finished my head. All that remained was the blue satin gown spread across the bed. It was very old fashioned, with little puffed sleeves, oodles of lace covering the boobs, which would make me look even bigger, and a giant red bow at the waist. I never would have designed it for a girl of eighteen, but it was perfect for a first dance…, if I had been thirteen.

Mom left me standing while she went downstairs to answer the bell. I gazed at myself in the mirror. I was not beautiful like Mitzi and Jeannie, nor even cute like Daisy. Yet, I was not ugly. My teeth were even and white. My eyes appeared gigantic, magnified by trifocal glasses. My date probably would not be turned on, but he wouldn't want to throw up either. The biggest question was if I could hold my breath for three or four hours, and which was going to be worse, standing in those heels or sitting in the girdle and bra?

Bounding back through the door, Mom gathered the blue satin of my gown and held it for me to step into.

"Hurry. It's okay to keep a boy waiting a little, you don't want to give him too much time to think.... They might get cold feet."

Stepping into the dress, I held it against my bust while Mom started working the zip up the back. "How does he look?"

"Who?"

"My date, of course. Did you catch his name?"

"Suck in, the zip is catching. I really didn't pay attention to the name. He seems quite manly. Robust, even. Let's see. Some sort of animal."

My breath sucked in. "Oh God! Not Moose. Please tell me it's not Moose Hanahan. He's going to kill me."

"It could be, Dear. I really didn't notice. He's not my date."

"Mom, you don't understand. Moose Hanahan hates me. His hands are the size of baseball mitts. He could tear me to bits. Jeanie thinks this kind of thing is funny, she's not going to get beat to smithereens."

"Now, Ruby. You're only anxious, no one is going to beat you up, least of all this nice young man." She straightened my puff sleeves and red bow, then removed my glasses which propelled me into a hazy, unfocused world. "There's mad money in your purse, and your bra. You'll be fine. Hurry down, a lady doesn't keep her gentleman waiting too long."

I tried to breath deeply to quiet my nerves, but the blasted bra and dress were too tight. My only consolation was that if Moose didn't actually kill me, I would be able to strangle Jeanie for getting me in this predicament. After pausing at the top step I descended slowly and entered the kitchen where Mom was regaling everyone with exaggerations about my latest paintings. The two fellows turned as I entered and..., neither was Moose.

Jeanie stepped forward. "Ruby, this is Newton Chapman, he's a senior in physics at the University. He can tell you all about the Theory of Relativity. Newt, this is my cousin Ruby, she's an artist and designer."

Newt was at least six feet and built like a tank, yet when he took my hand his grip was so gentle I barely felt it. Jeanie introduced her date, I hardly noticed him. Mom pined his corsage among the layers of lace on my bodice. Before I could get grounded we were side by side in the back seat of a new Plymouth. He was still clinging to my hand.

"Ummm, Jeanie said you could explain…, Relativity."

"Yea, it's all relative." He slid closer. "You smell like a flower garden." He breathed deeply, as if soaking in my aroma.

"Errrr, do you like to dance?"

"Love to," he whispered. "Jeanie said you were beautiful. I had no idea."

He was silent for a while, with only the hypnotic hum of tires on pavement filling the aether.

"What do you design?"

"Women's clothing, you wouldn't be interested."

"I love fashion. Nothing could be more lovely that a pretty girl in a pretty dress. Tell me about yourself. All about yourself. I want to know everything about you."

I could feel the tension leaving my body. It was going to be a long evening, a very long evening, and I was going to enjoy every moment of it.

CHAPTER THIRTY-THREE

By Any Other Name

The other shoe conked me on the head. The financial gods had obviously become tired of playing with Mom and me, it was time to kill any hopes we had of becoming a success. First, the front steps of our home began to crumble resulting in a bone crushing bill, then the fifty-year old floor furnace that provided all our heat died. We had never had heat on the second floor, now we only had a glimmer of warmth in the kitchen. Our only option was to take a loan from Papa Henry. Soon we would owe everyone in town. As a business we had to have heat, we certainly could not ask patrons to undress in a refrigerator. The only logical solution was for me to drop out of school and begin earning money full time. But, Mom would not hear of me quitting. We were all dangling between the proverbial hard place and somewhere even worse.

To top everything, Doctor Frank called me to his office. In my condition I could only assume the worst possible reasons and expected to be tossed out of school, which would perhaps help our momentary financial condition, but also meant I'd never amount to anything.

Once more the IN CONFERENCE–PLEASE WAIT! sign was plastered on his door, so I had to pace and sweat. The sign forever seemed to be on the door these days. I always had to wait, and it was the same bunch of guys who needed the conference, Butch or one of his sleazy buddies. Well, they were the yuckiest boys in school, perhaps they required extra help. Anyway, having to wait gave me time to think, which was never a healthy time with my overactive imagination. Was I finally going to get the ax? Had someone been spreading lies about me? Why would anyone lie, when the truth was damning enough? My hyperactive creativity and non–existent self esteem always joined in tormenting me. At last, Butch Spence sauntered out, hitched his pants and strutted away. Butch was getting sloppy, he had not grinned at me.

Again I was motioned into the office and placed in the upright chair before the Dean of Men's gigantic desk, while Doctor Frank signed several papers before dumping them unceremoniously into the OUT basket. He leaned back, hands clasped behind his head and gazed at me.

I fiddled with the hem of my skirt, making sure it was pulled as low as possible over my knee. The room was quiet dark since the heavy curtains had been drawn against the afternoon sun. Soon, I would be willing to confess to any sin, I simply could not stand the gloomy silence beneath his withering gaze.

"I've been extremely pleased with your progress," he said at last. "Professor Silver has shown me your work from the Senior Art Lab. Your ability to capture the human body is truly amazing."

"Thank you, Sir." I swallowed deeply. Was he being nice before the death blow?

"You are probably wondering why I called you in today."

"Ye…, yes Sir." Okay, here it came.

"I can tell, you always expect the worse. Did your father abuse you? Beat you, that sort of thing?"

I nodded. "Sometimes."

The corners of his mouth turned down. "Never could understand how anyone could hit a defenseless child, especially one as lovely as you."

Unlocking the bottom drawer of his desk, he drew out a heavy brown envelope and placed it between us.

"Ruby, I have a…, sort of business proposition. I know you're desperate for money. For instance, if your cousin doesn't purchase lunch, you never eat. I've never even seen you buy a donut or Coke."

"I don't want to get fat."

"Nonsense, you don't have an ounce of extra fat."

He pushed the envelope towards me. "I have a friend in New York. He handles, shall we say, special projects for very wealthy people. He has a client in Switzerland, an industrialist, with peculiar tastes. My friend needs this illustrated. He is offering a lot of money, especially for someone in your situation."

I put my hand on the envelope, but Doctor Frank placed his over mine.

"I don't want you to be shocked or distressed. The story is very explicit and some might consider it filthy. However, you are the only person I know with the talent and imagination to pull this off. My friend is offering fifty dollars a page. I would think, something like the drawings in your carrier."

Suddenly I felt cold. Doctor Frank was telling me he had looked at my drawings of Fifi, without actually admitting it. Was he threatening me, or only trying to allay my fears?

He withdrew his hand. "The story is poorly written and contains many French and German words as well as some in a language I don't know. Anyway, you're a smart girl, I think you can figure it out."

It took some effort, since I knew neither French or German and obviously didn't have a clue about some unknown language, but after studying the pages gained a gist of the story. I could understand why the Swiss man was an industrialist. The entire story consisted of girls being captured and turned into living machines, or at least living parts of a huge plant.

"Can I rewrite the story so it makes sense?"

He nodded.

"I won't kill anyone, like here on page three where the girl is pumped up and explodes. The girls will be helpless and uncomfortable, but not hurt. I couldn't stand to hurt anyone, especially a girl. I'll have to look up a lot of the words. It will probably take about twenty pages. Would that be too much?"

"That sounds about right, I'll talk with my friend. Twenty pages at fifty dollars each. That makes one thousand dollars, more than you need for another year of collage. Oh, and Ruby, this shouldn't go beyond this room. Normally I would not touch something like this, but I know you need the money. I only want to help you."

"Thank you, Sir. I do need the money."

"And, you aren't offended."

I hesitated, feeling absolutely filthy for agreeing to do things like this to girls, even on paper. But, he was right. I desperately needed the money. Mom and I were already stretched as far as we could go.

"No Sir. Thank you. When do you want them?"

"Sooner, rather than later. At least by the end of this term." He glanced at his watch. "You'd best run along, you're already late for class."

I stopped off at the ladies room and threw up. Putting Fifi through his paces to entertain Jeanie was one thing, turning innocent girls into living machines was quite another. But, Mom was barely keeping her head above water. I either had to drop out of school and work full time, or I had to become a prostitute. An art prostitute, but a prostitute none the less.

CHAPTER THIRTY–FOUR

Propositions

Somehow I survived until Good Friday. Nothing was going well, especially the Swiss story which somehow always seemed to exceed my grasp. Perhaps my brain was shrinking, or maybe I was simply exhausted. It had been so long since I slept more than a few hours a day, it felt as if I was walking in a fog. Thankfully, Tri–County along with most of the other universities had Spring Break the week following Easter. If I could stay awake through church I could sleep for a couple of days and catch my breath. I vaguely remember stumbling in from class and putting my head on the kitchen table, only to rest for a few minuted.

When I came to, Mom was gently shaking my arm.

"Wakey wakey, sleepy head." A broad smile lit her face. "Time to get up, you don't want to be late for Easter Service."

Slowly, I put one foot in the floor, then pushed the other from beneath the covers. "How? I was in the kitchen."

"William carried you upstairs and helped me get you undressed."

"But…. I have a lots to catch up on."

"You have gobs of sleep to catch up on. You're going to take it easy for a few days. Anyway, your girlfriend called."

Now I knew I was still dreaming. "What girlfriend? You don't mean Jeanie."

"No, the Johnson girl. She'll pick up up this afternoon."

"Mitzi? Pick me up?"

"Is there an echo in here? Yes, she's invited you to the beach this week."

"The beach? I don't have anything to wear at the beach. Mom, I've got loads of work to do."

"Well, you won't be doing it at the beach. I will let you take your art carrier. But, no books. No studying. Jeanie brought over a suitcase and some of her play suits, those should be fine for the beach. You won't need a swimsuit, the ocean will be far too cold for swimming." She sat beside me. "Listen, Ruby. Mitzi said she wanted to talk business with you. I assume she wants some special outfit, perhaps a wedding dress. Whatever she wants, you agree. We're desperate for work right now."

"Mom, please don't say wedding dress. I'd die if I had to make a wedding gown for Mitzi."

"I know, Sweets. But, one day she's going to get married, and it isn't going to be to you." She hugged me tight. "Come on, Sugarplum. People in our place can't have hopes, all we can do is muddle through."

*   *   *   *   *

Not long after Easter service Mitzi zipped in front of our house in what appeared a brand new bright red sports car. Mom pushed me through the door and down the steps before Mitzi had a chance to change her mind. After Mitzi stuffed my suitcase in the trunk and wedged my art carrier behind the only two seats big enough to hold a human, she held the door while I plonked into the extremely low seats and swung my legs inboard without showing more than a couple of inches of panty girdle. Before I could get settled, Mitzi had hopped in and clamped a wide strap across my lap.

"What's that?"

"It's a seat belt, Silly! It'll keep you from tumbling out in case I take a corner too fast." She put her hand between the belt and my tummy, as if checking to make sure the belt was tight. "It also gives me an excuse to feel you up a little, which is convenient when you're on a date."

"A date?"

"Sure, you're my date this week, so you'll have to be on your best behavior. You don't want me to have to spank you...," she gave a wink, "or do you?"

All this time I had been trying to glimpse her left hand, the ring finger to be exact, yet Mitzi had done a monumental job of keeping it hidden. After excruciating moments she wiggled her fingers before my nose.

"Nope, no bangles as yet. Th' boys have been laying low."

I let out an audible sigh. It seemed almost as if she sighed with relief also.

Without another word Mitzi squealed away from the curb and shushed around the corner so fast I almost slid out of the seat. Perhaps I did need the belt. Soon we were out of town and heading southwards towards the coast. I had only been to the beach a few times, and had no real idea where we were heading. All the while, Mitzi kept up a steady stream of chatter about nothing in particular, and yet somehow made every word seem exciting. Soon I was up to date on all of her escapades at university, her favorite classes and regular dates. I learned her grandparents had built the beach house during the Depression, and how much she and her father loved going to the old place, especially during the winters when the beach was deserted. I also learned that it was her mother who insisted the house be upgraded and turned into a summer rental, which had become a tremendous point of contention between her parents.

She glanced at me. "You think rich people don't have problems. We're only people. We hurt like anyone else."

We were quiet for a long time. Occasionally she would change gears when passing slower traffic, but otherwise kept both hands on the steering wheel. We came up behind a string of cars and Mitzi shifted down to third and worked her way around each car as if it were parked. After we cleared the last auto she shifted back into forth, but instead of moving her hand to the wheel, she let it settle onto my thigh. Her touch was like an electric charge, it was all I could do to keep from moaning. Her fingertips delicately made circles in the soft space between the bottom of my girdle and the stocking tops. Slowly, I placed my hand upon her leg. She was soft, yet firm, warm but cool. She was not wearing anything except panties beneath her pants, which enormously increased my excitement. What could be more erotic. I was a boy wearing a girdle and stockings, she was a girl dressed like a boy.

We both stared straight ahead. The white strips on the asphalt rushed from the distance, then disappeared beneath us. At last, she gave me the tiniest squeeze and returned her hand to the steering wheel.

Why on earth had Mitzi invited me to the beach? What kind of business proposition did she have in mind, or was she interested in some other type of arrangement? All

I knew was that whatever she wanted, I would give, even if it destroyed me.

*   *   *   *   *

At last we neared the coast. After traversing a wide band of marshes atop a causeway no wider than the road, we entered a long barrier island. Mitzi pulled into a tiny general store where we purchased enough eggs, bacon, bread and goodies to keep us from starving. They only had one, particularly pathetic looking steak, but we bought it anyway, then I selected several juicy baking potatoes and a large head of lettuce with a bag of carrots on the side. At the last moment I tossed in several cans of Spam.

Her nose wrinkled. "You eat that stuff?"

"I'll make you a sandwich you can't resist."

"Yuk!" Her tongue dangled out.

"If you like it, you do the dishes. If not, you do the dishes."

She tickled me. "That doesn't sound fair. I'll have to think about it. Anyway, maybe I'll do the cooking."

"You don't look like the cooking type."

"I suppose you are."

She had moved very close beside me. We were in the back of the store, between two tall racks of caned goods. Her hand drifted down my back and came to rest on the roundest part of my fanny.

"Tell you what. If I like your marvelous sandwich, I'll decide on your punishment." Her lips were inches from mine. "If I don't like it, I'll also decide. Doesn't that seem fair?"

"Sounds perfectly fair to me." Our lips brushed.

"Remember," she whispered. "I like to be in charge."

After Mitzi payed from her thick wallet, we loaded everything and headed down a long street between mostly weather beaten and unpainted houses. Those facing the beach were bigger and more substantial or perhaps less dilapidated, depending on your point of view, those away from the beach smaller and more decrepit. The farther we drove the more space opened between the houses. At last, we left the main settlement and took a bumpy dirt road onto a higher strip of land. Just before we ran into the ocean, we came upon a gigantic and rambling two story house. Actually, since it perched atop tall poles, the house was really three stories and to crown everything there was a flat platform atop the steep roof.

"My God! Is this your place?"

"Yea, horrible isn't it. Once Mother got started, she just couldn't stop. Those Hanahans are nothing if not outlandish."

I must have looked as stunned as I felt, because Mitzi almost died laughing.

"Didn't you know Mother was a Hanahan? Yep, Moose is my second cousin. I have to put up with him at every family gathering." She looked thoughtful for a moment. "Maybe that's why money goes to Mother's head. She started as poor as you."

I tried to think of something to change the subject. Moose was not a topic I wanted to think about. "The house is so big I'll get lost. Maybe I should tie a string to the front door."

Again Mitzi laughed. "Don't worry, we'll only use the bottom floor. The top is all bedrooms. Well, the lookout all the way up there is a great place to sun in the buff." She made a face at the monstrous house. "You can sleep about a dozen bodies in there, more if you use the couches. We'll sleep in Mother and Dad's rooms which are side by side." She glanced at me. "If you'll feel safer, I can sleep upstairs."

"No, why would you do that?"

"We'll have to share a bathroom. That was Mother's biggest mistake, putting bathrooms between every two bedrooms. Renters like to have their own bath, even if the whole family uses one bath at home." She shrugged. "Go figure. People are funny."

Mitzi pulled beneath the house and we began to unload. It took several trips to get everything up the stairs, but soon the groceries were properly stored, water was turned on and the furnace fired up. She grabbed my suitcase and led into a huge bedroom at the front corner of the house. A picture window and sliding door looked over a deck to the surf beyond. The deserted and windswept beach stretched far to left and right. For several minutes I stood, mesmerized by the rollers sweeping in, only to crash with a thunderous roar against the sand. Gulls and terns wheeled overhead, while a long train of pelicans skimmed the wave tops.

With a start I raised from my revery when I realized Mitzi had opened my suitcase and was methodically removing each item.

"You don't have to do that, I can unpack."

She held a pink play suit I had made for Jeanie at arms length, then against herself as she turned right and left before a full length mirror. "This is so cute. Not for me, but you'll look adorable in it." She placed it on a hanger, then took our a dress. "Oooo, another stunner. It's really short, did you design this?" Another hanger. Next she held up Jeanie's girdle. "Wow, now this baby looks firm. Is this one you're breaking in for Jeanie?" A strange smile crossed her face. "You don't have to blush. Jeanie told me a lot about you. She has some crazy ideas, but loves you very much."

Methodically, Mitzi moved each piece of my underwear from the suitcase to a drawer, then lined my makeup near one of the two sinks in the bathroom.

"No pants?"

At last I found my voice. "Mom won't let me wear pants. She says girls have too big fannies to wear pants."

"Do you wear girdles all the time?"

I nodded.

"Even to sleep!"

"Sometimes."

She made a face. "I know, whatever your mother wants. Do you always follow your mother's directions?"

"Of course, don't you?"

Mitzi smiled that strange flicker of the lips. "Hardly ever."

She clicked my now empty suitcase shut and placed it in the closet.

"My room is through that door. Since the toilet and shower are in their own spaces we usually just keep the bathroom doors partially open. If my snoring gets too bad you can always shut them."

"Mitzi, sometimes I have bad dreams and cry out at night. I..., I hope I won't disturb you too much."

"Certainly not. Jeanie says if I turn you over and rub your back you'll settle down. That's good to know."

"My gosh, what else has Jeanie told you about me?"

"Everything. I wanted to know every little detail and Jeanie was very accommodating." Once more the faint smile. "I have a way of getting information out of people. Now I know all your secrets."

Her eyes bore into me, as if she was searching for something.

"Well, that's incorrect," she continued. "I don't know everything. What kind of dreams do you have?"

Suddenly, I felt naked beneath her stare. I didn't want to say anything, but my mouth wouldn't stay shut. "That I've been abandoned. Alone in the rain and dark. That I've been thrown out with the trash and I'm all tied up and can't get free."

"Don't you ever have nice dreams?"

"Sometimes, after I have my injection." I could feel heat building in my face.

"And, then you have naughty dreams?" She grinned and touched a finger to my nose. "We'll have to investigate those thoughts sometimes. There appears to be more to little Rudy than meets even my eye."

I wondered, exactly what did Mitzi know? Obviously not everything, or she would never have taken me to the beach.

While Mitzi unpacked I wandered through the house. Actually, she had run me out of her bedroom. Funny that she had handled every piece of my clothing, yet would not let me even see her unpack. The house was essentially bedrooms surrounding a large two story open space. Across from our bedrooms was a gigantic stone fireplace with a raised stone hearth just right for sitting. Once the fireplace had been real, but now there were massive gas logs where the fire would have been. There was a controller which allowed the fire to be adjusted from a gentle flicker to a roaring inferno. It didn't take long for the room to become toasty once the gas logs were jumping with heat. In front of the fireplace was a long couch, in between the floor was covered by a thick and comfy sheep—skin rug.

The front wall was all glass that opened onto the same deck as my bedroom. In the middle was a strange pool with a folding cover. After opening some valves and flipping several switches a hollow thumping came from beneath the pool.

Mitzi settled back on her fanny. "It'll take a day or so for the filter and heater to get the water just right."

"What is this? It's too small for swimming."

"It's a hot tub. You soak in it."

"Well, I don't have a swimsuit. You'll have to soak alone."

Mitzi rolled her eyes. "This is a beach house. I'm sure we can find you something to wear." Once more the tiny smile played across her lips. "Otherwise, since this is an all girl week, clothing is optional."

That evening I fixed omelets, bacon and biscuits. Once more Mitzi was animated and chatted contentedly throughout the mean. In some ways I was learning a lot about her, but in others she was as enigmatic as a Himalayan monk. She had driven to the beach wearing boy's trousers, yet now that we were alone she had switched to a skirt and lightweight panty girdle. Nothing about Mitzi made any sense, yet everything about her was absolutely captivating.

After the meal she went back to the main room while I cleaned. They had a dishwasher but I was used to doing everything by hand. Not only that, I really was not sure how to make the blamed thing run. When I emerged Mitzi was stretched out on the sheepskin rug before the fire. Her eyes were closed. I was not sure if she were awake or asleep. She had started a record of romantic music by Tchaikovsky and the melodious strings filled the room like a pink light. Quietly, I opened my art carrier and retrieved my sketchbook.

Just as I was finishing a second sketch, she opened one eye.

"You're drawing when you could be ravishing me?"

"First I sketch…. Then I ravish. You probably don't remember, I drew you once before."

She looked blank. "How could I forget something like that?"

"In the fourth grade. We were studying Mexico and Miss Simmons let me make a poster of a dancing girl for our fiesta."

Mitzi groaned. "How could I forget? You had me raise my arms like I was dancing, then added that bright skirt and blouse with the other dancers in the background." She had flushed red. "Was I the first girl you asked?"

"No, you were the last. I thought you would reject me, like all the other kids.

For a moment, her eyes closed, as if she were calling up memories.

"I remember you as the strange little boy who didn't know the difference between the boy's and girl's restroom. You'd wait quietly in line with the girls until one of the teachers sent you with the boys. I though it was cute."

She patted the sheepskin, then held up her hand. "First, let me see how ugly you've made me."

Settling, I held the sketchbook above her.

"Lord, I look frumpy. Are my cheeks really that round? And my boobs, I look like a Holstein!"

"You look marvelous."

Before I knew what had happened, she pulled me down and rolled atop so her knees clamped my arms. She was surprisingly heavy, not so that she hurt me, but such that I felt cornered and slightly out of breath. Suddenly, she leaned forward with her chest only inches from my face. At any moment she could lower her full weight onto my face and suffocate me with her breasts. Her breathing came in deep heaves, while I could only manage slight pants.

Her voice was a hoarse whisper. "I told you I needed to be on top. I don't want to hurt you, but I could. What should I do with you?"

Gradually she lowered her weight onto my chest, it was becoming difficult to breath. "Anything," I gasped.

Down came her breast, covering my mouth, then my nose. For thirty seconds, perhaps a minute she pressed, then pulled away only to cover my lips in a furious embrace as her tongue entered, tentative at first, then deeper than any boy had ever kissed me. As quickly as it began, her attack ended. She lay beside me, one arm cradling my head, the other lightly across my waist.

"Sweet, sweet Ruby," she whispered, "such a delicate little flower."

We rested quietly, her fingers delicately tracing the tummy panel of my girdle. I was boiling inside, yet afraid to move, terrified I would break the magical spell she had woven around us. At long last she sighed deeply.

"Time for bed. You've had a trying day and need your beauty sleep."

Gently she kissed my cheek, then helped me up.

My head was exploding with questions as I slipped into a nightgown and removed my makeup. What had just happened? Was this planned, or had things simply gotten out of hand? Was it a test? Had I passed, or miserably failed? I could hear her changing in the next room. Her door was partially open. I could easily peek at her, she would never know. Yet, I would know that I had invaded her privacy. Perhaps she wanted me to look. What did she want? Oh Lord! I had no idea what was happening.

As I turned down my bed she walked in. Instead of a flowery nightgown like me, she was wearing an oversized sweatshirt emblazoned with the University logo, certainly with nothing more than panties beneath since it barely reached her thigh. While helping me into bed her fingers slipped across my still girdled fanny.

"Good girl. No naughty thoughts tonight."

After tucking the covers beneath my chin, her lips caressed my forehead.

"Nite, nite, Ruby. Sleep tight, no dreams tonight."

She clicked off my light. The room was incredibly dark with only a dim glow from a nightlight in the bathroom. The roar of surf filled the darkness. Occasionally, an especially heavy swell sent shock waves through the house. My mind and body were dancing with excitement. Surely, I was going to lie sleepless for hours. My eyes closed, only for a moment.

* * * * *

The sun simmered high above the horizon. It seemed that only moments before I had been in complete darkness. Somewhere in the distance a clock chimed..., eight, nine, ten. Ten o'clock. It couldn't be. I slipped from bed and tiptoed into the great room. Mitzi was hunched over a heavy table near the front wall of glass doors. Glancing up, she closed what appeared to be one of my sketchbooks.

"Morning Sleepyhead. There are still biscuits from last night and fresh coffee. We have grape, strawberry or peach preserves."

I picked up the sketchbook. It was the one containing all my Fifi drafts and what I had worked up on the Swiss story. Swallowing hard, I glanced at Mitzi, knowing she now though I was filthy.

"Mitzi.... I...."

"That's very interesting. We'll talk about it later." She turned toward the kitchen, then looked back. "You really are talented. I can't imagine how you pack so much emotion into a few pencil lines. Come on, I'm starved."

Following breakfast Mitzi helped me dress in the pink play suit before we walked miles up and down the beach collecting shells and bits of nature's treasure tossed up by winter waves. I felt like a kid in a toy shop as each new shape and color emerged from the sand. Mitzi carried a plastic bucket while I scurried this way and that, squealing as the cold waves chased me up and down the beach. After we returned to the house, exhausted but happy, I arranged my hoarded delights on the cusp of a dune and sketched while Mitzi washed accumulated salt spray from the windows and decks. For lunch I crisp–fried portions of spam and spread gobs of mayonnaise on thick slices of bread for my somewhat famous sandwiches, all washed down with ice cold Coke. At first Mitzi turned up her nose, but by the third sandwich she was a convert.

After a nap we drove to a dock overlooking the marshes and filled a bucket with blue crab. Now it was Mitzi's turn to shine as she taught me how to boil crab and break into the succulent meat with nutcrackers and hammers. She was ten times faster, so she ended up feeding me most of her crab. Even with a towel tied around my neck as a bib I ended up with as much on my face as in my mouth.

We didn't nap after eating, but did stretch out on the sheepskin in front of the fire while more Tchaikovsky filled the air. Once more Mitzi regaled me with her endless escapades. She talked more than Jeanie, but not as much as Daisy. And, her stories were a lot more interesting. She was quiet, then hunched up on an elbow and looked down into my eyes.

"Don't you ever date?"

"Sometimes. Jeanie sets me up with her friends, but they never call me again. I try to be friendly, but I must be doing something wrong. You must have had dozens of boyfriends."

Her head slowly shook, she glanced at me, then looked away as her eyes filled with sadness. "I've had dozens of lovers, never anyone I'd call a boyfriend. Boys want to screw me 'cause I have these boobs. No one is interested in what's inside my head..., or my heart. Sometimes they hurt me. It's like I'm not a real person, just a rubber doll."

Her fingers traced my lips. "That's why I like you so much. You never push, never hurt me, even though you love me. I can see it in your eyes."

Once more she was silent, then as quickly as she had become serious she bounced up. "Come on, the tub should be ready by now. Let's find you a suit."

A short while later she tossed me a small bundle of bright blue stretchy material emblazoned with multicolored flowers. At first I thought the swimsuit was far to small, but after I'd wiggled into my Playtex brief I discovered that swimsuits were designed to stretch even more than girdles. The bottom was like a boy–leg brief with a bib front that just covered my boobs. The straps tied behind my neck. Since the back was open down to my waist I was certain I would pop out if I leaned over, but the material seemed to cling like a second skin. By now Mitzi had donned a two–piece suit in shimmering red. The top was designed so it made her appear even bigger and the bottom definitely fit like her skin.

It took both of us to open the thick cover over the pool. Immediately, steam started drifting into the cool night air. Mitzi flipped one switch and the water sprang to life, churned with bubbles. A second switch turned on a single bulb set deep in the bottom. While holding my hand, she had me step onto a seat, then down into the pool itself. At first I felt like a lobster about to boil, then I was able to slowly lower myself until I was sitting neck deep in churning bubbles. Mitzi slid in next to me so our hips were touching. The only sounds were the throbbing jets and roaring surf. Overhead, a million dots of light sparkled against jet black darkness. Silently, Mitzi's hand slid into mine.

After half an hour the jets died and Mitzi helped me from the pool and wrapped us in a gigantic towel. I was so relaxed I could barely stand. Soon I was out of the swimsuit and brief and into my nightgown, then into bed. This time instead of kissing me goodnight on the forehead, Mitzi brushed my lips. I was fast asleep before she left the bedroom.

*   *   *   *   *

The next morning was a repeat of the previous day, except I fixed a gourmet breakfast before we walked. After lunch Mitzi brought out a thick photo album that documented the beach house. The second half also contained a history of Mitzi and her parents. Well, mostly Mitzi and her father with their spaniel. In the later photos you could tell the dog had gotten really old since most showed Mister Johnson carrying her up or down the stairs, or Mitzi holding it's head.

Taking several photos out of the album, Mitzi lined them on the table.

"This is Curly. For years she was my best friend and Dad's constant companion. Dad and I cried for days after she went to doggie heaven. She's buried under that marble slab next to the walk." Mitzi brushed at her eyes. "I want you to paint a picture of Curly for Dad's Christmas. Something like this, in the prime of her life. Can you paint from a photo?"

I nodded. "I won't paint this photo. I'll paint what I see in my mind, using all these photos and what I know of you and your father. You'll have to trust me. I can only paint what I see inside."

"Agreed. Make it the same size as *The Gift*, so Dad can mount them together in his office. Mom despised Curly for shedding all over the place, she wouldn't want the painting in our house. Okay, how much do you want, this is a business arrangement."

"I'll need to purchase the canvas and have the frame made. Lets see..., perhaps fifty dollars, would that be too much?"

"Fifty dollars! My God, you're a worse business woman than I thought. How about five hundred."

"I could never charge you that much, not for a Christmas gift for your father."

Acting as if she were pulling out her hair, Mitzi screamed.

"Don't you understand anything about business? You're not giving me a gift, I'm buying something for Father. You're the artist, I'm the client. Here, let me show you."

She hopped up and returned with a pad of paper and an ink pen. Several minutes later she signed the bottom of the page and pushed it in front of me.

"Sign here.... Now, print you name and put today's date. It would be better if we had witnesses, but this will have to suffice. Do you know what you've just signed?"

I shook my head.

"That's because you didn't read the contract."

"That's because I lov.... That's because I trust you."

"Love and trust have no legal bearing." Her finger ran down the page. "I'm the party of the first part. Here I contract with you, the party of the second part, to paint a picture of Curly. Here is the size. It is to be ready by Christmas Eve, when I will pick it up at your home. For this service I agree to pay you five hundred dollars. I further agree to pay you half today and half when the painting is delivered. If I approve of the painting I agree to give you a big kiss. If I am displeased, I promise to turn you over my knee. The last part probably isn't legally binding, but I thought it added a nice Mitzi Johnson touch."

She put out her hand.

"Agreed?"

"Mitzi, I...."

She tapped the paper.

"If you don't agree, you've just signed a paper giving me the right to pull up your skirt, pull down your girdle and tan you fanny right now."

Taking her hand, I pulled her towards me. Our lips met.

After we finally came up for air, Mitzi whispered into my ear, "I probably should spank you anyway, just on principle."

Later, Mitzi made a show of counting out the first payment and made me sign a receipt before putting the money in an envelope and hiding it in the bottom of my underwear drawer. After we shared a Coke and some chips she marched me back to the table and placed the large sketchbook before me.

"What's this?"

"It's my planning sketchbook. I lay out projects, try idea, that sort of thing."

"I can see that, what I want to know is," she flipped open the book to a Fifi story, "what type of drawing is this?"

"It's..., sort of like a comic book. A special comic book for a special person."

Mitzi rolled her eyes.

"Ruby Jones! Tell me about these drawings!"

After swallowing deeply several times, I explained about Fifi and how the stories had started. I ended by explaining the latest adventure intended for Jeanie's Christmas.

Mitzi flipped through several pages, then tapped a drawing with her red fingernail.

"Tell me about this drawing."

"The girls have taken Fifi to Egypt as their maid. He's been put into a Harem costume and locked into golden chains."

"You said he. Is Fifi still a boy, or has he become a girl?"

"He's both. A boy when being punished, a girl when he serves his cousins. It wouldn't be right for a boy to see them undressed and, you know, take care of them."

Once more Mitzi rolled her eyes.

"You mean, if you were my maid you wouldn't be able to look at me?"

"Well, of course not. You wouldn't want a boy seeing you without clothes or washing you in the tub."

"My God! I couldn't imagine anything nicer! Go on with the story."

"Anyway, the girls take Fifi to the Souk, that's Arabic for market, and leave him to be fitted with a special gag. See, here's Fifi locked to a stool while all these scruffy men watch his mouth being sealed tight."

"That doesn't look too comfortable."

"It's not suppose to be. After all, Fifi tried to run away, he's being punished."

"Why? I mean, why did he try to run away?"

"I don't know. He loves his cousins and they love him. When she's a good girl Fifi is treated very well, she wears beautiful clothes and expensive jewelry, yet she always revolts and must be punished. Maybe they're all a little looney. Perhaps I only want to make Jeanie happy..., and me happy."

Mitzi slowly went through each page several times, letting her fingers linger over the drawings.

At last, I couldn't stand the tension any longer.

"Are you going to have me arrested and sent to prison?"

She stared at me, her expression blank as an empty page of my sketchbook.

"Why? Why on earth would I do something like that?"

"Because I'm filthy and draw filthy pictures. You won't tell on Jeanie, will you?"

Slowly, her face brightened.

"When I was in France I spent lots of time in book markets and saw many adult books like this. Not as original, not as well drawn, not as humorous and certainly not as erotic. No, Ruby. I would never have you arrested. The next time I'm in Paris I'm going to see if I can find a publisher for your stories. You and Jeanie can split the royalties."

"Oh!"

"Oh, indeed," she whispered. "Now, tell me about this." She plopped the Swiss story on the table. "It's clear you didn't write this and from your sketchbook you don't have a clue what to make of it."

"I'm.... We need the money. Doctor Frank.... He said not to talk about it."

"Doctor Frank? Ah, that greaseball at the college. He gives me the creeps. Okay, this Frank guy offers you money if you illustrate this nutcase story..., if you can call it a story."

"I though I understood. I only skimmed it before I agreed. But now..., there are all those strange words, and the guy enjoys hurting girls. I can't do that. I don't mind drawing girls all tied up, but I can't just hurt them."

She patted my hand. "Okay, settle down. Lets see what we can make of this mess. How much is he offering you?"

"Fifty dollars a drawing, for twenty drawings."

"Wow." She let out a whistle.

"I know, it's a lot. I'd probably be able to stay in school."

"Ruby, he's ripping you off. You do professional work. It'll take you hours to complete each page." She shook her head. "It's too bad I'm not a veterinarian."

"A vet?"

"Yea, there's a lot of men in this world who need neutering."

Since Mitzi had lived in France and Switzerland she was able to understand most of the unusual word structure of the story and even recognized the mystery words as being Romansh, Switzerland's fourth language. I didn't know they had three. By late afternoon we were able to begin bringing the story together. First we agreed to change it from stark realism to a more gentle fantasy. The bloodthirsty monster became a misunderstood eccentric bent on creating the perfect living machine. The girls were hired rather than kidnapped, the bondage permanent but not brutal. Then I started adding a little humor and eroticism.

A problem we could not solve was the man's motivation, especially about one of the girls. Most of the girls were simply pieces of machinery, but one girl received the brunt of his anger, and the tenderness of his love. It just didn't make sense. At first we decided to take our mystery girl out of the story entirely, but the plot became even less clear without her. We were at a standstill.

Fortunately, Mitzi came up with the perfect name for our sometimes hero, which sent us off in another tear of creativity. He became Baron Clyster, which meant Baron Enema in French and pretty well summed up his personality.

"When I was in school in Paris I lived with a French family with three daughters. If any of us had tummy problems, we all got clysters..., and they only had one bathroom and it was downstairs. Lord, what a mess."

"Gosh, that sounds like Momma Jean. At least we girls had our bathroom on the same floor."

Mitzi broke out laughing. When she finally got herself under control she wiped her eyes on a tissue. "Every day I discover how much we're alike. No wonder I love you." She glanced away. "I mean, no wonder I like you."

She drifted to the window. After staring at the surf for a while, she almost whispered.

"Lets take a stroll down the beach. Be sure to bundle up, it's getting chilly."

We walked together, but separate. My stomach was churning. How could I have wounded her so much? I was certain she would abandon me again. I was always hurting the people I loved, yet I never understood how or why. How could I be such a terrible person? I deserved to be tortured a thousand deaths. I should be one of the unfortunate girls in Baron Clyster's clutches.

Mitzi took my hand. After a while she stopped and rubbed my hands between hers.

"You're freezing, I've got to get you inside." Her face lit with excitement. "I understand Baron Clyster now. He's captured someone like you."

"Like me?"

"Yes, a girl who's actually a boy…, or a boy who's actually a girl. I don't know how I think of you. But, our good Baron has captured this beautiful girl who is not really all girl. Does he hate her, or love her? Does he keep her imprisoned or free her? For our story he keeps her, but makes her into the perfect machine in his perfect factory."

"Oh Mitzi, Mitzi, Mitzi! You're wonderful, you're marvelous, you're perfect."

This time I didn't wait, I kissed her as I had always wanted to, like I was a boy kissing a girl. We hugged and danced and kissed while a giant wave sent water swirling around our naked feet. At last, Mitzi swatted me on the backside.

"I can also be a terrible bitch when I'm hungry, and I'm really hungry. Let's see what you can do with that mangy steak. If it's tough, I may have to eat you."

I nestled close to her cheek.

"Would you really eat me."

Her tongue ran lightly across my lips.

"Every inch of you. Every delicate, soft, tasty morsel.... Then I'd expect you to eat me in return."

CHAPTER THIRTY–FIVE

Dateline

The next day we worked like fiends bringing all our ideas for Baron Clyster to life, or what passes for life when the main character is a fictional madman. By midday our original draft was so convoluted it became clear we needed a fresh start. While I fixed sandwiches for lunch, Mitzi got out a blue fiberglass case and dusted off her old Underwood typewriter.

"I did many a book report on this baby," she said, plugging in the cord. "I hope the ribbon is still good."

Rolling a sheet of paper, she pecked out a few words.

Baron Clyster and the Perfect Machine

"Looks pretty good. Do you think living would work better than perfect?"

She painted out perfect and typed in living.

"Yep, that works better," she cooed. "How about fix me another Spam sandwich." She glanced at me and winked. "Them things is addictive."

Through the afternoon Mitzi typed pages while I penciled in a few remaining changes and began laying out each drawing. By six o'clock we were exhausted, but we also had a complete manuscript and the layup for twenty-one panels. I needed the last to bring the story to a proper conclusion. Anyway, for a thousand dollars I could give Doctor Frank an extra drawing.

Mitzi yawned and stretched. "I'm dead. Let's take a walk and have an early night. We have a busy day tomorrow?"

"Oh?"

"It's a surprise."

Hand in hand we trudged about a mile up the beach, letting the cold waves Swirl up to our knees. As we turned to head back, Mitzi made a strange noise, as if she were trying to start a conversation. I waited, she didn't normally have trouble saying her mind. Finally, it tumbled out in a jumble.

"Ummm, Ruby, you don't have, er..., a contract, ummm..., or anything with that nutcase Professor do you?"

"Doctor Frank? No, why would I? We have..., sort of a gentleman's agreement."

"Yeah, but you aren't a gentleman.... Neither is he. I don't trust anyone with three first names. Who would name their child Richard Paul Frank. It's like his parents couldn't decide what name to use."

"Don't be silly! He's got a PhD or something. I don't know, maybe he has two or three. Neither of us has anything."

"Okay, okay! Don't get your girdle twisted. You know my Father is on the Board at Tri-County. This Frank guy has raised a lot of money, but no one is sure where it's going."

I hugged her hand close to my chest. "I'm sorry. I didn't mean to speak sharply. It's just..., Mom and I need this money. I'd be much happier drawing you than the evil Baron, but...."

"I know, you need the money."

Neither of us said anything until just before we reached the beach house.

"Mitzi, have we had out first spat?"

"Now, don't you be silly. Anyway, love..., er, friends can disagree and still remain friends."

She kissed me on the forehead, then the tip of my nose. "You have the cutest nose. Wish mine was that small."

"Well, I wish I had some boobs. Looks like we're both out of luck."

"Not necessarily. There's a doctor in New York who can make boobs bigger or smaller. Perhaps he could take half of mine and give them to you."

"You wouldn't really do that, would you? I mean, have them made smaller. You wouldn't be you."

Her hand drifted down to my tummy, then lower. She had never touched me there, and I certainly had never considered doing that to her.

"A lot of changes can be made to the body these days. You would still be you, but you would also become something completely different. I don't know, I have to think about it more."

I was not at all sure what she meant, yet I knew she was thinking of something monumental, something that might change my life completely. But, what would it do to our relationship? That was the important thing. I could not let her do anything that would tear us apart. One day she would get married. Until then I had to cling to her with every ounce of my strength.

*   *   *   *   *

All through breakfast Mitzi could hardly contain herself. From a lifetime of experience with Jeanie and Daisy, I knew she was planning something diabolical. Soon as I had finished the dishes she sat me on the couch and had me close my eyes. After a few moments I felt something placed in my lap.

"Okay, open wide!"

It was a package wrapped in bright pink paper tied with a gigantic red ribbon. There was a card that read,

Red Ruby, Red Ruby
It's payback time!
Happy Unbirthday.

"Now I'm Alice?"

"Oh, you guessed that too quick. Go on, open your present."

I carefully unwrapped the box, taking as long as possible so Mitzi's excitement could build. I was at a complete loss and had not the slightest idea what trick she was playing on me. At long last I removed the top and lifted out a very heavy duty open bottom girdle.

Mitzi strutted about and stroked an imaginary mustache.

"Well, Mon Amie, can you guess?" she said in her best Hercule Poirot voice.

"It's your Always 21 girdle"

"In that, Mademoiselle, you would be incorrect. I tell you, it is **your** Always 21 as I predicted the first time you made me wear it. Mon Dieu, Hastings, it is time for payback."

The girdle felt as if it weighed ten pounds and was constructed mostly of stiff satin panels and steel bones. Standing, I held it against my middle. It was beautiful, but deadly.

"I couldn't blast my way into this in a week."

She nibbled at my earlobe and whispered, "Come on Ruby. Today is a special treat for both of us. If I could stand it all evening, you can make it through the day. Anyway, you're Fifi today and don't have any say in what happens."

I nodded. "If I die, at least you wont have trouble stretching me out in the coffin."

Mitzi stood silently with her arms crossed during the ten minutes it took to struggle into the girdle, then had to help zip me since my panties kept catching in the heavy hooks. The stockings almost killed me since I couldn't lean over very well. Again, she had to help, this time to close the back garters. While she was attaching the garters she took the opportunity to do a lot of poking, prodding and tickling back there and I was incredibly agitated by the time she finished. After my padded bra, the one that inflated me from an A to a B Cup was fastened, I stepped into white pumps and simply had to gaze at my reflection in the mirror. My body was firmly contained from above the bust to well below my hips. My tummy was absolutely flat and the back panel had turned my tush into a single, well-controlled mound. Some women were girdled like this all the time, but it was a completely new feeling for me. My waist was a couple of inches bigger than Mitzi, so I was really compressed. I tried to take a deep breath, which only served to make my tiny boobies swell more dramatically.

After my makeup, which Mitzi oversaw with excruciating detail, she helped me into my prettiest but also shortest slip and dress, then doused me with her favorite perfume. A tiny patent clutch just big enough to hold a compact, lipstick, two super tampons, an ink pen and my glasses completed my costume. That meant I had no money and no identification. More important, being stuck with a clutch, which had no strap, meant at least one of my hands was occupied all the time. In a way, it was as if I were partially bound, which made me feel even more completely under her control. As a final check she had me walk across the bedroom and back several times, making tiny adjustments in my dress or hair until I at last passed her inspection. My biggest problem was that the girdle wanted to keep me ridged, while the spike heels made my fanny swing. It was going to be a long, long day.

To drive home my situation, she next took me into her bedroom and stood me facing a corner while she dressed. Having her so close and doing intimate things while I stared at the wall made me even more frustrated. When I was at long last allowed to turn around she stood before me in the satin blouse I had made for her, men's trousers, asexual shoes, hair severely pulled back and no makeup. She appeared half girl and half boy, or at least like a beautiful woman wanting to be half boy.

"Okay, Sweetie Pie, you're my date and you'd best be a good girl." Her hands worked down my satin hips and around to my fanny, her tongue slid delicately across my lips. "Baron Clyster has ways to deal with pretty young things who misbehave."

After we finished smooching she had to completely rework my lipstick.

I had to sit boldly upright during the hour drive into the city. Fortunately we were in a sports car, which allowed Mitzi to zip into a tiny space on Meeting Street not far from all the best shops. We began with leisurely window shopping so people could gape at the girly-girl, me, being lead around by…, whatever they though Mitzi might be. It wasn't clear which she was enjoying more, the attention I was receiving or the ruckus she was causing.

We window shopped for a while more before she guided me into an upscale men's store and straight to a display of expensive blue jeans.

"Mitzi," I whispered. "Mom will never let me wear jeans."

"Don't be silly, I wouldn't let you wear them either. These are for me."

"You? Anything that fits your hips will swallow your waist.

She held a pair against her waist.

"See, even a size smaller will be far too big in the waist."

By this time a smarmy salesman approached.

"May I help you ladies? Jeans are becoming quiet popular among the fair sex."

I frowned at him, but he didn't go away.

"May I suggest this style, Madam? Or this? And, perhaps a pair of these?"

Holding the first pair against Mitzi, I shook my head. The second pair were better, the final ones the best.

"We need one size smaller in these. This other pair is worth a look, you'll need to try them on."

Mitzi made a face at me, them tossed the strap of her bag over my shoulder. Now I had to keep track of two pocketbooks. A few minutes later she emerged in the first pair.

"Okay, I can salvage those. Try the other pair."

More waiting. The salesman looked more uncomfortable than I felt. I could see him trying to figure us out. Were we friends, lovers, relatives? Who was in charge. Even I didn't know the answers, yet when it came to clothing I was definitely in charge. I would not let Mitzi wear anything that detracted from her beauty.

When she came out, she slowly turned around so we could admire the countryside. I had to admit, the jeans made her fanny look stunning, but the entire waist area would need adjusting, which was not going to be easy with all that colored stitching and rivets.

"Can you fix them?"

Nodding, I pointed toward the mirrors. "I'll need to mark some darts. Will you wear them with flats or heels."

"Heels, of course. These will be a fashion statement."

"They'll be a statement alright. Hold still."

I borrowed the Salesman's chalk and marked darts at all the seams and two smaller ones on either side of the back seam. Since it was clear I was too restricted to reach her feet, I had to let the salesman mark the hem, taking into account she would be in heels. All this time the salesman and I were handing off the pocketbooks and marking chalk.

"Right, let's do the other pair."

Without blinking, Mitzi unsnapped, then unzipped the jeans and peeled them off, revealing a baby blue panty girdle and dark gray stockings. Both the salesman and I almost swallowed our tongues. As nonchalantly, she climbed into the second pair and I marked them. Afterward, I marched her to the changing room to finish dressing. One view of her in the girdle and stockings was all I could manage.

After she paid, Mitzi took my purse and before I realized what she was doing, unsnapped the clasp and took out the two tampons.

"Now, I know you had a pen in here," she said, digging deeper into the purse. "Ah, here it is." She turned to the salesman, my tampons in one hand, the pen in the other. "Do you have a slip of paper I could have?"

The salesman stared at the tampons, his face growing redder by the minute. I'm sure he though I was having my period. Anyway, flashing a pair of super tampons in a men's store was not something most women would consider. Following a lot of fumbling, the man came up with the back of a sale flier. Mitzi printed at the top, *Contract*. Next she added, *Design woman's jeans*. She smiled at me.

"Darling, you can design jeans that would fit women?"

I nodded. "But, who would purchase them?"

She smiled sweetly. "Don't worry your pretty head. You design 'em, I'll sell them." Turning to the salesman, she extended her hand. "Thank you sir, you were most helpful."

Following her from the store, I almost ran to catch up, which was not easy in that tight girdle.

"Mitzi, I can't believe you did that."

"What?"

"Everything. Taking off your pants, showing my tampons. Everything."

"Didn't you enjoy yourself? I thought you were going to pop your cork when I took off those jeans. You should have seen your face."

Taking her hand, I held it against my cheek. "I did enjoy seeing you like that, and fitting the jeans, and even having you flash those tampons. I thought the salesman was going to have an attack. He'll probably whack off over you tonight. But, I love you so much. I don't want you hurt. I don't want people to think bad of you. I don't want you to think terrible things about me."

"Oh, sweet baby. You're so special to me also. This may be the last time I see you alone. My life is getting so hectic, with business and school and Mother wanting me to get married. At my age she was already a wife and mother. She can't understand that things are different now. That I'm different. That I don't particularly like men. I don' t hate them, I just don't want them screwing me. It's been so wonderful being with you. No pressure. No demands.

You just follow my lead like a little puppy and you make me feel very important. Let's have a beautiful day."

"I just don't want you hurt…, except maybe by being put in this girdle, which is killing me."

"Good. That's exactly what you need."

*   *   *   *   *

We took a carriage ride through the old part of the city, then enjoyed lunch at a street-side table. The weather had warmed beautifully and the shops were filled with locals and tourists. Mitzi had to help me in the ladies room since the only way I could pee pee was to straddle the toilet, which required about six hands to make sure everything stayed dry. At one point we were both laughing so hard the lady in the next stall surely thought we were having a party.

We simply cycled through most of the shops, as if Mitzi was only interested in what they were stocking and the prices. Since I had no money and Mom made my clothing, I was only interested in what was fashionable. I didn't let current fashion dictate my designs, but it was important to know what women were purchasing. We would visit a few shops, then go into one of the old churches or pubs or theaters. Mitzi seemed to know the history of every ancient building and who shot who over someone's wife or lover, and how the pirates got their loot into town, or where some first this or that took place. In some ways it was like being on a school field trip, except the teacher was interesting as well as beautiful. Of course, it didn't hurt that she let me put my arm round her waist or that she had the erotic habit of nibbling my earlobes, which simply drove me wild.

It was getting near dinner when we entered a small but elegant shop in a delightful little alley. Immediately, I felt uncomfortable. All the designs were outdated and drab.

They were for little old ladies. The few customers were as decrepit and ancient as the styles. Well, the ladies really weren't that old but they should have been.

"Mitzi, lets get out of here. This place gives me the creeps."

"Why, this is a very upscale shop. Look at the name on this suit..., and look at the price. Don't you think I'd look good in this?"

"That wouldn't look good in purple, much less in drab gray. It would help if you added a gay blouse and shoes, maybe a double strand of pearls. Even then it would make you look fifty, maybe sixty. You want clothing to make you look younger, not older. Well, unless you're an underage teen trying to buy a drink."

"And you know about such stuff? The strongest thing you drink is Coke on ice."

"I do go out with Jeanie, you know. She tries to get a beer now and then. Anyway, there's nothing here for you."

She made a face. "How about this case of jewelry. There are several lovely pieces. What do you like?"

After studying the case for a while I pointed. "This little heart pendant is very nice. It would look lovely on you, especially with the matching earrings. Oh, and this bracelet just screams your name."

"How about this platinum and diamond pendant. I could wear it right between my boobs, that should attract some attention."

"It would attract attention alright! Like you need something to draw attention to your boobs. I threw up my arms. "Mitzi, sometimes you drive me to distraction."

By now we had gotten the attention of everyone in the shop and a crinkled old lady hobbled over. "May I help you young people," she said with a quivering voice."

"Yes you may," answered Mitzi. "But first I must send this naught child outside to cool off. Ruby, outside. Sit on that bench until I'm finished here."

"Mitzi, I...."

"Ruby! Outside!"

"Yes, Mother." I stuck out my tongue.

It must have taken her half and hour, but at last she sat beside me.

"I'm sorry, Mitzi. I only want you to be beautiful. I don't mind if men stare at you, I just don't want them to think you're a..., well, you know."

"A prostitute?"

"Well, a loose woman."

"Is that why you want me in girdles?"

"No, because you look better, and you feel so nice and smooth. And, because, I don't know, I just like it. You didn't buy that awful pendant, did you?"

"Perhaps. We'll see. Come on, there's a restaurant near here I want to try."

"Mitzi, will you help me in the bathroom again. I'm about to drown."

"That's what you get for drinking all that Coke. See, drinking can get a girl in trouble."

Soon as we entered, I knew the restaurant was far out of my price range. Mitzi spoke French with the Maître d' who immediately showed us to a secluded table. I didn't know if that was to give us privacy, or because we were two females, one very feminine and flat chested, me, and the other overloaded and butch, who were clearly more than casual acquaintances.

Before long we had gigantic, leather–bound menus. Actually, Mitzi returned my menu and announced she would order for both. Instead of sitting opposite me at the small table, she had her setting moved next to me so we could talk. It wasn't long before her hand was on my knee, then beneath my skirt. We did talk, but in hushed whispers, except when we were giggling. The waiter brought Mitzi a glass of wine and my crystal goblet of water was decorated with a slice of lime and a hibiscus flower.

Next came oysters, which I definable was not sure about. But, she kept sliding them in my mouth. Once they get between your lips, there's only one place for them to go. She said they were to awaken my libido. Since I had no idea what a libido was, I had no idea if that was good or bad. Following came Crab Imperial for me and shrimp 'n grits for her. She fed me much of her shrimp and I fed her most of my crab. Both were the best dishes I had tasted. She also kept slipping me sips of her wine, which soon had my head spinning.

While we were waiting for desert of Bananas Foster, Mitzi stepped behind me and placed something over my head. I looked down and nestled in the tiny valley between my breasts lay the ruby heart.

She kissed me gently on the neck and whispered, "Rubies for my Ruby. You know what happens when you're tricked into a necklace?"

"I become your slave."

This time she kissed me full on the lips, in front of God and everybody.

*   *   *   *   *

I don't remember the Bananas Foster, or the drive home. My heart was so full of happiness I could have burst. Mitzi helped me undress and into my rubber brief and swimsuit.

"Go start the hot tub." she said. "I'll be out soon as I change."

By now I knew how to switch on the bubbles and tiny light in the bottom of the pool. To make everything cozier

I switched off all the other lights, cranked up the gas logs to high and started the Tchaikovsky. I had barely slipped into the tub when Mitzi appeared wearing a thick terry robe. She towered over me, staring up at the Milky Way far overhead. Slowly, her fingers loosened the belt and let the robe fall free. She was like a Greek statue in alabaster. But, instead of her red suit, now she wore only a rubber brief and the night air. Moments later she was beside me, her hands behind my neck.

"We don't need these ol' straps, they get in the way."

The front of my suit peeled away, then she helped me out of the bottom.

I scarcely remember when we left the tub, or snuggling on the sheepskin before the blazing fireplace. I do recall tumbling deep beneath the sheets while the wild surf crashed and roared against the beach, and the taste of her flesh as I worshiped every inch of her being. Then we slept, tangled, each within the others arms.

CHAPTER THIRTY–SIX

Endless Night

Once more the sun was high when I awoke, this time to the clack of typewriter keys. Sometime during the night we had peeled out of our Playtex briefs. Mine was neatly folded on the nightstand while Mitzi's was tossed far across the room. Slipping on a housecoat and sandals I yawned my way to the great room. Mitzi was hunched over the typewriter, a steaming cup of coffee in one hand while she pecked away with the other. She glanced up and stopped pecking.

"I was ready to call the undertaker."

Mumbling something unintelligible, I plopped next to her. "Ugggg. My head."

"I told you to lay off the Coke." She rolled the sheet of paper from the typewriter. "This is a draft contract. Mr. Green at the Bank will contact you about the final version."

"Final version? Of what?"

"The contract. Ruby, are you awake or not?"

"I'm not sure. Explain in tiny words so I can understand."

"It's very simple. That shop you hated is owned by my grandmother. I'm hiring you to design some livelier outfits and accessories. The clientele is older, but not yet in the grave. Grandma's present designer must be ninety and her clothing looks it. Also, here at the bottom it states you're also to design some girl's jeans, those are for me, but I'll let Grandma pay. She likes when I show initiative."

"Mitzi." I took her hand. "Yesterday was wonderful, and last night was the most marvelous experience I've ever had."

"Oh? Well, I thought you might like it. Consider it an early Christmas present." She glanced at her watch. "Look, it's already late. We need to close up here. I'm suppose to attend a concert with Mother and Dad tonight." She began stacking the papers she had been working on. "I typed a final version of our story, it's in your sketchbook. Be sure to read through the contract. Let me know if you require any changes." She waved her hand at me. "Hop to, go take a shower and get dressed. You smell like a rubber girdle."

With that, she was off to the kitchen. I felt old and very tired. The previous night had been the most exciting and delightful of my life, yet to Mitzi it was nothing more than an amusement. Something to pass time at the beach when things got too boring. How could I ever hope to understand someone so utterly different? How could I love her so desperately, while I meant less than nothing to her? When would I learn I was a big zero?

We cleaned till the house was spotless, then packed and got underway. My heart was so heavy I said nothing for hours. Mitzi drove like a demon, but slowed as we neared home.

"Ruby, when you finish those drawings you are not to take them directly to Doctor Frank. Once he gets his hands on them you will have nothing. He can cheat you and the courts would be powerless to help. It would be your word against his. He's a man, a professor, and an upstanding member of society. You're a boy living as a girl. You know who the court would believe."

"But, he said he'd give me a thousand dollars for the drawings."

"He can say anything. Take William or Papa Henry with you, and maybe a pair of brass knuckles. Only, don't just walk in and give your work away. Look, at least do this. The Bank has a large camera thing that makes copies of artwork for insurance companies. I'll have Mr. Green set up a safe deposit box for you. As you finish pages, put them in large envelopes and store them in the box. When I come home for university I'll photograph them. At least you'll have a high resolution photo of each page."

"Okay, if you think it's necessary. It just doesn't feel right to question my betters."

"Betters? Ruby, Sweetheart, he isn't your better. He's only older and a man. That doesn't make him better than you."

We drove in silence. There was so much I wanted to say, how I worshiped her and could never live without her. But, I was only a plaything, a momentary diversion to fill her spare time.

When we were a block form my house, Mitzi pulled to the side and stopped.

"Ruby, Dearest. We can never do this again. I can't keep shutting down my feelings. This week has been heaven and last night ecstatic, but I'm being unfair to you."

"No! I love you, with all my heart."

"I love you too, but can't you see how hopeless this is? No matter who I marry, no man is going to let us be special friends. We've got to stop, before I completely ruin your life."

"Please, destroy me. That would be better than living without you."

Closing her eyes, she slowly shook her head.

"No, Sweetheart. It's over."

She rammed the car into gear and squealed from the curb and into our drive. Neither of us said a word as she unloaded my bags and then tore away. She did not look back. This time I knew our relationship was over.

*   *   *   *   *

I did what I always did when my heart was breaking. I began working like a fiend, eighteen hours a day as long as I could stand it. Then I'd crash and sleep for a few days before starting the cycle over again.. Mitzi's down payment on the painting got Mom and me back on our feet, and every time I completed a group of designs I'd get a check from her grandmother. The Baron drawings were progressing well, and I did as Mitzi ordered. Soon there was a thick stack of envelopes in my safe deposit box. However, the painting of Mitzi's puppy simply was not advancing at all. I tried sketching her running, jumping, playing and even sleeping. Nothing seemed to catch the essence of a real dog.

Schoolwork, on the other hand, was progressing well. Since I had absolutely no social life, there was noting to waste my time.

Actually, I did have one diversion, spending time with Big Mike and Jake. There could not have been a less likely combination, yet they were much more like big brothers than William or Buddy had ever been. With my Ladybug beetle and their huge van being the most visible vehicles in town, we could always spot each other, even in the dark of night or pouring rain. We'd flash lights, honk horns and wave like fools every time we passed, which would remind me to bake them more cookies or cakes or take them burgers and Cokes. They were always roaming around helping Snowbirds heading to or returning from Florida, and they listened to the police and highway patrol radios to find stranded motorists. I painted a watercolor of Ladybug with its hood open like a mouth chasing them down the road while I ran behind. They liked it so much they insisted William hang it in the Chevy showroom, which led to another article in the paper and a lot of publicly for me and the dealership, so I suppose having weird friendships was not such a bad thing after all.

The day finally arrived when all of the Baron Clyster drawings were complete and photographed. Mitzi had placed the originals in a leather folder in my safe deposit box so they would be ready for delivery to Doctor Frank. Just before the Bank closed, I entered and retrieved the folder. Quickly counting the envelopes to make sure all twenty–one were there, I tied the folder shut with a strong red ribbon and drove out to the Chevy dealership to pick up William who had agreed to go with me to see the good professor. After all, I was going to get a thousand dollars in cash. Mitzi had been right, it would be unsafe not to have a strong man along. I smiled to myself, thinking of what Mitzi would say, 'Well, my dear, men do have *some* uses.'

William was tied up in a meeting with the owners of the dealership. I waited. And waited. And waited. Sounds of argument came from William's office. I waited more. Now it was pitch black outside and the school building would soon be closed and locked. I thought about that thousand dollars. How much Mom needed that money. I checked, Big Mike and Jake were out on a call. I though more about that thousand dollars. Damn! I was a big girl, if not a big man. I could handle this on my own. I did not have to be a shrinking violet all my life.

Soon I was in Ladybug heading for Tri–County. Big Mike and Jake's van appeared from the darkness. I flashed my lights, honked and waved. They returned my salute.

Onward I drove through the deepening darkness. All the while I kept counting that thousand dollars, counting the bills Mom could pay, and relishing the thoughts of her finally being proud of her little boy–girl. I screeched to a halt before the main steps and hopped out. The school building was almost completely black, but a dim light flashed from a slit between the curtains of Doctor Frank's office. Was he still in, or had he simply forgotten to turn off his lights? Racing to the top of the steps, I peeked through the tiny slit.

Doctor Frank was leaning against his desk talking to a boy in front of him. Well, actually, they weren't talking. They were kissing. Then the boy dropped to his knees and began fiddling with Doctor Frank's trousers. Something pink and gigantic came out, many inches long and several in diameter. The boy took the end into his mouth, just barely, the thing could scarcely fit between the boy's lips. Like a lightning bolt it hit. I understood what was happening. I wanted to turn away, to run, to vomit. All I could do was stare through that slit. I had no idea a man could be that big, no notion any boy would take it in his mouth, nor an idea any boy would then try to swallow the whole thing.

Vice–like fingers clamped onto my right arm. Seconds later more hands secured my other arm, easily twisting my wrist back and upwards between my shoulder blades.

"What in hell are you looking at, Cunt?"

"She's spying on the Professor. Christ, get her inside."

"No. Help, you're hurting me. I came to see Doctor Frank."

"You're gonna see him alright, Bitch."

"Butch Spence! What are you doing here? Let me go this instance. Agggg! That hurts."

"It's nothing to what you're gonna feel if you don't shut up. Come on, get her to the Professor."

We burst through the door as Doctor Frank was pumping his thing deeper into the boys mouth. Both of them looked more surprised than I had been.

"What the shit? Get that bitch our of here."

"She was snooping, right outside your window," screamed Butch. "She's seen everything."

Doctor Frank nonchalantly pulled his thing from the boy's mouth and stuffed it back into his trousers, as if nothing at all had happened.

"Well, well. If it isn't our little jewel."

"I..., I didn't see anything, Professor. I have your drawings. Just give me my money and I won't ever say anything."

He calmly took the folder, untied the ribbon and glanced inside.

"They're all there. Twenty—one of them, but you only need to pay me for the twenty we agreed on. An even thousand dollars and I'll be gone."

His face broke into a wide smile. "Were you actually stupid enough to think I'd pay you? I knew you were a social dwarf, I never imagined you were an idiot."

"She isn't very smart, Professor," said Butch. "No one will believe her anyway. We can probably let her go."

"Don't be an idiot," shot Doctor Frank. "She knows everything and if there's one thing this bitch can't do is keep her mouth shut. Which means.... We have to shut it for her. Put her hand together in back."

I tried to resist, which was more than futile against two hulking boys. Doctor Frank snatched the ribbon from the folder and wound it tightly about my wrists. This was nothing like Jeanie tying me with bows. The ribbon was wound ten times tighter and tied in an impossible knot.

"Please, that's too tight. You're hurting me!"

Before I knew what was happening, he spun me around and swung his palm against my face. If the boys hadn't caught me I would have collapsed onto the floor.

"That'll teach you to spy on me. Take the cunt to the cemetery. Leave her car near one of the entrances. When you finish with your fun, hit her in the head and leave her body near the drunks. Everyone will think they killed her." He laughed. "Someone should do something about that cemetery, it's really not a safe place."

I was bundled into the back seat of my beetle with one of the guys while Butch climbed behind the wheel. At first he couldn't get it started.

"Don't give it so much gas, you'll flood it."

"Shut up, Bitch," he drew back his fist, like he was going to smash me in the face.

"You shut up, idiot! Ruby, what do I do?"

"Take your foot off the gas. Turn the key, it'll start."

After a couple of tries, he got it started and we lurched off as he let his foot off the clutch too fast.

"Butch, you can't do this. You'll end up in the electric chair."

Again the guy threatened me with his fist.

"I told you to shut your trap, cunt. Next time I'll drive this fist down your throat."

"She's right." Butch looked back over his shoulder and almost ran off the road. "Sucking off th' Professor is one thing, this is another. We can't do this."

The fellow in the back seat slapped Butch beside the head. "You shut ya' trap too. Drive, dammit!" He turned his attention back to me and started rubbing between my legs. "Too bad we won't have time to fuck you in th' pussy and ass. I'll bet you're a fuckin' virgin and I ain't had no fresh pussy in a long time."

For some incredible reason my mind realized I actually was a virgin. I had slept with Daisy and Jeanie as sisters, not to mention Mitzi on our wild night, yet I had not made love to any of them, at least not like a boy. I had never reached a climax and was not sure I could. At least I was not going to die as an old maid, I was going to die as an idiot, and I deserved what was coming.

An oncoming vehicle flashed its lights. A horn beeped. I turned in time to see Big Mike's face flash by. That was the last time I would see him, or William or Buddy. I'd never hug Daisy or Jeanie, never kiss Mitzi. Mom and Momma Jean flashed through my head. I hadn't finished Mitzi's painting..., hadn't designed her jeans. Everything was over. I had failed everyone.

Butch bounced onto the sidewalk and slid to a stop outside the Confederate Cemetery. Another car screeched behind us. After being hauled out of the back seat, they drug me down the winding paths and stopped beside one of the tombs. Two of them forced me to my knees while the other fiddled with his zipper.

"Dammit, Dammit, God Dammit! Th' fuckin' zipper...."

At last the zipper opened and he fished out his erect meat and rubbed the head across my mouth. Suddenly, slime spurted over my face.

"God Dammit, see what you've done."

He started to slug me, but the other boy forced him aside and rammed his thing deep into my mouth. I was gagging and suffocating, all I could do was bite as hard as I could as my throat was filled with more slime.

"Ahhhaaa! Th' whore bit me. I'm bleeding to death."

Butch was standing over me, a broken piece of cement in his hand.

"Do it! Fuck her and bash her head in."

Butch shook his head.

"Do it, Asshole, or give me the rock."

They fought a moment, then the concrete lifted and something slammed into my back. Everything went black, then stars, then screaming and dull thuds. Again all was black.

*   *   *   *   *

Someone gently turned me over and wiped my face. I was lifted, up, high into the air. With the greatest effort my eyes opened.

"Mi…, Big Mike. Please. Please help…."

"I've got you now, Miss Ruby. Don't you die on me. I've got you."

For a final time, all went black.

CHAPTER THIRTY–SEVEN

Bells and Rings

Light came several times among hushed voices, yet I never could reach them. Always they remained just out of reach. No matter how hard I tried no one could hear my screams. I was alone, so very alone.

Then the light returned. It took forever to understand this was not Heaven…, or Hell. It was Jeanie's room and she was sleeping beside me. I tried to call her, yet nothing came from my mouth. Her eyes fluttered. She placed an arm around me.

"Is little Ruby back among us?"

All I could do was nod. At last I managed, "Drink."

After pouring ice water into a glass, Jeanie lifted my head and let me sip.

"Get…. Get up. Late for work."

"Whoa. Baby isn't going anywhere."

Then the darkness returned.

I came and went. Always a different face greeted me. Then some spark seemed to refill my lungs and I was alive once more. Now I remembered what had happened, but there was no memory at all from the cemetery to Jeanie's room.

"How long?"

"Many days. Doc Pricher kept pumping you with happy juice. He said sleep was your best medicine."

"But, they killed me."

Jeanie helped me sit up. "Well, they didn't do a very good job."

"Butch hit me in the head with a big block. I felt it."

"What you probably felt was Big Mike's knee when he attacked."

"Big Mike? I thought he was taking me to Heaven."

"It was close. When Ladybug didn't respond to his greeting, Big Mike knew something was wrong. It took them a while to find your car. Only Butch Spence would have been dumb enough to leave something like the Beetle run up on a sidewalk. Anyway, Mike and Jake grabbed tire irons and charged into the cemetery. All the shouting led them directly to you. Fortunately, Butch and one of the other guys were fighting over the rock, so they didn't see Mike and Jake till the last second. By then it was too late."

"Oh Lord! The guys didn't kill anyone, did they?"

"Close. Mike says it's because all those cookies have made him weak. You'll be glad to know those three assholes are now heroes."

"Heroes? You've got to be kidding."

"The story in the papers is that a bunch of drunks wantonly attacked three upstanding young leaders of tomorrow and left them for dead in the cemetery. One revived enough to call the police. The three were rescued. If you can believe it, this attack has finally spurred the city to clean up the cemetery."

"And..., Professor Frank?"

"Last seen taking a position in Toronto."

"With my drawings."

"And over a hundred thousand unaccounted dollars from Tri–County."

"Mitzi? I suppose she's laughing. She told me what would happen. I got greedy. All I could think about was getting that money for Mom. Now I've lost the money and my drawings. She must think I'm totally stupid."

"I have no idea what she thinks, but stupid probably isn't one of them. She's been taking her turn sitting with you and I've seen her doing a lot of praying."

I kept rubbing my face. I could feel and taste their slime all over me.

"Jeanie, will you help me bathe. I've never felt so filthy."

"Sure, Baby. Let me run a nice hot bath."

"I'm sorry to be so much bother."

She pulled my head against her breast. "After all the times you've taken care of me, I'll gladly give you a million bathes if it makes you feel better."

We desperately clung to each other, as if our lives could melt into one. But in my mind I could only see Butch squirting into my face and his taste filled my throat. I knew I'd never get the sight out of my mind, or the taste from my mouth.

*   *   *   *   *

It took weeks for my full strength to return, but I was now a changed person. Everything was my fault. I had been greedy. Only I could have been so careless and stupid. I could not even go to the police. After all, I was a boy living as a girl. My entire life was a lie. My dreams of breaking free and becoming something were all lies. I was nothing and would never be anything.

I dropped out of school, buried myself under work. Every day I though about killing myself. But, I was too much of a coward to do even that. No, that was not true. There were things I had to do first. Mitzi's painting. I had to finish her painting, yet I could not begin. Whenever I stared at a canvas all I saw was Butch Spence squirting in my face. Jeans, I had to design the jeans, yet I could not. And the contract. I had signed a contract with Mitzi. How could I kill myself when I had promised to be her slave? So many other duties. Duties, always duties. Mom? How would she earn a living without me? What would happen when Jeanie became sick? Who would take care of her? And, Mitzi. How could I leave Mitzi. Oh, Lord. How could I leave Mitzi.

Day by day I sank deeper into myself. My only answer was to work harder, longer, anything to keep from thinking. Sixty hours a week, seventy, one hundred hours were not enough. Summer came and disappeared, Autumn began, then grew old. I gave up eating, sleeping. Work, only work.

At times I would stare at a canvas for hours, trying to force my hand to paint, yet all I saw was Butch. My eyes closed. This was the end, I simply could not live another day.

As my eyes opened, Butch was no longer before me. Now I could see only Mitzi and her puppy. With a shaking hand I penciled in the big stone fireplace. Oils squirted from tubes, brushes appeared in my hand. Yes, the fireplace, with real logs and real flames. Next, Mitzi, partially in shadow, part glowing with life and flames. Yes, Mitzi as I remembered her from the fourth grade. Still slightly gangly, but the beauty was already in her cheeks. Pigtails, tied with pink ribbons. One across her shoulder, the other behind. That little gingham jumper with the big pockets and a handkerchief peaking out. Her eyes, large, huge, with their deep stare of knowledge that frightened all the boys. Sleeping at her side lay Curly, head resting contentedly in Mitzi's lap while dreams of rabbits and balls and sticks filled her head.

Hour after hour my vision became life on the canvas. I was starving, thirsty. Mom forced a Spam sandwich into my left hand and held an iced glass of Coke to my lips. At last I took my smallest brush and lettered, *Buddies*, followed by *Ruby*, then lay down the brushes and palette before settled into a chair. Never had I been more exhausted, or more alive. Mom knelt beside me.

"Ruby, my sweet Ruby. It's marvelous, beautiful, wonderful. The best you've every painted. Mitzi is alive, staring at us from the fireplace. It's as if she's peering deep into my heart."

"Mom, do you hate me? I lost the drawings, the thousand dollars."

"Of course not, I love you more than life itself. You're my baby, you'll always be my baby."

I tried to stand, my legs gave way.

"I don't think I can get upstairs."

"That's alright, Baby. William will carry you.

My eyes closed.

* * * * *

By Thanksgiving I was feeling much better. Instead of helping cook, I mostly napped on the couch. No one seemed to mind. Perhaps they were happy not having to eat my pecan pies. The next week I cooked a giant batch of cookies, picked up a half dozen burgers and visited Big Mike and Jake. We all did a lot of hugging and crying, but I've never enjoyed a burger more than sitting in their greasy little office. There's simply nothing like munching with true friends.

Now it dawned on me that I had made no plans for Christmas. For most of my life I hated the thought of the

Holidays. It was a time of dreary weather and dashed hopes. I never received even the simple toys I dreamed about, and a couple pair of socks and an orange was worst than no gift at all. Santa always forget our house or left a piece of coal in my striped sock hung on the mantle. How different life had become. All I could think about was filling other people's dreams. Fifi and candy for Jeanie, dresses for Daisy, exotic delicacies for Mom and Momma Jean. Tickets for Papa Henry and William to watch Buddy play in his first Bowl game. A whole packet of naughty comic books for Buddy.

I had the painting for Mitzi's father, but what could I get for her? My mind was a complete blank. After all, I had made such a fool of myself, there really was no way I could mend our relationship. She was a lost cause. That was a part of my broken heart I could never mend. Well, it was probably best to keep our relationship strictly on a business basis. She would stop by on Christmas Eve, I would give her the painting, she would give me the final payment. Purely business. No emotional attachment. Simple, straight to the point, no emotions. The painting was framed, wrapped in bright paper and sealed with a huge red ribbon. What could be simpler?

The day finally came. Jeanie, Daisy and I practiced carols. Mom and I planned the menu. I began cooking. William and Buddy set up the tree, we all pitched in with the decorating. Mom worked on the eggnog and everyone sipped a little special recipe. The clock ticked. At last Momma Jean and Papa Henry arrived. Now, Christmas could begin.

For hours we ate and drank and sang, then ate more, followed by even more drinking and singing. Around nine o'clock the bell rang and Mom led Mitzi into the kitchen. I breathed deeply. This was business, nothing but business.

I brought out the painting. We shook hands. She handed me an envelope, I placed in on the mantle. Then I saw it. The diamond on the third finger of her left hand. It was gigantic and sparkled like it was filled with fireworks. My heart stopped, then slowly sputtered along. I could not breathe. The day had finally arrived. Mitzi was engaged. I tried to speak, nothing came out.

Mom handed Mitzi a glass brimming with eggnog.

"Here, Mitzi, won't you join us in a glass of Special Recipe? Ruby's grandmother developed it years ago...."

They walked away and everyone gathered around Mitzi. I could see she was showing them the engagement ring. There was a lot of oohing, giggling and whispering followed by several rounds of congratulations. I was frozen, unable to think or move. This at last was the end. As Mitzi herself had said, no husband would let his wife have a special relationship with another woman, much less a boy playing at being a girl. If only she would leave, so I could run and cry. Instead she, laughing with my family while I died.

Suddenly, Mom grabbed my right hand and drug me into the middle of everyone.

"Ruby, come see what Mitzi has."

Mitzi took my left hand and dropped to one knee. Taking the engagement ring from her finger she held it against mine.

"I can't go on this way. I've loved you since grammar school. Ruby Jones, would you do me the honor..., would you make me the happiest woman.... Ruby, will you be my wife?"

"Wah.... What?"

"She's asking you to marry her," screamed Daisy and Jeanie. "Don't be a Doofus. Tell her yes."

"Yes. Yes! Oh, God, Yes!"

The ring slipped onto my finger.

Then she kissed me, like I'd never been kissed, while I melted into her arms.

CHAPTER THIRTY–EIGHT

Satin Mists

With me, nothing was ever easy. All this happiness before I remembered I had nothing to give Mitzi for Christmas. The only thing to do was admit my failings.

"But Darling, you've just given yourself, what more could I ask for," she replied. "If it make you feel better, I don't have a present for you either." She gave her classic grin. "However, I do have a little something for us to share."

She handed me a thin box, which I tore into with my normal reserve. Inside was a thin book with a gold embossed leather cover. Across the cover was emblazoned, **Baron Clyster et la Maquine Vivante.**

"I had to translate it into French, but they also plan to publish an English version. Next they'll bring out, **Les Aventures de Fifi.**"

"But, Mitzi. How? Doctor Frank stole the originals."

"Actually, he stole proof copies. I knew you were too trusting to check what I was doing. When I photographed the originals I simply made a duplicate set of proofs."

"What's that?"

"That means your brilliant professor now has a set of completely black photos. I had no idea he'd try to kill you. I figured he'd be satisfied to steal your work."

"But...."

"That's why I'm marrying you. You're too trusting to run around free. I'm keeping you on a tight leash from now on." She stared deep into my eyes. "I hope that's alright."

"Woof, woof." Was all I could think to say.

*   *   *   *   *

Planning a wedding for two girls was not the easiest undertaking, even if one of them was a boy in dresses. There was no doubt I was going to be the wife and everyone agreed I should be in a wedding dress. What wasn't so clear was how Mitzi should dress. Two frothy dresses in white satin seemed slightly over the top, yet I didn't want to see her in a man's tux. In the end I designed a girl's outfit of black satin trousers and white coat with tails. Her blouse was cut even lower than my dress, which left no question as to her gender, while also giving me something to gaze at. I was to wear a satin and steel Merry Widow that almost cut me in two, while Mitzi selected a lightweight panty girdle and bra in baby blue. Other than that, I left my dress and trousseau completely to Mom. After all, I was her only daughter and she had dreamed of my wedding for years.

At first, neither the Methodist or Baptist Church would agree to marry us since I, the boy, was to be the wife in a dress, and Mitzi, the girl, would be the husband in pants. We approached the Unitarian Minister who readily agreed to marry us, for a substantial contribution to cover costs. At this point both the Methodist and Baptist Ministers changed their minds. We finally decided on the Baptist Church with the Methodist and Baptist Ministers sharing the service. By this point I was so confused I began voting for elopement.

Bridesmaids, groomsmen, invitations, service, cake, rehearsal dinner, wedding feast and refreshments all fell into place. As the selected date approached Mitzi and I settled into a state of numbness, but Mom became more agitated by the day. Finally it became evident that something was desperately wrong. At first I decided it was only natural stress, yet slowly I had to recognize we were approaching a disaster.

On the morning of my wedding I had just climbed from the tub after a long soak. In an hour it would be time to begin dressing. Mom entered and wrapped me in a large towel, then had me sit on the edge of the bed. Placing an arm around my shoulders she drew me close.

"Sweetheart, there is something I must tell you."

"I'm okay, Mom. Mitzi is very gentle with me. She'll teach me all I need to know."

"No, it's nothing like that." She hesitated, cleared her throat and stared into the distance. "You must know a deep secret about me. One day you will find out. It is best I tell you now, rather than let you discover it later. This is to be the happiest day of your life. I don't want you to look back and wish I had not been part of it."

"Mom, that's silly. Of course Mitzi and I want you part of the wedding."

"That may change after you know the truth."

"Now you are being silly."

She bit her lip and took a deep breath. I could see tears forming in the corner of her eyes.

"When your Father and I first married..., before he started drinking so much, we decided on two children. A boy and girl. Except, we had your brothers. I desperately wanted a little girl, but your father was adamant. Two brats were enough. One night he came home extra drunk and treated me very badly. I though about leaving him, but soon I discovered I was pregnant with you. It was like a sign from God. Your father had raped me, but God was giving me a daughter to make up for everything."

"Mom, you don't have to tell me all this. I love you, that's all there is to say."

"No, Ruby. There's much more. I was convinced you were a girl. Doc Pricher thought you'd be a girl. It didn't matter that your father wanted me to get rid of you. God had given you to me and nothing could go wrong."

"But, everything went wrong." I whispered.

She nodded. "When my time came we went to the hospital. All signs were normal. Then, you turned sideways, as if you didn't want to come out of me. Doc would turn you, but you'd turn back. Hours passed. I became weaker and weaker. I don't want to make excuses for what happened, but I became so befuddled. The pains would not stop. Hour after hour while Doc became more and more frantic. He said he could only save one of us. I said, save my little Ruby, but your father and his parents demanded you be sacrificed. They said I was needed to take care of your brothers. That you were a curse, not a gift from God."

By now, Mom and I were sobbing. I knew I had caused her suffering, but I never realized it started before birth.

"Doc was ready to cut me open when you turned right way around and just popped out. But by then I must have been delirious. When they handed you to me, you weren't Ruby at all. You were another mother's baby. I kept screaming for my Ruby. I pushed you away. I didn't want to touch you."

"I'm sorry, Mom. I didn't mean to disappoint you. I couldn't help what happened."

"Of course not, Ruby. Nothing was your fault, it was all mine, and I've been punished for it every since." She sobbed more, then caught herself. "Doc must have given me something to quiet me. I remember, the room was mostly dark. You were in a box like thing, right next to my bed. They said you were very weak, very sick. But, I knew you were sick because my Ruby was inside you. If only I could open you up, I would find Ruby and you would get better. There were sharp knife like things in a drawer. I struggled out of bed. It was so hard. I must have fallen several times. At last I reached the drawer and got one of the knives."

We were both crying so hard she could barely speak. I knew what was coming, what she would say, but I didn't have the power to stop her.

"I took the knife and split you open, just as I had done with so many chickens. That's how I treated you, just like a chicken."

"Mom, please stop. You don't have to tell me."

"Yes, I must. But, there was no Ruby, only blood. Oh God. All that blood."

"Enough. Please, Mom. No more."

"A nurse entered just in time. Doc Pricher saved you, but you were damaged for all time. I did that to you. I tried to kill my own baby. I can never live that down."

"You don't have to. Everything is alright now."

"That's when they took you, gave you to Jean. For a long time I thought you were dead, then I realized you were my Ruby. Jean and I have fought for you every since that day. I should have told you, should have given you up. Jean loves you so very much. She could not have been a better mother. But, I just had to get you back. Even though it tore the family apart. I had to get you…, just had to."

"You do have me. You'll always be my mother, just as Momma Jean is my mother. I love both of you, and can't stop because you were sick when I was born."

"But, I tried to kill you. I would have. I understand that you won't want me in your wedding. You've got Mitzi to take care of you. You don't need me any more. I'll leave you in peace."

"You'll do no such thing. You'll help me get dressed and make sure I get to the church, just as we planned. When the Minister asks who gives this woman, you and Momma Jean will join Papa Henry and William and answer that you do. And, when he asks if you accept Mitzi as a part of our family, you'll answer that also. Mom, you gave me life as a boy and tried to take that away. Then you gave me life as a girl, and that washed away all the bad part. You and Momma Jean just fixed up a little mistake one of the Angels made. I got delivered a little beat up, that's all. Everything's fine now."

"Sweet, sweet Ruby. Are you sure?"

"Positive. Now, help me get dressed, I'll never get in all this stuff by myself.

Instead of moving we clung to each other, sobbing as if our hearts would pour from our eyes. All I could think of was how terrible Mom's life had been and how much better it would have been if I had died. It never dawned on me that I might have been taken advantage of or cheated out of being a boy, all I could imagine was Mom's pain and suffering. We might still have been there but Momma Jean and Jeanie arrived to help get me ready. It only took seconds for Momma Jean to understand what had happened. Soon she and Jeanie were also crying right along with us.

At last Jeanie began tickling me. "Well, it's sure going to be a lot quieter around here. I was beginning to think the only way to get Ruby out of the house was to sell her to the Gypsys."

At first I didn't understand what was happening, then it sunk through my thick head.

"Even Gypsys aren't that hard up," said Momma Jean. "Come to think of it, perhaps that's how I can get two other little gals out of my hair." She wiped her eyes, then added, with a wistful look. "Who ever would have imagined that Ruby would be the first one of my daughters to be married. God really works in mysterious ways."

Jeanie tickled me again. "Be sure to take good notes. We expect a blow by blow of everything Mitzi does to you on your honeymoon."

"In your dreams," I said. "That's strictly for us to know."

"You mean it won't be in the next Adventures?"

"Well, if it is, you won't get a copy."

"Girls, girls." Mom blotted her eyes. "It's getting late. Time to get Ruby trussed up."

It took all three of them to get me into the Merry Widow and heels, but it wasn't long until I was squeezed into everything except the dress itself. While Jeanie worked magic on my face, Mom and Momma Jean piled my curls into elaborate swirls. At last I was helped into the mountains of satin and lace and zipped tight. Mom pinned on my veil and started to pull it over my face.

"Ruby dearest, marriage isn't a fifty–fifty proposition. It takes one hundred percent from both parties, sometimes that isn't enough. Mitzi worships you and you love her, but there will be times things don't go right. It will be your duty and her duty to work it out. We love you, but a marriage is a two person affair." She lowered the veil. "Right now you're a girl and our baby. But, when Mitzi lifts your veil and kisses you, you'll be a woman and her wife. You'll never be a girl again, but you'll always be our baby."

Big Mike and Jake arrived in a new van and whirled us to the church. Everyone except Papa Henry, William and I disappeared into the sanctuary while we waited in a tiny cubicle.

After two lifetimes, Lohengrin started and they guided me down the aisle. All I could see through the mist of my veil was Mitzi, waiting at the alter. Thank God we had practiced, because all I could think about was how beautiful she was and how much I wanted her to take me in her arms. She vowed to love, protect and cherish me, then her ring slipped onto my finger and locked against my engagement ring. It felt as if a ring was being set into my nose. I was hers. I vowed to honor, cherish and obey her, then my ring slipped onto her finger.

The Ministers said a lot of other words, then someone added, "What God has joined together, let no man put asunder. Mitzi, you may kiss the bride.

She lifted my veil and gently brushed my lips. Then, her strong arms encircled me and our lips locked in an endless embrace. That's when I knew Mom had been correct. I was now a woman. Never again would I be a boy in a dress. I was a woman, and my husband's wife.

*   *   *   *   *

That was years ago, yet I remember it all as if it happened yesterday. I could not have children, of course, but Mitzi could. To everyone's amazement I was still fertile, at least a little. It took a long time and gobs of money, not to mention loads of science and perhaps some divine intervention, yet we managed to have two children, a beautiful girl and boy. I could not be a mother, yet once again intervention let me nurse both our children, which made Mitzi extremely happy.

I am still the world's worst business woman. Most of the time Mitzi keeps me straight. Not always, but most of the time.

William finally found the courage to marry Becky, and Buddy was picked up by a Professional football team. Unfortunately it is up north somewhere so he freezes his buns off every winter. I suspect it's good for him.

Daisy is still Daisy. Playing the piano and looking for the perfect husband. Actually, I think she enjoys playing at looking more than finding someone. Jeanie is my most special friend. I look after her when she's down, and put up with her when she's up, yet I love her in ways I could never express. It's like she and I are two sides of the same coin, forever joined, yet looking in different directions. The two of us are able to see all things at all times.

Mom and Momma Jean will always be my mothers, and no matter how old I become I am their baby. Although I work mostly as an artist and designer, nothing on earth is more fulfilling than sitting beside Mom at the sewing machine transforming fabric into beauty.

And Mitzi. Oh, my Mitzi. She is my loving husband, and I am her devoted wife. Which is how fate commanded it should be.

BOOKS BY JILLIAN ALLEN

MISTRESS HELENA – Imagine a world in which the gentle hero becomes a damsel very much in distress, within a story charged with excitement, danger and intrigue. Enter this creation from noted author, Jillian Allen in the first book of the epic novel, MISTRESS. MISTRESS is an adult erotic romance intended for mature readers of both genders.

MISTRESS ANNE – The adventure continues in the exciting second book of MISTRESS. What impenetrable secrets surround Helena, head of the powerful Palmsdale companies? What dark power is held by the enigmatic Intruder? Can Victor possibly choose between the energy of Helena and the allure of Anne. It soon becomes clear who will wear panties, what is not apparent until the exciting climax, is who will wear the pants.

Made in the USA
Lexington, KY
08 April 2017